# Anyone But Him

THERESA LINDEN

# PRAISE FOR *ANYONE BUT HIM*

"*Anyone But Him* had me hooked from the start! How did good girl Caitlyn Summers wake up next to bad boy Jarret West? Theresa Linden unravels the mystery layer by layer as Caitlyn questions whom to trust, who has changed, and how an unfinished investigation may be the key to it all. Caitlyn's quest for truth won't be complete until everyone's motives are brought to the light, including her own. Told through Caitlyn's eyes, *Anyone But Him* will keep you doubting, guessing - and maybe even falling in love - alongside her."
**~Carolyn Astfalk, author of contemporary inspirational romances, including *Stay With Me* and *Ornamental Graces***

"I don't often re-read books but once in a while, one touches me, and I become so connected with the characters that I must revisit them from time to time. *Anyone But Him* is that kind of book. The author has a lot of elements going on in this story - mystery, romance, amnesia, and a pro-life message. How she intertwines and weaves all these pieces together is perfection. There were so many scenes that I read numerous times because they were so captivating."
**~Leslea Wahl, author of award-winning *The Perfect Blindside* and *An Unexpected Role***

# BOOKS BY THERESA LINDEN

CHASING LIBERTY TRILOGY

*Chasing Liberty*
*Testing Liberty*
*Fight for Liberty*

WEST BROTHERS SERIES

*Roland West, Loner*
*Life-Changing Love*
*Battle for His Soul*
*Standing Strong*

SHORT STORIES

"Bound to Find Freedom"
"A Symbol of Hope"
"Made for Love" (in the anthology *Image and Likeness: Literary Reflections on the Theology of the Body*)
"Full Reversal" (in the anthology *Image and Likeness: Literary Reflections on the Theology of the Body*)

http://theresalinden.com
Library of Congress Control Number: 2017918741

Hardback: 978-0-9976747-5-0
Paperback: 978-0-9976747-4-3

First Edition, Silver Fire Publishing, April 2018

Cover: Theresa Linden

Editor: Lisa Nicholas

# DEDICATION

This book was originally titled "Life After Mistakes" but was retitled to avoid sounding like a non-fiction, self-help book. But the possibility of having a wonderful life even after making big mistakes is the message of this story, so I am dedicating this book to everyone who has made big mistakes in their life. I hope you come to believe that God is much bigger than your mistakes, and He can't wait to forgive you, shower you with grace, and give you a mission for the sake of the Kingdom.

# ACKNOWLEDGMENTS

I am grateful for the encouragement and assistance I have received from several talented authors: Carolyn Astfalk, Leslea Wahl, Don Mulcare, Susan Peek, Corinna Turner, Barb Grady Szyszkiewicz, and my editor Lisa Nicholas. These authors have helped me to grow as a writer and have encouraged and supported me through this project. Last but not least, I will always be thankful for the love and support of my husband and three boys, who have helped me in countless ways.

*"Therefore, if anyone is in Christ,*
*he is a new creation;*
*the old has passed away,*
*behold,*
*the new has come."*

~2 Corinthians 5:17

# Chapter 1

A STRANGE TAP-TAP-TAPPING sucked me from a dark sleep, making me aware of something warm and comforting draped over my waist. An arm? No, not possible.

Shadows shifted, a breeze tickled my cheek, and a burst of light turned my closed eyelids orange. The tap-tap-tapping started up again, my last hope for sleep slipping away. Inhaling a deep breath of lilac-scented air, I reached to adjust my pillow, but pain made my hand shoot to my throbbing head. Why did it ache so? I never got headaches.

I opened my eyes and tried focusing on what should've been my closet door. Curtains swished in the breeze and a drawstring tapped the window frame. The window didn't belong there.

The thing draped over my waist moved. It *was* an arm! Then a hand touched my side and slid over my abdomen. A man with a deep, sleepy voice said, "You still mad at me?"

Wide awake now, I stopped breathing. I threw back the covers—and the hand—and tore out of bed.

"I guess that's a *yes*," the man said.

In my mind, jagged, edgy lines zipped in every direction, splintering off again and again over the picture of my life, turning it into a puzzle. What was a guy doing in my—

I stood in the middle of a large shadowy room, next to a queen-size bed with a curved headrest behind it and a bare-chested man in it. A dark old-fashioned dresser with a huge mirror dominated the opposite wall. The room had three closed doors that probably led to a bathroom, a closet, and the way out. This was not my bedroom.

"It's Saturday. Come back to bed, Caitlyn." The man lay with his face in the pillow and his arm stretched across the bed in the exact spot where I had been. He turned his head, maybe to look at me but dark curls covered his eyes. He looked familiar. Did I know him? Why was I in his house? In his bed? Certainly we hadn't—

My stomach tightened. "No, I—I think I..." With my eyes fixed on him, I backed to the window and the blowing curtains. Any chance it was a sliding glass door and I could make a break for it?

A gust of wind sent the curtain twirling and light scattered the darkness in the room. I caught a glimpse of myself in the mirror. My hair had none of its natural curl but hung down, straight and red, over my shoulders. I wore a pastel pink sleep teddy and—

My heart shot into my throat. Was I wearing only a sleep teddy that barely covered my panties? I crossed my arms over my chest, which was adequately covered, and scanned for clothes.

My toes sunk into a fluffy dark-blue rug on a hardwood floor. Two antique armchairs flanked a big wooden chest against the wall. A worn cardboard box sat askew in the corner, seeming oddly out of place in the otherwise tidy room. Not a stitch of clothes anywhere.

What had I done with my clothes? Or what had *he* done with them? And what else could I use to cover myself? A wave of nausea washed over me. Head throbbing and hands trembling like mad, I grabbed the bedspread and gave it a good tug.

He grasped at it and said, "Hey! Just 'cuz you don't want to sleep in..." as I whisked it from the bed. He made one last swipe for the bedspread, then pulled the sheet up to his chest and locked it down with his arm.

I wrapped the dark flowery bedspread around myself and

tossed the end of it over one shoulder, making a sort of toga. Where was my purse? My cell phone?

"I still don't get why *you're* mad at *me*." The man rolled over and threw back the sheet, revealing a lean but muscular physique. He pushed himself up, swung his bare legs over the edge of the bed, and sat with his back to me. Dark curls hung past his wide shoulders. He wore nothing but dark blue shorts or maybe boxers.

The trembling increased. I shot wild glances to each side, looking for something to arm myself. Who was he? How did I end up here?

He groaned, rubbing his face. "Really, I should be mad at you. You were the one out late. With no explanation. You ever gonna tell me why?"

Not sure how to answer, I watched his reflection in the mirror. When he dropped his hands, I gasped and staggered back. The puzzle of my life quivered, and all the pieces scattered. "Jarret West?"

Okay, so at least I knew him. I shook my head, shocked that I'd found a degree of comfort in that thought. Jarret West?

He looked older or maybe tired. And rather than the faint, trim goatee I remembered, he had that stylish unshaven look of today's young actors and models. Maybe he hadn't bothered shaving for the past few days. No, that didn't seem like him. He'd been one of the vainest guys in high school.

His haughty eyes narrowed as he gazed at me through the mirror. "What?" His tone held a note of challenge.

"Oh, I... um." I backed up until the curtains licked my back. Not wanting to make him mad and desperate to figure this mess out, I forced a smile. "I'm sorry. I don't know how I got here."

Where was here? I'd been inside Jarret's house before. His younger brother Roland was one of my best friends. Expensive furniture and displays of antiques filled every room of their gigantic house. This looked nothing like their house. "I'm not sure where I—"

"You wanna go look for your car? Is that it?" He stepped to the dresser and opened a low drawer.

So much bare skin and in such an intimate setting! I squirmed and turned away.

"I wish you'd tell me why you up and left it somewhere. I'd like to know what happened. Don't I have a—"

"My car?" What was he talking about? I was only eighteen. My parents weren't rich. How could I afford a car? "You mean my dad's van? I'm sure it's at home." My parents must be worried sick. I'd never stayed out all night unless for a sleepover... with permission... at a *girl*friend's house. What did I do last night? How did I end up in this mess? I tapped my throbbing forehead. Why couldn't I remember?

"Huh?" He glanced at me through the mirror as he pulled his jeans up. "What's the matter with you?"

"What happened last night?"

"I don't know." He shoved a wallet into his back pocket and jangled some keys but didn't seem interested in getting a shirt. "I hate when we fight." He turned around. His eyes looked softer, maybe a little sad. I had never seen him like that before. He'd always struck me as an insensitive, rude, and conceited guy.

I stepped back again and bumped the window. "No, I mean, what happened to *me* last night?"

Bare chested, long hair hanging loose, he walked around the bed, eyes on me. "You don't remember? Are you feeling all right?"

I reached for my aching head, and the toga slipped.

Jarret stepped into my personal space.

I gasped.

He stepped back.

Grasping wildly at the bedspread, I remade the toga and held it in place as I moved away from him. He followed until I wound up backed into a corner.

His eyebrows twitched. He stopped uncomfortably close and brought a hand up to my head.

I jerked back, knocking my head against the wall. Not that I thought he would hit me but... I shivered and crossed my arms over the quilt.

He put a palm to my forehead. "You're not hot."

"I—I have a headache."

"Yeah?" With concern in his eyes, he brushed the hair from my forehead.

My skin crawled. I shoved his hand away and darted past him. "Yes, a little one." I lied. It felt like a bomb had gone off inside my head, and my stomach rumbled as if I had eaten bad clams. "But really, I can't remember how I got here. And..." I gulped, hating to ask the next question. "Do you know where my clothes are? And my purse?" I slunk to the other side of the bed, scanning the floor.

"You don't remember how you got here?" He cocked an eyebrow and raised his voice. "You came home in a cab. You don't remember that? I want to know where your car—"

"Home? Okay, but that doesn't explain how I got *here.* I took a cab home... and then came here? Why? Where else was I? I mean, what was I doing?" I tried one of the doors. A nightlight showed a large, tidy bathroom that smelled of soap and manly cologne.

Jarret stood motionless on the other side of the bed, staring at me with his mouth hanging open. "What... were... you doing? You're asking me?"

"Yes." I held his gaze then dropped mine to the bed. I'd shoved the thought aside but had to face it now. We'd crawled out of the same bed. The answer was obvious. Needing to hear him say it, I pulled the toga tighter, sucked in a breath, and waited.

His mouth fell open again, his eyes narrowing. Why didn't he want to answer my question?

I gripped the bedspread so hard my fingernails pressed into my palms through the fabric. How could I ever have wound up in a situation like this? This was like bad casting for a horror movie. Some of my friends might have found themselves in this situation. But not me. I always said "no" to drugs and to sex before marriage. I didn't even swear. And I always said "yes" to my parents and to Jesus. This could never be a chapter in my life. There was no possible way this was happening to me.

"We didn't, I mean..." Relaxing my death-grip on the bedspread, I set my jaw, determined to get an answer. "Did we, did we...?" I couldn't get the words out.

His mouth curled up on one side and his eye twitched. "Make love?"

"Have sex?" Could one really call *doing it* with someone they didn't like *making love*?

He turned away, inhaled, turned back, exhaled. "You don't remember making up?"

My heart plummeted to the floor. My eyes watered, making me blink rapidly. I couldn't have. I was waiting for marriage. Could he be lying? "Where are my... my clothes?"

"Where are your— I think you'd better go back to bed. Maybe you're dreaming. Somehow. Maybe. Could you be sleepwalking, sleep talking?" He crept toward me. "Why don't you lie down?"

"No, thank you." I backed away. My lips wouldn't stop trembling. "If you could give me my clothes, I'll be on my way."

He shook his head. "No." He pointed to the bed. "Lie down."

I shook my head. "I don't want to. You can't keep me here. I need to go home. My parents are probably worried sick."

His face drained of color. "Your parents?" With something like panic in his eyes, he grabbed my shoulders. "Baby, you need to lie down."

Disgusted by his touch, I tried twisting from his grip. "Please, don't call me *baby*."

"Something must've happened to you." Still gripping my shoulders, he moved me to the bed. "Maybe we should get you to the hospital."

"The hospital? I'm not going to the hospital. There's

nothing wrong with me!"

"No, I'm gonna call a doctor. I'll call Mike. You remember Mike? Did you know he's a doctor?"

"Jarret, no, I'm not going to—" If he went to make the phone call, I could try the window. I'd need to grab some clothes. "Okay, I'll lie down. You call the doctor. What's his name? Mike? You go call Mike."

With jail warden eyes, he watched as I crawled back into bed. Then he went for the middle door. He gave me and the window a funny look before leaving the room.

The door clicked shut.

I jumped out of bed. The toga fell to the floor. I tore open the bottom drawer, the one from which he'd taken the jeans. Two neat stacks of jeans filled the drawer. I grabbed a faded pair and shoved my foot into it. They fit tight at my hips, loose around my waist, and hung way past my feet. As I zipped up, I dashed for the window.

When I pushed back the curtains, my blood ran cold.

A little wooden deck came off the back of the house, outside the bedroom window. A tree with a twisted trunk grew nearby, casting its shadow on the cushioned patio chairs and teak table on the deck. Jarret, still shirtless, sat hunched at the table with a phone pressed to his ear. He glanced at the window.

I let the curtain fall.

Had he kidnapped me? Maybe he'd drugged me. But why me? He had no need for money and no interest in my type. He always chased the pretty, flirty, vain girls.

I flung myself onto the bed and wrapped my arms around my waist. My head still ached and my stomach churned, but I didn't feel different in any other way. Had I really lost my virginity? To *him?* I could never get that back. Burying my face in the pillows, I sobbed. *Oh Lord, how could I have let this happen? What have I done? Why did he do this to me?*

# Chapter 2

A DOOR SLAMMED and jarred me awake. The front door? Dad must've been off to work, and that meant Mom would come knocking on the bedroom doors in a few minutes with her daily chant: *Time to get ready for schoo-ool.* The house would soon fill with the abominable noises of my brothers and sisters fighting over the bathroom.

*Oh, just a few more minutes.* My body felt like a lump of clay, weighted down and molded into the bed. Sleep never felt as good as it did in the morning when I had to get up. If only I didn't have this grinding headache.

*A headache.* That probably accounted for my crazy dream, the nightmare. I giggled at the thought of lying in the same bed as Jarret West, being anywhere with him for that matter. I inhaled and exhaled slowly. *Thank you, Lord. It was only a dream.*

*Jarret West.* Why would I dream of him? Why not Roland, whom I adored, or one of the other nice boys in the Catholic teen group? Or anyone but him. But dreams didn't have to make sense. Still, why would he come to my mind? I hadn't seen Jarret or thought about him for the past two years. He was probably keeping himself busy with all the girls at college, robbing them of their virginity, if they still had theirs.

My thoughts turned to my best friend. *Poor Zoë.* Dating Jarret had made her the envy of all the girls, but she'd hated being pregnant in high school. She'd wanted to hide it at first. Then came the morning sickness and all the physical changes.

She'd lost some friends. And her parents hadn't taken it well.

A knock sounded on the door.

I moaned and buried my face in the pillow. "Just a few more minutes." I should force myself to get up. Mom always tried to wake me before the others so I could have first dibs on the bathroom. I was the oldest—it was only fair. If my body would just cooperate. I sank deeper into the pillow.

*Oh, wait.* I didn't need to get ready for school. It was Saturday. Was it Saturday? No, no, it wasn't Saturday. Why did I think it was Saturday?

My cheek brushed a big damp spot on the pillow. I lifted my head and looked at it. Why was my pillow wet? Had I been crying in my sleep?

The bedroom door opened.

"Hey, baby, you awake?"

The sound of Jarret's voice sent an involuntary shudder coursing through my body. I rolled over to face him, my gaze falling upon the dark flowered bedspread, the dresser with the big mirror, and the room I had never seen before today.

Jarret West stood in the doorway, dressed in jeans and—*oh good*—a shirt. A white tank top. Not much of a shirt but better than nothing.

Could I still be dreaming? I sat and pulled up the disheveled bedspread, tucking it under my arms.

He sat on the foot of the bed and gawked at me.

"Why are you doing this?" I tried to steady my voice.

"Hey, uh, Mike's here. You wanna get dressed?"

I flipped the covers back to show him I wore jeans.

"You, uh, wanna put on some of your own clothes?" He gave a nod toward door number three. "Not that you don't look hot in my jeans, but..." He gave me a crooked smile.

My stomach twisted. "My clothes are in there?"

He shrugged and sort of nodded.

"Could you please leave the room?"

He gave another nod and rolled his eyes.

When the door clicked shut, I tore out of bed and threw

open door number three. I stared in amazement.

The closet was as big as my bedroom at home. Granted, I'd gotten stuck with the smallest room on account of my younger siblings shared a bedroom. Men's clothing hung on one side, organized by type and color. Women's clothing hung on the other, with no obvious organization. Cubbies on the back wall held folded clothes and miscellaneous items. Shoes in neat rows on the floor lined the walls.

I flipped through the dresses. What was my denim jumper doing here? And my aqua sundress... my white linen dress... my black, my brown, my plaid...

My chest tightened. Something was terribly wrong. How could he have gotten all my clothes from home to this place? Where did my parents think I was? Why couldn't I remember yesterday?

A wave of nausea and lightheadedness washed over me. The answer became clear. I'd been drugged.

In high school, I had heard about a date rape drug. A guy could sneak it into a girl's drink. She'd be out of it and he could—

I sucked in a breath. "It happens so fast," Zoë had told me, "that you don't know anything's wrong until it hits you hard. Then you're so tired you can't keep your eyes open. You're in this strange dreamlike state where you feel like you're floating."

I had never thought to ask Zoë how she knew about it. Could she have known from experience? Had Jarret ever used it on her? Rumors surrounded that boy, some of them pretty bad.

My hands trembled as I searched my memory. Had I ever heard anything like that about him?

A knock came again and a muffled, "Are you dressed?"

"No!" I yanked the denim jumper from the hanger. "I'll come out when I'm done. I need a few minutes." I pulled the jumper over my head and dropped the jeans. Okay, a dress really wasn't the most practical outfit for what I planned to do, but I was absolutely not going to wear his clothes, not if I could help it.

Would the shoes be my size? I slipped my feet into a pair of brown sandals. They fit perfectly.

Now, to make my escape. I stepped out of the closet and scanned the room. What could I stand on to climb out the window? I headed for the wooden trunk and the antique armchairs. The trunk was a good height, but it didn't budge. I grabbed a chair by the arm and yanked. It scraped across the hardwood floor, the sound ripping through me.

I froze, my heart pounding.

No one came through the door, so I continued, this time lifting the chair so it wouldn't drag. It slipped in my hands and cracked against my shin. Stifling a yelp, I limped to the window.

Anxiety mounting, I pushed back the curtains and stepped onto the chair. The window was open, so I had only to deal with the screen. Not finding any tabs, I gave it a shove. It didn't budge. I tried lifting it a little and then shoving. The bottom corner popped out.

Voices came from the other side of the door.

"Just a minute!" I shouted, ramming my palm against the screen. It popped halfway out. I pushed, twisted, then wrestled it from the window, hoping the scraping sound didn't reach Jarret and the doctor on the other side of the bedroom door. The screen finally came free and clattered to the deck four feet below.

I sat on the windowsill and swung a leg outside. It would be an easy jump, but I'd better hurry. They may have heard the noise. Any second now—

The bedroom door opened. "Caitlyn?" Jarret's voice.

Heart racing, I swung my other leg outside and said a quick prayer for safety.

"What are you—" He rushed toward me. "Caitlyn, no!"

I cast one frantic look over my shoulder. Then I jumped. I landed on my feet but fell to my knees. Would he follow? I scrambled to my feet, flew down the steps, and ran past a tall lilac bush and into the backyard.

Thick bushes grew between trees along the back edge of the yard, leaving no obvious way into the woods. A high wooden fence ran along one side of the yard, so I dashed to the other side. The neighboring lawn had the unkempt look of an abandoned property. Just my luck: I'd find no one there to help me. I sprinted through the long grass and nearly made it to the next yard when someone grabbed me from behind.

"Caitlyn, stop!" Jarret squeezed my wrist.

I pulled away then remembered it would be more effective to push. So I shoved my captive arm toward him and twisted it fast. Breaking his grip, I took off running.

An instant later, his arms slid around my waist and held me tight. His chest pressed against my back, his face over my shoulder. "Hey, stop."

The feel of his body against mine increased the surge of adrenaline through me. I could get free of him and I knew it. To accomplish it, I simply needed a bit of space between us. With a grip on his arms, I twisted my shoulders and tried turning my whole body.

Thwarting my plan, he lifted me off the ground.

My blood boiling with frustration, I considered kicking his knee or taking a groin shot. A few more self-defense moves came to mind, but I needed my feet on the ground. I needed some space. Of course, Jarret did have long hair...

I reached over my shoulder, grabbed hold of his long locks, and yanked.

He cussed and lessened his grip.

I slid down and got my feet on the ground. He moved to tighten his embrace, but I twisted my body and got the space I need to—

A grunt escaped me as I cracked my elbow into his gut. He groaned. As he leaned forward, I took my elbow to his chin. He staggered back. I lunged, ready to knee him in the groin, but then stopped.

What was I thinking? This wasn't a cage match but an escape mission. I turned and dashed for the woods.

The bushes at the back of the yard grew close together like a wild hedge. I plunged into them, making my escape. Branches, like a hundred daggers, sliced my arms and legs but I forced myself through.

"Caitlyn, hey, stop! You don't want to go back there."

Beyond the bushes, the undergrowth thinned enough for me to pick up my pace. I ran. Branches cracked beneath my feet and birds fluttered overhead, but it didn't sound like he was following. Once farther away, I'd risk a look. Right now, I needed to figure out my destination, the depth of the woods, and where they came out. Finding no obvious paths, I dashed between the wider spaced trees and bushes.

The woods had a pale, surreal quality, the green tones softer, the dirt a lighter shade of brown, the scent like a candy store or maybe root beer. They didn't remind me of the South Dakota woods I knew. Maybe the stress of the moment affected my perception.

I made a studied glance to either side. My gaze caught the shaggy, peeling bark on the trunk of a tall tree, lobed leaves on shrubs, branches with toothed leaflets, and a tree covered by thick vines. No, I had never seen woods like this before.

My heart pounded and my mind raced as fast as my feet. How had I gotten into this situation? I would never have gone anywhere alone with Jarret... willingly. Did Roland suspect what Jarret had done? Did anyone know where I was? If he had all my clothes brought here, he must've had a plan, one that he'd been working on for some time. Maybe he'd made it look like I had run away. Oh, how miserable my family must've been!

Leaves stirred overhead. I glanced up and saw a squirrel scurry from one branch to another. Bugs chattered but no wind blew. Everything, besides me and the squirrel, seemed still and calm. I leaped over a dead tree and ducked under a low branch. The branch caught my sleeve, making me need to stop to free myself. I took the moment to try to catch my breath and then raced on. My pace had slowed to a jog despite all my efforts, but I wouldn't stop, not until I found help.

Jarret had held me so tightly, yet I had freed myself. I smiled. It didn't seem possible. He obviously worked out. I liked to take walks, but I was thin as a pipe cleaner. How had those self-defense moves popped into my mind? Maybe I'd seen them on TV. But they had come to me in such detail. And I hadn't hesitated to use them.

Light showed between the trees about a hundred yards ahead. I ran out of energy to carry on. Panting for air, I forced myself to the edge of the woods.

The wooded area ended at a strip of grass along a newly paved two-lane road. A few scattered, mismatched houses stood across the street: a little ranch with a three-car garage, an old graying bungalow, and a vinyl-sided split-level. They each had a deep yard, a long gravel driveway, and naturally growing clusters of trees between and behind them.

I could go for help. Lungs struggling for air, I propped myself against a tree and gasped to catch my breath as I scanned the woods behind me. He must not have followed, but I wasn't going to wait longer to be sure. I stepped out of the woods.

A shiny black Mercedes Benz rolled down the road, approaching. It slowed then came to a sudden stop in front of me.

I sucked in a breath, my heart pumping double-time. Jarret didn't drive a Mercedes. Maybe someone had come to help me.

The passenger-side door flew open.

I braced myself to run.

A man jumped out of the car. *Jarret!*

I gasped, my mouth going dry. I staggered, wanting to dive back into the woods, but in an instant, he was upon me.

He latched onto me from behind, his arms like tentacles entrapping me.

"Let go!" Drained of energy, I couldn't fight him. Maybe I could slip out of his vice. I tried to drop down. He dropped down with me, and we both ended up on our knees.

"You'll run." He spit his words into my hair.

"Of course... I'll run." I gasped to draw in air. "Why... don't you... let me go?"

"I can't do that."

I wiggled and twisted. He lessened his grip, so I turned to face him and plopped down in the grass. He stayed on one knee as if waiting to pounce.

"But I don't... I don't want to be here."

"Yes, you do. You belong here."

We stared at each other for a moment, both of us breathing hard.

"Come on back," he said. "We'll talk. Something happened to you. I don't know what, but we'll figure this out."

"Why can't we... talk... at the police station?"

He chuckled and stood, holding out a hand to me. "Come on."

I reached as if I would take it but then jumped up to run. I turned, bolted, and smacked into a wide, solid chest.

"Hey there, Caitlyn. Whatever are you doing?" The thug had to be seven feet tall. He had smoothed-back dark hair, a clean-shaven chin, a white scar under one eye, and the strangest pale eyes I had ever seen. He planted a hand on each of my shoulders and grinned down at me.

"I don't suppose you remember Mike?" Jarret said.

I didn't answer. He must've known I didn't know him. Something about Mike made me reluctant to speak, but I pushed past the discomfort. "So, Mike, you must be the doctor Jarret told me about."

Mike's grin broadened. "That I am. I hear you're having something of a day." He spoke with a definite Southern drawl. Who was he pretending to be?

"Did you drug me?" I said, glaring at Mike.

"Come on." Jarret grabbed me by the arm and tugged me

to the Mercedes.

# Chapter 3

"WHAT DID HE just put in the eggs?" I dropped the peroxide-soaked cotton ball I'd used to clean the scrapes on my arms and straightened in my chair, wanting a look at the small white container in Jarret's hand. He turned away from the kitchen island and slid the mystery ingredient back into the refrigerator. It wasn't milk.

"Please, Caitlyn," Mike drawled, tapping his fingers on the table. "It'll be a right quick exam." His impatience clashed with his professional "doctor" demeanor.

I sat opposite him at one end of a long, thick-legged, formal dining room table. Carvings on the edges of the table gave it an elegant look, despite the scrapes and wear. While too big for the breakfast nook, it would've fit well in the empty dining room on the other side of the kitchen. A huge antique painting of a rifle-toting man on a horse filled the wall behind me, as if someone thought hanging it in the same room as the monstrous table would tie it all together.

The antique pieces clashed with the clean, contemporary feel of the house. Sand-colored walls without a single smudge, dent, or handprint. Pale kitchen cabinets and shiny black appliances. If I hadn't seen Jarret yanking things out of cabinets and messing up the marble countertops, I could've believed no one lived here at all, that this had all been staged.

I crossed my legs and hiked my skirt high enough to expose the bleeding gashes on my shins. I'd ruined my denim jumper. As soon as they'd dragged me back to the house, I'd changed into a camouflage skirt and an army-green t-shirt. If an opportunity to escape presented itself, I'd be ready.

Jarret had kidnapped me. But why? Did he have mental problems? He'd done mean things before. He once made his younger brother, Roland, miss school by locking him in a room of their house for a whole day. Roland was fourteen then, Jarret sixteen. Did Jarret have a reason for it? Had he a method to his madness? Or was he just mad?

Mike leaned back and folded his arms. His gaze shifted from me to the sliding glass patio doors. He looked like he'd rather be fishing. No, he probably played golf. But maybe he owed Jarret a favor and had to convince me to take his mind-altering drugs before he could go. Or whatever devious thing Jarret wanted him to do.

With a sigh, I dragged a cotton ball down a scrape on my leg. If only I'd succeeded in getting away, the bodily damage would've been worth it. I should've stayed in the woods instead of rushing through them. He hadn't followed me into them. I could have hidden, sneaked out later, and found my way home. How could I have known he would drive around—

"Caaaitlyn? The exam, please." Mike's tone bore a strong resemblance to my father's when he wanted me to do something to which I was diametrically opposed, like eating stew for dinner.

I glanced at Mike but wanted to keep my attention on Jarret. "Did *you* see what he put in the eggs?"

Mike groaned.

Jarret looked up as he zealously whisked the eggs. "Don't worry, you'll like 'em."

"I'm not hungry."

He snickered. "Yeah, right. Have you ever skipped a meal in your life?"

"Of course. I'm Catholic." In fact, I fasted twice a year: Ash Wednesday and Good Friday. My stomach always hated me for it, rumbling at mealtimes and making me nauseous within the hour. Thank God the Church prescribed only two fast days.

"Not counting Lent." Jarret gave a cocky grin.

My cheeks warmed as I realized he'd read my mind.

"Dear, may I inquire?" Mike said. "Is there a history of mental illness or other disorders in your family?"

"Mental illness?" Jarret stopped whisking and shot Mike a horrid glare. "She ain't crazy. There ain't no crazy people in her family."

Mike withstood Jarret's glare, expressionless for a moment, then he exhaled and lifted his hands in frustration. "Well, it need not be that extreme. Are her parents still living?"

Jarret's mouth fell open and he glanced at me. "What does that matter?"

"Yes, my parents are still living." Done cleaning my wounds, I secured the lid on the peroxide bottle and pushed it aside.

"What about a thyroid disorder? An untreated thyroid—"

"No. Something happened to her."

"As a *doc-tor...*" Mike emphasized the word and paused. "I must consider all possibilities."

Jarret bristled at the word *doctor,* as if Mike had challenged him for leadership of their little duo. What was their arrangement?

With a father as rich as his, Jarret could pay his accomplices well, but his youthfulness and lack of education could be a source of insecurity. Maybe the two of them would get into it and I could silently depart. *Yes,* I could help generate friction between them.

Jarret mumbled something and returned to whisking the eggs. They had to be getting to the soft peak level. When would he stop? Of course, with that secret ingredient...

I craned my neck to glimpse inside the bowl, but Jarret tilted it toward himself as he worked.

"Caitlyn, if you would simply allow a check-up..." His fake Southern accent grated on my nerves. People didn't really talk like that. Except sometimes on TV. When they were acting. "...

we might get some answers." Mike tapped the shiny black doctor bag on the table.

"No, thank you. How do I know you really are a doctor? And besides, I have my own family doctor. Why don't you let me see her? I'm sure she's not far. Where are we, anyway?"

Jarret chucked the whisk over his shoulder to the sink and dumped the frothy egg mixture into a skillet. It immediately hissed. He muttered something—probably a swear word—then yanked the skillet off the stove and lowered the flame. He glanced at Mike. "Don't you have an ID badge or something to show her?"

"Oh, sure." Mike stood and swung a hand to his back pocket as he approached. "You can have this." He pulled a business card from his wallet, tossed it to the table, and got his phone.

Stopping near me—too close for comfort—he tapped his cell phone then twisted toward Jarret. "What *did* you put in the eggs? My stomach is beginning to take note. I hope you're fixing to give me some."

My attention zeroed in on the image on his phone, a portrait of a teenage girl with sleek brown hair and a slight smile. She sat poised with her head tilted, looking like a teen model. She'd probably had her picture done professionally by a glamour studio with make-up artists. "Is that your daughter?"

Mike turned his cell phone to himself and tapped the screen. "Is *what* my daughter?"

"The picture. The girl." I pointed to his phone as he continued tapping it.

He set his phone nearby. He'd pulled up an on-line listing that showed his professional portrait, name—Michael A. Caragine, MD—bio, and the address and phone number of the medical facility where he worked. The business card had the same information.

"The 'girl'? Why, she's a young woman. Besides, how old do you think I am? Since you obviously do not recall me, I get a second chance at your first impression." He peered down at me through pale eyes and grinned. His eyes... were they green or gray? He continued staring, waiting for my opinion, no doubt hoping for a favorable answer.

"Hmm." I hated to look him over.

His wide chest and slight paunch strained the cotton fabric of his designer gray polo shirt. The upright and relaxed way he carried himself gave him an assertive, professional air that countered the thug-like impression created by the thick scar under his right eye. His hair—shiny, dark brown, and smoothed back in a man-bun?—could have come from *Just for Men* hair color, but he did have all his hair. Fairly handsome, he had a strong, clean-shaven jaw and few wrinkles, not counting the bags under his eyes. Overall, he struck me as a clean, vain, gentlemanly, and professional man with a few quirks. Probably pushing forty.

"Well? Your guess?"

I shrugged and decided to go with the lower number in my estimate range so as not to offend his pride. "Thirty-five."

"Thirty-five?" He laughed, snatched his phone, and returned to his seat at the table. "Not yet, sweetheart. I'm only thirty."

I glanced at the business card and flicked it away. "I could have one of those made up and put anything I wanted on it. Caitlyn Summer, hmm..." What title would I use? "Caitlyn Summer, Private Investigator." Liking the sound of it, I folded my arms and gave a satisfied grin.

Jarret laughed. "Yeah, you could use that title, all right. Only you got the last name wrong."

"Back to the matter at hand. I've given you proof. So, how about it? You have a bathrobe, don't you? You could put that there on..."

Jarret jerked his head toward Mike.

"... and I could examine you right quick in the bathroom or in your bedroom if you prefer. I'm worried that you—"

"What, do you think," Jarret snapped, "she has cuts or

bruises she don't know about? I'm sure she'd feel it. Besides, she can check herself in the mirror."

Mike shook his head. "Try to help me out here, Jarret. Y'all want answers or not? Caitlyn, I—"

"No." I folded my arms. "The only cuts I have came from Jarret hunting me like a lion after its prey. But I do have a headache. Probably from the poison you gave me. Maybe it's wearing off."

Jarret and Mike exchanged glances.

"What can you tell me about yestuh-day?" Mike said.

"Ask Jarret. I don't remember *yestuh-day*. I don't remember how I got here at all. What kind of drug did you use on me anyway?"

"What's the last thing you do recall?"

I made a face. What difference did that make? The last thing I remembered was... was... Memories and images tumbled in my mind. Was I still attending high school? Was I a senior? No.

An image came into focus: my graduating class all in caps and gowns, huddled for a group picture. Roland came up to me afterward, a look of humble pride in his gorgeous steel-gray eyes. A few strands of his dark hair had fallen out of place and hung over his forehead. He looked so handsome in black. Of course, he always wore black...

Realizing I was smiling, I forced a frown. "What difference does it make? Can I use the phone?"

"The phone?" Jarret slid a plate of scrambled eggs and buttered toast in front of me, his gaze traveling up and down me.

My skin crawled. I turned my eyes to the plate. All that work for plain old scrambled eggs?

"What's with the camouflage outfit?" His eyes held a glint of humor.

I flashed a curt grin.

Smirking, he stepped back behind the counter. "What d'ya want to drink?"

"Poison."

His cocky look and the arch of his brow showed he had tired of my attitude.

I pushed the eggs around with a fork. They didn't look strange.

Jarret returned with a tall glass of milk.

I dropped my fork onto the table. I wouldn't take my chances.

He took a swig of the milk, set the glass in front of me, snatched the fork and took a bite of my scrambled eggs. "See? No poison." He set the fork down, leaned back against the counter island, and gawked at me.

"Can you recall the day before yestuh-day?" Mike wasn't going to let up until I gave him something.

"Umm." The eggs did look good. Should I try them? I said the *Prayer Before Meals* in my mind and tasted the eggs. Light, fluffy, melt-in-the-mouth delicious. What *did* he put in them? "Sure, I remember the day before. I umm..." I was sitting on my bed, the papers I'd received from South Dakota University spread out around me, trying to decide how to spend the summer. Happy butterflies danced in my stomach as I thought about college. I couldn't wait. All through high school, I'd looked forward to college even more than summer vacation. This summer would be a long one. I'd reached for the phone to call Roland when Mom shouted, "Caitlyn, I need you to watch the kids while I run to the—"

I snapped from the memory. Why was I thinking about that? That wasn't yesterday. When was that? I finished the eggs—with no ill effect—and grabbed the toast. "I don't see what difference it makes. May I *please* use the phone? Mom's probably wondering—"

"How old are you, Caitlyn?" Mike said.

Jarret should know. I was the same age as Roland. I gave Jarret a look to say "as if you didn't know" and answered, "Eighteen."

Jarret's eyes snapped wide and his mouth fell open. He

turned away and leaned over the counter, looking like he might vomit.

"So, are you still in high school?" Mike continued to pry. What was his game?

I shook my head. "Jarret, why don't you tell your little Southern friend all about me? It's not like you don't know."

Moving in slow motion, Jarret turned and sat in the chair nearest me. Trembling? "You're not eighteen, Caitlyn. You're twenty-two."

I laughed. "Oh, I'm twenty-two. That makes me older than you."

He shook his head. "I'm twenty-five. After high school, I went to college for four years. I have a bachelor's degree in anthropology. I wanted to get my..." His eyes flickered and he shut his mouth.

Could it be true? No. And if it were— "I still don't see why I'm here. With you. What do you want with me?" Heart quaking, I struggled to keep the emotion from my voice. "Why are you doing this?"

He gave me a blank stare then raised his hand. I jerked back though he didn't look angry. With his other hand, he tapped the gold band on his ring finger.

"So?"

He grabbed my left hand. I pulled away but then looked at my hand. There on my ring finger, where I expected to see my chastity ring, was a gold band and another ring with an opal set between two diamonds.

I gazed at the rings in disbelief then looked at him. "We're... married?"

He frowned. "Don't sound so excited."

The blood drained from my face, my neck, my chest. I forced myself to breathe. "This isn't real. I don't see how..."

He huffed and got up from the table, the chair legs scraping the floor. "Are you done with that?" He grabbed my empty plate.

Mike dug through his little black bag and pulled out a

stethoscope and something else, maybe a pen or one of those "doctor" flashlights. After hanging the stethoscope around his neck and stuffing the flashlight into his pocket, he scooted his chair out and stared at me. Then he stood and approached slowly, as if he thought I might attack.

"Now, if you'll oblige, I'll simply take a peek at your eyes and head. That there shouldn't be a problem, should it?"

"Well, um..." I leaned away from him.

He had his fingers in my hair before I could voice an objection. *Oh well, what would it hurt?* He could look, but only at my head.

"Mmm." He moved my head to one side and the other as he inspected me with all the gentleness one might expect from a doctor. "Mmm-hmm."

"What?" Jarret propped his hands on his hips and stepped closer. I shot him a warning look, and he stepped back.

Mike stooped, lined his face up with mine, and held his little flashlight-thingy up. I tried to hold still and focus on his seriously pale irises, while he tried to blind me by shooting a beam of light into each eye. He did it a second time then straightened and snatched my wrist.

I blinked to get rid of the green spots the light had caused.

After a minute of staring at his watch, he dropped my wrist and shoved the earpieces of the stethoscope into his ears.

"Don't," I said, but he did.

He placed the chest piece here and there on my back, over my shirt, and then on my chest. He seemed like a doctor.

Yanking the stethoscope from his ears, he spoke. "How's your vision, Caitlyn?"

"My eyes are fine. I just have a terrible headache."

He held his hands out in front of me. "See if you can squeeze my fingers."

I made a disgusted face and did not comply.

"She's got her strength and reflexes," Jarret said. "Believe me." Glaring at me, he rubbed his chin where I'd hit him earlier.

Mike returned to *his* end of the table and dropped the instruments into his doctor bag. Sitting, he rested his clasped hands on the table and leaned forward, his pale eyes fixed on me. "Caitlyn, there's a right good-sized lump and bruise on one side of your head."

I touched my head, my finger going right to the sore spot. *Oh! A bump!*

"I do believe you've got a concussion, and you've obviously got amnesia." His eyes narrowed with a thoughtful look. "My dear, do you have any idea what on earth happened to your head?"

"Amnesia? I have amnesia?"

Mike turned to Jarret. "I suggest you take your wife in for a CT scan and..." He lowered his voice. "Well, you'll want to check..."

Jarret had been standing as still as a stone statue ever since Mike had said *amnesia*, but now he blinked and made a quick nod. "Yeah, yeah, okay. Your clinic?"

"The clinic? Why, no, it's Saturday. We're closed." Mike cast a long look out the sliding glass doors.

"Oh yeah?" Jarret gave an annoyed smirk. "You got the key, don't you? And that place has the equipment, right? Can't you do a CT scan?"

"Well, sure, I suppose."

"Amnesia?" I whispered to myself. Could I really have amnesia?

# Chapter 4

MY EYELIDS HUNG at half-mast. The second we'd returned from the clinic, my body had been drawn to the couch. Its soft cushions and plush throw pillows beckoned me to curl up and fall into a deep slumber. Unfortunately, my parched throat had diverted me from the couch to the kitchen, where I now stood searching for a cup.

I opened another kitchen cupboard: dinner plates, dessert plates, and a tissue box filled with... batteries? Interesting.

Maybe I should've put up more of a fight when Mike insisted I take a sedative before the CT scan. Jarret hadn't wanted me to have a sedative, at first. That was the main reason I did. I'd fallen asleep to the buzzing, clicking, and whirring of the CT scanner, and I woke to Mike's grinning face hanging over mine.

"That's a girl," he'd said. "Time to get up."

Having no clue what had happened to my head, I'd been relieved when Mike had given me a clean bill of health. Whatever that was worth.

I cracked open another cupboard and found spices, olive oil, cooking spray, and a carton of dog treats. Dog treats? My gaze swept the kitchen floor, the sun-drenched breakfast nook, and the part of the living room I could see over the kitchen island. No fur, scratches, dog toys, or food dishes.

Jarret and Mike carried on a whispered discussion behind the half-closed door of a room off the empty dining room. If only they would close the door completely and I could sneak out or take the phone. Every minute or so, Jarret glanced, his eyes narrow and glum. They must've been working out the next part of their plan. Maybe they were waiting to see if I bought the amnesia and marriage lines. Maybe I did have amnesia. It would explain a lot. But that I had willingly married Jarret West? That mountain was too hard to climb.

As I opened another cupboard, a Ziploc bag stuffed with packets of hot sauce from a Mexican restaurant fell out. I tried to shove it back but couldn't find room in the crowded cupboard. Plastic containers filled the top shelf. On the lower shelf, bottles of vitamins and medicine surrounded a stack of bowls, leaving little room for much else. The kitchen had seemed so clean and new, with shiny marble countertops, natural maple cabinets, and sparkling black appliances, but I felt more at home with every packed cupboard I checked. I'd always had too many things and not enough room.

Opening another cupboard over the island, I finally found them. Glasses. I wrapped my fingers around a pretty, blue-tinted glass and went to the sink.

As I turned on the water, the phone rang. My heart skipped a beat. The phone sat at the end of the counter. Would he let me get it? I was much closer to it than he was. I lunged and snatched it up on the second ring.

"Hello?"

"Caitlyn?" His voice—I recognized his voice!

"Roland! Is it really you?" My heart danced in my chest. "You found me!"

"What?"

"I need your help," I said, my voice high and hurried. "It's urgent. I don't know where I—" A hand snatched the phone from me. I spun around.

Jarret hung up the phone and shook his head. "No phone calls yet."

My bottom lip trembled. Was he the jail warden and I the prisoner? "But it was Roland."

"Was it?" Jarret said with indifference. Did he expect

Roland to find me? Did Roland already know where I was? He wouldn't be in on it, on this evil, twisted scheme. He didn't have a devious bone in his body. Maybe I shouldn't have said it was him. Maybe now Roland would be in trouble.

"Why can't I talk to him? He already knows I'm here."

He shoved his hands into the front pockets of his jeans and stepped past the dinner table. "I don't know." He faced the sliding glass door. "Maybe you can. I need to think."

Clinging to hope, I stared at his back. Then a shadow shifted and a voice sounded in my ear—

"So, take my advice," Mike said.

I jumped. I hadn't heard him approach, but now he stood right behind me.

Jarret turned. "I will."

"Good." Mike's tone held authority, his expression concern. "Call if you need me. Or, uh, if her memories return. Remember, I would like you to call right away, should that occur. She may have some confusion about her memories." He gave me a strange pasty-eyed look as if he refrained from saying more. Then he grinned at Jarret. "Well, I'm going to go chase the little white ball. Take care."

I knew it: he was a golfer.

Jarret walked him to the door, where they exchanged a few last whispers. I thought Mike said, "Maybe you should tell her." Then they both looked at me.

As the door closed, a dull feeling of dread rolled over me, like the shadow of a storm cloud, at the thought of being imprisoned with Jarret. He seemed different from when I knew him in high school. More devious, if that were possible.

"Maybe you should tell me what?" I said.

"Why don't you come sit down?" Jarret grabbed a framed picture from the bookshelf, sat on one end of the couch, and propped a bare foot on the coffee table. He wore his hair in a low ponytail and had a look of concentration or a scowl on his unshaven face. Maybe it was the look he got when scheming. I'd seen him annoyed and angry, usually at Roland, with his lip curled up on one side and his eyes narrowed. I'd seen his vain and cocky look too, with his brows arched and a coy smile on his face. What would he look like if he ever really smiled? Maybe he never did. Maybe he was an unhappy man.

I dragged myself to the living room but stopped behind the loveseat. The room appealed to me. It had a fairly uncluttered, deceptively peaceful look, with splashes of dark blue and brown among paler beiges and cream colors. Light streamed in through wooden blinds over the front bay window and made stripes on a puffy brown leather armchair. A flat-screen TV hung on the opposite side of the room, by a bedroom door, two baskets of unfolded laundry under it. And a shelving unit of books, little framed pictures, and decorations lined the far wall behind the couch.

I had yet to wrap my mind around what he'd told me so far. Did I believe him? Was I ready to hear more? No. Not yet. "I think I'd like to take a shower, maybe lie down."

He shrugged and indicated the bedroom door with a grand sweeping gesture. "Let me know if you can't find something."

I stopped at the bedroom door. It was a trivial question compared to the weight of everything going on now, but I couldn't help but ask, "Do you have a dog?"

"What? No. Why? Do you… want one?"

"No, I just saw… I mean, I was just wondering."

I spent longer in the shower than I ever had in my life. The water came down in pulsing streams, relaxing my back and neck. Our shower at home dribbled on one side and sent cockeyed streams out the other so that I had to keep repositioning my head to get the conditioner rinsed out of my hair. And here no one banged on the door and shouted, "Hurry, I have to pee!"

Goosebumps formed on my arms as I stepped out of the shower. I dried with a huge, soft, royal blue towel, then I stuffed an arm into the smaller of the two white robes that hung on the wall. Obviously, they were *his* and *hers*.

His and hers. Could I really have amnesia? Could I really

be married to him? Why couldn't I remember a single detail about what should've been the most important event in my life?

No. I never would've married a guy like him. My perfect husband would love Jesus more than me and love me because of my love for Jesus. He would be faithful and gentle and have a heart for others. Jarret was selfish, vain, and prideful. He swore and drank. And he wasn't a virgin. But then, I wasn't either. Anymore. Could that be true? Were we really married? I had intended to remain pure as a sign of my love for God, not to mention out of respect for myself and my future husband. I'd romanticized my wedding night, when I'd give myself to another for the first time, when two would become one and possibly create a new life!

I sighed. Had I done something wrong, made some foolish mistake that brought me to this terrible situation? If only this were a nightmare from which I could wake up.

"Wake up, already!" I said as I opened the bathroom door.

On the far side of the bedroom, the long brown curtains inflated like a balloon, twisted, then flattened against the screen. When had he fixed the screen? He must've been busy while I took a shower.

My gaze dropped to the bed, now sloppily made, and to a framed photograph that lay on it. Was it the one he'd grabbed from the bookshelf? Guess he wanted me to see it.

Pulling my robe closed at the chest, I picked up the picture. As the image came into view in the dim light, I gasped. A bride and groom held hands in the dark open doorway of St. Michael Church. Jarret was the groom and I the bride!

As if touching something evil, I tossed the picture onto the bed and stepped back. *No!* It didn't have to be true.

Not wanting to believe it, I turned to the dresser to find clothes. The first drawer I tried held men's underwear. I shoved it closed.

He could've easily used an image editing program.

I eased open another drawer: guys' socks and

handkerchiefs. With a huff, I slammed the drawer.

People manipulated photos all the time.

The next two drawers had all girl things, so I picked out what I needed and headed for the closet.

A girl simply couldn't believe her eyes nowadays.

In the middle of the floor lay the denim jumper I'd worn earlier, stained with grass and torn from my experience with thorn bushes. I picked it up and sighed. It had been one of my favorite outfits. Maybe I could repair it.

What was I thinking? My life needed repairing first. I needed to get home.

I whipped the jumper across the room, and it landed on the box in the corner near the closet door. My gaze fastened to the ratty, two-foot square, cardboard box. It sat at a crooked angle as if it had been shoved there in a hurry, not as if it had been placed there for storage. One flap hung out, the edges were ragged, and black scribbled-over letters marked the sides. In such a tidy little house, it seemed out of place.

I knelt on the floor by the box and opened the flaps. Three shiny yellow boxes sat balanced on top of an old slide projector. I pulled out a thick stack of loose papers and manila folders, a tape dispenser, a glass ashtray, an old camera, and from the bottom corner of the box, a new digital camera.

A new camera? I took it and sat on a crumpled mess of sheets and blankets on the bed. Maybe the camera held pictures I'd remember or pictures that might explain things.

Before I could figure out how to turn it on, a light rapping sounded on the door. The door opened and Jarret stuck his head into the room.

"Hey, uh, did you want to— Is that my camera?"

I shrugged and held it out to him.

Eyes on the camera, he came over and took it. "Or is it yours?" He sat beside me on the bed.

I pulled my robe closed at the neck and curbed the impulse to scoot away from him.

He turned the camera around, examining it. "We have the

same kind. I lost mine the other day. Took yours by mistake. Remember that? No, you don't remember that. Anyway, this must be mine. Where'd you find it?"

I pointed to the box in the corner, wishing I had put all the junk back into it.

"Oh, yeah," he said, staring at the mess.

"What is all that stuff?"

"Ah, it's from work. We're moving to a newer building. I was cleaning out some cabinets. Those old slides and files need to be put with their projects instead of... Well, I thought I'd bring the junk home and sort it out. I guess I dropped my camera in the box. The guys were looking for it."

"The guys?"

"My coworkers and Mike. I gave them your camera by accident." He stared at me for a moment, thoughtfulness and compassion in his eyes.

A rush of heat assailed me. It felt odd having him look at me like that. He'd given his girlfriend Zoë—my best friend—the same look during her pregnancy, whenever she moaned or struggled with something or simply looked uncomfortable.

"Does your head still hurt?" he said.

I nodded.

"Want something for it?"

I shrugged. "I thought you had a degree in anthropology."

"I do."

"Why are you working at a doctor's office?"

"I'm not. I work for a private company that does cultural resource management. I'm leading the field investigation at a future construction site."

"That sounds boring."

Irritation flickered in his eyes but faded when he spoke. "Well, I've only got a BA. There's only so much I can do."

"So, where does a doctor fit in?"

"Eh, he's not with us as a doctor. He's been studying archaeology. He's getting experience." He stood. "I'll get you something for your headache. You get dressed. I wanna go find your car."

"Do I have to go? Can't I just stay here?"

He stopped in the doorway and gave a crooked grin. "Do you still want to run away?"

I opened my mouth but didn't answer.

"Yeah, you have to go."

# Chapter 5

THE AFTERNOON SUN reflected off Jarret's mirrored sunglasses. He slouched in the driver's seat of his Dodge Ram and palmed the steering wheel, driving like a man at ease with himself, his life, and his truck.

"Where're we going?" I couldn't get myself to ask my other questions. What had Mike meant when he'd said Jarret should tell me? Why wouldn't Jarret let me talk to Roland? Why did all of this feel so wrong?

"Mmm, I dunno. Just gonna drive around." While appearing completely relaxed, he rode on the bumper of a midnight blue minivan.

I groaned inwardly, wanting to go home. I should look for an opportunity to get away.

We had left a housing area of newer, cookie-cutter homes, drove down a long road with older homes and farmlands, passed over a highway, and now headed toward a busy strip mall. Across from the strip mall, a digger dumped a load of orange dirt onto a pile of more orange dirt, carving out a foundation for a new construction. Nothing looked familiar.

"The dirt is orange." I stared as we passed the digger. Orange dirt clouds billowed out around it.

"Yeah. We're in North Carolina. Didn't I tell you?" He sped up, gripped the steering wheel, and whipped around the minivan.

My stomach leaped into my chest. "Do you have to drive so fast? North Carolina? That's clear across the country from home."

"It's weird, you not knowing stuff." He slowed a wee bit and relaxed his grip on the steering wheel.

"So, what are we doing in North Carolina?"

He glanced at me before answering, a strange, irritated look crossing his face. "Don't blame me. *You* wanted to be here."

I shook my head, not believing him. I loved everything about South Dakota, its history of cowboys and Indians, its rugged landscape, prairies, and buffalo. South Dakota had inspired countless miniatures I'd painted over the years. I loved my church and neighborhood. The tiny house in which I grew up. My friends. Miles and miles away.

My heart raced as I visualized the vast stretch of land between me and all that I held dear. Why would I ever want to leave all that?

Jarret cocked his head and cracked his neck. "Look, you have an Associate in Criminal Justice and Police Science. And you found this job with—"

"I have an associate degree? In criminal justice?" The thought thrilled me but I sighed. I couldn't remember any of it.

"Yeah."

"I don't remember going to college." I gazed down at the yellow car ahead of us as its bumper sticker came into view: *If you can read this...* I pressed my foot to the floor as if I had control of the brakes. The truck moved too close for me to read the rest.

He smiled. "Well, you did. You and Roland got the same degree, only he's still going, working on his bachelor's or something."

"Why won't you let me talk to him?" The words flew out, emotion with them, and my hands balled into fists. "Maybe Roland can help me remember. He can tell me what happened in college and help me get to this point, my life now. With you. It's hard for me to understand how I ended up like this." Jarret shouldn't have mentioned his brother. Roland's voice sounded in my head, saying my name. I needed his help. I needed him now. He'd always been a good friend, a calming presence in my life. He could help me.

Jarret snickered. "You talk like your life's over, just 'cuz you can't remember how we ended up together." He glared. "You think you would've married me if you weren't in love with me?"

Turning away, I gazed at an orange dirt smudge on the window and spoke in a lower voice, more to myself than to him. "I'm not your type. And you're not mine. How could we ever have been attracted to each other?"

He let out a long, hard sigh. "No, I am not ready for you to talk to Roland." He tapped the brakes, glanced in the mirrors, and raced recklessly across oncoming traffic, heading for the crowded parking lot of a grocery store.

My hand shot up to the glove compartment to steady myself. I read the big red letters of the store sign. "Piggly Wiggly? That's a strange name."

"Yeah, for a grocery store. You used to say it sounded insulting." He cruised from one end of the parking lot to the other, then up and down the rows, his head turning from side to side like the *terminator*. The truck crawled slow enough for me to jump out if I wanted to.

I laughed to myself. What a silly idea. Still, I found my fingers inching to the door handle. I would have to fling the door open and jump. He'd stop the truck and get out. But I could run to the nearest gas station and ask for help. Then again, I might get hurt trying to exit a moving vehicle. I'd feel stupid needing his help.

My finger brushed the black door handle.

Jarret's hand slid onto my other hand. He laced his fingers through mine, his eyes shifting toward me.

Flinching at his touch, I sighed and dropped my hand to my lap. It was a stupid idea anyway. Maybe inside the store, I'd find an opportunity to get away. I had to. I couldn't stay here with this man I'd never liked and didn't trust. Why wouldn't he let me speak to my family? Something wasn't right—

He pulled out of the last row and turned toward the road.

"Wait!" I said.

He released my hand, slammed a foot to the brakes, and jerked his face to either side. "Where? Did you see it?"

"See what?"

Driving with determination, he turned the truck around and pulled into a parking spot at the back of the lot. He reached one hand to the door handle and the other to the keys in the ignition. "Your car. Did you see it?"

"My car? I don't remember having a car. What does it look like?"

Hand sliding off the door handle, he blew air out his mouth and re-gripped the steering wheel.

"Can't we go in?" I sounded desperate.

"You need something?" That strange look of concern came to his eyes.

My face warmed. It didn't seem possible that he could have those feelings for me. "I—I do need something."

"What?"

I huffed. "Do I have to tell you?" *Think, think, what do I need?*

He huffed. "Why can't you tell me?"

"I'm a girl." I narrowed my eyes, trying to appear indignant. "Sometimes a girl needs things that are private. I shouldn't have to explain."

"You don't need any of that."

"How do you know?"

He grinned in a way that made my stomach turn. "I'm your husband."

"So you say." I grabbed the door handle.

He latched onto my other hand again. "We'll go in, but you hold my hand the entire time. And don't try anything stupid."

"Stupid?"

"Yeah, like trying to run or get attention. I know how you feel about me. I see it every time you look at me. So, if you try anything, expect me to do something about it."

"Like what?"

The grin slithered back onto his face, and he waved his brows.

My skin crawled and I turned away.

Hand in hand, we crossed the huge parking lot and stepped into the air-conditioned store. Jarret grabbed a basket instead of a cart, and we weaved through customers in the produce department.

"Need any fruit or vegetables?" He didn't slow one bit.

"No." I shivered, my skin turning to goose flesh from the cool air. Wanting to fold my arms for warmth, I wrapped one arm around my waist and tried to wriggle my sweaty hand from his.

He tightened his grip. "So, what do you need?"

I clenched my jaw. My brain kept searching for an escape route, but Jarret's words in the car made me reluctant to attempt anything. "Let it Be" by the Beatles played overheard and Jarret hummed along. While I considered myself to be a girl who trusted God's will for her life, this just didn't feel right. I didn't want to "let it be." I wanted to go home. Why wouldn't Jarret let me go? Did I stand a chance of getting away from him in the store?

We cruised up and down the aisles. Jarret spent a considerable amount of time in the ethnic food section, comparing enchilada sauces. I grabbed random items on impulse: a can of barbecue potato chips, a can of mandarin oranges, a bag of miniature chocolate bars... olives, pickles, sardines. I didn't remember liking sardines. Or prunes. But for some reason I had to have them.

"What's with the shades?" Jarret said. We walked to the refrigerated section in the back corner of the store.

"I don't know." I stared at my reflection in the black sunglasses I'd grabbed a few aisles ago. Something about them spoke to me. They reminded me of something... gave me a strange feeling. Maybe I'd meant to buy some before. I dropped them into the nearly full basket Jarret carried at his side.

"What do you want for dinner anyway?" he said.

"Oh, whatever my mom's making." I flashed a fake smile. It felt good to give the snotty reply.

"Right. Knock it off. This is your home now. Give it a chance." Jarret stopped by the meat department and set the basket on the floor. "Let's grab some dogs."

*Give it a chance.* His words echoed in my mind. Should I give it a chance? Could I give it a chance? None of this made sense. Why wouldn't he give me some space?

No, I couldn't do this—live with a man I didn't like and so far away from my family. How would I ever get my memory back like this? No, this required drastic measures.

As Jarret picked up a pack of hot dogs, a girl some distance away shouted, "Jarret West!"

We both turned.

A sixteen- or seventeen-year-old girl bounced up to us. She wore formfitting jeans and a skimpy top with spaghetti-straps. Blond-streaked brown hair fell over one eye. Her other eye, the one glued to Jarret, shimmered with thick make-up. "Hey, ya, Jarret," she said in a sweet Southern voice.

"What's up?" Jarret shifted to face the girl, the hint of a smile passing his lips. He assumed the same coy, self-confident attitude he used to take in high school whenever he spoke to a pretty girl.

"Wow," the girl said. "What're y'all doing here?"

Did she really have to ask? I found my eyes narrowing and forced myself to avert my gaze. I had no reason to feel jealous. What did I care whom Jarret associated with?

Then it happened. The opportunity I had been looking for. The girl stuck out her hand to Jarret. Jarret held a pack of bun length Ball Parks in his left and my hand in his right. His right hand twitched. Then he let go.

Air hit my sweaty palm and sent a cool chill through me.

I sucked in a breath and stumbled back a step.

"I didn't know you lived nearby." The girl gushed with adoration. "Are you coming back to our school this year?"

Jarret mumbled something, his attention entirely on the girl.

I turned and bolted. The grocery basket— I saw it in my peripheral vision but too late. My foot crashed into it with a jolt of pain. The basket slid. I sailed forward. A display of hot dog and hamburger buns broke my fall. I hit the cold hard floor and grunted, packages of buns sliding onto me.

"Hey, baby, you all right?" Jarret hovered over me, his expression changing from concern to amusement. He grabbed my hands and yanked me to my feet.

"I'm fine," I said, bottom lip trembling. I was back in high school, walking into the tetherball pole and tripping over my own books.

Jarret pulled me to himself, his arms slithering around my waist. He turned me so we both faced the girl, then he spoke over my shoulder, his musky cologne assailing my nostrils. "Do you remember my wife?"

The hair on my neck quivered. My face burned. I had probably turned every shade of red.

"Sure, I think so." The girl extended a hand to me.

I forced a smile and shook the girl's hand. "Charmed."

"Can't wait to see you when you come around again." The girl beamed at Jarret, another gushy smile, and bounced off.

I exhaled, still trembling. "You can get your hands off me now," I said with disgust, prying at his warm, muscular forearms.

"I don't know if I want to." He buried his nose in my hair, took a deep breath, then released me. "Let's get out of here. Did you get everything you wanted?" He snatched a pack of buns from off the floor.

A few minutes later, we were through the checkout and back in the truck. He shoved the key into the ignition. Before cranking it, he gave me a long look. "You're probably wondering what that girl—"

"No, really, I'm not." I flashed a smile. "I don't care. I just want to go home." I didn't need to know. I needed to go. I needed to return to my family home and figure out what had happened to me. Jarret was Jarret. I was under no illusions about him. He could do what he wanted.

~ ~ ~

Our second stop came after a fifteen-minute drive down a busy four-lane boulevard, past restaurants, strip malls, a fire department, and spa. Jarret turned down a road behind a new car lot, drove past a little church and a few houses, and pulled into a shady, sprawling two-story apartment complex. He gave me a sideways glance as we crawled through the half-empty parking lot.

"Who lives here?" I said. The apartments looked older but well maintained. They had sloping tan roofs, cream siding, burgundy shutters, low bushes, and towering trees that cast inviting shadows on the lawn.

Jarret drove to the back of the half-mile complex and stopped.

I eyed the buildings. Did he expect to find my car here? Should the place jog a memory?

He stared at the back of the parking lot, where a group of young men and teenage boys rode skateboards back and forth. One practiced jumping, the board following his feet into the air like iron to a magnet. Another spun on the back wheels of his skateboard. One guy sped up a ramp and did a turning jump. He and his skateboard landed together on the pavement, but then his foot slipped off the board and he fell. Without hesitation, he jumped to his feet and rolled on. Another boy took a turn at the ramp.

"Do you know them?" I said.

Jarret shrugged and drove back through the complex and out onto the road.

We rode in silence for a long time, down another busy

road, then to a rural road, and back into a more populated section of town. Finally, he pulled into the parking lot of a tall, two-story brick building. White pillars rose up on either side of a fancy door. It looked like a real-estate brokerage. A white sign with big black letters hung out front, displaying the names “Wright Investigators” and “Guardian Investors.”

“This is where you work,” he said.

“Really?” Eyes wide, I looked again. “Wright Investigators?”

“Yeah, you guys are in the back half of the building. I think some investors have the front. It was a real-estate brokerage but they moved out.” He looked at me, the muscles of his face twitching. “I wish you remembered something about yesterday. Anything.”

“Well, what do you remember?”

He gazed at the building before answering. “We both went to work. Then I saw you here at lunch because...” He glanced at me.

“You came up to my work? Why?”

He frowned. “I, uh, I wanted to bring you your camera in case you needed it. I also told you I’d be late getting home. You said you’d make dinner.” He shook his head. “But I came home to an empty house. No message. Nothing. I tried calling you. You didn’t answer your cell phone. No one was at Wright Investigators.”

“You tried calling my work?” Something about his expression and words gave me the impression he was hiding something, but I didn’t know what to ask him.

“Yeah.”

“Did you try my boss or a coworker’s cell phone?”

“No, I figured you’d tell me your deal when you got home.” He rubbed his temples, his eyelids heavy. “But it was late, after dark. You came home in a cab, told me to pay for it, and went inside. Then you were just gonna walk right past me. No explanation. Nothing.”

“Did I have a purse or my phone?”

"Huh?" He looked at me. "No, nothing. You probably left it all in the car. But maybe... you were mugged." He frowned. "I really don't know." His voice rose in anger. "I don't know what happened to you. You wouldn't tell me a thing, just said you wanted to lie down."

"Well, I do have that bump on my head. I was obviously hurt."

"I know." His tone softened. His eyelids flickered. "But why didn't you tell me that? Instead, you avoided my questions. You made me so mad."

"Were we upset with each other yesterday? I mean, earlier. Like, did we fight at lunch?"

He blinked a few times and averted his gaze. His mouth opened as if he had something to say, but then he shut it. Was he keeping something from me?

"Do we argue a lot? I remember when I was in high school, how you used to yell at Roland. Do you shout at me like that?" Maybe I shouldn't have asked, but I wanted to know.

Still not looking at me, he shook his head and threw the truck in gear. "No."

# Chapter 6

I FOLLOWED MY friends Peter and Roland through the woods down the rocky path that led to the waterfall. My heart floated above me, free as a drifting cloud. My stomach growled, but other than that, I hadn't a care in the world. A bird chirped and another replied. Something made a tap, tap, tapping sound.

*The curtains? Oh.* I was not in the woods.

I sighed and tried to cling to the dream for a little longer. I preferred the dreams to the reality, but reality slithered in like a snake and my dream slipped away. Somewhere in this unfamiliar little house where I now lived, halfway across country from home, lurked Jarret West. Though he'd slept on the couch without me asking him to, I dreaded seeing him this morning.

Throwing the covers back, I sat up. The smell of bacon wafted through the window. My stomach growled as if in greeting to the wonderful smell. Then my stomach did something else. Churning? Maybe I wasn't in the mood for bacon. An uncomfortable lump formed in my throat. My hand shot up to it. Maybe I wasn't hungry at all. The hunger pang dissolved into a wave of nausea. Ugh. Maybe I was going to be sick.

As the nausea abated, I gazed at the dancing curtains and twisted my wedding bands the way I used to twist my gold purity ring whenever lost in thought. Sometimes I would run my finger over the little cross inside the heart or take the ring off and read the inscription inside: *True love waits*. Nothing had meant more to me than finding true love, the man God had prepared for me, my future husband and father of my children.

Over the years I'd romanticized it more and more. It would be love at first sight, but we wouldn't let on at first. We'd grow closer through shared projects and friendships. Various tests, trials, and misunderstandings would prove the depth of our love until one day... "I've loved you since the day we met," he'd say on bended knee. "I know God brought us together, and I want to love you for the rest of my life. Will you marry me?"

A tear rolled down my cheek. Had we waited for marriage? Or did we marry because we'd already rushed things? How had he proposed? Did he get down on one knee and say something terribly romantic? Or was it something more like: "Hey, babe, why don't we get hitched?" What was our wedding night like? Did we go on a honeymoon?

With a sigh, I staggered from the bed to the closet and stared at my clothes. *I might as well get dressed.* A pink-flowered sundress fell off the hanger and into my hands but, noticing its big red belt, I put it back. I didn't feel red, pink, or flowery today. The aqua button-front dress had always been a favorite. Nah, too cheery. I settled for a dress I'd never seen before, a knee-length with a dark print and short sleeves, black pockets and trim.

After dressing, I considered hanging out in the bedroom longer, to avoid him, but my stomach disagreed. So I forced myself to leave the comfort and privacy of the bedroom and to face my destiny.

A pillow and blanket lay on the couch, papers and cups cluttered the coffee table, and jeans and a shirt littered the floor. The lived-in living room tempted me to clean, even though it didn't feel like my house, but my stomach urged me on to the kitchen.

Jarret rifled through an overhead cabinet while mumbling into the phone pressed between his shoulder and ear. He wore loose white pajamas with a V-neck so low it hung half off one shoulder, exposing the brown cord of a necklace. A curl hung loose from a messy ponytail that he'd probably slept on.

All through his high-school years, he'd portrayed the image of male vanity, from the expensive clothing that emphasized his masculine physique to his long dark curls pulled back in a neat ponytail and his well-trimmed goatee. Every detail of his appearance and attitude had mattered to him. He'd created an image that attracted girls and commanded the respect and fear of boys. Even his twin brother, while roughly identical in appearance, couldn't match his vanity.

Now he seemed at ease with a comfortable, shabby look. Was he only this way around me?

As Jarret brought plates down from the cabinet, he caught sight of me. He mumbled into the phone, pressed a button, and slid the phone toward its cradle. "Hey. You sleep okay?"

I nodded and forced myself to stop staring. "Not as good as I would've in my own bed."

"In your own—" He shut his mouth and smirked, then scooped scrambled eggs onto two plates. "Right. Well, I hope you want scrambled eggs again. I made bacon."

A sudden rush of nausea overtook me. My hand shot up to my mouth.

"Don't tell me you're not hungry, 'cuz I know better."

Did he know better? How well did he know me? Of course, my eating habits had never been a secret. My friends made fun of me all through high school. I ate whatever I wanted and even brought snacks to every other class. Never gained an ounce. They drank Slim Fast for breakfast, ate salads for lunch, swore they didn't eat dinner but still gained weight.

I forced myself to smile and say, "Breakfast smells good," even though I no longer wanted to eat. Why did I feel the need to be polite to everyone, friend or foe?

As I sat at the end of the table, the nausea passed. Maybe

I did need to eat.

Jarret slid a plate of bacon and eggs to me and another to the place next to mine. When he returned to the kitchen, I got up and slid the second plate to the other end of the table. There was no need for us to sit so close.

On the way back to my seat, I noticed three thick books stacked in the middle of the table. Photo albums? I reached for one, but he came to the table with a mug of black coffee and a glass of milk, so I withdrew my hand and sat back down.

Sliding the second plate back to where he'd first placed it, he sat in the chair next to mine. "Aren't you hungry?" Eyes on me, he sipped his coffee.

"Sure, I'm hungry." I lifted the fork and poked at the eggs.

He turned toward the books. A breath later, he said, "You... wanna look at these?" Moving in slow motion, he took the top book down and slid it toward my plate.

It had a thick, satiny white cover and, in the middle of it, an oval picture of a bride and groom. I leaned in for a better look and gasped. Jarret was the groom and I the bride.

The fork fell from my hand.

He blinked a few times, then gazed into my eyes. "I'm not lying to you. You're my wife and I love you. These are wedding pictures." Lowering his head, he talked to his plate. "I wish you'd look at them. Maybe it'd bring back your memory."

"All right. I'll try." I did seem happy in the picture, smiling, laughing as I gazed into his eyes, a white veil blowing behind me. He smiled too. He wore a trim goatee, not the completely unshaven look he had now. What was the look in his eyes?

Aware of his attention, I opened the book and saw pictures of myself with my mother and sisters. My sisters wore frilly pale-aqua dresses. They must've been flower girls. Mya was my bridesmaid?

"Did Zoë come to the wedding?" I shouldn't have asked, but the question was out.

He shifted in his seat and gave a little nod. "Yeah, she was there."

I wanted to ask, "With your baby?" but I would've only said it in spite. I knew the answer. Neither one of them had been ready to care for a baby.

The next picture showed Jarret with Roland, Mr. West, my father and brothers, and even Peter. I suppressed a giggle. Every picture showed Peter in an awkward pose. In one, he was doubled over laughing while everyone else stood poised for the camera. He held his hands up in another, and a few yards away a glaring Jarret pointed at him. Oh, how they hated each other. Did they still? And where was Jarret's twin brother Keefe?

The next few pages showed the wedding, the wedding party, and other pictures taken inside St. Michael Church. Flowers, candles, decorations... It all looked so real. Could it be true? Was it possible all these pictures could be fakes?

Between glances in my direction, Jarret pushed his eggs around and tapped his fork on his plate.

"So, when was this? When did we..." I couldn't bring myself to say *get married.*

"Almost a year ago, end of June. Got our first anniversary coming up." Fork sliding from his hand, he gave me a lingering look.

"I'm sorry I don't remember any of this."

"Yeah."

"I don't mean to hurt your feelings, but it's hard for me to accept. I don't see how it's possible that we... What do you even know about me?"

He leaned back, wiped his face, and clasped his hands behind his head, sitting with his elbows out. "What do I know? You like cute things," he said, eyes to the ceiling. "Puppies and babies and such. You love taking long walks. You paint miniatures, mostly of South Dakota." He rolled his eyes. "We don't have any in the house 'cuz, well, you give them away to friends and family and, you once gave one to a total stranger."

A smile flickered on his lips, only to be replaced by a glower. "Your favorite color is, well, you don't have a favorite color because you like them all, but you tend toward shades of green and violet. And I don't know what else to tell you. I know you. You're my wife." He slumped forward, resting his arms on each side of his plate.

All those things he said about me, they were true. It just didn't seem real. "What ever happened to me and Roland?"

He huffed and shook his head. "I don't know. I don't know what happened to you and Roland. You told me you were good friends. You told me it wasn't meant to be more than that. You weren't seeing him when you and I..."

"Really?" My voice came out high, my forehead wrinkling and brows lifting against my will. How could that be true? I had wanted Roland to ask me out for years before he finally did. I was so drawn to him. He was mysterious, handsome, kind. He hadn't a single fault. We were planning to go to SDU together.

"Well, can we visit him?" I said. "Can I talk to him?" A glimmer of hope fluttered in my heart. What reason would he have for saying—

"No."

"No?" I pushed the photo album away, my stomach clenching and a weight falling in my heart. I'd seen enough. I had a lot of thinking to do. It was really all too much. How could it be true? What would have ever drawn me to Jarret? We were nothing alike. If I could talk to my mother or some of my friends—

"Caitlyn, we're not in South Dakota. We can't take a little drive and go see Roland. We're in North Carolina and I'm your husband." A troubled, stormy look came over him, and he was suddenly leaning into my space.

I gasped in shock, my lips parting. Before I could protest, he cupped the back of my head and smashed his lips to mine. A warm, intense, fleeting kiss.

"I need you to remember me." Fire smoldering in his deep

brown eyes, he got up and stomped away, disappearing into the room off the front of the house. The door slammed shut. A second later, he opened it to keep an eye on me.

He wouldn't drop his guard.

# Chapter 7

AN HOUR LATER, I finished my breakfast. Jarret had barely touched his. I scraped food into the garbage disposal, thinking of the hungry children in China and Africa. I thought of my brothers and sisters at home. We never threw anything out. Someone always wanted whatever someone else didn't. Maybe I should've wrapped it and put it in the refrigerator, but Jarret probably didn't eat leftovers. My nose wrinkled at the thought of eating something from his plate. With a sigh, I flipped the disposal on. Then I washed dishes and wiped the table to the sound of weights clanking and an occasional grunt from the room off the front of the house.

Half an hour later, when he still hadn't come out, I decided to explore. I did live here, right? It wasn't like I was being nosy.

Sunlight sneaked through the blinds on the front window in the living room, forming stripes on the leather chair and carpet. A mess of junk covered the coffee table: empty pop and water bottles, a plate, a TV remote, a pile of papers, and some of the folders I'd seen in the old box. Throw pillows were tangled up in a blanket on the couch.

I folded the blanket and, as if by habit, brought it to my nose. The scent, a manly odor combined with musky cologne, stirred something inside me. It was pleasantly familiar. I took another sniff and placed the folded blanket on the back of the couch.

The bookshelf had much to explore. Trinkets decorated

each shelf: rocks, pillar candles, shells, and framed pictures. Between two candles and a grapefruit-sized amethyst geode, stood an eight-inch statue of Saint Catherine of Siena, my confirmation saint. The rocks probably came from Jarret's collection. Roland had told me about it, how he even had rough rubies and an emerald. A hunk of pink quartz sat like a bookend against a set of blue books. Next to an old vase I found a vibrant bluish-green rock, and between the framed pictures, a shiny black rock, a clear rock, a gold one...

I picked up one of the pictures and smiled. A young, teary-eyed girl held a bundled baby in her arms. As I set the picture back, I noticed two more pictures of girls holding babies. They looked like teenagers. Who were they?

"Looking for a good read?"

My insides jumped at the sound of Jarret's voice. He stood in the doorway of the weight room, wiping his sweaty neck with a towel and watching me.

"Just looking around," I said, not sure why I felt guilty.

"Yeah, good idea. Maybe you'll remember something." He crept toward me, like a man afraid to scare off a wild animal.

"Do you remember your detective novels?" Coming up beside me, he pulled a book from the shelf and stared at it while he spoke. "Maybe the stories would all seem new." He handed me the book, a G. K. Chesterton novel.

I rubbed the smooth book cover. *The Man Who Was Thursday*. It looked new. "I read this in high school."

"Not *that* one." He gave a weak smile, a flirty look in his eyes. "I gave you that one."

"Really?"

"And these." He pointed to a section of books, then withdrew one and handed it to me.

I balanced it on the Chesterton and ran my hand along its glossy cover, a coffee-table book titled *South Dakota Parks and Forests*. While I did not remember it at all, it moved me. I loved to lose myself in photos of South Dakota landscapes. But not now. I returned it to the shelf.

We did have a lot of books. A few familiar titles of mysteries and detective novels popped out at me. There was a section of Westerns, probably his. Archaeology and geology handbooks, also his. And a dozen coffee-table books. Mine?

"Why don't you read something you don't remember? Or listen to music. Remember these old things?" Jarret slipped a CD from the top of a stack of CDs. "Here's one you like." The flirty look intensified as he pushed the CD into my hands.

My face warmed. I stared at the CD, wishing he wouldn't stand so close. *Switchfoot?*

Out of the corner of my eye, I glimpsed movement at the base of his neck, a rhythmic pulsing movement. For a moment, I could focus on nothing else. This really meant something to him. *I* meant something to him.

He continued staring, then finally spoke. "I'd, ah, like to take a shower."

Relief flooded me. I took a deep breath and glanced at him. "Okay."

He made no move to go.

"Go ahead." I backed up and gestured toward the bedroom. "I won't go anywhere."

"Uh, never mind. I've got some things I, uh, need to do first, I guess." He slipped past me and went into the bedroom.

Returning the CD to the stack, my gaze fell on a wallet-size photo that leaned against books: Jarret's twin brother Keefe in the brown Franciscan habit. "Oh, that's right..." I picked it up, remembering that after high school he'd pursued a vocation as a Franciscan Brother. That explained his absence from the wedding photos.

Keefe and Jarret were so similar in appearance, yet so different in personality. It would've been strange, but I wouldn't have minded waking up as Keefe's wife. He was the considerate, gentle twin. Jarret had always tried to control him, making him do the dirty work of his schemes. Until Keefe broke free.

The bedroom door swung open. Jarret came out in denim

shorts and a red t-shirt. He returned to the weight room to do... whatever.

With a sigh, I set the picture down and searched for a book to read. Hmm...maybe a Western.

Sometime later, I woke on the couch, a Louis L'Amour book in my arms and the aroma of grilled hot dogs wafting in the air. My stomach grumbled. Where was Jarret?

As I sat up, someone knocked on the front door. The book fell to the floor. The patio screen door slid open, and Jarret appeared in the living room.

The knock came again. I scooted to the edge of the couch, intending to answer the door, when Jarret dashed for it.

He shook his head. "Let me get it."

Jarret cracked the door open a foot or so and mumbled through the screen. Judging by the tilt of his head, he spoke to someone short.

I slunk closer to listen.

"No. She's busy," Jarret said. "What d'ya want?"

Irritation shooting through me, I put my hands on my hips and glared. *She's not busy. She's a prisoner stuck in a strange nightmare.*

"I noticed y'all didn't leave for church today. Is Mrs. West sick?" said a young boy with a cute Southern drawl.

"No. Yes. I don't know. What d'ya want?"

"I'm selling candy bars to get money for Little League. Mrs. West always—"

"We just went to the store. We don't need any candy."

The boy didn't respond, but he must not have gone away. Jarret sighed and leaned against the doorframe.

"Can I ple-e-ease speak with Mrs. West?"

"I already told you, she's busy." Jarret sounded heartless. Didn't he like kids? How could I have married someone who didn't like children? I wanted a houseful of them.

"But she always buys candy from me." His comment and disappointed tone pulled at my heart strings. "And I saved the peanut butter cups fo' her. See? I only have one left, and I put it in my pocket so no one else'd see it."

"Mm. I'm sure she'd want that."

Unable to stand another second of this, I yanked the door open.

"Hey!" Jarret's hand shot out for the door.

"Oh, come on. Won't you let me talk to anybody? He's a little boy, for goodness sake. What do you think he's going to do?" I gave the boy with the candy box a smile and pushed open the screen door.

An eight- or nine-year-old boy stood on the front porch. He wore cut-off jeans, a purple t-shirt, and tennis shoes with no socks, and his straw-like, sweaty hair stuck out from under a baseball cap worn backwards.

"Hi, what's your name?" I said.

"Hi, there, Mrs. West. I'm selling candy."

"That's Bobby." Jarret scowled.

"Would you like to come in?" I said.

"No, he doesn't want to come in." Jarret whipped out his wallet. "How much are your stupid candy bars?"

"A dollah each. I saved this one fo' you." Bobby held up a pack of Reese's Peanut Butter Cups.

"He kept it in his pocket," Jarret mumbled. "Get something else."

"Oh, that's my favorite." I took the warm candy and selected two others.

Jarret flipped three dollars into the candy box. "See ya, kid." He reached for the handle of the screen door, but I pushed my shoulder against the frame.

"Y'all having hot dogs?"

"Yes—"

"No." Jarret drowned out my response.

"What's the matter with you, Jar—" I said.

"I love hot dogs," Bobby said, oblivious to our tension.

"Would you like to join us for lunch?" I pushed the screen door open further.

"He's not allowed." Jarret tried to pull the screen door closed, but I blocked it with my body.

At the same time, Bobby said, "I sure would, Mrs. West," and made a move to come in.

Jarret cut him off. "Go ask your mother."

"Okay. Save a hot dog fo' me." Bobby hopped backwards, then he turned and bolted down the sidewalk, candy bars banging against the box.

I smiled, watching him run. Then I frowned at Jarret. "Don't you like kids?"

Jarret squirmed. "Sure, I like kids."

"Well, you're awfully rude to little Bobby."

He shook his head. "Bobby's over here—" His eyes went wide and he dashed for the back patio. "...ten times a day on the weekends."

I followed. I grabbed the condiment tray and carried it outside, dodging as a horsefly zoomed past me and into the house. "So, what's wrong with Bobby visiting us? He seems like a nice little boy. He even knows my favorite candy bar."

Smoke billowed from the grill. Armed with tongs, Jarret rescued hot dogs, tossing them onto a serving plate. "I don't know. Bobby's nosy, and he's a big gossip." A blackened hot dog rolled off the plate and onto the deck. Jarret snatched it with the tongs and with a pitcher's move whipped it over the neighbor's fence. He placed the last few uncooked hot dogs on the grill.

I stared at the neighbor's fence. "I can't believe you threw a hot dog into the neighbor's yard. Won't they be mad?"

He never answered, so I went back to work, setting up for the picnic.

A bit of the weight I'd been carrying lifted at the thought of Bobby visiting. It would be a nice way to spend the afternoon and would give me something to do other than dwell on my present misery. Besides, my family always gathered with friends to relax and cook out or share a big home-cooked meal on Sundays after Mass.

*Sunday?* Was it really Sunday? We'd missed Mass! Could I really have married a man who didn't go to Mass on Sundays and holy days of obligation? "Jarret, don't we go to Mass?"

Jarret faced the grill and tapped hot dogs with the tongs. "Yeah, sure we go."

"Well, it's Sunday and it's getting late. When do we go? I mean the last Mass must be around noon, right?"

Tongs in hand, he turned toward me. "We go at eleven-thirty. And, yeah, we missed it. Don't worry about it." He continued poking hot dogs.

I plopped down in one of the chairs at the patio table, and my arm knocked the ketchup over. "Don't worry about it?" What kind of man had I married? "I never miss Mass on Sunday."

Setting the tongs on the grill's side table, he turned around again. One brow lifted and his expression turned cocky, as if I'd accused him of being a heathen. "Are you worried about committing a mortal sin? I made you miss Mass. It's my fault. Don't worry about it. We'll go next Sunday."

"You don't care about committing a mortal sin?" I righted the ketchup and simultaneously knocked over the mustard.

He shook his head, rolled his eyes, and exhaled. "It's not a sin. You're sick, and I'm taking care of you."

"I'm not sick." I stood, flung my arms out, and glanced at my perfectly healthy body. "I'm perfectly fine."

He also looked over my perfectly healthy body, though at a slower pace. "If you were fine, you'd remember being my wife."

I slumped down in the chair.

Ten minutes later, as I neatened the plastic forks and spoons, Bobby raced into the backyard, still carrying the candy box.

"Hi there, Mrs. West, Mr. West." He climbed onto the deck and flopped into the dining room chair that I had insisted Jarret carry outside since there were only two patio chairs. "I'm not allowed over till I sell all the candy."

Jarret gave a satisfied grin and gestured with the tongs. "Better get going then."

"Well, how many candy bars do you have left?" I said.

"Don't even think about it." Jarret pointed the tongs at me and gave me a sharp stare.

Bobby opened the box and started counting. "One, two, three, fo'..."

"What?" I said to Jarret. "Think about what?"

"I'm not buying all those."

"... nine, ten, 'leven..."

"Why not? It'll take hours if he has to sell them all. Besides, there're only six houses on the street. Who's going to buy them?"

"Not us. There're other streets. Don't worry about him. He goes all over."

Bobby kept counting. "... eighteen, nineteen, twenty..."

I glared at Jarret.

"What?" He made a defensive shrug. "I'm not my father. You and me struggle to make ends meet. I can't go spending twenty dollars every time Bobby has a fundraiser."

*Yeah.* He stood there in his designer denim shorts and red Armani t-shirt, saying he didn't have the money. His father was ridiculously rich. They lived in a big castle-like house. Jarret must've had everything he wanted growing up, including a shiny red car as soon as he turned sixteen. I couldn't see him ever struggling to make ends meet.

"Don't look at me like that. I haven't bought myself clothes since college. Well, except for my shoes." He looked down at his bare feet.

"I've got twenty-three. I think Mrs. Bannista would buy some. Only Momma says she's a diabetic and I shouldn't go over there. What's a diabetic? And maybe the Gregorich family... with all their kids, but they're on Butternut Street and that's pretty far. And Mr. West looks hungry. Will y'all save me a hot dog? At least one?"

"You can have as many hot dogs as you want. Mr. West is

going to buy all your candy bars, Bobby."

Bobby jumped up. "Really? Oh, wow, Mr. West. You hate buying candy."

Jarret groaned and brought out his wallet. "Here." He flung a twenty at Bobby and it landed on the deck. "Sell the other three to somebody else."

"Thank you, sir, Mr. West." Bobby retrieved the twenty and shoved it into his pocket. Then he handed the box to me. "Pick which ones y'all want. You can keep the box. I'll put the last three in my pocket."

"Good idea." Jarret rolled his eyes.

I pulled out three chocolate covered raisins, thinking they would suffer the least from being stored in a pocket, and put the candy box in the kitchen. We could have candy for dessert.

The chips, prunes, sardines, and sunglasses from yesterday's shopping trip still sat on the countertop. The sardines had been tempting me all day, so I snatched them up on my way outside.

Jarret had made a plate of food for Bobby and was making another plate. As I sat at the patio table, he stopped in the middle of scooping baked beans onto the plate. "Oh. I made hot dogs, and you're gonna eat that?"

"I'm sorry." Embarrassed, I started to get up. "I'll go—"

"No. Sit down." Resignation showed in his tone. "Eat what you want. Let's say prayers."

I bowed my head, amazed that Jarret really prayed before meals. Did he start before or after we married?

After the closing *Sign of the Cross*, I cracked open the sardines.

"That looks gross, like fish bait," Bobby said. "You really gonna eat that?"

"Yes."

Bobby talked between bites and talked with his mouth full for the rest of the lunch. "Momma says Mrs. Cook's daughter and all her grandchildren are coming to live with huh. I hope that's true, 'cuz there ain't no kids on this street, and I have to go all the way ovah to...

"I heard Dad talking to Mr. Sweda about our street. Y'all know they're gonna bring in construction trucks and bulldozers toward the end of summer? I can't wait! Dad says they're gonna make the street longah...

"When I sold Mrs. Patterson some candy, she told me..."

When we finished eating, I stacked dirty plates and utensils.

Bobby leaned back in the chair, sipped his orange soda, and gazed at overhead branches. "Say, Mrs. West, I heard Momma and Mrs. Patterson talking. They were wondering when you'd be having a baby."

The ketchup and relish slipped from my hands, crashed to the deck, and the relish jar broke near my feet. I gasped and stared wide-eyed at the mess. A strange feeling overtook me. This had happened before. On some other day in the past, I'd stood in the kitchen, staring at a mess of salsa and applesauce. Frustration and misery had flooded my mind as I'd dropped down to clean it up. Then Jarret had come...

"I'll get it." Jarret dashed into the kitchen. He'd said that before, but it wasn't this house, this kitchen...

"Momma says maybe y'all too busy with careers and don't spend enough time trying." Bobby kept babbling. "And Mrs. Patterson thought that was funny..."

I picked up the bottle of ketchup, thankful that it was made of plastic, my mind still on the flashback.

A second later, Jarret returned with a crinkly grocery bag and a roll of paper towels. "I'll get it," he said again. "Go sit down."

"Mrs. Patterson says that Mr. West—"

"Bobby!" Jarret shot him a hot glare. "Mind your own business. You can't go repeating everything you hear. Didn't anybody tell you it's not nice to be nosy?"

"What about Mr. West?" I said, uncertain if I really wanted to know. I sat down and watched Jarret wipe relish off the deck.

Jarret shot Bobby a death glare hotter than the last one.

Bobby shut his mouth, and Jarret finished cleaning the deck. The second he straightened, Bobby said, "Hey, Mr. West, can we play ball?"

"No." Jarret stomped into the house with the bag of broken glass.

"Ple-e-ease." Bobby hopped up and followed Jarret into the house.

A cabinet slammed and I jumped. The faucet came on. "Get out, Bobby."

"Ple-e-ease."

"No."

"Ple-e-ease."

All the begging tugged at my heart, if only Jarret—

"All right." His voice held intense exasperation. "Ten minutes. Then you go. Deal?"

"Deal." Bobby dashed back outside and leaped off the deck.

Scowling all the way, Jarret stomped into the shady backyard. He stood with one hand on his hip and sighed as he waited for Bobby to get the ball and gloves from under the deck. Bobby tossed Jarret a glove and jogged to his position near the neighbor's fence. Bobby threw the ball. Jarret lunged to catch it and threw it back, right to Bobby's glove. Bobby threw again. Jarret raced and lunged to catch it, then whipped it directly to Bobby.

I watched for a minute then finished clearing the table and wiping down the patio furniture. With everything clean and in order, I had nothing to do but watch them, so I made myself comfortable on the top step of the deck.

Jarret frowned and muttered under his breath, but an occasional smile broke through and not only when he made Bobby reach to catch the ball. Something about his smile drew me. Maybe because I rarely saw him do it.

"What happened to yuh new ball?" Bobby caught and threw the ball.

"I dunno." Jarret reached overhead and barely caught the ball. "Don't worry about it. This one's fine." He whipped it back.

Bobby's next ball sailed too far away from Jarret. Jarret sprung for it. He reached. He took to the air. His glove skimmed the ball. Then he fell and slid through the grass, coming to a stop on his side. "Caught it." Victory written on his face, he waved the glove in the air.

Bobby laughed, making me laugh.

Jarret smiled at me as he got up and brushed himself off.

Before long, I couldn't stop smiling. Jarret had stopped frowning and seemed to enjoy himself. Maybe he wasn't as mean and tough as he acted. He and Bobby probably played ball all the time. Maybe he *did* like kids. Maybe he put on a front to protect his image. Or maybe he didn't want Bobby to find out I'd lost my memory and report it to the neighbors. Or maybe—

"Hey." Bobby dropped the ball and jogged to the bushes at the back of the yard. "I know where yuh new ball is." Using his foot, he rooted through bushes and weeds. "Last time we played I threw it back yonder. Then those girls came over, and you made me leave before I even had a chance to find it."

"Never mind." Jarret glanced at me.

"Girls? What girls?" I said.

Bobby searched through weeds. "I dunno. Two girls, older than me. I think they go to high school."

"Was I home?"

"Nah, it was just me and Mr. West."

"Never mind." Jarret's scowl was back in full force. "Time's up, anyways. You need to go."

"Here it is!" Bobby stooped then straightened with a clean white baseball in his hand. "Found it."

"Good. Time for you to go." Jarret stomped over and snatched the ball from him.

"Who were the girls?" Tension forming in my chest, I stood and folded my arms. Not that I was jealous. It was just that...

Eww, what a louse! Was it the night I'd come home with a head injury? I was out in a car accident, getting mugged, or whatever, and he's home with two girls. Was one of them the adoring girl in the grocery store?

"Your mother's calling you, Bobby," Jarret said. "Better go."

Bobby jerked his face toward the house. "I don't hear her."

"Well, I do." Jarret snatched the glove from Bobby and took it, along with his glove and the two balls, to the deck.

Bobby made his goodbyes and dashed through the side yard.

With one foot on the bottom step, Jarret peered up at me, the worry of a trapped rat lurking in his eyes.

"So, you had girls over while I was out, huh? Was that the night I came home late?"

"I didn't *have* girls over. They came over on their own. We know them from our volunteer work. Not sure how they got our home address, but one of them needed advice."

"Our volunteer work. Right." Like I was going to believe that.

"Yeah, maybe it's hard for to you to believe, because you can't see the real me right now, but that's what we do." He climbed the steps, eyeing me as he passed by.

Before he made it to the patio door, not satisfied with his answer, I grabbed his wrist. It was the first time I'd touched him on purpose, and I immediately regretted it.

He stopped, his gaze dropping to my hand then lifting to my face. His eyes held no anger but flickered with a distant and even hopeful look.

Flooded with confusing thoughts, I released him and turned away.

He came up behind me and spoke low over my shoulder. "I don't cheat on you."

# Chapter 8

OKAY, SO MAYBE he wasn't cheating. But why could he have girls over the house, and I couldn't talk to Roland on the phone?

Arms crossed and fists clenched, I paced the bedroom floor. The smell of burnt hot dogs wafted through the room. A housefly buzzed against the screen, and the curtains hung like limp flowers in the still air.

What kind of a relationship did we have? Whatever it had been, it couldn't remain this way. If my memory never returned and I was stuck with him, he would have to change.

I stopped by the dresser mirror. Sad green eyes gazed back at me. I was a married woman. *Sigh.* Marriage was a sacrament, after all, a sacred institution. I was his and he was mine. Forever. For the love of God, I would try to make it work. I folded my arms and paced around the bed, toward the window.

Forever his. How would Jarret feel about abstinence? Saints Cecelia and Valerian practiced abstinence in their marriage.

Jarret married and abstaining? Maybe he would go along with it for a little while. Wait! Since I couldn't remember getting married, could I get an annulment? What were the rules for that?

*Rules.* Maybe I should set some rules for Jarret. And if our relationship mattered to him, he'd follow them. I stopped pacing. Jarret following someone else's rules... Ha! That would be the day. He set the rules. Everyone else had to follow them.

I tensed with determination. That was about to change.

I yanked open the bedroom door. The weights clanked on the other side of the house. Jarret grunted. I stomped to the weight room and stepped into the doorway.

There he lay on a bench, sweaty and shirtless, pressing weights with his legs. When he saw me, he let the weights clang down and sat up.

"What's up, babe?"

The sweat on his collarbone reflected light from the window, drawing my attention to his muscular but not overly bulging physique. I'd never cared for the bulky powerlifter look, but his trim, defined biceps and triceps, deltoids and pecs snagged my gaze and wouldn't let go.

Taking a breath, I turned to the doorframe. "Would you please put a shirt on? We have to talk. And my name's Caitlyn, not babe."

I sat on the couch in the living room and waited for him to join me. A moment later, he sauntered from the weight room to the kitchen. Dressed now.

"Want something to drink?" He opened the refrigerator.

"No. I want to set some rules." I made sure to sound firm, determined.

He grabbed a bottled drink and came over, his lips curling up into a crooked grin. "You want to set some rules, huh?" He took a swig of the red drink and wiped his mouth with his arm. Then he sat across from me, slouching on the loveseat.

"That's right. I don't need you to tell me about the girls, but I do expect—"

"I was helping them." He came across cool and collected, as though nothing bothered him. "It's what we do."

I put up a hand. "I don't want to know. And I don't need to know how things were between us. I'm beginning to think you controlled everything, and maybe I was your naive little slave girl."

He huffed and gave an eye-roll. "Like that would ever

happen."

I continued. "I don't know. And I don't care. What's done is done. But since we are married—Yes, I believe you now—and since there's nothing I can do about it, I'm going to tell you how I want things to be."

He smirked again, then frowned and looked away. "Lay it on me."

"When I'm not here, no girls in the house. And, unless it's work related or I'm standing right there, I don't want you talking to girls on the phone. You said you don't cheat, fine. But I don't want the slightest temptation in your way. Okay?"

He didn't look at me. His mouth stretched out, but I couldn't decide if it was a smile or a grimace. "Okay, Caitlyn. And let me tell you what I want."

As his brown eyes turned on me, I felt my resolve melting. What would he want? I was his wife, after all.

He leaned forward and set his drink on the coffee table. Then he snatched a pen, scribbled something on the corner of a page of junk mail, ripped the corner off, and handed it to me. "I want you to stop thinking of me like I'm sixteen years old. I'm not the same. If I was, you wouldn't have married me. Why don't you give me a chance?"

"What's this?" I read the scrap. He'd written the name *Kelly* and a phone number.

"Call her. Talk to her. Maybe she can help you understand a few things." He stared through sullen eyes. "Deal?"

I shrugged. *Kelly?* Why should I call Kelly? He probably told Kelly what he wanted her to say.

I spent the rest of the day avoiding him. When he sat in the living room watching baseball, I hung out in the bedroom. I stuffed the scrap of paper he'd given me between the jewelry box and a candle. Then I rearranged my side of the closet, organizing the dresses, shirts, and skirts according to whether I recognized them or not. I put all *my* clothing on one end of the closet rod and the rest on the other. As I moved the unfamiliar dresses and skirts, a few of them caught my eye.

The colors, the styles... they were simply perfect, so I put them in the middle, separating them from the clothes I couldn't imagine having selected for myself.

None of the shoes looked familiar. But then again, the ones I remembered wearing were old and worn. If it was three years later than I remembered, I had probably thrown them out.

On the top shelf of my side of the closet, I found a big plastic container of my things. My heart stirred as I pulled it from the shelf and carried it to the bed. Tears welled in my eyes as I pored over old photo albums and mementos. A folder held the artwork I had saved from grade school. It pained me to flip through the pictures; my artwork was atrocious in those early years. Nothing like the miniatures I'd learned to paint in high school. I unfolded my grandmother's handkerchiefs, finding inside clay figures made by my sisters and brothers. My sister Priscilla had made a ladybug. My youngest brother Andrew made a super hero, one with a cape, maybe Batman or Superman.

The ballerina doily my mother had made for me sat folded on a little box. As I lifted the doily, a scraping sound came from outside. I set the doily down, went to the window, and pushed back the curtain.

Jarret hovered over the grill, his arm muscles flexing as he scraped it clean. He would probably be outside for a while. I could explore the rest of the house.

Leaving the mementos and the box on the bed, I headed for the kitchen. I'd gone through a few cupboards already, so I cracked open one I hadn't checked. A cute, cat-shaped tin of herbal teabags sat on the lowest shelf. I loved brewed iced tea. Searching a few cabinets, I found a pan and put some water on to boil.

As the water heated, I dug through drawers. The one under the phone was a mess: an actual phone book, loose papers, and appointment books on one side; pens, pencils, and miscellaneous junk on the other. I pulled out the appointment books and mindlessly reached into a cupboard for a coffee mug.

With my hand on the handle of a mug, I froze. I hadn't checked that cupboard before, yet I knew the mugs were there. My heart skipped a beat. I wanted to tell someone.

Jarret stood out on the deck, his back to me, still scraping away at the grill. I didn't want to tell him. He might get too hopeful. Or he'd get upset, wondering why I remembered where we kept the mugs and not something about him.

I set the mug on the countertop and flipped open an appointment book. A business card fell out, landing face down. Someone had made three vague entries on the month of January: "Shelby 7:00," "Mr. Carr 3:30," and "Call Dee." And that was it. It wasn't my handwriting, so it must've been Jarret's book. He obviously wasn't big on writing down his appointments.

My attention shifted to the business card. Flipping it over, my heart lifted with a mix of amusement and joy. *Caitlyn West, Private Investigator, Wright Investigators*. So, that's why Jarret laughed when I'd said I could have my own cards made up. I had!

Still smiling, I opened the next appointment book and found notes scribbled on every page. All of it in my handwriting! How strange to see my own handwriting and not remember writing any of it. Notes filled the pages from January to May. Was it May? It felt like summer. Of course, we were in North Carolina. It had to be warmer here than in South Dakota.

I flipped through the book. When I reached the last filled-out week, my heart stopped. On a Wednesday was the note: *A-Z Women's Choice Clinic 2:00 p.m.*

Women's Choice? An abortion provider.

I couldn't tear my gaze from the words. Why would I have an appointment with an abortion provider?

Jarret no longer scraped the grill. He squatted and wiped the shelf under it.

Was I pregnant? I tried to find something in the other

entries that might make sense of things. There were names, times, and addresses but nothing detailed. Then toward the end of March, I found *Dr. Stillman 10:15 a.m.*

If only I had my cell phone, I could look up the doctor. Wait! Hadn't I seen— I tore open the drawer and grabbed the phone book. Flipping through the yellow pages, I found the physicians... the OB/GYNs... Dr. Henry Stillman.

I gasped, my body tingling with shock. I'd had an appointment with an obstetrician.

The sliding screen door opened. My heart jumped into my throat.

Jarret came inside. "Something wrong?"

I shut my mouth and shook my head, the tingling sensation spreading.

He went to the sink and cranked the water on, then washed his hands and forearms. "Your water's boiling."

"What?"

"On the stove."

"Oh." Stepping to the stove, I shut off the burner, then I stared through unblinking eyes as the bubbles died down in the water. Was I pregnant? I didn't feel pregnant, and I didn't have much of a belly. I did, however, often feel nauseous. Maybe it wasn't because of Jarret.

Why would I have an appointment scheduled with an abortionist? The hairs on the back of my neck stood as my mind turned over the sickening thought, and a shudder replaced the tingling sensation. Rather than pass through me, the shudder turned into trembling, my body shaking the way it did in the cold.

Leaning against the counter near the stove, Jarret stared at me while drying his arms on the clean kitchen towel. "You cold? Making tea to warm up?" He slid the cat-shaped tin toward me.

"What?"

"Something wrong?"

Unable to process his question as my own questions

weaved through my mind, I stared back.

"Want me to make it?" He opened the tin and dropped four teabags into the water.

"Am I..." Heart pounding against my ribs, I cleared my throat and tried again to get the question out. "Am I pregnant?"

He gave a little smile and glanced at my belly. "Yeah."

A rush of feelings mingled inside me: relief, excitement, fear, anxiety. "Why didn't you tell me?"

"I don't know." He frowned and shifted his position in an agitated way, rubbing one arm and leaning against the counter again. "You don't seem to like me too much, so I didn't know how you'd take it. Thought it might be best for you to get comfortable with me before you find out about him. Her. Whatever." He reached out and touched my arm, sending a strange, unwelcome sensation through me. Then his hand traveled down my arm, but I pulled away before he touched my hand. He looked away, in the direction of my appointment book.

"I guess I should've figured, you know, with my nausea and strange cravings, but—" I leaned past him and closed my appointment book. "Was I happy about the news?"

"Of course." He reached for me again but then shoved his hands into the front pockets of his denim shorts.

"Were you?"

"Happy?" His face flinched with a look that flickered from hurt to something else, something wishful maybe, expectant. "Yeah. Heck, yeah." He must've lost control of himself; his hands flew out of his pockets and latched onto my arms. "Gosh, Caitlyn, I love you. I want us to have a baby."

Backing away, I tried to make sense of the appointment with the abortionist and the unrestrained love in his eyes.

"Don't be upset about it. You're going to get your memory back. It's gonna be okay."

"Were we happy?"

A look of pain shot through his eyes, and he shook his

head, but he said, “Yes.”

# *Chapter 9*

MONDAY CAME AND I thought Jarret might go to work.

He didn't. He spent an hour of the early morning on the back deck, talking on the phone. Talking to people at his workplace or mine? I'd heard my name a couple of times, his voice traveling through the open bedroom window, but I hadn't caught anything else. After a while, I heard him banging around in the kitchen. Then the savory aroma of fried food and fresh coffee wafted through the window, so I decided to get up and venture out.

After a quiet breakfast of French toast and decaf coffee, I excused myself to the bedroom, took a long shower, and decided to wear a dark-green flowered sundress.

I stuffed my arms into the sleeves, ready to pull the dress over my head, but then stopped. Tossing the dress onto the bed, I ran to the dresser mirror and turned sideways. Excitement zipped through me as I ran my hand over my abdomen.

Oh! My belly did protrude a bit. Funny, I hadn't noticed the little bump sooner. Was a living, growing person really floating around in there?

A burst of motherly love and joy warmed my heart. *A baby*. I caressed my baby bump, desiring to communicate love to the little one hidden inside. How had I failed to realize it was there? Safe within me and yet not me, an entirely different person, made and loved by God, infinitely loved by Him.

As I dressed, I thought of all the shouting, fighting, and worrying I had been doing lately. Had the baby sensed it and worried too?

"I'm sorry, my little one." I rubbed my belly. "No matter what that father of yours says or does, I am not getting angry again. You will have peace and joy from now on."

With that resolution, I decided to spend the day avoiding Jarret. I wanted time to organize my thoughts. Nothing made sense. No girl sets an appointment with an abortionist unless she is upset about her pregnancy, about her life. How could I ever have planned to get rid of my tiny baby? I must've been so miserable that I couldn't think straight. Did my emotional state have something to do with my memory loss? Was my life so horrible that I couldn't think about it anymore? Maybe I had been running away when I got the bump on my head. Maybe... with the amnesia, God had given me a second chance at life—my life, the baby's life.

I scanned the closet, wanting something to organize, but I had already sorted my side. I'd made the bed. The dresser was already neat. The floor vacuumed. Discovering that the master bathroom needed cleaning, I opened the little window over the toilet and set to work. I gave half a thought to climbing out the window, but it was narrow and high, and trying to escape would make me feel anxious. The baby didn't need that anxiety. Alone in the bathroom, I could find peace.

After scrubbing and shining every possible surface, I decided to organize the bathroom closet. Little bath soaps, salts, and colorful oil balls filled one shelf. My sisters would have a blast with them. The towels, all soft and new in pretty blue and aqua colors, smelled so fresh I could sniff them all day. But the closet was already in order, so after a thorough investigation, I closed it and left the bathroom.

As I stepped through the doorway and into the bedroom, my relaxed mood ended and every muscle in my body tensed.

Jarret stood by the bedroom window, gazing outside. He turned. "Are you okay?"

"I'm fine." Hoping to stave off the tension, I took a deep breath.

"You've been in here all day." He walked to the foot of the bed.

"Have I? What time is it?" I glanced at the clock on the dresser. It was half-past four. "I was just cleaning."

"Oh." His gaze darted around the room as if he had something to say.

"Is something wrong?"

"I don't like you breathing cleaning fumes." He sounded bossy, looked bossy. His jaw even twitched.

Who did he think he— *Relax. He can say whatever he wants. It doesn't matter.* "Okay."

"The baby."

*The baby? He was worried about the baby?* My heart tingled and a little weight lifted from it. "I only used baking soda and vinegar."

He nodded, satisfied. "That's good." His gaze went to the open bedroom door, his steps soon following. Then he stopped. "Oh, hey." He faced me and leaned a shoulder against the doorframe. "I don't know what you were gonna do with the chicken. But it's thawed now, so I gotta do something with it today. Oh, and Mike's coming over."

"Mike? Why?"

"He called to ask about you. I said he could come over."

"Is he bringing anyone? A wife?"

"No, he's not married."

"Does he have a girlfriend?"

"Uh..." Jarret squinted, thinking. "I don't know. Yeah, I guess he does. He talks like he does, but I've never met her. He didn't say anything about bringing anyone. I think he wants to see you, make sure you're all right." Pushing off the doorframe, he turned to leave but stopped again. "Hey, uh, think you could help me with the chicken? I don't really know how to cook."

"All those breakfasts you've been making...?"

"Yeah, eggs and cooking on the grill..." He shook his head and shrugged, looking a bit embarrassed. "...that's the extent of my skill."

A smile forced its way to my face. He smiled back, his eyes holding more emotion than I could handle. So, I left the room ahead of him.

I went as far as the kitchen island and rested my arms on the countertop. "What are you planning to make?"

"Uh, chicken." He walked around the island and set the package of raw chicken breasts between us.

I tried not to laugh. "How are you going to cook it? What are you going to have with it?"

"I don't know. What do you want?"

"Well, what do you like? What ingredients do you have?"

He opened the pantry next to the refrigerator and stepped back so I could see. "What do you need?"

I wanted to keep my distance and stay mad at him for what he must have put me through, but he seemed so helpless. As the oldest child in a big family, I had grown accustomed to helping my younger brothers and sisters. Sometimes I'd felt like a second mother. I loved that feeling, being needed. The more someone needed me, the more it warmed my heart.

Coming around the counter, I opened a low cabinet to get my favorite cookbook.

"You know where the cookbooks are?" He sounded shocked, hopeful.

"I've been snooping around," I said, though I hadn't really checked this cabinet yet. Another thing I just *knew*. "Do we have spinach?"

"Boy, do we."

"Wow, really?" I flipped pages in the cookbook.

"You've been on a spinach kick. You sent me shopping for some last week, so we've got canned, fresh, low sodium. Whatever you want."

"Perfect." I smiled. "Let's make Chicken Florentine."

I had Jarret put a pan of water on the stove for the pasta

and then make salads. Next, I had him pound out the chicken and cut it into strips, while I got out salt and pepper and prepared a dish of flour for dredging. Then I had him wash and cut the spinach, but his first cuts were too small, so I took the knife from him and pushed into his space.

"Like this." I proceeded to show him how I wanted it cut, but he only stared at my face. "Are you paying attention?" My cheeks warmed under his gaze.

"Yeah, I got it," he said, without having even glanced at the spinach. He did move closer though, so that I now felt his body heat.

"Good." Woozy from the closeness, I set the knife on the cutting board, rather than hand it to him, and went to the stove to flip the chicken. "So, why don't we have sweet Southern accents like Bobby and Mike and the checkout lady at the grocery store?"

"We haven't been here that long?"

"How long does it take fo' a gal ta pick up a Southun drawl?" I batted my eyelashes and smiled, a bit shocked at myself for such flirtatiousness.

"You'd make a fine Southun belle, baby, but it ain't gonna happen in a yea'." He brought the cutting board to the kitchen island and leaned on the counter, his long-lashed, brown eyes on me.

My cheeks burned. He stood so close, his passionate gaze drawing me in. The rough kiss he'd given me yesterday flashed into my mind. I suddenly felt as helpless as Scarlett in the presence of Ashley Wilkes.

"Ma'am," he said in a low voice, his gaze flitting around my face, "what can I do fo yuh now?"

My heart flipped like a fish out of water. My mind went blank. Was it his dark chocolate eyes, his manly cologne, or the seductive tone of his voice? I opened my mouth to reply, with no idea what to say.

His attention went to my mouth. His lips parted. He leaned and—

The doorbell rang, and I breathed.

Jarret straightened and spun his face to the front door. "It's Mike. I'll get it." He crossed the living room, yanked open the door, and greeted Mike with a loud, "Hello." Mike shouted his own greeting back, still standing outside.

I took a deep breath, my heart still hammering in my chest, and forced my attention back to dinner preparations. I got out the cooking wine and tossed a chunk of butter into the skillet for the sauce. Mike's interruption couldn't have come at a better time. I would've regretted kissing Jarret willingly, on impulse, an act of passion with no underlying love. It might have affected my ability to think clearly, and I really needed to understand why I married this man.

My hand lifted to my lips. Was I really going to let him kiss me?

"We missed you at work today." Mike stepped inside and slapped Jarret on the back. "You *are* leading the field work, after all. Nobody else can count the fingers on their hands independently."

The butter sizzled. I scraped diced garlic and onions into the skillet. Did we have a second skillet for the spinach? I flung open the pan cabinet.

"I called. I was on the phone with Chuck for an hour," Jarret said defensively. "Didn't he get things together?"

The garlic and onions released their heavy aroma. I tossed butter into the second skillet, added the spinach, and turned up the heat. How much wine for the sauce? I checked the recipe, pushed the onions with a spatula, and added the wine.

"Oh, I suppose, but not like you do. There is a certain organization to your methods that others seem to lack. You are coming in tomorrow, I hope and pray."

"Yeah, I don't know." Jarret led Mike toward the kitchen.

"Well, the boss was none too pleased with your absence. And I hear you have another day off scheduled. You are aware of the deadlines and our future relocation."

They neared the kitchen island. I grabbed the cream from

the refrigerator, checked the recipe, and pushed the spinach around in the skillet.

"How yuh doing, Caitlyn? You're looking good," Mike said as he passed, his pale gaze lingering on me.

"Just fine, sir," I said in my best Southern drawl. "Dinnuh will be served right shortly."

Mike grinned and exchanged glances with Jarret.

Plain faced, Jarret shrugged, giving the impression he didn't understand Mike's surprise at my new accent. He stepped into the kitchen, grabbed the salads and the dressings, and carried them to the table.

"Does your head still ache?" Mike sat at the head of the table and smoothed his hair back.

"No, sir. My headache's done gone." I touched the bump on my head. "Still a little sore, but only if I touch it."

"Have any of your memories returned?"

Should I tell him about the brief memories, the flashback of dropping salsa and applesauce, the recollection of where we kept the mugs and cookbooks? "No, sir, not a thing." It wasn't a lie, really, since they weren't full-fledged memories.

Jarret drained the pasta into the sink, turning his head as the steam billowed up. He scooped it onto plates, then lined up the plates by me so I could add chicken and spinach.

"Well, y'all remember, you may get some memories back that don't quite make sense. It is possible t'experience disjointed memories. Perhaps, even, you may link faces or impressions to experiences in a way that does not reflect the reality."

Jarret slid a plate of Chicken Florentine to Mike. "What are you talking about?"

"Well, I mean, as she recalls experiences there, ah, may be some, well, some inaccuracies. Don't let it trouble you. It's all part of the healing process. I really want you to let me know once it happens, if it happens."

"I would love to have my memory back," I drawled as I joined them at the table, taking the seat next to Jarret.

"I'm gonna take you around," Jarret said with a frown. "When you're ready, I want to take you places we've been. Maybe it'll help."

"I've been ready." I batted my eyes, forcing back feelings of annoyance and replacing them with the docile disposition of a sweet Southern belle.

"You're not ready. You can't even accept that you're my wife."

*I do accept it.* I couldn't get myself to say it aloud, so I held his gaze for an uncomfortable moment.

"We are nearing the deadline, Jarret."

When Mike spoke and took the attention off me, my body relaxed and I took my first bite of the Chicken Florentine. It was delicious.

Jarret stared at me for a moment, instead of looking at Mike, who seemed to be waiting for a reply. Then Jarret leaned toward me and whispered, "You eat without praying now?"

I gasped and stopped chewing. I *hadn't* prayed. I always prayed before I ate, even in restaurants. Ever since I could talk, I prayed. I prayed even if I had to pray in my mind because I was with someone who didn't pray.

I swallowed the food in my mouth, my eyes locked on Jarret's.

He gave the hint of a grin, put his hand to his forehead, and said, "Let's thank Our Lord for what we got." Then he made the Sign of the Cross and muttered the *Prayer Before Meals* all by himself. Mike said, "Amen, let's eat," rubbing his hands together. Jarret picked up his fork.

"About that deadline," Mike said with his mouth full. "You know we have the entire north area and the formal garden to investigate."

"I told Chuck to—" Throwing an irritated glance to the ceiling, Jarret shook his head and chewed. "Well, how many students showed up today?"

"Same as ever. Chuck had them working in teams, one

team comparing the historic and current maps of the site, another going over the evidence for the paths around the grounds, another organizing and categorizing the artifacts recovered thus far."

"No, no, no. They need to get to that north section—"

"Artifacts?" They both looked at me when I spoke. "What artifacts have y'all found?"

"We've unearthed iron tools, ceramic pots and shards, even a bronze bowl," Mike said.

"And a few pieces of jewelry." Jarret set his fork down and gazed into my eyes, communicating pride of accomplishment but also love for me, maybe appreciating that I had taken an interest.

I felt the warmth of a blush again and my heart convicted me. There was more to him than I realized. I ought to give him a chance.

"It's the site of an 18$^{th}$ century plantation," Jarret said. "Only parts of the structures remain. We're there to collect artifacts and to reconstruct and retain the history before it's lost with the new construction."

"Since you've found artifacts and parts of a historical building," I said, having to force myself to maintain eye contact with him, "won't that stop the new construction?"

Mike and Jarret looked at each other.

Jarret shook his head. "Not usually. It's—"

A cell phone blared out the first few bars of the song "Calling Dr. Love." Mike peeked at his phone then pushed out his chair. He stepped into the living room before answering it.

Jarret must've lost his train of thought. He shoved a forkful of food into his mouth and glanced from his plate to me every other second as he chewed.

I felt as uncomfortable as a schoolgirl on a blind date. "So, um, I noticed we don't have any barstools." I glanced over my shoulder at the kitchen island.

"No." He took another bite and chewed, still staring.

"And I was wondering... This table seems awfully large for

the breakfast nook or dinette or whatever you call this. Wouldn't it fit better in the dining room?"

He nodded as he chewed but appeared entirely disinterested in the subject. Couldn't he add anything to the conversation? Or couldn't he offer an explanation for the strange arrangement?

He looked away. Staring at Mike now?

I looked too. Mike sat hunched on the arm of the loveseat, his back to us. Shielding his mouth with his hand, he mumbled into the phone. Then he flung his arm out, gesturing widely, and raised his voice in a defensive tone. Maybe he was fighting with his girlfriend.

It was none of my business, so I returned my attention to Jarret. "What about a little table?" I said.

Jarret looked at me.

"Maybe one of those tall tables with the tall chairs. Don't you think that would work better in here? Did we ever think of getting one? I mean, doesn't it look a little awkward the way it is?"

He grinned but the look in his eyes said I'd insulted his manhood. "I'm not my father. I don't have endless cash at my disposal. It never bothered you before."

"I'm sorry." Heat assailed me and I averted my gaze. I hadn't meant to belittle him. "I was just wondering. I didn't mean—"

"Pardon the interruption." Mike returned to the head of the table. "Now, what were we discussing?"

I elected to drop out of the conversation and resigned myself to smiling politely at appropriate times. Jarret and Mike dwelled on work. After dinner, I offered a selection of candy bars for dessert and set myself to washing dishes.

"I've got dirty dishes in the den," Jarret said and pushed out his chair, but then the landline phone rang.

I could take one step and reach it, but the warning in Jarret's eye told me I wasn't allowed. He took the call in the living room.

Assuming "den" meant the weight room, I went to retrieve the dishes. The den was a *man cave.* A monstrous black weight-set loomed before me, standing seven feet tall and stretching out with benches and weights from the door to the window, taking up most of the little room. Against the wall, sat a seven-drawer computer desk. It was cluttered with cups, little flash drives, papers, and the camera I'd found a few days earlier.

Curiosity overtaking me, I sat down to look things over. The papers came from Jarret's work, judging by the logo: Englehardt, Cultural Resource Management. The left-hand drawers held boxes of envelopes and unused checks, USB flash drives, thin black cords, and miscellaneous office supplies. The bottom drawer on the right had files labeled with neat hand-printed tabs: gas bill, electric bill, phone bill...

As I pulled out the credit card file, Mike darkened the doorway.

"Looks like Jarret's going to be awhile on the phone." He stepped into the den.

I set the file on the desk and turned the chair to watch him peruse the room.

"Jarret has quite the weight set."

"He does. I guess he likes to stay fit." I had unintentionally dropped my accent. Why did he make me so uncomfortable? He *was* a doctor, after all? "Mike, can I ask you..." I sucked in a deep breath and resolved to trust him, at least with this one question. "I don't know what happened to me, but, I mean, you checked me over, so do you think the baby's okay?"

His expression showing compassion and a hint of amusement, Mike squatted before me.

I tried to avoid staring at the ugly scar under his eye, but I couldn't help wondering how it got there. Probably a childhood accident or something innocent like that.

His pale green eyes conveyed sincerity and comfort as he gazed up at me. "Your baby's fine, Caitlyn. I checked its heartbeat with a fetal Doppler."

"A what? You did?" Joy rushed into my heart at the words "your baby" and my hand shot to my tummy.

Eyes dropping to my waist, he smiled and nodded. "If you'd like, I can check again."

"No, that's okay, if you checked already. I—I didn't know."

"You know now. And you'd best take care of yourself. No more running off through the woods and getting your head banged up."

"In the woods? What makes you think I was in the woods when I got my head—"

Averting his gaze, he laughed and straightened. "I meant no more running off like you did Saturday morning. Who knows what you were doing Friday night." He stared past me. "Say, is that your camera?"

"What?" I turned to see. "Oh, I think that's—"

Mike reached for the camera just as Jarret poked his head into the room. "What're you guys doing in here? It's nice out. Let's go sit on the deck."

"Sure. That sounds fine," Mike said.

"I'll be out in a bit," I said.

Jarret gave me a nod and his gaze slid to Mike, as if he suspected Mike made me uncomfortable.

As soon as they left, I grabbed the camera. I'd meant to look through the pictures stored in it. When Jarret had taken it from me, I had forgotten all about it.

It took me a minute to figure out how to view the pictures. Most of them were boring. A field with orange markers, a section of land where the grass had been taken up, the same section dug out, a row of stones in red dirt, a spread of dirty tools evenly spaced on the ground... So far, I'd found no people, other than a guy and a girl standing in the background of a picture of dirty pottery. The dark-haired man dwarfed the petite girl. His posture, arms out and palms turned up, made him seem angry or defensive. The girl stood rigidly with one hand on her hip and the other a raised fist.

Jarret was in the next picture.

I smiled.

He pointed to the neck of the dirty piece of pottery he held, his self-assured attitude coming across. Was it the confident look in his eyes? The tilt of his head? His mouth was open as if the camera caught him speaking. He had such nice, shapely lips for a guy.

What was I thinking?

I clicked to the next picture. The couple stood in the background of this picture too. They were kissing. The next few pictures were as boring as the first, so I decided against viewing the rest and set the camera on the desk.

Switching gears, I picked up the credit card file. One could learn a lot from a credit card statement. I opened the file and reviewed the top statement. *April.* We used the card to eat out twice a week. We seemed to have a favorite restaurant, El Sombrero's, and we liked to try new places. We shopped at—

*Wow. Jarret shops at the Supermart!* With his expensive tastes, I found it hard to believe. Of course, he did say we struggled to make ends meet.

A charge to the Indian Fort Hotel caught my attention. Why would we stay at a hotel in the town where we lived? I flipped to another statement: *March.* Another hotel charge. And the month before that... an airline ticket? According to the description, someone had purchased a single ticket to South Dakota.

# Chapter 10

AS IF VERIFYING what he'd claimed the other day—that his culinary skills were limited to eggs and cooking on the grill—Jarret made omelets for breakfast. The two of us ate in sleepy silence under the yellowish glow of the overhead light in the eat-in kitchen. Outside, gray clouds stretched across the sky and the birds seemed to have forgotten how to sing, creating a sullen atmosphere that matched my mood. After breakfast, I offered to wash the dishes, but he said he'd do them. So, I wandered about the house.

He didn't do the dishes. Instead, he cleaned the table and spread work papers on it. Then, with one knee resting on a chair, he leaned over the table and shuffled papers and 35mm slides around as if working a puzzle. Every now and then, he held a slide up to the light, squinted at it, and jotted down a note. He barely seemed to notice me.

At first the lack of attention had given me a sense of relief and I'd curled up on the couch to try to finish the Western I'd started. But I soon found myself staring at the fly that had been buzzing around the house yesterday and was now flitting around in circles, trapped between the window and the screen. Trapped and restless. I sighed, identifying with it.

My ears perked every time the phone rang. It rang a lot. Jarret always took the calls outside. Most of the time, when he returned the phone to its cradle in the kitchen, he looked grumpy. Sometimes he muttered under his breath.

I had just finished washing the breakfast dishes and

gotten out the whole-wheat bread to make sandwiches for lunch, when he came grumbling back inside with the phone.

"What's the matter?" I said, mildly interested.

"Nothing. Just work." He gathered a few papers and made a pile on the table, clearing room for us to have lunch.

By noon, the rain clouds had passed and a gentle breeze blew through the house. We sat at the table eating lunch, each lost in our own thoughts. With every bite of every meal, my thoughts turned to the baby and my heart stirred.

When I lifted my tuna, tomato, pickle, lettuce, and cheese sandwich to my mouth, a tomato slid out. It landed on the heaping pile of potato chips on my plate and knocked a few chips to the table. As I reached for the chips, my napkin slid from the table and fell to the floor.

I pushed my chair back and looked at it. A question popped into my mind, halting me from retrieving the napkin. I turned to Jarret instead. "Jarret? Did I drop something?"

"Huh?" One cheek bulged with a bite of his sandwich. His gaze darted to the floor and back to me.

"I mean, not recently, but before. Like, salsa and applesauce?"

"What?" he asked with a mouthful of ham and tomato sandwich.

I sighed. Why didn't my words come out right? Maybe I should've kept it to myself. It was probably nothing. "Never mind."

He swallowed. "Did you..." He cleared his throat and took a swig of water. "Did you say salsa and applesauce?"

"Yes, I—I was just wondering. Did I ever drop salsa and applesauce on the kitchen floor?"

His face froze. The sandwich slipped from his hand and fell apart on his plate. "You...remember that?"

"Sort of. It didn't seem like it was here, though."

He shook his head, a desperate, anxious gleam emerging in his brown eyes. "It wasn't here. Tell me what you remember."

The emotion radiating from him startled me but then touched some deep place in my heart, making me want to give him more. "Okay. Well, Sunday, when I dropped the pickle relish, I got this frantic, sick feeling and I think a memory came back. I saw broken glass, red slop, and an ugly mess on the kitchen floor. Salsa and applesauce, I think. And you were there. You helped clean it up. And..." Turning inward, I searched for the words to explain how it had made me feel. "An overpowering emotion struck me the day it happened, something wonderful and violent inside me, something I don't understand."

Looking up, I found him blinking back tears, his forehead wrinkling.

He wiped his face, glanced at the ceiling, and looked at me with the hint of a smile. "You remember that? You're getting your memory back." He stretched his arms across the table and rested his hands two inches from mine. "That was the first time we kissed. You kissed me."

Once I processed his statement, my eyes popped open and my temperature spiked. "Our first kiss? *I* kissed *you*?"

"Yeah." One of his hands jerked, as if he were dying to stretch those last two inches and hold my hands.

"I don't remember that." I resisted the urge to pull back. It wouldn't kill me to let him touch me. I should hold his hand. Maybe it would spark something. Our first kiss? If only I could fully remember. "Tell me about it."

"It was at my house. You were getting ready for the Salazars' visit. And we hadn't been talking for a few days, 'cuz—"

The phone rang. We both looked at it and then at each other. It rang again and he sighed. On the third ring, he got up to answer it and carried it out to the deck.

"Yeah, this is Jarret."

After taking a deep breath and exhaling slowly, trying to regulate my mood, I took another bite of my sandwich. I hadn't meant to be nosy, but his voice traveled into the house.

"Hey, hey, I want you to calm down. Calm down!"

I stopped chewing. That did not sound like a work call.

Jarret sat on the top step of the deck, facing the backyard. "I need you to listen to me... Heather, listen! It's going to be okay."

I dropped my sandwich. *Heather?*

Mumbling into the phone, Jarret got up and paced back and forth on the deck.

I pushed my chair out and stood. As I slid the screen door open, he caught my gaze and gulped as I approached. I stopped directly in front of him and folded my arms. "Heather? Really, you're talking to a girl?" Just when I was beginning to believe I'd had it wrong about him... "Has she been calling all day? You said it was work."

He shook his head. "Hold on," he said into the phone. "I'll explain in a minute," he whispered as he moved past me.

I stared, dumbfounded as he went back into the house. Explain what? One minute we're discussing our first kiss and now he's talking to another girl. "Give me a chance," he had said. *A chance for what?*

Irritation building, morphing into anger, I followed him into the house. "Who's Heather?"

He turned and gave me the once-over. Backing away, he whispered into the phone, "Now wait. Slow down. It's not as bad as it seems."

I gave him a fierce, narrow-eyed glare. All the rumors I'd heard about him in high school rushed into my mind. Was Heather a girlfriend?

He put up his index finger and mouthed, "One minute." Mumbling into the phone, he turned and headed for the weight room.

"Oh, no, you don't." I zipped past him and blocked the door with my body.

Jarret pressed the phone to his chest and whispered to me, "I need to help her. I'll explain in a minute."

I let out a disgusted, "Her?"

He rolled his eyes. Then he touched my arm, which he had to know would make me move out of his way. But I hadn't moved far enough, and our bodies brushed as he slunk into the weight room.

Skin crawling, I scooted back more.

He gave me a glance and proceeded to close the door, whispering into the phone before it clicked shut.

I strained to hear his low voice, now muffled by the door, unable to make out anything, until he said, "The baby."

I jerked back. *The baby?* Did he mean our baby? Or some other baby? Heather's baby? Was he cheating on me? My eyebrows drew together. My heart slammed against my ribs with hard, angry thuds. I did not need this.

This was the father of my baby? Why had he bothered saying I shouldn't think of him as being sixteen? He was no different. How did I end up with him? Why hadn't I seen it before I married him? Could I really have been so blind? He must've seduced me with his smooth ways. What a fool I had been.

I stomped to the bedroom and snatched Jarret's wallet from the dresser. I pulled out all the bills, maybe a hundred dollars' worth, and stuffed them into a canvas purse I found hanging in the closet. As I headed for the front door, I saw movement out of the corner of my eye.

The weight room door opened. Jarret leaned against the doorframe, the phone still pressed to his ear, mumbling low.

He could have his private call. I was out of here. How could I possibly maintain a peaceful disposition for the baby when I had to deal with his games?

No sooner had I touched the front doorknob than Jarret dashed over. He slid between me and the door, peered down his nose at me and shook his head slowly. "Just wait," he said maybe to me, maybe to Heather.

I stepped back and made a face to show my disgust. "You can't keep me here. I don't care if I have amnesia, and I don't care if I am your wife. I don't want to live with you." I regretted saying such harsh words. I never said things like that.

My words should've stung him, but his eyes only flickered. Then he lowered his head and spoke low into the phone. "So don't tell them yet. I'll go with you if you need me to."

The nerve! I growled then shouted, "Get out of my way!"

"Uh, yeah. I gotta little problem here." He gave me a glance. "Don't be scared. I promise you'll get through this... All right. Bye." He pressed a button and tossed the phone to the leather chair.

I glared, stars popping out one by one in my vision. "So, how many girls *are* there?" Self-control abandoned me and I lunged at him. It didn't feel real as I smacked my palms against his chest. I had never shoved anyone in my life.

He yielded to my violence, making no effort to resist me. His back cracked against the door and his head rolled back. He winced.

"You don't know what that was about." An aura of calm surrounded him. Did nothing disturb him? "Why don't you let me explain—"

"I don't know what it's about, huh?" Did he think I was stupid? "I'm right here. I *heard* you." I grimaced with anger. "Let me guess: is she pregnant?"

He inhaled and, avoiding my gaze, nodded.

"Yours?"

With an air of exhaustion, he exhaled loudly and pushed off the door. "I'm a married man. Married to *you*." He stood too close.

I scooted to the loveseat, snatched up a decorative pillow, and whipped it at him. He dodged out of the way. "Married! What does that mean to you?"

His arms shot up in an agitated gesture, and he started pacing back and forth behind the couch.

"I told you I didn't want you talking to girls!" I shrieked. I hated losing control to anger. I needed to calm down for the baby. Sucking in a deep breath, my bottom lip trembled. Why did I care what he did? If he wasn't my baby's father, I wouldn't care at all.

He ran his hand through his hair and stopped by the bookshelf. Was he looking at our wedding picture?

"So, Jarret..." With a few deep breaths, I had composed myself but I couldn't avoid the accusing tone. "Who went to South Dakota last month?"

He spun to face me, irritation in his eyes. "What?"

"I saw the credit card bill. One plane ticket to South Dakota. Was it for me? Was I trying to get away from you? Did I want to move back home?"

He sighed and stomped past me, stooping for the pillow I had thrown. "No. I went back home." He whipped the pillow onto the loveseat and snatched up the phone from the chair.

With jerky, angry movements, I grabbed the purse I had inadvertently dropped and slung the strap over my shoulder. Then I followed him to the kitchen. "Alone? Why didn't *we* go? Was it a little vacation? I am your wife, right? Shouldn't I have been with you?"

He set the phone in its cradle, grabbed the edge of the countertop, and leaned into it a few times, rocking back and forth like a nervous child. Then he pounded a fist to the counter, took a deep breath, and glanced in the direction of the sliding glass doors. A squirrel sat on the patio table.

Leaning against the opposite counter, I glared at the back of Jarret's head. "Well? Why didn't I go?"

He glanced at me over his shoulder. "You couldn't go. It was a last-minute thing."

"What was a last-minute thing?"

Straightening, he folded his arms and turned to face me with a sulky, stubborn look.

"Aren't you going to tell me?"

"I'd like you to remember it for yourself."

A surge of anger made my eyes snap open as wide as they could go. How could anyone make me so furious? "Tell. Me. Now."

His gaze skittered to the floor. "I, uh, I went to see Zoë."

"Zoë?" I searched through my memories, trying to fit pieces together. Zoë had broken up with Jarret after the baby. They'd avoided each other after that, for the most part. She hadn't dated anyone in her sophomore year of high school, but then over the summer she'd met someone. Was she still seeing him? How long ago was that? Why would Jarret fly back home to see Zoë? Zoë had once told me he'd taken the break-up hard. Did he still love her?

A burst of irritation coursed through me. Why wouldn't my memories fall into place! My gaze snapped back to Jarret, who still stared at me through sulky eyes. "You went to see my best friend, your ex-girlfriend, without me? Did I know about it?"

Eyes narrowing, he snapped, "Of course you knew."

"Really?" I let out an angry laugh. "So, we must have an open relationship. That sounds like me."

Expression softening, he stepped toward me. "Zoë needed help. I went to talk her out of making a big mistake."

I shook my head, struggling to access more memories, not sure what to believe.

"I told you already," he whispered, closing the distance between us, "I don't cheat on you." With smoky eyes locked onto my face, he brushed his fingertips down my arm.

Liking and hating the sensation from his touch, I twisted away from him. Too many questions filled my mind for me to trust him. "So, who stayed at the local hotel? I saw the charge from the Indian Fort Hotel on our credit card statement. Me? Needing a break from you? Or, let me guess..."

He leaned a hip to the countertop and stuffed his hands into the front pockets of his jeans, squirming as I spoke.

"Another girl?"

"Caitlyn, stop." Head shaking, he rolled his eyes and sucked in a breath. "She needed help. It was your idea, you said—"

"Oh? Was she pregnant?" At some point, I'd started smirking. He was such a louse. How many children did he have?

"Not by me." He stepped toward me again, so I darted to the other side of the island counter. "*I* don't cheat on *you.*"

Something in the way he said it gave me pause. Was he accusing *me* of cheating? But that wouldn't be possible. No matter how miserable my marriage became, I would never cheat on my husband. Jarret had probably made the insinuation so he could get the attention off himself.

"So, you're just a pregnant-girl magnet?" I said.

With a huff and another eye roll, he opened his mouth as if he had something to say. A full two seconds later, he said, "Why don't you let me explain?" His hands shot up and out in an angry gesture that made me jump. "All of this, this was your idea. I'm a, uh, I'm a counselor. And so are you. We help troubled teens. We volunteer at the—"

The doorbell rang.

Jarret gave me a *don't try it* look, and we both made a mad dash for the front door like a couple of kids after the last open swing on a playground.

Heart thumping, I reached the door first. I wrapped my hand around the doorknob, but then he wrapped his hand around mine. His touch, slimy as a slug, slithered down my spine, so I slid my hand away and backed up.

He opened the door only enough to see out. A cuss word escaped him. He gave me a glance and then stepped outside, pulling the door closed behind him. "You're kidding me. What are you doing here?"

The door clicked shut.

# Chapter 11

I TRIED TO turn the front doorknob, but it wouldn't budge. Jarret must've held it. I peered through the peep hole but could only see the back of his head, so I slid behind the leather chair, adjusted the blinds, and peered out the front window. Except for Jarret's car, the driveway was empty. And I couldn't see who was standing on the front porch, but I spotted a black canvas suitcase. Was it a girl? Was it Heather?

I pushed the window open slowly so as not to make any noise.

"I don't want your help," Jarret said.

"Why not?" The voice sounded like Roland's.

Heart pounding with hope, I lunged for the door and tried the knob again.

"Open the door!" I pounded on it. Was it Roland? I tried to get a view from the front window again.

"Let me stick around for a few days. I'll try talking to—"

"I don't want you around. Don't you get it? She thinks she's eighteen. She hated me when she was eighteen. Didn't she?"

Roland gave no audible answer.

"And she was in love with you. Wasn't she?"

Again, no audible reply.

"All she remembers about me is what a bad a—"

"Just let me talk to her." Roland spoke over Jarret's complaint. "I think I can help."

"You're not gonna help. You're gonna make things worse.

I already have to explain why..."

I turned without thinking and smacked into the back of the leather chair. Stumbling past it, I rushed for the patio doors. I squeezed around the chair at the end of the dinner table and yanked open the screen door a little too roughly. The screen door flew open, banged against its track, and slid back, hitting my arm as I escaped the house.

The second I stepped outside, the smell of lilacs and the chatter of birds assailed my senses. A squirrel scampered off the patio table and over the railing, where it disappeared. Sunspots on the deck warmed my bare feet as I hurried to the backyard.

Jarret was not going to send Roland away!

I jogged through the cool grass along the shady side of the house and past flowering bushes in the front landscaping. Then I saw him, and an enormous weight lifted from my heart, rising and dissipating in the sunlight.

Roland, my pale and handsome knight, stood on the porch with his hands stuffed in the front pockets of his black jeans. His hair, dark and wavy, was shorter than I remembered. He shook his downcast head, then sighed and looked up at Jarret.

Clutching the doorknob with one hand, Jarret waved his other arm as he ranted. Halfway across the yard, I could hear him. "Hell, she don't even remember that we—" His gaze fell on me. He let his hand slide from the doorknob and shut his mouth.

Roland turned. His gray eyes and thick dark brows had always conveyed the strength of steel and the gentleness of a dove. When he smiled, my heart melted. "Caitlyn!"

I ran to him and fell into the safety of his arms. A rush of relief, love, and peace filled my troubled soul as I relished the feel of his arms around me and the scent of shampoo and freshly washed clothes. "You came."

"Oh, my God," Jarret mumbled, defeat heavy in his voice.

Stroking my hair with one hand, Roland held me tightly with the other. "Yeah, and maybe Jarret will let me stay for a visit."

Not wanting to release him, I turned my head to speak to Jarret. "Please, please, can he stay?"

Jarret's face twitched all over, his jaw, his mouth, his cheeks. He inhaled and held it. "If that's what you want." He said it without making eye contact and then flung open the front door and stomped inside.

I paused and watched him go, a twinge of guilt teasing at my chest, then I took Roland's hand and gave him my full attention. "Oh, I can't believe you're here. Let's sit and talk." Releasing his hand, I sat on the edge of the porch and dangled my legs over the landscaping.

Roland stared solemnly at the door for a moment, then he tore his gaze from it and sat beside me. "How are you doing?"

"Terrible." I couldn't take my eyes off his face. Just seeing him gave me comfort, but something about him seemed different too.

"Jarret says you have amnesia."

I reached for the sore spot on my head and gingerly touched the bump. "Oh, tell me I'm not really married to him."

Roland bumped his shoulder against mine and gave me a sweet smile that stirred my feelings for him. "Now, Caitlyn, give him a chance. He's different from when we were in high school."

I grabbed his hand. "That's what he said. So when did he change?"

Roland shrugged. "There was always some good in him."

"Struggling to get out," I said and giggled.

He smiled and bumped me again. Roland always found the good in others, like a prospector searching for gold or precious minerals. He had broken through the layers of willfulness, pride, and arrogance of Jarret's outer crust and discovered something good and worthy of love. He had seen the flesh in Jarret's heart of stone, the glimmer of light in his dark soul, the speck of goodness hidden by the fog of selfishness.

I wished I had Roland's gift. Maybe then I'd understand why I'd married Jarret, of all people.

"What ever happened to us?" I searched Roland's eyes, but he only shrugged. "I feel the same as I always have about you. When did my feelings for you change?"

He stared across the street to where a car pulled into the driveway of a little ranch house that resembled Jarret's house and the other six houses on the cul-de-sac street. He gave no answer.

"Oh," I said. "My feelings didn't change. Yours did?"

"No, it wasn't like that. If you think about it, if you really think hard and look into your heart, I think you'll understand."

"Understand?"

"Ever since we met in high school, we've been close friends. I don't know if I've ever had a closer friend than you. But it just never went to the next level. Something was missing. We tried." His emotionless tone said he spoke of ancient history.

"But I do feel romantic about you." Tears welled in my eyes.

"Uh." Roland glanced over his shoulder at the door and turned back with a pink face. He lifted his hand, hesitated, then grabbed my hand and rubbed it with his thumb. "I did too, Caitlyn, but we were better as friends. I didn't end it." He released my hand and ran both hands down his thighs.

"I did?"

"You told me about Ling-si."

"Ling-si?"

"We met her our first year at SDU. She's Chinese."

I giggled. "I figured, you know, with that name."

"Yeah." He smiled and gave me his shy look. "We all became friends right away. It was as if we had known her for years. Then one day toward the end of our first year at college, you told me she liked me, said I should ask her out. Which I didn't understand at first, because I always thought it was you and me. But you told me to look into my heart. You said I was your closest friend, and you weren't interested in anyone else, but you didn't think we were meant to be a couple. So, I thought about it for a few days, and I realized my feelings for Ling-si were different than my feelings for you."

Heart aching as if I'd just been dumped, I sniffled and tried not to let the tears escape. "Are you still seeing her?"

He nodded. "I think we'll get married someday."

"You do?" My heartache eased, and I felt a burst of happiness for him. "That's wonderful, Roland. I can't wait to meet her."

He gave me a funny look.

"Again, I mean, or remember her. That would be better, I guess. I'd like to remember. I would really like to remember how I got myself into this... situation." I was going to say *mess* but I didn't want to offend Roland with my negative feelings for Jarret.

Roland had always been defensive of Jarret no matter how Jarret treated him. When he came to school with bruises, he said he got them messing around. I suspected they came from Jarret. I knew for a fact that Jarret's schemes had plunged Roland into trouble at home and at school, even causing him to serve hard detention time. But he never sought revenge. He wouldn't even tell on Jarret. Roland was the real treasure. In those years of brotherly neglect and torture, where any other child would've hardened in anger and sought revenge, he had grown in patience and mercy. Any girl would be blessed to marry him.

"Ling-si must be special."

He smiled. "Let's go inside."

"Yeah, Jarret's probably seething," I said.

Tilting his head, Roland gave me a playful look. "Now, Caitlyn. Give him a chance."

I carried a black ceramic plate to the table and gazed through the patio doors. The cornflower blue, early evening sky and the lilac-scented breeze reflected the joy in my heart, the joy I'd felt ever since Roland arrived.

Roland and Jarret talked together out on the deck, their voices traveling through the screen door.

"I'll handle this my own way." Jarret faced the grill and flipped hamburgers with a long-handled spatula.

"What's *your* way?" Roland sat on the deck rail, a glass of water in his hand. "I mean, what're you going to do? And, and why can't I help?"

Except for our brief conversation on the porch, I hadn't spoken with Roland at all. He hung out in the weight room while Jarret worked out, then he watched him change the oil in his truck. When would he talk to me? He probably felt it necessary to tame Jarret first, to bring him around to his way of thinking.

I could wait. Since Jarret wouldn't let me go anywhere or do anything outside the house, all I had was time.

Hugging the black plate to my chest, I studied the table. Roland would want the black plate. Where should I put it? The table seated eight. I had placed an orange plate on one end, for Jarret, and a blue plate on the other, for myself. Would Jarret let Roland sit next to me? Probably not. Unless... I set the black plate on one side of the blue plate and relocated the orange plate to the spot across from it. We could all sit together. I returned to the kitchen for silverware.

The smell of charred hamburgers wafted into the house and Jarret uttered a curse. I glanced outside in time to see him do an arm-waving, hamburger-rescuing dance by the grill.

Roland laughed and turned to look inside the house. Our gazes connected. I smiled. He smiled back, and my heart melted.

"Look, I didn't ask you to come here." Jarret tossed the last hamburger onto a serving plate and turned a knob on the grill.

"I know. But I think I can help. Why can't you ever accept my help?"

"Help?" He snorted. "You're not gonna be any help. You're

making things worse." Jarret glanced inside.

I looked away.

I arranged the condiments between the three plates and brought out the baked beans and potato chips. If only we had a vase for flowers. It would make the perfect finishing touch. I could clip some lilacs from the bush in the backyard. Nothing compared to the sweet scent of lilacs in bloom.

Wanting to find a vase, I returned to the kitchen. If this were my house, where would I keep vases? I yanked open the cabinet under the sink and a bunch of plastic grocery bags fell out.

The screen door slid open.

"What're you looking for?" Jarret set the burgers on the table and moved the black plate to the opposite end.

I straightened. "Nothing." I shoved the bags back under the sink, closed the cabinet door before they fell out again, and scurried to the end of the table. "I thought we could all sit together." I snatched the black plate and placed it back where I wanted it.

"That sounds nice." He gave me a cocky grin.

I flashed a fake smile. He huffed.

Roland stepped inside and instinctively took the chair by the black plate. "Need help with anything?"

"No," Jarret said with finality. He sat at the head of the table, leaving me the place adjacent him and opposite Roland. Not exactly how I wanted it but *oh well.*

I opened the bag of hamburger buns and put one on Roland's plate. "Can I get you something to drink?"

"He knows where the refrigerator is." Jarret spun his face to Roland, saying, "Grab me a Coke."

Roland popped up to do his bidding. Was I like that? Did I run to fulfill his every desire? *Ugh.*

I took a bun for myself and set the bag by Jarret's plate.

"Nice." He snatched the bag and got out his own bun.

Roland returned with Jarret's Coke, a glass of water, and an iced tea. "You still like iced tea?" He held it out to me.

Flattered that he knew me so well, I smiled and took it.

"Ni-i-ice." Jarret narrowed his eyes at Roland. "So where do you plan on staying for your helpful visit?"

"I thought—"

"Can't he stay here?" I had stabbed a hamburger with my fork and moved it toward my plate but ended up dropping it on the table.

"Here?" Jarret's glare deepened. "Are you..." He raised a brow at me. "... gonna let me sleep in our bed?"

My mouth fell open and a wave of heat washed over me.

"I didn't think so. We only have one couch."

Roland shrugged. "I can sleep on the loveseat or on the floor. You have sleeping bags, don't you? I don't mind."

"That sounds great." I inched forward on my seat and propped my elbows on the table. "Doesn't it, *dear*?"

"Great." Jarret slumped back in his seat and exhaled like a deflating balloon.

After saying grace, we ate without speaking, stealing furtive glances at one another.

Roland broke the silence. "So, Caitlyn, what are some of the last things you remember?" Roland reached for the mustard at the same instant Jarret did. He backed off.

"Don't ask her that," Jarret said, glaring. "Why would you ask her that?" He squirted mustard on his burger and set the bottle by me.

"Well, I... why not? Why wouldn't I ask her that?"

"You," I said in answer to Roland, while offering him the mustard. "I remember you."

His eyelids fluttered and his mouth wrapped around the word *oh* but it never became audible. "I'm sorry," he whispered to Jarret. He faced me again and accepted the mustard, but it took him a moment to get out his next question. He was probably trying to foresee the answer and Jarret's response before he asked. "Have you checked out your photo albums or videos?"

"We don't have any videos," Jarret said.

"Jarret showed me the photo album with pictures from our wedding." Peter's poses in the photos came to mind, and my lips quivered as I suppressed a giggle.

"That's good. Right?" Roland gave Jarret a hope-filled look. "Did that help?"

Jarret and I shook our heads, then exchanged a glance.

"Don't you have classes?" Jarret said to Roland. "You're working on your bachelor's degree. Quarter ain't over yet, is it?"

"Yes. No." Roland brought his hamburger to his mouth but then returned it to his plate. The way Jarret glared at him probably had something to do with it. "We're in the last two weeks. I'm getting A's. I got permission. There's stuff I can do on-line. It's not a big deal."

"It's his own business," I said. "I'm sure he knows what he's doing. Roland's always been responsible. You just don't want him here."

Jarret turned his hardened glare on me. "That's right. I don't. You're *my* business, and I don't want him messing things up for me."

"For you?" His selfishness amazed me. That, and his jealousy. He did nothing to hide it. Jealousy disgusted me. It showed insecurity, fear, weakness. Maybe that explained his obsession with weightlifting. He felt weak and had to prove his strength to himself, to others. No, I didn't believe that. He didn't feel weak. He simply knew the strength of my feelings for Roland, and he didn't want to lose me.

His hard expression melted. "For us," he said, his voice weak and breathy. "You, me..." In a barely-audible whisper, he added, "...and our baby."

Judging by Roland's confused look, he hadn't heard it. But an ache wormed its way into my chest. Did I really cause those feelings in him? How had he fallen in love with me?

# Chapter 12

MALE VOICES, ONE soft and one loud, traveled through the closed bedroom door. I inhaled and yawned. Where was I? I sat up, got a glimpse of the gaudy room of mismatched antique furniture, and remembered. *Oh yeah, the nightmare.* I swung my legs off the side of the bed, stretched, and yawned again.

"Fine. You're right. I'm sorry I'm acting like such a heel," Jarret said to someone in the living room. "This is hard for me too."

"I get it." The second voice was softer. "Don't worry. I'm sure I can help. I'll tell her about the summer it all started."

"Yeah, tell her about our summer, but don't let her go anywhere. And when I get home, I need a shower. I've been washing up at the bathroom sink."

Who was he talking to? Wait— Remembering, I jumped to my feet and my heart started thumping. *Roland!*

"Why can't she go anywhere?" Roland came to my defense. "Don't you think it might help? Maybe if she—"

"Help? She wants to leave me," Jarret whined, but then his voice turned accusing. "What are you here to help her do?"

"Ah, she's not going to leave you. Don't you want to help get her memory back?"

I went to the window and opened the curtain. Sunlight glittered through the trees. The grill was still open and a chipmunk sat on the deck.

"And keep her from making phone calls, unless she wants to call Kelly. Yeah. Tell her to call Kelly."

"What? Jarret, you're sounding like a—"

"Just do it. You can't let her try to call home. You know her mother never warmed up to me. She'll blame me for this." In a lower voice he said, "And, besides, she doesn't know."

Ears perking up, I spun toward the closed bedroom door. Who doesn't know? Me or Mom? And *what* doesn't "she" know?

"You didn't tell her?"

"Not yet. Let's wait." He paused. "I need to get dressed. I'm going to be late. If I miss any more work, I'll lose my job. Of course, with you here, I'll probably lose my wife. You get her to remember that she *is* my wife, and don't spend all day yakking about your past together. In fact, don't talk about it at all. Whatever she doesn't remember about you, she doesn't need to know."

"Jarret, relax. She fell in love with you. Why don't you try to be the guy she fell in love with? The way you're acting now—"

Something bumped in the living room and someone grunted. Then Jarret mumbled something in his mean voice. Why did Roland put up with him?

"I'm sorry," Jarret groaned. "That was uncalled for."

I jerked back, shocked. He apologized to Roland?

Hearing nothing more, I turned toward the bathroom.

The bedroom door flew open and Jarret stormed into the room, the two of us colliding. "Oh, you're up."

"I was just going to the..." I pointed to the bathroom. Why did he make me feel the need to ask permission to do anything?

"I gotta grab some clothes. I really need a shower." He darted to the closet. "But I'm running late." He pulled his t-shirt off over his head.

I turned away.

Clothes rustled in the closet. "I'm going to work. I hate to leave you while you still have amnesia but..."

Keeping my back to him I said, "It's okay. I don't mind."

"Yeah." He came up behind me. "I know you don't. *I* mind."

"Well, I only..." I faced him, my reply dying on my lips. He stood so close, and he hadn't buttoned his white dress shirt. Heat sliding up my neck, I glanced every which way, trying to avoid looking at his bare chest.

"You'd rather be with him," he said, wrestling a black belt into the belt loops of his beige Dockers.

"I'm sorry." I meant it. "I'd like to remember us. I—I remember dropping the salsa."

"Yeah, well, work on it." He darted into the bathroom. The water went on, things clanked on the sink, and a minute later, he left the house.

At the sound of the front door squeezing shut, I sighed, my body relaxing from head to toe. Then a surge of excitement put me into motion. Now to see what Roland wanted for breakfast.

"I overheard you two talking this morning." I poured a second bowl of Toasty O's for myself—and the baby. I'd offered Roland everything I could think of for breakfast: pancakes, French toast, omelets, fried eggs over hash browns, and fruit cups and toast. But all he wanted was cereal.

"Did you?" Roland spooned the last few O's into his mouth, drank the milk from his bowl, and sat back.

"I don't understand why he doesn't want me to call home." I scooped up a spoonful of cereal, trying to conceal my intense desire to know the answer. Would he tell me something that Jarret didn't want me to know? "And what did Jarret mean when he said, 'she doesn't know'?"

Roland blinked and his gaze shifted to the glass doors. "Uh, it'll all make sense when your memory returns. I don't think you want to rush anything."

"What do you mean? The sooner I remember everything, the better."

"Yeah, I agree. But it's not like we can just rattle off everything that happened in your life and you're suddenly going to remember."

"But it could only help, right?"

He took a breath. "When things happen in life, we get time

to process them. If it's all just thrown at you..." He shook his head. "I don't think it's a good idea."

What had I needed time to process?

Apparently not wanting to continue the conversation, Roland stood and took his bowl to the sink. His lack of openness troubled me. I'd have to find a way to get the information out of him later. Certainly he'd be here for a few days. I lifted my spoon to my mouth. "What day is this?"

Roland returned to the table. "It's Wednesday."

The spoon fell from my hand and splashed down in my bowl. My heart seemed to skid to a stop and nausea rippled through me. "Wednesday?" I whispered.

One thought filled my mind, one image: the appointment written in my own handwriting in my appointment book. Wednesday at two o'clock, I was scheduled to visit an abortion clinic. It was probably a consultation, but I couldn't squelch the feeling that this was the day my baby would have died. Had my mother known about this? Was this the thing Jarret thought I didn't know?

Trying to push the miserable thought from my mind, or at least get some perspective, I took my bowl to the sink and dumped out the cereal I could no longer make myself eat. Whatever tragedy had led to my amnesia, I now saw it as a gift from God, a second chance, a way to start anew. My baby would not die.

As I washed the breakfast dishes, Roland wiped down the table. "Hey, when we're done here, I've got something to show you."

"You do?" I perked up a bit. Roland was another gift from God, someone to hold onto in the storm.

"Yeah, and maybe it'll help you put the puzzle of your life back together." Roland tossed the wet washcloth he'd been using into the sink and headed for the weight room.

Drying my hands with the kitchen towel, I followed. Morning sunlight streamed in through the window, shining on the metallic bars of the weight-set and making line patterns on the carpet. I sat on the end of the weight bench—after spraying it with Lysol and wiping it with the kitchen towel.

Roland had switched the computer on, and it now hummed softly. He gazed at the monitor, tapping his thumb on the arm of the chair while he waited for the computer to boot up.

I sighed watching him. He typed a few things, slid the mouse around, and shook his head when something didn't work out. His pale skin, smooth dark hair, thick eye brows, steel gray eyes... Oh, he was handsome.

I snapped from my thoughts. I shouldn't think of him like that, being married and all, but having him around sure made my situation bearable.

"If Jarret hadn't let you stay, I was going to leave." My hand shot up to my mouth. The words had just flown out. I shouldn't have said it.

Roland stopped typing and turned concerned gray eyes to me. "Aw, you can't do that."

"Oh, yes I can." Deciding that I had the right to feel this way, I jumped up. "I'm sorry, Roland, but I just don't like him. He's mean. He's controlling. He's no different than in high school. And I think he..." Gaining a thread of self-control over my speech, I choked back the rest of my sentence. *He cheats on me.*

Roland opened his mouth. His brows twitched. He blinked. Then he faced the monitor again and moved the mouse. A minute later, he said, "He's not himself right now. With you not remembering why you like him, he's all messed up." Another pause. Eyes still on the monitor. "I'll admit I was shocked when it finally came out, you and him. But I knew it was right. You two needed each other." A glance. "You still do."

"Why? I don't get it." I lifted my arms, then let them fall back to my sides. I resisted the urge to rest a hand on the back of his chair.

"You need someone who needs you. And he needs you. He's a totally different person with you."

Eyes to the ceiling, I blew out a breath and tried to avoid saying anything negative.

Roland swiveled the chair toward me and touched me, placing his warm hand on my arm and drawing my gaze to his serious eyes, which now stared intently at me. "Do you trust me?"

Warmth radiated from his touch and moved my heart. "Yes, I trust you," I whispered. *More than anyone*, I kept myself from saying.

"Then believe me when I say Jarret loves you. And you love him." He spun the chair again, turning toward the monitor. "Oh, here, I got it." He stood and motioned for me to take the chair. "These are the emails you sent me the summer you two got together. Some of them have my reply on them, but most of them don't. I just sent you new emails, and those don't show up in my mailbox."

I got comfortable in the chair, and he leaned over my shoulder, the scent of his shampoo teasing me. "You've kept my emails all this time?"

His pale face flushed carnation pink. "I keep stuff. I have Peter's too. I have everybody's." He grabbed the mouse and clicked on a message. "This is the first one you sent after you got to our house."

"Could you explain that to me again? Why was I living at your house?"

"Uh." His gray eyes shifted upward, then back to me. "Remember Nanny, our live-in maid? You always liked her."

The image of the plump, middle-aged woman with curly gray hair came to mind, and I smiled. I'd first met Nanny the day Peter and I had come uninvited to Roland's house and I had seen the West castle for the first time. "Of course, I remember her. I haven't forgotten *everything*."

"Well, Nanny had an operation. Papa wanted someone to live there over the summer so she could heal without worrying about cleaning and cooking. When Papa heard you were looking for summer work, he thought you'd be perfect for the job. You know how to cook and clean. You're nice and responsible. And since Keefe, Jarret, and I weren't expected home for the summer, it seemed like a perfect fit."

"*Seemed* like." I shook my head and then focused on Roland's email box, half-excited and half-afraid of what I might discover.

# *Chapter 13*

*HEY ROLAND,*

*I'm here at your house. Mom, Dad, and the whole gang came to move me in. Don't worry, I don't have that much stuff, just two suitcases and a box. My sisters are "helping" me unpack. Mom's trying to keep the boys out of trouble. They just want to slide in their socks down the long hallways. You probably did that when you were little.*

*Your father is so nice to us. He told my family to come over any time, stay the night if they want. I hope you don't mind, he offered them your bedroom and your brothers' rooms. But they won't take him up on it. Mom's a homebody. I think Dad would do it. He's in the poolroom right now, playing a game with your father.*

*I hate to sound mean, but I can't wait until my sisters leave. They're playing house in the walk-in closet in my room. My dresses are in piles on the floor. I think they're being used for beds.*

I laughed to myself. That sounded right. My sisters would've loved exploring and playing make-believe in the Wests' house, even in a walk-in closet. Excitement rising by degrees, I glanced at Roland, who stood admiring Jarret's weight-set. "I can't believe I lived and worked in your house. I hope I didn't break anything."

He dipped his head and almost laughed.

*My room is the guest room nearest the Digbys' suite. Do you like how I call it "my room" already? Your father wants me close to Nanny in case she needs me at night. I'm excited about staying here. I've always loved your house, or should I say castle? I shall pretend I am the maid of the West castle. All the princes and knights are away.*

*Well, Sir Roland, I hope your summer will be as fun as mine. I must go now. I guess someone ordered pizza. Looking out my window, I see the delivery boy outside. His mouth is hanging open, and he's gawking at your house. You'd think he had never seen a castle before.*

*Bye! Caitlyn*

In the next email, I claimed everything was going fine, I enjoyed working hard and trying to make Nanny happy. I liked feeling needed. And I also admitted that I hadn't broken anything.

I exhaled. "Oh good. My question answered."

The weights clanked, then Roland came over and looked at the monitor over my shoulder. "What?" He squinted. "What question?"

Shaking my head, I decided not to explain. I hadn't outgrown my klutziness yet, so I should probably keep my mouth shut. Chances were, I'd broken something.

I read a bit more. Mr. West had asked me to call him Ignatius, but I couldn't get myself to do it. And he also told me to take more breaks and relax in the evenings. He thought I worked too hard.

I looked up, turning from the monitor to Roland, who leaned against the wall. "I admit it sounds incredibly fun. But where were you this summer?"

"Me?" Still leaning against the wall, Roland crossed his legs at the ankles. "I was still at SDU, taking summer classes and hanging out with Ling-si in my spare time." A smile passed his lips, and his eyes held a sweet look I'd never seen before. He lifted a shoulder. "Keep reading. Maybe you'll find something."

Taking a breath, I got back to work. The subject line of the next message showed that several replies were in one email. Roland must have replied to my emails and I'd replied back. My heart pitter-pattered with excitement at the thought of getting to read his responses, but I scrolled to the first message to read them in order.

*Roland,*
*You'll never believe who showed up yesterday. Okay, maybe you already know, but I don't think so. You would've warned me. Yes, I'm talking about Jarret.*

My heart skipped a beat. This was it. Jarret had now entered the picture.

*I was strolling down the front hallway on my way from Nanny's room to the kitchen, when the front door flew open and Jarret, carrying two suitcases, stomped into the foyer. When he noticed me, he dropped the suitcases and shouted toward the staircase for you. I told him you weren't here. His mouth fell open and he said, "Keefe?" in a whispery, wishful way. I giggled and said, "Doesn't he live in a monastery?" Then his eyes narrowed with suspicion and he said, "So what are you doing here?" I just said, "Nanny," because I figured he knew her situation. And I politely asked what he was doing here. Boy, did he flip out. "It's my house!" he shouted. Then he stomped back outside and dragged in more suitcases, piling them up in the hallway.*

Picturing it in my mind, I sat back and folded my arms. "Look, Roland, he doesn't seem any different to me. I can't understand how I could've possibly…"

A silent moment passed, the two of us staring at each other.

"Well, you did," Roland said, matter-of-fact. "You fell in love with him, so keep reading."

*When he dropped the last suitcase onto the pile, he walked away, leaving his blockade of luggage behind. I stopped him and offered to move it all upstairs. He said no. Can you believe it? I guess he wanted poor old Mr. Digby to do it. But I didn't want it blocking the hallway. I needed to get Nanny in her wheelchair to the dining room for lunch in an hour. So when I heard the shower go on in the upstairs bathroom, I lugged it all upstairs and piled it in the hallway, between his bedroom and the bathroom. I mean, I left him a little path. But, boy oh boy, was he mad. He hunted me down, fire in his eyes, and barked, "I told you to leave it." He could've been talking to a dog. Then he asked me twenty questions and gave me his opinion about my living and working arrangement.*

*I noticed something odd while he was ranting. A brown tag peeked out the front of his shirt at the collar. If it wasn't Jarret, I would've thought it was Our Lady's Brown Scapular. My scapular tends to hike up whenever I'm behaving badly. Any chance Jarret wears the Scapular? No, never mind. I'm sure that's a silly question.*

*I hope this email doesn't make you worry. Maybe I shouldn't send it. Really, I'm not worried about him being here. I've hardly seen him in the house, except for those two encounters.*

*Don't worry, my prince. I can handle the dark knight.*
*Caitlyn*

I scrolled up, anxious for Roland's reply. Then seeing how short his message was, I sighed. Oh well, he'd always been a man of few words.

*Caitlyn,*
*What's Jarret doing there? Is he going to stay? He won't answer my calls. I thought he had field study. If he stays, are you going to? Papa's not going to like this. Email or call. Just call. Roland*

A warm rush of happiness started in my heart and spread through my whole body. Roland cared about me! How could that have changed? My gaze slid to him.

Face to the window and with daydreaming eyes, he stood with a foot propped up behind him on the wall and his thumbs in the front pockets of his jeans. A second later, he turned and caught me staring. "What?" His bewildered expression made him even cuter.

"Nothing." I sighed and slumped back in the chair to read more, my message now.

> *My Dear Prince Roland,*
> *Stop worrying. I shouldn't have sent that last email. Or maybe I should've worded it differently: Your dear brother has arrived. He showed up one day, but I haven't seen him since.*
>
> *It's really no big deal. You are right, though. Your father is upset about it. The two of them fight whenever they cross paths. I think they even had a fistfight out back. And your father's been home much more since Jarret got here.*
>
> *The reason Jarret is here: I overheard him say that his favorite instructor was unable to lead the field study, so he backed out too.*
>
> *Your father insists he either get a job or go with him on his assignments. Apparently, Jarret is not interested in either option. He'd rather stay here and boss me around. He doesn't like my hair down when I'm anywhere near the kitchen. He shot a hairband at me the first time he saw me making lunch. "Don't let Nanny see you like that," he'd said. Then he told me not to go upstairs except to clean the bathroom. He wants me to clean it on Mondays and Thursdays. My, but isn't he a bossy one?*

"My thoughts exactly," I said. Then I gave a little headshake. I'd written the email, so of course those would be my thoughts.

*I know he used to boss you around. Didn't it bother you at all? I try not to let it bother me. I just make a game of it. I carry hairbands in my apron, and if I ever see him in the house, I make a big deal of putting my hair up, then I look around and say, "Oh my, oh my, I hope Nanny doesn't catch me with my hair down."*

*Your father told me not to do anything for him, not even his bathroom. He said I'm only to do what Nanny says. I still brought clean hand towels down to the basement. Jarret wants them by his weight set. Your father caught me one day and got on Jarret about bossing me. I tried to say I didn't mind, but they didn't stop fighting long enough to hear me. So now Jarret doesn't boss me. But he makes me stop cleaning and leave rooms that he wants to be in: family room, game room, dining room... I think he's trying to be a pain but I don't mind. It gives me something to offer up. I think maybe I'll put flowers in his bathroom after I clean it Thursday. :)*
*Your maidservant, Caitlyn*

*Caitlyn,*
*Bad idea about the flowers. He'll think you're coming on to him. You wouldn't want him to think that. And Papa said not to clean his bathroom, so don't.*

My eyes snapped open wide. Had I placed flowers in Jarret's bathroom and he'd taken it the wrong way? Is that how it all had started? I refocused on the email, eager for the rest of Roland's message.

*Hey, I thought about your question about the Brown Scapular. And, yeah, he could be wearing one. Why not? I don't think the Virgin Mary intended for only saints to wear it or she wouldn't have promised that whoever dies wearing it won't go to hell.*

*How is Nanny? How much longer before she's back on her feet? All right, I can hear you. "Stop worrying." Fine. I'm*

*getting ready to meet Ling-si. We're going camping with some of the others from the Dead Theologians. By the way, Ling-si loves your emails. She laughs hysterically when she reads them. Do you tell her the same things you tell me?*
*Roland*

*Dear Roland,*
*I share a few different things with Ling-si, I suppose. She is a girl. It's different. But here's something I'll share only with you, except I won't share all of it. I'll have to keep some of it private because it's personal to your brother.*

*Jarret came home drunk last night. Correction: this morning. Around three in the morning, loud voices outside my window woke me. I peeked out my bedroom window and saw a car in the circular driveway, a guy standing by the open driver-side door, and Jarret lying on the ground. Jarret was upset and slurring something about his car being parked at some bar. The guy helped him to the porch, told him his car would be there in the morning, and left.*

*After a long while, I heard the front door open, but not close. I snuck from my room and down the hallway and watched Jarret from the shadows. I wanted to make sure he got the front door closed and that he made it upstairs in one piece.*

*He stood swaying in the middle of the foyer and then turned and looked straight at me. "Stop hiding an' step into the light," he slurred. So I did. I stepped into the moonlight that came in through the open door. He propped himself up against the wall and stared at me. I asked if he was all right. And he told me I was beautiful, using a cuss word that I won't repeat. Isn't that funny? I told him he was drunk, and he never would've thought that otherwise. He said he thought it all the time, but he never would've said it. Then he said the older I got, the prettier I got.*

*So. That was shocking. Jarret thinks I'm beautiful! Ha ha! I'll have to ask him about it now that he's sober. Maybe not.*

*Anyway, he was so intent on getting his car that he called a cab. Since he was in no condition to walk, much less drive, I got dressed and went with him.*

*I don't think he remembers last night at all. He keeps asking me questions. I'll let him wonder. Oh, by the way, you're right. Jarret wears the Brown Scapular. Who would've guessed?*

*You probably won't get this email until you get back from camping. Did you have fun? Tell me all about it.*
*Caitlyn*

A strange tingly feeling tugged at my heart. Jarret wore the Brown Scapular. I mentally re-created the scene I'd just read, trying it on for size, transporting myself to the Wests' house and to the foyer, dark except for the moonlight. And to Jarret, drunk and holding himself up with the wall. He'd told me I was beautiful. Even now, knowing he'd married me, it seemed hard to imagine him thinking anything nice about me. He'd always treated me with cold indifference, to say the least.

"Something wrong?" Roland squatted by my side and glanced between the monitor and me.

"Oh, it's just that all through high school, I had the distinct impression Jarret didn't like me. I always felt like such a clod around him, clumsy and awkward compared to the type of girls he liked. How can he think I'm pretty?"

"Well, the only reason he didn't like you back then was because you were my friend." Roland pressed his lips together and glanced to one side, as if not sure how to word the rest of his response, or maybe not sure how much to divulge. "For a time there, he didn't like any of my friends. But he didn't have a reason not to like them."

"And that changed? How?"

Roland's gray eyes shifted and held a strange, distant look. "Jarret changed. You'll have to trust me on that. And his opinion of you must've changed when you guys got to know each other. Have you ever formed an opinion of someone because of one little thing, then you get to know them and you realize you were wrong about them?"

I shrugged, but my heart convicted me. Yes, I'd jumped to conclusions about others in the past. And I was doing it now. I was judging Jarret based on his past mistakes.

# Chapter 14

I SAT BESIDE Roland in the shade of the front porch, kicking my feet into and out of the sunlight. Birds sang happily in the trees. Crickets buzzed and chirped in the dense woods that surrounded the little street. The sweet smell of flowers and grass lingered in the air. And Roland looked fine in his black, button-front shirt and jeans. Everything felt right.

Except for my stomach. It kept making weird, sproingy noises.

Since breakfast had been so light, I'd made up for it with lunch. We had tuna fish sandwiches, potato chips, chicken noodle soup and salads. I'd eaten prunes for dessert. Maybe I shouldn't have.

"I'm sorry, Roland. The emails haven't helped. I don't like Jarret any more in the emails than I do now. I don't get it. He sounds like a drunk. How could he ever have appealed to me?"

Roland sighed then gave me a serious look for a whole second before he spoke, making my heart stir every which way. "Sometimes Jarret's qualities are hidden and hard to find."

"I guess I should use my detective skills." I said it seriously, but he smiled and dropped his head to laugh.

"I don't know what to tell you, Caitlyn. You should talk to Jarret. Have him tell you about the summer you two fell in love. You never explained it to me. But you haven't read all the emails. Keep reading. After a while, I got the impression that you and he were friends. You rode the horses together and took walks. Selena came up, and the three of you did everything together."

"Selena? Really? I met Selena?" In high school, Roland had told me stories about the fun and beautiful Mexican girl from Arizona, the daughter of his father's close friend. I had always wanted to meet her. Figures, I did and couldn't remember it at all.

"Toward the end of summer, something you wrote made me realize your relationship with Jarret was deeper than you were letting on." With the hint of a smile, Roland leaned close and bumped my shoulder. "Keep reading. Maybe you'll see what I mean."

"I suppose." I took a deep breath, my gaze resting on the swaying leaves of the dogwood tree in the front yard. "I don't want to read anymore today. It's so nice out. I'm tired of being here. Let's take a walk or call a cab." An idea popped into my mind. I jumped up. "Yes! Let's go to my workplace."

"Ah, Jarret doesn't want you going anywhere." Roland stood and stretched.

"So? He's not my father. He's my husband. I still can't get over how he dragged me clear across the country, so far from home."

"No, you got that wrong. You're the one who wanted to move to North Carolina. Before you moved out here, you told me you had a job opportunity you couldn't pass up." Standing face to face, Roland stared intently into my eyes as if determined to make me understand. "Do you know what Jarret gave up for you? I couldn't believe he agreed to it. He wanted to get his master's from the University of Arizona. He put that on hold for you."

Stunned, I tried to absorb this revelation. It did not fit the image I had of Jarret. Maybe he had changed, but maybe he still had some changing to do. "Oh, well, that was nice. But must I do everything he tells me? Can't I do things that I want to do?"

"He's afraid you'll run away. He's afraid of coming home and finding that you've gone. Do you know what that would do to him?" Gaze dropping and emotion flickering on his face, he took my hand with the slightest possible grip then released it. "It would break his heart, Caitlyn."

Moved by Roland's concern for his brother, I sighed, but I wouldn't give up, couldn't give up. I might find answers at my workplace. I took Roland's hand in a firm grip. "Don't you want to be a private investigator?"

He shrugged. "Well, yeah. That's what I'm going to college for. Maybe I'll work with the police or the FBI."

"Okay. Then call Jarret. Convince him that we should stop by my workplace. I want to learn as much as I can about last Friday and, well, what specifically do I do on the job?" I squeezed his hand and smiled. "I'm a private investigator." Excitement raced through my veins. "Let's go see what I do. Wouldn't you like to know? Maybe we can work together some day."

Roland stared at me while thinking it over, making me want to lose myself in his deep gray eyes. Then he glanced up and down the street. "All right." Grudging reluctance gave way to a hint of excitement. "I'll call him. Do you know where your workplace is?"

I bounced on my toes. "Mm-hm. Jarret showed me. We pulled into the parking lot, but we didn't go in."

"Okay. Give me a minute." He took his cell phone from a back pocket and strolled down the driveway.

I dashed inside to change into one of the more professional outfits in the closet. I chose a straight tan skirt and a pale-blue button-front blouse from the group of clothes that I couldn't imagine myself wearing. Then I grabbed a matching purse. What would I put in it? I didn't have a wallet or anything. I tossed the purse and ran to the bathroom. Checking my face in the mirror and running my hands through my miserably wild-looking red curls, a thought flashed in my mind. *Jarret thinks I'm beautiful?* Pushing the thought back, I stuffed my feet into black pumps and hurried outside.

Roland sat on the front porch. He twisted around and looked me over. "Whoa! You look great, like a regular professional." He stood up, smiling.

"Thanks." The compliment pleased me, making me stand tall, though I couldn't stop swinging my arms. "Did you talk to Jarret? What'd he say?"

"They found your car."

My heart skipped a beat. "What? Who did?"

"The police. They had it at the impound lot. Guess Jarret called around this morning. He's bringing it here. Should be here any minute."

"Wow, where'd they find it?"

"I don't know. Some park around here. He said your purse and everything was still in it. Didn't look like it had been touched."

Confusion drew my eyebrows together and made me bite my lip. "That's strange. What could've happened? Did they check for fingerprints?"

"Uh, I don't think so. I guess Jarret never reported it stolen."

Ten minutes later, a dusty dark-blue Honda Accord pulled into the driveway and Mike's shiny black Mercedes stopped at the curb. Jarret climbed out of the Accord and stood tucking the back of his white dress shirt into his beige Dockers. I followed Roland over to him.

"Hey, Jarret," Roland said. "That's great they found her car. Part of the mystery solved, huh?"

Jarret looked me over twice and then flat-out stared.

My cheeks burned. Did it bother him to see me dressed up or to know I was going to my workplace? I folded my arms, feeling cold and self-conscious. *He thinks I'm pretty*, I reminded myself.

"So what park did they find it at?" Roland said. "How far is it from here?"

Jarret continued staring, wearing a brooding look now. He stuck his hand out to me. "Here's a set of our keys. I don't know where yours are."

I took the keys from him.

"Car runs fine," he said. "Your purse is in there. Nothing else seems to be missing."

"Thanks." I glanced away, then back.

He gave a nod and kept right on staring, conveying something I didn't understand. Not anger, not attitude. Something more like vulnerability.

"So, it's okay if we run up to her work, right? I think it's a good idea to see what they can tell us." Roland sounded positive and cheerful, even though Jarret hadn't looked at him once. "Hey, so, um, where'd they find the car? What park was it? Maybe we can check that out too."

Jarret finally looked at his brother, giving him a squinty-eyed glare. "You're not taking her to that park."

"Why?"

Jarret's upper lip twitched. Fire flashed in his eyes. "Because I said so."

I bristled at the bossy reply.

Jarret caught my expression, dropped his gaze, and took a breath. "God, this is hard for me," he whispered, shoving a hand in his hair. Then he spoke to Roland again, his voice calm. "Look, I don't know what happened to her there. But I'm not comfortable with her going back there without me. Got it?"

Roland nodded. "Yeah, sure. You... want to come with us up to her work?"

Jarret glanced over his shoulder at the black Mercedes that waited at the curb. "Can't. Gotta get back to work." He took a few steps backwards down the drive. "Keep her safe and be here when I get home."

He gave me one last look. "Bye."

"Bye," I whispered back, barely finding my voice as I wavered between compassion and irritation.

# Chapter 15

I DROVE THE Honda Accord myself. And it felt natural, except I didn't know where I was going, I drove way under the speed limit, and I turned down a few wrong roads. The drive may have taken a bit longer than it should've, but between me and Roland, we finally found the two-story brick building with the tall white pillars out front.

"Wright Investigators?" Roland's eyes sparkled with a look of admiration, maybe even jealousy.

"Cool, huh?" Pride and excitement propelling me to action, I swung the car door open and led the way.

We stepped into a classy foyer with huge artwork, high ceilings, and an elegant chandelier. A contemporary but empty waiting area stretched out to the right, two halls came off the left, and across the room from us stood a tall reception desk with no receptionist.

"The place looks empty," I said, a bit disappointed but not ready to give up. We could still snoop around a bit.

"Someone's got to be here. There's music." Roland approached the reception desk and drummed his fingers on the marble top.

Classical music played softly, competing with a low droning sound that came from down a hall. Roland scavenged through the little waiting room while I studied the signs behind the desk. The second floor and a few first-floor rooms belonged to Guardian Investors. Two first-floor rooms belonged to Wright Investigators.

"Hmm," I said, two minutes later, tired of waiting for a receptionist.

"Yeah." Roland glanced at his watch. "Let's find their office."

Relishing how Roland understood me even without words, I led the way. Metal plaques by the doors showed that Guardian Investors occupied the four rooms in the front of the building, so we headed to the back of the building and found an open door.

I raised a fist, ready to knock on the doorframe, when Roland nudged me.

"The door's open. Let's just go in," he said.

Feeling a bit like a trespasser, I peeked into the room. An old wooden desk with a phone, computer, and a blue coffee mug—but no receptionist—faced the door. Four tan filing cabinets lined the wall behind it, and open doors leading to other rooms flanked the cabinets.

"Where is everyone?" I said.

He shrugged and nudged me through the doorway.

Heat billowed through the entrance, making this room considerably warmer than the rest of the building, warmer even than outside. A tall fan stood by an open window, turning and humming, trying to bring in cooler air. The seating arrangement consisted of a few metal chairs with dark-red cushions arranged along two walls. Art nouveau posters decorated the walls, and a life-size wooden statue of Sherlock Holmes held open the door we had come through.

"The place has character." Roland studied Sherlock.

Voices, barely audible over the hum of the fan, traveled from the door to the right of the desk. Roland glanced at me and nodded toward the door.

"Should we just go back there?" I still felt like a trespasser.

The voices grew louder and a woman shouted, "Then check again!"

"Sure," Roland said. "You work here, don't you?"

I gave him a wide-eyed *I guess so* look. Before I stepped through the door, someone called my name. A neatly-dressed wiry man with shaggy brown hair and a scraggily beard approached me, his arms wide as if he expected a hug.

"Hello." Not recognizing him in the least, I put up my hands to block the hug.

He laughed and glanced over his shoulder at the others in the office, one woman and two men. They huddled together at a desk in the middle of the room, various states of joy and shock overtaking their faces as their eyes found me.

"Caitlyn!" The woman, forty-something with short black hair and a gray skirt-suit, took one hand from her hip and adjusted her black-framed glasses. She stepped around the desk and raised her arms as if she, too, wanted a hug. Did everybody at my workplace give hugs? Was I that close to my coworkers? "How are you?" the woman drawled.

"I'm fine and you... Who are you?" I accepted the woman's firm embrace, but the others would have to settle for handshakes.

"I—" The woman started to answer, when the shaggy man cut her off.

"Son of a gun. You do have amnesia." He checked me out through wide, half-crazed eyes, as if I'd come from outer space. "Well, then, I guess we ought to introduce ourselves." He stuck out one hand and used the other to swipe the stringy hair from his forehead. "I'm Mitch."

I shook his hot, dry hand. "Hi, Mitch. Sorry, I don't remember you."

Mitch chuckled oddly, without showing it in his expression. He motioned me over to the other two men, the woman following.

The older man remained by the desk. A foot taller than everyone else, his bald head, dark goatee, and grim expression suggested he'd make a good bouncer. He mumbled something to the younger man, who immediately snatched the dress shirt draped over the back of a chair and shoved his arm into it.

"This is Victor," Mitch said.

Expression still grim, the older man reached for my hand. "Caitlyn." His voice, low and comforting, had no Southern accent. He shook my hand then adjusted his tie.

"And this is Sean."

Sean, a blond about my age, fumbled with the buttons of the shirt he'd just put on over his white t-shirt. His gaze flitted from his shirt to me, to Mitch, back to me, and then to Roland. He finally reached a hand out and gave me a quick handshake and a shy nod.

"And," Mitch said, "I probably should've introduced her first..." He turned to the woman. "Our boss, Candice Wright. And she doesn't like to be called Candy." In a loud, laughing voice, he added, "We do *not* call her Candy."

"That's enough, Mitch." The sharp look in Candice's eye, her short retro hairstyle, and the low waistline of her skirt gave her the air of an old-fashioned Nancy Drew. "We've been worried about you since your husband called. He said you have amnesia?"

Since the others made me uncomfortable, I clung to Candice's gaze. I needed to trust at least one of them so I could find out all I could. "I do. I woke up Saturday not remembering anything about the past two or three years."

Candice blew out a breath and shook her head. Folding her arms, she paced toward the windows. "We've been trying to figure what could've happened to you. But your workday last Friday went smoothly." Her eyes narrowed with a look of concentration. "Your husband said you got home late. He was hoping we could give him an idea as to why, but we all left work around five o'clock. No one knows what happened to you after that."

With a glance at me, Sean's face flushed. He turned to the window with the fan and tugged at the front of his shirt. Bothered by the heat or something else?

"Yeah," Mitch said. "You spent the morning working with me on the Whitney case. After lunch, you went with Sean to pick up photos and supplies. Uh, what else did she do?" He tapped his lips, thinking.

"Jarret came up at lunch," Sean said, his Southern accent heavier than the others. All eyes turned to him, their expressions saying they hadn't known. In response, his eyelids flickered and mouth opened, the attention seeming to make him uncomfortable. Finally, he shrugged and shook his head. "Well, I saw her get outta his truck, so I reckon they had lunch together."

"That's right," I said, mostly to Roland. "Jarret told me that. He said we accidentally switched cameras so he came to trade them back. He uses his for work. I guess I do too?"

Sean nodded. "We took yer camera up to get prints made, y'know, when we picked up the other prints, y'know, after lunch."

"She doesn't know," Mitch said with a quirky grin.

Sean shrugged and faced the fan, the breeze rippling through the blond tufts on the top of his head.

"I don't think my camera's at home," I said. "Is it here?"

Victor went to the desk nearest the door, the messiest of the six desks, and sat down. How odd that the investigator with the neatest appearance, the only man in a tie, had the sloppiest desk. "Mind if I look in your desk?" he said.

I jerked back. "That's *my* desk?" I huffed in disbelief. Stacks of folders sat on either side of the computer monitor, loose papers and folders in front of the phone, and a pile of reference books in the back corner. Stuffed in between things: a pencil holder, an electric pencil sharpener, a mug, and who knew what else. On the corner of the desk, ready to fall off, lay a little yellow notepad with the name "Adeline" scrawled on it. I picked it up and tossed it farther onto the mess, to where it wouldn't likely fall. "My desk is a mess."

"You're busy." Victor gave me a grin and a wink.

"Don't make excuses for her." Mitch snickered.

I scanned the rest of the room. So maybe the other desks looked neater, but the office wasn't exactly something I would show to a prospective client. Boxes were stacked everywhere, next to desks, lining walls, on top of mismatched file cabinets. Every desk had a computer and additional strange electronic equipment with tangles of cables and wires that resembled Medusa's hair. My cluttered desk wasn't so out of place. I obviously worked hard.

Victor yanked open a low drawer and dug through its contents. "This is where you keep your camera, but it's not here."

"I think you left with yer camera," Sean said. "Y'know, at the end of the day."

"My, my, my." Mitch put his arm around Sean's shoulders, but Sean shrugged it off. "But don't we keep a close eye on Caitlyn."

Jaw twitching, Sean shook his head and blushed. He turned his back to me and muttered something to Mitch.

Mitch chuckled. "Watch your language, Sean."

With a sigh and click of her tongue, Candice marched to my desk. "Children. They're like children around here." She turned the computer on and pushed through the pile of loose papers. "Friday was mostly office work for you. You recorded several phone calls for three different cases."

Candice patted a stack of folders on the desk. "You should review the cases you were working on." She flipped open a manila folder. "You've kept good records on the computer. Here are the file names of the cases you've been handling." Before I could see them, Candice closed the folder and handed it to me. "Maybe something will ring a bell."

She started to walk off but stopped and gave me and then Roland a curious look. "How'd y'all get up here? Did you find your car?"

"Jarret picked it up today," I said. "It was at the police impound lot. I guess they found it at a park."

"What park?"

I shrugged, feeling like a child in Candice's presence. I should know what park, but Jarret hadn't said. It wasn't my fault.

"You'll want to find that out." Candice came across like the boss with her *you should know that* tone of voice, the way she carried herself, and the respectful fear she commanded from the others.

Candice held Roland in a thoughtful gaze. "Who's your friend?"

"Oh, I'm sorry. I should've introduced him. This is Roland. He's my, uh, my..."

"Brother-in-law." Roland reached for Candice's hand. "Roland West, Jarret's younger brother."

I sighed. Roland said it so easily. *Brother-in-law*. It didn't seem fair. I wouldn't have minded one day saying that Jarret was my brother-in-law, but Roland...

"Yes, I see some family resemblance," Candice said. "So you're helping your sister-in-law get her life back together?"

Roland smiled, his gray eyes shifting to me. "I'm trying."

"Roland's working on his bachelor's in police science," I said with pride.

"Hmm." Candice sized him up. "We're awfully busy. A lot of lawyers depend upon us. Maybe someday you can work for me. And feel free to help Caitlyn look through files. We'll consider you an intern."

She turned away before Roland could reply. "Mitch! I need you back on the phone. Double check the details of the Brooke contract. We needed that information yesterday."

Mitch raised his hands. "I'm on it. I'm on it." He scooted off to one of the desks against the wall.

"Sean," Candice barked, "spend a few minutes getting Caitlyn back in the game. Make sure she can find the computer files. Give her a brief overview of the cases she's been working on."

My stomach clenched. I came here hoping to learn more about my life, hoping the place would bring back memories. But I couldn't remember one thing about performing my job. What could I possibly do with my cases?

Candice strode toward the door, a commanding air to her. "And you, Victor—"

"I'm late for an appointment." Victor jumped up from my desk and the chair rolled into the wall. "I hope you get back to your old self soon. We have another long-term covert surveillance coming up. Of course, if you don't regain your memory, I could always tell you the same stories. They'd all be new to you."

I smiled, not sure how I felt about working on covert surveillance with such a stern-faced man. "That sounds fun."

Victor shook his head, amusement in his eyes. "You say that now..." He strode to the doorway. "Mitch, follow up with the HVAC tech. We need that air conditioner repaired."

"You're not the boss of me," Mitch said, again with the weird laugh.

"I have an appointment, too." Candice glanced at the wall behind my desk. A clock hung between two huge city maps. She smoothed her hair and brushed her skirt as she headed for the door. "I'll be in the next room if you need me. But I'll be with a client so..."

I nodded. Candice did not want interruptions.

Sean pulled up a chair for Roland and one for himself. They sat on either side of me.

"I don't feel right digging through your stuff, but..." Sean riffled through a stack of files and pulled one out. He spread pictures and papers on my desk. Reaching for the computer mouse, he rolled his chair into mine.

I scooted back, not wanting to get in his way.

He opened a computer file. "This'll give y'all an overview of Caitlyn's most recent cases and contacts."

Roland and I leaned in to view the list he'd pulled up. Apparently, I'd been working with Victor on a fraudulent worker's compensation claim. The man claimed a work-related back injury, but after a three-week investigation, they obtained video of him golfing, pictures of him gardening, and more proof that his back was fine. That case was closed.

"Roland." Mitch motioned him over to his desk.

After giving me a glance, Roland got up. Mitch showed Roland something on his computer monitor and said something about South Dakota University's degree in Police Science.

"And there's this one." All business, Sean directed my attention to another file. I had a new case for a landlord who was suspicious of a tenant's activities. Some of the pictures I'd recently taken pertained to this case.

"We've got pictures that point to drug activity, but we need hard evidence." Sean gave a sly grin. "I was going to go in on this one."

"Go in?" I said.

He nodded. "Yeah, if I could get in there and see what they all got going on, you know, get some hard evidence." His blue eyes hazed over. Though he stared directly at me, he no longer seemed to see me, as if he had stepped into an alternate reality. "We'd have to watch the house, find out when no one was home, then I'd sneak inside. Or, I reckon it'd be better if I could get invited in. We'd have to find out what sorts of people get invited into the inner sanctuary, then I could pose as... I don't know but I'd bring a micro camera."

"A micro camera?"

He blinked, snapping back to the present. "You've used one. They're so small you can hide them in anything." He held his finger and thumb about an inch apart. "You clip it in a purse with a hole in it. But I use a pack of ciggies. Takes pictures or video." He got up and shuffled to a tall cabinet by the windows. A moment later, he returned and handed me a pen.

It looked like an ordinary black ballpoint pen with a silver clip, band, and tip. "Thanks?"

He took it from me and unscrewed it. "This half is pen. This half is camera and drive." He handed me the two parts and pointed to the top of the clip. "Camera."

"Wow. That's cool." I examined it, then put it back

together and returned it to him. He set it on my desk. "It looks like an ordinary pen," I said. "So, you'd go inside with the drug dealers and start taking pictures or video? That sounds dangerous."

Sean shrugged. "That's the fun part." After smiling at me for a long second, he flipped open a different file.

I stared at him, trying to figure him out. I was a detective, after all, so I'd better start acting like one. Sean had seemed uncomfortable at first, but now that we were one-on-one, he seemed fine. Maybe we were friends. "Hey, so...do you know Jarret?"

Sean glanced, then he focused his attention on the computer monitor. "Jarret? Your husband?"

Amused by his question, I smiled. Whom else could I mean? "Yes, Jarret, my husband."

Sean shrugged. "Sure, I know him. He comes up here sometimes. We've had a chat or two."

This gave me hope. Sean seemed like a friend, and he and Jarret had talked. Maybe he had some insight into my marriage. "What do you think of him?"

Eyes to the monitor and hand pushing the mouse around, Sean shrugged. "I don't know. He's cool. Maybe sort of the jealous type."

Jealous? I'd never give Jarret a reason for jealousy. If anyone had a reason to be jealous, it should be me, what with all the girls he talked to. "What makes you think that?"

Still not making eye contact, he took his hand off the mouse and started to wrap his lips around a word but then stopped.

"You can tell me," I said softly, touching his arm and giving a reassuring look.

Cheeks turning crimson, his gaze dropped to my hand on his arm. "Well, I don't know. The things he says, the way he looks at..." He shook his head and moved his arm, reaching for a photograph and breaking my hold.

"Mitch? Victor?" I laughed. With tousled blond hair and a

nice tan, a masculine jawline and sky-blue eyes, Sean probably turned a few heads. He was the only man at my workplace over which Jarret could possibly be jealous.

His tan cheeks reddening, Sean shook his head. "No. Jarret's cool."

"Do you think he and I got along?" I held my breath, anxious for the answer.

His eyebrows drew together, and he finally turned his blue eyes to me. "So, you don't remember much about him, your own husband?"

"No, I—I remember graduating from high school." I blinked rapidly, thinking back. "I...didn't like Jarret. Then...at all."

"Shoot. That'd be rough. Yeah, I guess y'all got along. You never came to work crying." He smiled but I sensed he held something back. "You never complained about him, not to me anyway."

He grabbed the mouse but then let go of it. "Hey, uh, I know y'all saw me Saturday. What were y'all doing?"

"What? Who? Roland just got here—"

"Naw, I don't mean him. You and Jarret."

"Saturday? We saw you?" Struck with curiosity, I recalled Saturday. "You must've seen us driving around? He wanted to find my car, so we drove to the grocery store and up here, but we didn't go in. I didn't see you."

He nodded. "You and Jarret both looked right at me. I was skateboarding in the back parking lot."

"Oh. You mean at the apartments. You were one of the guys skateboarding?"

He smiled and lowered his head, peeking at me sideways. "Yeah, I don't usually fall. I'm rad on a board."

I would've smiled at his comment but the revelation disturbed me. "Jarret didn't tell me I knew you, er, that I knew one of the guys skateboarding. I wondered who lived there and why we drove through the parking lot."

Sean averted his gaze and swallowed, his Adam's apple

bobbing. He reached for a stack of files on my side of the desk as he spoke. "I don't know, Caitlyn, but don't ask him about it. Don't tell him I said anything. I'm sure he had some other reason for being there. You know, probably knows someone else who lives there or something." He slapped a file down in front of me. "Anyway, this is the big one."

I dropped my gaze to it, but my mind remained on Saturday. Why would Jarret have taken me to Sean's apartment and not even spoken to him?

The bright label on the file folder caught my eye. And the words written in my sloppy printing with what looked like a black Sharpie: A-Z Women's Choice Clinic.

# Chapter 16

THE SQUEAK OF the front door opening made me glance up from a cookbook and tuck my hair behind my ear. The sight of Jarret strutting into the house, dress shirt half unbuttoned and hanging out, made me suck in a breath. His unkempt look appealed to me in some strange way.

Our eyes met and a smile flickered on his face. He stopped near the door to his weight room. "How's it going?"

"Okay." My mind sorted through appropriate wifely comments. "How was your day?"

He shrugged. "Don't feel like I got anything done, kinda distracted." A lingering gaze told me I was the source of his distraction.

The temperature in the kitchen suddenly getting to me, I racked my brain for something else to say. "Dinner's almost done."

"Smells good. Think I got time to work out?"

The thought of Jarret asking me for permission overwhelmed me. "I... sure."

I prepared salads and rinsed dishes, and Roland set the table, while Jarret clanked around in the weight room and showered. Twenty minutes later, he returned dressed in jeans and a rock concert t-shirt with a low neckline. Coming to stand on the opposite side of the kitchen island, he watched my every move.

Oven mitt on one hand and knife in the other, I peeled the foil back from the glass baking dish I'd set on the island counter between us. Heavenly aromas filled the kitchen, making my stomach rumble. I couldn't wait to—

"Lasagna. For real?" Attitude heavy in his tone, Jarret's lip curled and he drummed his fingers on the countertop.

Did he know I'd made it because it was Roland's favorite? Yes, he must've. Oops. I should've thought that one through. What was Jarret's favorite?

"Don't you like lasagna?" I cut large squares and arranged them on plates. One plate I slid toward him, two more I carried to the table.

"Yeah, sure. Who doesn't like lasagna?" He took a seat at the head of the table. "So, you went shopping, huh?"

I nodded and sat adjacent to him, across from Roland.

Roland flashed a smile and pushed aside the folders he'd been sifting through. "Smells delicious." He slid the plate closer. "I love lasagna. I haven't had lasagna since—"

"Get me a Coke," Jarret said to Roland, who popped up obediently. Then Jarret turned to me. "What else did you get at the store?"

I had to push back irritation over Jarret's bossiness and Roland's puppy-like obedience before I could answer. "Lots of things. Ice cream, beets, cereal, pizza rolls, milk... Roland paid for it."

"Well, ain't he nice?" Jarret seemed like a different person around Roland. He resembled the teenage Jarret I remembered, the arrogant, controlling one who, when that control slipped away, swore, glared, and lost the ability to use proper English.

Roland handed him a Coke. Jarret thanked him with a nod.

"Well, I didn't have any money," I said. "Do I have money?"

Jarret huffed and cracked open the Coke. "Of course you do. Except, I, uh, I canceled our credit cards." He peered through grumpy eyes. "I thought your purse had been stolen. I canceled everything Saturday. I'm sure we'll get the new ones soon. But, well, I'll go to the bank and get you some money. How much do you want?"

"I don't know. I should have *some* money, shouldn't I?" I'd explored the contents of the leather-trimmed corduroy purse that he'd found in my car. The wallet contained a five-dollar bill, a few of my business cards, credit cards—useless now—and a pocket of change. Other items in the purse included a wide-toothed comb, a compact, lip balm, a plastic rosary, a notepad, several pens, and two candy bars. Except for my business cards and a photo of my family, it could've been anyone's purse. Nothing felt familiar. More importantly, I'd found no cell phone and not a single note or address to investigate.

"What happened to the money you snagged from my wallet?" Jarret's tone held a trace of annoyance. "I had about eighty bucks in there."

As he spoke, a thought occurred to me. Jarret had searched my purse first. Would he have taken anything from it? I shook my head to rid myself of the idea. Why would he have? "What? Eighty dollars? I forgot about that. It must be in one of those purses."

"Those purses?" His voice rose. "Those are *your* purses. You still act like—"

"So, uh, should we pray?" Roland said with a shy glance at Jarret and then at me.

After the blessing, Jarret took a swig of Coke and leaned back in his chair. "So, what do you need money for?"

I chewed and swallowed before answering. "I don't know. Do I have to give you a reason?" Dad used to ask Mom that same question and it never seemed to bother Mom. Why did I find it so annoying? Maybe all married couples handled the money situation that way.

Jarret gave Roland a rude glance, as if he blamed Roland for my offending question.

"Best lasagna I ever had," Roland said, tipping his chin to me. He was good. He knew how to deflect anger.

Jarret glared at his plate and picked up his fork. "Well,

no, I guess you don't need a reason."

"Good. Because I don't have one." Having no money simply added to my feelings of powerlessness and captivity. Maybe he saw it like that too. If I had money, I might use it for a one-way plane ticket.

Jarret poked his lasagna with his fork. "It's just that you don't usually go shopping... without me."

"I don't?" I scrunched a brow.

"We go together, or you make me do it." The hint of a smile passed over his lips, fading as quickly as it came. "If you don't tell me what you want the money for, how am I to know..." His jaw twitched and he winced as if struggling interiorly between what he wanted to say and what he should say. "Well, how much do you want?"

"I don't know. None, I guess." I'd just find the eighty dollars and not worry about it.

He shook his head and turned his dark eyes on Roland. "So, what else did you two do today?"

Roland detailed everything we'd learned at work: my recently-completed assignments, my current assignments, the loss of my camera... But he claimed "client confidentiality" when Jarret asked to see the folders Roland had brought home. Jarret's face twitched. He scraped his chair out as if ready to fight, but then he glanced at me and scooted it back in.

If I wasn't there, what would he have done to Roland? Roland did say Jarret needed me. Did my mere presence encourage him to use self-control?

"So, who was there?" Jarret finally cut into his lasagna. "Who was at Wright?" He gave me a sideways glance.

"Oh, everyone, I guess." I found myself gazing at the low neckline of his shirt. In the emails Roland had shown me, I'd claimed Jarret wore the Scapular. Did he still? He didn't seem like someone with devotion to the Blessed Mother.

"Everyone?" Jarret caught my eyes on his chest and a smile flickered on his lips, a look of longing in his eyes. He probably thought I was admiring his build, not checking for a Scapular.

Face burning, I dropped my gaze. "Candice, Victor, Sean, Mitch... I guess that's all, right?"

"Yeah, that's all. That's the gang. Who did you..." He shoved a forkful of lasagna into his mouth.

*Who did I what?* What bothered him about the people I worked with? Sean had insinuated that Jarret was jealous of him. And we *had* driven by Sean's apartment. *Hmm....*

"Did you tell Roland what we did Saturday?" I used a cheerful voice. I wouldn't ask him directly.

"What do you mean?" Eyes on his plate, he took another bite.

"Driving around?" I looked at Roland. "Did he tell you?"

"Uh, yeah. He said you guys went searching for your car."

"Did he tell you who we saw?"

Jarret's gaze snapped to me. He opened his mouth but then shut it and shook his head at his plate.

"No." Roland watched Jarret, probably noticing his sudden discomfort. He didn't ask the obvious question *who?*

I smiled at Jarret. "Why don't you tell him? Tell him who we saw?"

Jarret shook his head at his plate again and fidgeted with his Coke can. "Nobody. We were looking for your car."

"Really?" I maintained my pleasant, nothing-bothers-me expression and tone. "Are you going to pretend you don't know what I'm talking about?"

His eyelids fluttered. Frowning, he met my gaze. "Okay. We saw Sean."

"Is there a reason you thought my car would be at Sean's apartment?" As the question left my mouth, I realized what that would imply, and my voice and expression softened mid-sentence.

"No," he whispered. "It didn't, it didn't make sense to look there." His weak voice and the sad look in his eyes made his answer seem like an apology.

Not knowing how to respond, I picked up my fork and turned my attention to my lasagna.

Jarret's eyes remained fixed on me.

I shouldn't have brought it up, and he should stop staring at me like that. I chewed self-consciously and swallowed hard. I reached for my iced tea as he reached for his Coke.

He still stared.

"We're going back to Wright tomorrow," I said, wanting to break the tense mood. "There's more I want to look into. And I'd like to get back into my job. I was doing research for an attorney who has a case against an abortion provider. Did you know that?"

He nodded. "You told me." He took a bite and finally stopped staring.

I exhaled. "I was relieved to find out I was working on that case."

"Oh, yeah?"

"I saw an appointment with A-Z Women's Choice Clinic in my appointment book in the kitchen. That's why I asked you if I was preg—" *Oh no.* My heart stopped beating and my face froze. I shouldn't have said that.

His fork clattered to the table and his eyes turned hard. Then he scraped his chair back and stood. "You would never..." He shook his head as if the rest of the sentence was too terrible to utter. "I'm taking a walk." He stormed out of the house.

As soon as the front door closed, Roland broke the distressing silence. "Why'd you say that, Caitlyn?" His accusing gaze pierced through me. "You know what he's been through. I don't think he's gotten over that."

"Oh. I—I didn't know how he'd taken it back then. Not really." I thought back. Jarret had practically forced Zoë to have an abortion. It wasn't until the day of the appointment that he'd come to his senses—largely due to Roland's intervention—and he'd gone after Zoë to stop her. Then he'd stayed by Zoë's side throughout her pregnancy, only to get dumped after the baby was born. Had he truly regretted pushing her to abort the baby?

Tension flooded my face and forced me to frown. "I'm sorry, Roland. It's just that, when I first saw that appointment, I thought..." Unable to think of a nice way to word it, I blurted out, "Do you know Jarret has girls over when I'm not home? And he talks to girls on the phone and there's a hotel bill on our credit card and..."

Roland shook his head. "What are you saying? Jarret wouldn't, I'm sure he doesn't... He loves you."

"Well, maybe you're wrong." I threw my fork at my plate and it bounced onto the table. "I don't recall Jarret having the highest standards. And when I saw that appointment in my book..." I motioned toward the kitchen and found myself waving my arms as I tried to explain. "Well, I figured I was so depressed over our relationship that I must've lost my mind. I can't remember anything, Roland." My voice scraped out high and my forehead wrinkled with the turmoil of my emotions. "Try to see things from my view. You're so protective of him, but he hasn't always been worthy of your protection, your defense. And me... Have I changed so much? I feel like the same girl I was in high school, with the same hopes, the same goals, the same values. If you had ever told me I'd wake up one day as Jarret's wife..." Lips trembling out of control, I squeezed my eyes shut and bowed my head.

"Caitlyn, your lasagna!"

I jerked back, locks of my hair dragging through the sauce.

He tossed me a napkin. "Now that you know the appointment wasn't to... to get rid of, well, now that you know..." He reached across the table and grabbed my hand.

Eyes welling with tears at his touch, I dropped the napkin and met his concerned gaze.

"Are you pregnant?"

A tight smile stretched across my face. "Yes."

"That's great. That's wonderful." He squeezed my hand. "You'll make a great mother. And give Jarret a chance. I know he'll be a great father." Releasing my hand, he sat back and joy lit his expression. "I'm gonna be an uncle."

Tears ran down my smiling face. No words could describe the happiness the baby inside me gave, but why had I ended up with Jarret? Why not Roland?

"I think you're wrong about him cheating on you. You should talk to him."

"I know." Roland might have been right, but I wasn't ready for that.

# Chapter 17

THE HUM OF the fan in Wright Investigators nearly drowned out the playful chirping of the early morning birds. I inhaled. I loved the aroma of coffee and the fresh, dew-drenched air that the fan sucked in through the open windows.

Roland sat beside me, hunched over my cluttered desk. He looked nice in his gray short-sleeved dress shirt, although his suitcase had left it terribly wrinkled. And his dark hair still had the waves I adored, though it was much shorter in back and on the sides than it had been in high school. It gave him a more mature, suavely handsome look.

Glancing at me, he cleared his throat.

I averted my gaze and returned my attention to the computer monitor. *Back to work. We aren't eighteen anymore. And Roland isn't the one I fell in love with.*

Appointments, confirmations, observations, interviews—

The hum of the rotating fan seemed to buzz in my ear. And Mitch… Did he ever stop muttering and snickering to himself? And what were Candice and Victor arguing about in the back of the room?

I sighed, refocusing on the monitor. What was I looking for anyway?

Roland seemed to have a clear idea about whatever he was doing. He made his way through a stack of files, staring at each one for a considerable amount of time before setting it in one of two piles.

Before I could think of something productive to do, my

stomach growled and my hand shot to it, my thoughts turning to the baby. I should find a snack before the hunger turned to nausea. I'd eaten a late breakfast, so I shouldn't be hungry yet. I had slept in to avoid a confrontation with Jarret. Roland must've slept in, too, or else Jarret had ignored him. I expected to hear him grilling Roland about our plans for today, but he'd puttered about the house in relative silence until he finally left for work. An hour later, I'd forced myself out of bed. After a breakfast of pancakes and eggs, I dressed in another professional outfit, a slender dark-blue skirt and coordinating top from the "I would never wear that" side of the closet. Then Roland and I had left for Wright Investigators.

I gazed with indifference across the room at Candice and Victor. Candice shook her head, obviously annoyed, and Victor raised his hands in a gesture of surrender and turned away from her. I caught the words "abortion provider" but not the rest of what he'd said before storming from the office. Which reminded me…

"Do you think I should reschedule my appointment with A-Z Women's Choice Clinic?"

"What?" Roland glanced.

"Well, since we've established that the appointment was work-related, maybe I ought to see what I can find out." I rolled a pencil back and forth on the desk.

He shrugged. "What would you say?"

I shrugged, picking the pencil up and weaving it between my fingers. He had a point.

Roland closed a file, dropped it into one of his two piles, and faced me. "Well, unless someone's seeking revenge, I don't think we'll find any leads in these."

"Oh?"

"These are closed cases, irrelevant, unless you were onto something or someone." He opened his mouth as if to say more, his gray eyes locking onto mine. He breathed, glanced to either side and leaned close. "Caitlyn, I was thinking," he whispered inches from my face, his eyes half closed and his thick lashes drawing my attention.

The smell of his cologne dazzled me, taking me back to the strong feelings I had for him at eighteen. I struggled to return to the present moment. "Thinking what?"

"I don't know how to say this, but you obviously abandoned your car at the park." He paused. "So, something happened to you there, probably something bad. Your purse was in the car, so you weren't robbed. So I wonder, I mean, I have to ask..." He pressed his lips together and then swiveled his gaze up to my eyes, the gray of his irises deepening. "Could you have been violated?"

His question shuddering through me, I sucked in a breath and jerked back. My mind reeled. I would've known the next morning, even with the amnesia, right? My thoughts turned to the morning I'd woken up shocked to find Jarret in the same bed. He'd said we made love the night before. But I wouldn't have known without him telling me. I hadn't felt violated. No, I couldn't have been. I wouldn't have allowed the intimacy with Jarret if I had been, and I would've had pain in more places than my head.

I forced myself to make a reassuring smile. "No, something else happened that night."

Roland's left eye narrowed as if he didn't share my confidence. "Are you sure?"

"I'm certain." I snapped my gaze from his and flipped open a file.

"It's the camera," Sean said. Wheels squeaking, he rolled his chair backwards to my desk and spun around to face us.

Heat assailed me, washing over my neck and cheeks and bringing the scent of my deodorant to my nose. Sean couldn't have heard Roland. Roland had whispered.

"What do you mean?" I said, hoping my embarrassment didn't show.

"Have you found your camera yet?" Sean unbuttoned the sleeves of his tan dress shirt and rolled them up. All morning, he had seemed entirely wrapped up in his own business at his desk, fidgeting with electronic gadgets, tapping the computer keyboard, and talking on the phone. "I think whatever happened to you has to do with the pictures you took."

"The pictures?" I exhaled, welcoming the new theory.

After pushing up his sleeves, Sean rested his tan forearms on loose papers on the edge of my desk. "You said your purse was still in your car. Anything else of yours missing?"

"Besides my cell phone? I don't think so, but I can't know for sure."

Sean nodded. "I remember, you took your camera with you last Friday at the end of the day. Maybe someone was watching you."

"Besides you?" Mitch said from his desk across the room.

Shooting Mitch a threatening glare, Sean opened his mouth but shut it again and ran a hand over his short blond hair. Then he pushed through the folders on my desk. "Maybe someone caught you taking a picture of them doing something, I don't know, illegal?" He slid pictures from a file and handed them to me. The top picture showed a teenage girl in a short skirt, walking down a sidewalk on a downtown street. Another picture showed the same girl opening a door. The sign above the door read: Sammy's Pub. The next three pictures were dark, taken inside the bar. The girl sat beside a man, talking to him in one picture and leaning toward him in the next. The two were kissing in the last picture.

"Tamara Eber. She's underage," Sean said, matter-of-fact, and slid more pictures from another file folder. "You had pictures for several cases on your camera. I bet whoever took your camera wanted the pictures, the evidence. They wouldn't have known we'd just taken the SD card in to get pictures printed."

The second set of pictures showed a man in an office building doing various office related things. I held them up to Sean.

"Gary Nicolan. Embezzlement and corporate espionage."

"Shouldn't you have a computer forensic engineer for that case?" Roland said.

Sean grinned and raised his brows. "That's me. I'm your cyber sleuth. We've got computer forensic software. I'll show you." He rolled his chair away a few feet then stopped, his gaze locking onto Roland. Judging by the fixed look in his eyes, his mind had taken a trip to an alternate reality, as it had the day before when he'd described the micro camera to me.

"First, I go on location to make a clone of the hard drive. Then, I work with it here. I can find and recover info from a computer hard drive, databases, servers, digital cameras, even fax machines and answering machines." He grinned and gave us both a glance, briefly flitting back to reality before he continued. "I can retrieve emails that were never saved, websites visited, deleted documents, uninstalled software. I can get stuff even if it's been deleted or if it's just fragments.

"When people use computers, you know, to commit a crime, they're awful careful to delete files and cover their tracks, but they don't realize the computer creates a trail. The toughest one I had was this guy who used an encryption program to create two separate spaces on the hard drive with two separate passwords. When his company went to investigate him, he gave them his password, but only the decoy data was found. He hid all the illicit data on the other space. They had no way of detecting it."

Roland tapped the pictures we had been looking at before Sean set off on his tangent.

Sean rolled back to the desk and looked where directed. "Oh, yeah. Caitlyn went undercover to get some pictures, identifying, you know, the suspect."

"Who's the client for the case with the underage girl?" I said, returning my attention to those particular pictures.

"The parents. They hired an attorney to go after the abortion guys."

"Why the abortion people? Why not the man with her? Isn't he guilty of statutory rape?"

"Yeah, but the parents weren't notified before she had the abortion. The parents say the boyfriend coerced her. And you know they need parental consent before they can do it. It's the law here. And the abortion guys, you know, they covered stuff up. It wasn't the first time." Sean continued searching through folders on my desk and setting a few of them in front of me. "You'll want to look at these." He rolled his chair back, toward his desk. "That ought to get y'all started. Let me know if—"

The phone on my desk rang and the three of us looked at it.

I turned to Sean. "Should I get that?"

He shrugged and slouched back in his chair. "It's *your* phone." Wheels squeaking, he rolled the rest of the way to his desk, reminding me of my younger siblings on the rolling chairs in an office supply store.

I snatched up the phone. "Hello? Um, this is Caitlyn Summer." Roland's headshake made me correct myself. "I mean West."

"Caitlyn? This is Melinda Myers. Y'all called me last week or the week before." The high, gentle voice made her sound young and very Southern.

"Melinda... Myers." Why did her name sound familiar?

Sean rolled his chair to my desk at top speed, bumping into my chair. "Sorry," he mouthed before pushing through a few files. He set a file in front of me and flipped it open. *Melinda Myers, underage girl who obtained an abortion from A-Z Women's Choice Clinic.*

"Oh, Melinda, I'm so glad you called."

"I'm sorry I didn't talk with y'all sooner, but I—I guess I was afraid."

"Afraid?" I jotted down the date and the words "afraid to talk" on the telephone record in the folder.

Roland read the note and looked at me.

"Well, not afraid, really," the girl said. "I mean, it's just my boyfriend. He doesn't want me talking with y'all, but now we're taking a break from our relationship. And you sounded kind of desperate to talk to me."

"Oh, I did? I mean, I am. So, you can talk now?"

Roland nodded, pushing a pencil and the telephone record to me.

"Did you want to talk on the phone," I said, taking the pencil in hand, "or meet somewhere?"

"I'm at Sandy Lake Park right now. Can y'all come here?"

"Now?" Dropping the pencil, I spun my chair to see the Indian Fort city map on the wall behind me. "Sandy Lake Park? Is that like a trailer park?" I jumped up and ran my finger along the map, trying to locate anything familiar.

"A what?" the girl said.

Sean showed up at my side and shook his head. Then he pushed my searching finger out of the way and tapped the map. Situated near a large golf course, Sandy Lake was a little park with a blue dot representing a lake. Sean continued to tap the map and mouthed, "We're over here. Fifteen minutes."

"Oh, I know where you are," I said into the phone, smiling and giddy. My first appointment—that I remembered—with a real live witness or informant or whatever. I slid a notebook and pen into my purse. "What time shall we meet?"

# Chapter 18

"SINCE YOU DON'T have your memory back, you can't go alone." Candice stood over my desk, hands on hips and her expression as strict as a schoolteacher... from the 1920s. "Sean's the only one free to go with you right now. And Roland will need to stay here."

I sagged in my chair, disappointment deflating me. "Oh, but can't Roland—"

"He's not licensed and bonded. Sorry." And with hardly a breath in between, she belted out instructions. "You'll need a recording device, an obvious one, and I want you to get permission from the girl to use it. Sean knows the procedure. This girl is young, under the age of consent, so you need to find out how old her boyfriend is and if the abortion clinic knew. And find out about her parents. Did they sign the consent form or did the clinic find a way around that? Remember, we're trying to prove that A-Z Women's Choice Clinic has a pattern of not following the parental involvement and mandatory sexual crime reporting laws. So ask the right questions. This girl could make a good witness. We'd have to get parent permission, of course, but we'll worry about that later. Find out her story first."

Candice turned on her heels but then stopped. The authoritative image melted as she faced me again. She spoke in the gentle voice of a friend. "Caitlyn, I don't think this appointment has much to do with your accident or whatever happened to you. And if you don't want to go—"

"I do. I think, getting back into the swing of things, I might recover some of my memory. That's what I hope, anyway."

Candice nodded. "Okay. But I understand if you need to do other things."

"Thanks." As I smiled to show my appreciation, a question came to mind, something I'd meant to ask earlier. "Hey, before I go, I was wondering, did you speak with Jarret when he called me off work Monday?"

Candice's curious look made me feel the need to explain.

"I want to find out everything I can about last Friday." I twisted my wedding rings as I spoke. "So I just wonder what Jarret said about it."

"Sure. I spoke with him. He said you wouldn't be coming to work that day and probably not for a couple of days. Naturally, I asked if you were okay." She laid her hand on my forearm, a motherly touch. "It seemed hard for him to get the words out. And I had to piece it together, but he told me you had amnesia. I was shocked. It's not your normal call-off. I couldn't help asking questions. Were you in an accident? Had you been sick? But he didn't seem able to say more, so I gathered he had no idea what had happened to you. After a stretch of silence, I thought our conversation had ended, but then he had a question for me, wanted to know if you were working on anything Friday that would've kept you out late. I checked your appointment schedule, found nothing, and that was it."

She smoothed her plaid 1920s skirt and folded her arms. "Of course, here at the office, we didn't leave it at that. We've all been thinking about it and trying to see if any of your cases held any clues. Could it be revenge? Could your bit of investigative work have been the key factor in someone's conviction? Could it have been someone you were following or someone following you? But who knows? It might have nothing to do with work. I checked police reports for that night for suspicious activity and other crimes. Victor checked police reports for the past several weeks, searching for possible patterns." Candice shook her head. "It may have been a first-time offender or simply an accident. I agree that you need to piece that day together better and see what you come up with."

"I think you're right." I should re-examine everything I did at work that day and talk to Jarret again about his lunchtime visit. He'd said he returned my camera. Had anyone been watching us? Did they know it was my camera? Could someone have wanted Jarret's camera?

As questions tumbled through my mind, I watched Candice cross the room. My gaze stumbled onto Victor. He sat at his desk in the back corner of the room, staring directly at me. When our eyes met, he gave me a slow nod and returned to his work.

In preparation for my appointment, Candice showed me the supply cabinet of recording devices, surveillance equipment, tracking devices, and special video and camera equipment. It was a private investigator's dream. I left Roland there, with Mitch, two boys in a toy store.

Before stepping through the doorway, I glanced back to tell Roland goodbye. He tore his attention from a contact surface microphone, which resembled a stethoscope, and gave me a brief look of concern. I responded with an eye-roll and a wave of my hand. Roland couldn't stop worrying about what Jarret would want. We both knew Jarret would not like this situation at all. He wouldn't want me *out on my own*.

I turned down Sean's offer to drive and drove him in my car. Twenty minutes later, we arrived at a sunny park where moms and preschoolers sat at picnic tables and on blankets beside a little lake.

Melinda Myers had said she would meet us at the picnic tables nearest the volleyball court. The park road wound past the lake, into and out of the shade. Opposite the lake, we found the volleyball court tucked in between a tennis court and a cluster of trees and picnic tables. The only people on this side of the park were an old man walking his dog and four teenage girls at one of the picnic tables. As soon as I parked, three of the girls took off. The remaining girl sat atop the picnic table and watched us get out of the car.

Sean grabbed the fast-food bag from the back seat.

"Great idea—about bringing lunch." I climbed out of the car and waited for Sean.

He handed me the bag of sub sandwiches, balancing the drink tray in his other hand. "Food relaxes people."

"It'll relax my stomach, that's for sure." My stomach rumbled as we hiked across the stretch of grass between the parking lot and the picnic table.

Melinda wore white shorts and a long, sheer purple vest over a tight black top that emphasized her shapely size-fourteen body. Her straight brown hair fell halfway down her back, and a blue crystal hung from a gold chain around her neck. Her heavy make-up didn't hide her youth. She couldn't have been over sixteen. Something about her looked familiar. Was she really involved with an older man? Had she really had an abortion at her age? A pang of sadness struck me.

I maintained eye contact with the girl as we neared, but I leaned to whisper to Sean, "Have I met her before?"

"Don't think so." He smiled at the girl and gave her a nod and a "hey."

Melinda responded with a little wave and jumped off the picnic table. She certainly looked familiar. Maybe she was in one of the pictures I had taken.

Clutching the bag of sandwiches with one hand, I reached into my purse with the other to grab a notebook and pen. I jotted down "check pictures" as I walked.

"You didn't sign that out," Sean said.

"What?" I glanced at my pen and notepad.

"The pen. You better get that back to the office."

"Oh." I looked at the black pen in my hand. Realizing I'd grabbed the spy pen by mistake, I shoved it deep into my purse.

Wanting to look friendly, I smiled as we neared the picnic table. Melinda stood with her arms folded across her chest, her body language saying she didn't want to shake hands. So I simply said, "Hi, I'm Caitlyn," and sat down.

Melinda nodded and slid onto the bench seat across from me.

Sean sat beside me and handed out sodas. "Hey. You probably figured Caitlyn would come alone," he said to Melinda. "I work with Caitlyn. I'm Sean." He stretched his arm across the table, offering his hand. Melinda shook it, ever so briefly. "I could go, you know, eat lunch in the car or take a walk or something."

I gave him a *no you can't* look, but Melinda said she didn't mind him being there, and she didn't mind being recorded.

After handing out subs, recording our introductions and the permission to record, I began. "We're trying to help a girl and her family. The girl had an abortion at the same place you, um, well, and without her parents knowing."

Melinda's expression remained blank. She sipped the soda. The gold chain around her neck reflected the afternoon sun, but the blue crystal that hung from it seemed oddly dull and roughed up.

"Do you know that's illegal?" I said. "Parents need to be notified in order for underage girls to have an abortion."

"I guess. But all you need is a letter."

"Right. Well, they got around that, and the parents were never notified. And the girl later wished she hadn't done it."

Melinda could have been a statue. She didn't even blink.

"So..." I bit my bottom lip. What could I say to get the girl to talk? "I guess the girl did it because her boyfriend talked her into it, but she wishes she had thought about it first. She and her parents are pretty upset because, well, if the abortion clinic had followed the laws, they feel she wouldn't have done it. So I, er, we—we're trying to show that the abortion company isn't following the rules. They're, um..."

"We thought maybe you could share your experience at the clinic with us," Sean said, taking a break from wolfing down his sub. He leaned forward and gave Melinda a little smile. "I'm sure it'd be hard but it could really help this girl."

Melinda nodded and smiled back. Sean had put her instantly at ease. Was it his smile, his relaxed attitude? "I'll help," the girl said. Within a minute she was sharing everything, answering every one of his questions, without even batting an eye.

"I'm fifteen... Yes, I'm seeing an older man... No, I won't tell you his age, but he's several years older... Yes, I was pregnant and would've had the baby. I wanted to go off with my boyfriend, but he has a career and can't just pick up and move. He didn't want me being pregnant... We're going to marry soon as I turn eighteen. Things will be different then... Yes, he came with me to get the abortion... No, he told them he was my cousin... Of course, he paid for it. I sure don't have that kind of money... No, we didn't want my momma and daddy to know. The clinic only needed a letter. Tony wrote it."

"Who's Tony?" Sean asked.

"My boyfriend."

"Did they know Tony wrote it?"

She shrugged. "I think it was their idea."

Whenever I asked a more personal question, Sean showed disapproval.

"Are you sure he's not using you?"

Sean tapped my leg with his foot and gave me a narrow-eyed glare and a slight shake of his head.

"Has he taken you to meet his parents?"

Sean jabbed my arm with his elbow.

"Does he talk about past girlfriends and their ages?"

A kick to the shin.

"Have you thought about how old he'll be when you're older?"

He stomped on my foot.

"People are so quick to judge." Melinda tilted her head and gazed into the distance with the look of a star-crossed lover. "Who can help who you fall in love with?"

"How did you meet?" I said, wondering where the creep

hung out to pick up young girls. Maybe we should be going after him along with the abortion provider.

Melinda smiled and her eyes turned heavenwards. "We met here. Me and some of my girlfriends were playing volleyball over there." She gazed lovingly at the patch of orange sand and the drooping net of the volleyball court. "He was watching us play..."

*Pervert.* Of course he was. How much older than her was he? Why did girls fall for that? Maybe he was handsome. He must've been smooth.

Melinda's eyes sparkled. She batted her long lashes and twisted her arms together as she spoke.

The poor girl. Melinda thought she was in love, but it wasn't real, and she would find out the hard way. She said they were taking a break from their relationship. Whose idea was that? Maybe Tony moved on to another underage girl. If only I could help young girls before they fell into these life-altering, destructive traps. I wanted to help. In fact, I felt called. I *needed* to help young girls.

A strong determination coursed through me. Yes, I would reschedule my appointment with the abortion clinic. Maybe I could—

Sean kicked my leg again.

"Ow." I rubbed my leg. I hadn't said anything, only thought it. What was his problem?

"Melinda asked you a question," he said. Then his head turned at the rumble of a truck pulling into the parking lot.

A charcoal Dodge Ram similar to Jarret's parked next to my Honda Accord. Sean jumped up from the picnic table and scooted to a tree ten feet away.

"What are you doing?" I glared at him. Had he lost his mind?

"Who's that?" Melinda said.

I turned.

Jarret strutted across the lawn, his gaze fixed on Sean. He wore dark work pants and a short-sleeved, slate shirt that hung loose and emphasized his muscular physique.

With emotions wavering between irritation and concern, I got up and approached him. I would not let him blow this interview.

As soon as we got within four feet of each other, he turned his scowling gaze on me.

"Jarret." I smiled as sincerely as I could in an attempt to calm his obviously cross mood. "What're you doing here? How'd you find me?"

His scowl faded as I stepped closer, a vulnerable boyish look replacing it. "I'm working right over there." He pointed toward the tennis court.

"You are?" I squinted to see past the tennis court, making out a distant road and, beyond that, a few scattered houses and a wide, rolling field. The grassy, nearly treeless field went on for miles. Something blue, maybe a tent, stood back there.

"I saw your car when I was driving by, going to lunch." His gaze flitted to the picnic table and then to Sean.

"Hey, Jarret." Sean stood with his back glued to the tree.

"Sean," Jarret said through gritted teeth. Then he faced me, the boyish look returning. "So, whatcha doing here?" He gave Melinda a cursory glance.

I moved closer to avoid being heard by the others. "I'm working," I whispered, touching his arm. His eyelids flickered at my touch. "I'm with a, oh, I guess, a witness or an informant or whatever. So, if you don't mind..." I turned him around, linked my arm in his, and walked him halfway back to his truck.

"So where's Roland?"

"He's at the office." I let go of his arm.

He stopped walking. "He should be with you at all times."

"Is he in trouble now?" My voice came out ugly, my pleasant expression gone. I forced the kindness back into my tone and my eyes. "He's going over something with Mitch."

"Yeah, so, what's *he* doing here?" He shot a glance at Sean.

I huffed. "I work with *him*."

He stared, the answer apparently not satisfying him.

Folding my arms, I huffed again. Sean had said he thought Jarret was jealous of him, so I should probably give a better answer. "Please, Jarret, just go. Candice didn't want me interviewing anyone alone, what with my memory all messed up. And everyone else was busy." I glanced over my shoulder. Sean stood with his back to us now, probably his attempt to show his disinterest in our conversation. I looked at Jarret again. "Why do *you* think he's here?"

"I'll tell you what I think." His lip curled up.

Unwilling to linger long on his hard eyes, I let my gaze travel down his long nose to the curl of his lip, to his rough jaw, to his clean neck, and... there. The throbbing at the base of his neck. I had to see it, the proof that he was more than the image I had created of him in my own mind. He was a real man. A man with blood coursing through arteries and veins. He had a heart. And the distance between us pained him.

"I think..." Mouth hanging open, he seemed unable to say more.

I met his gaze.

His eyes spoke words I didn't understand, words of pain and doubt and fear. He pressed his lips together, gave Sean a hard stare, and stormed away.

When his truck disappeared from view, Sean detached himself from the tree and returned to the bench.

I remained standing in the strip of grass, staring at the road and wondering. What was up with Jarret and Sean? Did Jarret have a reason to despise him? Still contemplating, I shuffled back to the picnic table.

"Who was that?" Melinda said, a lilt in her voice.

"*That* was Caitlyn's husband," Sean said, a bit cold and with his gaze sliding to me.

"He's cute," Melinda said.

# Chapter 19

WITH ANOTHER BAG of sub sandwiches, this one to appease hungry coworkers, Sean and I returned to the office. Sean held the door and studied me as I walked into the building, as if he suspected I had something on my mind. He was right. On the drive back, I'd wanted to ask him about his rocky relationship with Jarret. But the words wouldn't come. So, as we stepped into the dimly lit reception room of Wright Investigators, I forced myself to speak.

"Sean?" I stopped next to the Sherlock Holmes statue that propped open the door.

Sean walked ahead a few feet but stopped. As he turned to face me, his blue eyes glistened in the light from a window, a look of hesitancy in them. And something else I couldn't identify. He glanced over his shoulder toward the open door to the office. No one saw us.

"I need to talk to you before we go in."

"Talk to me?" A dazed, surfer-boy expression passed over his face.

I sat in one of the red-cushioned metal chairs and patted the one next to me.

After a few more furtive glances, he combed a hand through his windblown blond hair and sat. "What's up?"

"It's about Jarret. When I asked you about him yesterday, I got the feeling you held something back."

He stared blankly for a moment then lowered his head. "Nah. There's nothing to say."

"Well, I saw the look he gave you. And you clinging to the tree. There's obviously tension between you two. What's it about?"

He shook his head. "I don't know. I told you, he's jealous over you. A girl as pretty as you..." He gave me flirty smile. "...that's reason enough."

"Sean, please." I straightened in the chair, leaning toward him a bit, trying to convey how important this was to me. "I know it's like we just met, but you're so easy to read."

His cheeks flushed. He slouched back, rubbed his hair, inhaled, exhaled, and finally made eye contact. "Well, what do you want to know?"

"Have you ever had a confrontation with him?"

He stared out of the top of his eyes, the way a child might do when considering the safest way to answer. "Yeah, you know, we had a company picnic end of last summer, Wright Investigators and the Investors, since we're all in the same building, and we see each other all the time, it just seemed like a good idea—"

"Okay." I interrupted to get him back on track.

He inhaled and sighed. "I reckon I said something to you that maybe I shouldn't have, and Jarret was right behind me, but I didn't know it. It pissed him off. He shot me a dirty look. Then when we were playing football, you know, touch football, he tackled the crap out of me, even though we were on the same team. I had bruises for a week."

I suppressed a giggle and tried to offer a show of sympathy. "Okay. So, you said something inappropriate. What about last Friday? You said you saw us together at lunchtime. Were we getting along?"

"I don't know. I noticed you in his truck, that's all."

"Well, is there something else, something you know about him that I don't know?"

He shrugged. "I don't think so."

"Okay. Is there something you know about me that he doesn't know? Did I have any secrets from him?" I wanted to know but felt reluctant to hear the answer. I hated the idea that I would keep something from my husband, even if it was Jarret.

He nodded, staring at the floor. "Maybe."

"What?" Would I have to pry it from him? "Tell me."

"Caitlyn, naw, don't make me say more." He shifted, fidgeting with his shirt and shaking his head, squirming under my gaze. "I can't see that it has anything to do with— well, you're trying to find out what happened Friday night, right? I'll help you with that, and I'll help you with cases. But... why are you asking all this? What's it got to do—"

I touched his arm and squeezed it. "Please."

Eyes glazing over, he stroked my hand, then pulled away and folded his arms. "Ohhhh-kay." He shifted in the seat, licked his lips, rubbed his chin, and finally spoke. "Something happened, you know, about a month ago, maybe not that long, maybe more like two weeks and five days. It was a Saturday. You and I were undercover on assignment, attending a party at a suspect's house, posing as a couple."

He paused as if I needed a moment to understand what he'd said so far. "We were trying to find some stolen goods, a shipment of electronics. So we sneaked around, searched the house downstairs and then..." He leaned forward and rubbed his arm. "While searching upstairs, I heard someone coming and..." He gulped. "Well, we couldn't blow our cover. We weren't supposed to be upstairs. You know, the party was downstairs." A guilty look flashed in his eyes. "I—I kissed you."

"What?" I jerked back, a breath escaping. Even with all the lead-up, what he said shocked me.

"I was trying to protect our cover." He rushed his words. "What else would a couple be doing upstairs in someone else's house during a party?" His face flushed red again.

"I—I let you kiss me?" My brain couldn't accept the thought. I would not have allowed it...would I?

He shook his head. "Not really. You pushed me away and

backed up. But the bed was behind you, and you ended up stumbling and falling onto it. You asked what I thought I was doing. But then you heard them, too. They were right outside the door. They were coming. So, I made a move to kiss you again. You sort of let me, at first, then you slapped me. They found us sitting on the bed, you angry with me. I thought they'd tell us to leave or go back downstairs, but they didn't. They acted like it was no big deal, maybe didn't want involved in a lover's spat. When they left, we found what we were looking for. Later we got a, you know, a search warrant. Case closed."

"Oh." I turned away and wrapped my arms around my waist, feeling slimy and ashamed, feeling worse than when I first realized I'd lost my virginity to Jarret. *That* made sense to me now, being a married woman. But here I was a married woman, a pregnant married woman, kissing another man. I felt like I'd cheated on...my husband...and even my baby.

"If it makes you feel better..." He hunched forward, a sheepish look on his face. "I know you didn't want me to do it. You gave me a good talking to in the car. You were really mad."

"Does Jarret know?" It would certainly explain his behavior toward Sean.

He shrugged. "I hope not. I begged you not to tell him. But you saw how he looked at me today. Maybe he knows. You think he'd just give me a dirty look if he knew?" Sean's eyes narrowed as he considered it. "I kinda think he'd beat the tar outta me."

"Maybe I told him not to." Did I have that kind of sway over him? Enough to keep him from pummeling someone who'd kissed me, his wife?

The surfer-boy look returned to his blue eyes. "Hm. Maybe."

# Chapter 20

I HAD AWOKEN to the sound of the shower, water blasting for what seemed like an hour. Then I must've dozed off, because the next thing I heard came through the closed bedroom door: Jarret complaining to Roland. "Now I'm losing my job and my wife. Ain't it ironic that here I am an archaeologist and my entire life is in ruins."

Was his job really in jeopardy? Did he really think he was losing me? Had he ever really had me in the first place?

Roland replied in a soothing tone, his quiet words indistinct through the bedroom door, probably offering hope and encouragement and advice that would be lost on Jarret.

When I awoke the third time, I thought I'd heard the front door close. It was earlier than Jarret usually left for work, but he probably needed to make up for lost time.

Despite my body's protests, I crawled out of bed and dragged myself to the shower. I needed the early start to prepare for the appointment at A-Z Women's Choice Clinic. After a quick but comforting shower under hot, blasting water, I dried off, put on my robe, and took the blow dryer to my hair. I found a flat iron in a vanity drawer and decided to straighten my hair and part it low on one side. Then I searched for make-up.

I hated wearing make-up. It clogged my pores, looked unnatural, and took too much time to apply. Not to mention, I lacked the skill. But if I wanted to look the part—a fifteen-year-old, promiscuous girl—I'd better make an attempt. The girls pictured in my files all wore heavy make-up. I'd give it a try.

Half an hour later, I stood in the closet, flipping through dresses and sighing. My clothing was way too modest. But wait! There in the corner lay the denim jumper I'd ruined Saturday. I could work with that.

With the help of scissors and a white undershirt, one that I would've worn only under a full dress, I completed the image and stood gazing at myself in the dresser mirror.

Sleek and straight, my red hair cascaded over my shoulders and one eye, the way the girl in the Piggly Wiggly had worn hers. My eyes screamed for attention with ridiculously thick black lashes and shimmering brown eyeshadow. A touch of pink blush on my cheeks and shiny lip-gloss completed the facade.

I hadn't always appreciated my thin, shapeless figure, but my stork-legs sticking out of the "new" denim mini-jumper and my flatter-than-average chest did make me appear young. I could pass for fifteen.

Now to get Roland's first impression. I stuffed my feet into clogs and yanked open the bedroom door.

"I gotta run." Jarret strode from the kitchen.

Stomach dropping to the floor, I shrunk back. But too late.

As Jarret neared the loveseat, he glanced. Then he stopped dead in his tracks and did a double take. "What the hell?"

Mustering courage and gathering my resolve, I flashed a friendly smile and marched into the living room. "So, how old do I look?" I turned in a circle.

Jarret gave me a few fleeting glances, seeming reluctant to look at me. "You look like a... a ho."

"How old of a ho?" I meant to be funny, but his glare only darkened.

As Roland stepped around the corner, his mouth fell open and he made a few rapid blinks. Then he shook his head as if to pull himself together. "She's dressed like that for work.

She's pretending to be an underage girl who, uh, uh..."

"I rescheduled the appointment with the abortion clinic. I need to look fifteen, because of statutory rape laws in North Carolina. And my boyfriend will have to be, well, much older. We need to see what they will—"

"Who's your boyfriend?" Jarret's jaw and one hand twitched.

I shrugged. "I don't know. I'll make someone up."

"Are you going alone?"

Another shrug. "Whatever Candice wants. She doesn't know I rescheduled. I don't know what the plan was before. Do you?"

"I—I don't like you doing this. It's dishonest."

I huffed, offended. "What they do is dishonest. What they do destroys and kills, and some of it's illegal. We're trying to bring light to that."

"Two wrongs don't make a right. The Church teaches that."

"What?" I almost contradicted him, but I knew what he meant. *The end does not justify the means.* St. Thomas Aquinas had written something like that. But this wasn't the same. I wasn't doing something seriously wrong, was I? What about Pope Pius XII when he forged documents and hid thousands of Jews during Hitler's reign of terror? What about the Catholic "Just War" doctrine? No, I didn't have to feel guilty about this.

"Well, I don't like it. I don't like you walking into an abortion clinic for any reason. I don't care if this getup..." He gestured to my home-styled minidress, his narrowed eyes flicking over my straightened hair and made-up face. "I don't care if it is a cover."

"I don't like it either but I have to do this, Jarret. I have to find answers."

"Right." His tone conveyed doubt and irritation. "Well, do what you gotta do, and get that stuff off as soon as you can."

"You." He turned and pointed at Roland, who had gone to

the table as if doing his best to stay out of it. “Call me.” Jarret gave me one last look and stormed from the house.

# Chapter 21

"SORRY, CAITLYN. Would if I could, but I got things to do." Sean hadn't stopped soaking me in with his eyes since I'd stepped into the office.

Annoyed at his weakness, I folded my arms across my chest and huffed. How did girls who dressed like this tolerate the leering?

"Sean, look at my eyes. I'm talking to you."

He lifted his gaze to mine and gave a little headshake. "As much as I'd luuuv to, I absolutely cannot go with you to the abortion clinic."

Twisting to glance at Candice and Roland, who both stood by the special equipment cabinet, I lowered my voice. "Look, Candice won't allow Roland to go, so it's got to be you."

A chuckle came from behind me. I turned to see Mitch roll his chair back and mumble something to himself.

Jaw jutting, Sean gave Mitch a threatening glare.

I waited until Sean returned his leering gaze to me. "Please, Sean, I don't want to do this alone." Jarret hated me going to that place but, despite what Jarret thought, I hated it too. I couldn't go alone.

"Why don't you tell her the reason you won't go, Sean?" Mitch said, grinning. "Tell her who called you this morning."

"No one called me." Sean shook his crimson face and walked backwards, eyes on me, toward his desk.

"Wait. What?" I raced to him and grabbed his arm, anger rising inside. "Jarret called you? You're kidding." Didn't he trust me at all?

"No, I've just got stuff to do." He twisted his arm from me, sat at his desk, and flipped open a file. "Everybody thinks I don't work around here. I work."

"Hey, Caitlyn, you need someone to go?" Mitch stood and tucked in the front of his polo shirt. "I'll go."

"Victor can go." Candice marched from the special equipment cabinet to a desk in the back of the room.

Mixed feelings of relief and discomfort passed through me. With his odd personality, Mitch seemed like an entirely unlikely candidate, but Victor looked old enough to be my father. But if that's how Candice wanted it...

I stood at the special equipment cabinet, checking out recording devices, when Victor came up beside me. We exchanged polite nods. He remained silent for a moment, towering over me, making my mouth dry, and provoking questions in my mind. Did he shave his head or had he lost his hair? Did he wear the goatee to appear tough and unapproachable? How did the tie fit into his image?

"I'll have you know, I'm against this," he said, out of the blue.

"Oh, sorry." My temperature spiked under his hard eyes. "I'd wanted Roland to accompany me, but he's not allowed, and then Sean—"

"We're not just going up against A-Z Women's Choice Clinic." He spoke low, as if not wanting anyone to overhear. "We're going up against a giant. We're going against the whole industry, the culture, for that matter. We'll never win."

"But we're just the investigators for a case." Fidgeting with the recording device I thought I should use, I tried to understand the intensity of the anger he conveyed. "We're not the lawyers. We don't have to win. We just have to get the facts."

He stepped closer and switched the recording device in my hand for a smaller one. "As investigators, we're part of the team going against them. And abortion is big business. They don't take to challenges and threats nicely, always twist things around, get you on something. You're aware of the varying laws and how the age of consent is different in every state?" He cocked a brow. "Arizona's got some of the toughest laws with the age of consent at eighteen. Here it's sixteen. And the parental consent laws differ from state to state, too. Some states don't even have parental consent laws..."

Five minutes later, considering Victor's thoughts, I rolled my chair to Sean's desk and pleaded with him one last time.

With a great sigh, he flopped back in his chair and slapped his forehead. "Oh, all right. I'll do it. And I guess I can drive this time."

Once Candice agreed to Sean going, Victor strode to the door with purpose, then he stopped and motioned me over. He pulled me out to where only Sherlock Holmes could witness and said, "You're trying to piece Friday together, right? There's something you ought to know."

"Okay." Curiosity vied with discomfort.

He shot a beady-eyed glance at the door to the office. "You did not leave work at five last Friday and neither did Sean."

"I thought I had an appointment."

"Check the time of that appointment. I drove by around six o'clock and you and Sean were both here." He cocked a brow again. "*Just* you and Sean."

"Oh. Sean never told me that." I tried to remember what Sean had said, wondering if this new revelation could sync with it.

Victor rubbed his goatee and squinted. "I don't know if you've noticed, but Sean can be a bit obsessive."

I smiled. "I've noticed. He seems to love the whole detective thing and all the little gadgets that go with it. I have a friend like him..." My friend Peter popped into my mind, and his obsession with electronics. "...who likes electronic kits and makes his own—"

"Caitlyn." A concerned, fatherly look came over him. "Sean has a bad crush on you."

Heat rushing to my face, I shook my head. “What? Sean? I’m sure he doesn’t.” Of course, Mitch gave the impression he thought so too. But maybe Sean had one of those flirty personalities. “I think Sean’s just a bit—”

“He does, believe me. I’ve confronted him, but a lot of good that’s done. I’m not saying you returned those feelings or that you were in any kind of clandestine relationship. I’m sure you’re deeply in love with your husband. I don’t even know if you knew. But I do know you were upset with Sean that Friday, for whatever reason. You should talk to him and find out why. I’m telling you, Friday at six o’clock, both of your cars were parked outside the office.”

The conversation played over and over in my mind all the way to A-Z Women’s Choice Clinic. Had we talked about that kiss again or something else? And why had Victor driven by the office around six? I wanted to question Sean but decided to wait until after the appointment.

As we stepped inside the clinic, Sean grabbed my hand and rubbed my fingers, stopping at my wedding rings, convincing me of every word Victor had said. But then Sean whispered in my ear, “Get your wedding bands off, woman. You’re only fifteen.”

I barely managed to twist them from my finger before a woman greeted us in the waiting room. We took seats to wait for the appointment, and I dropped the rings into my purse, which reminded me—

With furtive glances at the receptionist, I turned the micro-video camera on and checked that the lens stuck out the hole in the side of the purse. A few minutes later, Emily called us back.

“I’m Emily, and I am sorry to keep you waiting, dear.” Emily was a Yankee. Tall and thin with dark spiky hair, dressed in a sleeveless black turtleneck, knee-length skirt, and heels, she could’ve passed for a clothing-store manikin. Not particularly pretty or ugly, she had a blemish-free tan complexion, dangling earrings, bright red lipstick, and no other obvious make-up. Her pleasant but insincere smile added to her manikin-like appearance.

"Please, come in." Emily made a graceful sweeping motion with her long arm, inviting Sean and me into the consultation room. Black-framed, modern posters of girls looking beautiful, self-sufficient, and all-important hung on walls of dark gray. The pale gray carpet and sleek black lamps, artistically placed, gave the room a stylish, contemporary appearance.

Another graceful gesture indicated that we should sit in the two black padded chairs on one side of a wide lipstick-red desk. Emily sauntered to the other side of the desk and eased herself into a high-backed, ergonomic chair.

"And who is your friend?" She gave Sean a long look as if sizing him up.

Sean and I glanced at each other as we took our seats. I placed my purse on the shiny red desk, making sure the camera pointed at Emily.

"Um, my friend?" I tried to act like a nervous girl who had something to hide.

"I'm Sean." He reached a hand across the table. Emily accepted and shook it in true manikin style. Sean was supposed to use a fake name, so either he couldn't come up with one, or he decided it didn't matter. Still thinking over Victor's warning, I had chosen the feminine version of his name: Vicky.

"So, how old are you, Vicky?" Emily said to me.

"I'm fifteen." I decided to keep my answers as short as possible and to hold a pout on my otherwise emotionless face, as Melinda had done, looking as much like a little girl's Bratz doll as I could.

"Is that gonna, you know, be a problem, 'cuz she ain't eighteen?" Sean reclined and rested his arm on the back of my chair.

Emily smiled and raised her chin, a condescending look in her eyes. "If we had better laws... I notice you, Vicky, don't have the local accent. Where are you from?"

The question made me gasp. I should've faked a Southern drawl!

Sean took it in stride. "Y'all got better laws in Ohio?"

"Ohio? No. So, are you Vicky's boyfriend?"

Sean shifted in his seat and gave me a wary glance. "Uh, yeah. Does my name have to be on anything? 'Cuz I'm, like, twenty-three and I think, uh—"

"No, Sean, your name doesn't need to be on anything. And I'll pretend I didn't hear your age or that you're her boyfriend, for that matter. As far as I'm concerned, you're just a friend."

She flashed a smile, flipped open a folder, and slid a couple of papers across her shiny desk. "You'll need to fill out a Medical History form. It's really straightforward. Just a few questions about your health and birth control methods. Were you using birth control?"

I maintained my Bratz doll pout and shook my head.

Sean snickered. "Would we be here if she had?"

"Maybe, Sean." Emily did not look amused. "Many couples don't use their birth control properly, and they end up pregnant anyway. So, I'd like to share that information with you. It will give you something to consider in the future. There are many options." She slid a few more papers toward us.

I bit back a reply. No matter how "properly" a person used birth control, a girl could still get pregnant. None of them was 100 percent effective.

"Now, because of your age, Vicky, we're going to need parental consent. It can be given by either parent."

Sean shook his head before she finished speaking. "No. That's not gonna work."

"My parents would kill me," I said without emotion.

Emily pursed her lips. "You can request permission from a judge and avoid—"

"No." Sean leaned forward. "We can't wait for that. And she can't tell her parents. They can't know about it. They can't know about us. They'd kill her *and* me." He gave me a sly grin, and I couldn't help thinking he had Jarret on his mind. "Can't we just take care of this quietly? I've got the money."

With eyebrows low over compassionate eyes, Emily slid another form across the table. "Why don't you take this form home? There's no need to make this difficult. If her parents *can't* know, then they don't have to know. But we need this form signed. Do you understand what I'm saying?"

He looked at me and shook his head, his blue eyes conveying the picture of naivety. "I can't ask either one of them to—"

"I know." She nodded slowly as if he should pick up on what she insinuated but didn't want to say.

"You mean *we* fill it out? What then? Do I sign her father's name?"

She gave another slow nod. "Now, I can't tell you to do that. But if I get this form back with her mother's or father's signature and a phone number, that's all I need."

He made a nervous laugh, sighed, and nodded. "Yeah, okay, I can take care of that." He gave me a glance, but it wasn't a nervous or relieved glance that fit with his acting role. It was more of a "we got her" look.

I nodded back. We had our evidence. Just as the girls had said, the woman insinuated we could fill out the parental consent form ourselves. And she had overlooked Sean's age, which would obviously make him guilty of statutory rape.

Emily leaned back in her chair and smiled, appearing satisfied that Sean understood her. She turned her smile to me. "How far along are you, dear?"

My pouty mouth suddenly trembled. Sorrow and disgust welled up inside me. This woman was perfectly at ease asking me how far along my unborn child was, all the while arranging to have it terminated. Unable to speak, I covered my trembling mouth.

*It's okay, baby, you really are safe with me,* I communicated the thought to my unborn child. *I'd never let any harm come to you.*

Sean grabbed and squeezed my hand. I turned away from

the woman I now despised and pressed my face to Sean's shoulder. He stroked my hair. "It's okay," he whispered, his voice soft and soothing. "We'll make everything all right."

*Pull yourself together. Don't blow the cover.* I took a deep breath, put my stone face back on, and sat up, returning my gaze to the woman with the sympathetic eyes. "I'm three months along."

Our mission complete, we gathered the forms and left the clinic.

"We did it," I said as Sean and I hiked to his car. The weight of misery I'd felt in the office lifted, leaving me with pride of accomplishment. Would this be enough for the case?

As Sean opened the passenger-side car door for me, his eyes fixed on some distant point. "Shi-oot."

I glanced around the parking lot, the two rows of cars down the length of the building, but didn't see whatever he saw. Sliding into the car, I closed the door.

Sean dropped into the driver's seat and slammed his door. I was about to ask him what was wrong when he said, "Shoot, shoot, son of a... son of a—" and slammed his palms against the steering wheel. "Son of a Mitch!"

I suppressed a giggle. "What's the matter, Sean?"

"Ain't that your husband over there?" He made a nod toward his window.

I finally saw what he saw and my stomach flipped. Four cars down in the second row, Jarret sat in his charcoal black Dodge Ram, glaring at us.

My heart jumped, landing with a sickening, guilty thud. He hadn't wanted me to go here at all, but he probably hated seeing me with Sean. Could he have known about Sean's feelings for me? Or about the kiss? "I guess I should see what he wants." I reached for the door handle.

Before I could open the door, Jarret tore out of the parking lot, tires squealing as he drove away.

# Chapter 22

"JARRET'S GONNA KILL me."

"He's not going to kill you."

Sean gripped the steering wheel, his knuckles white, and stole glances in the side and rearview mirrors. "He's gonna kill me. He called me this morning, you know, what Mitch said. That was true." He dropped a hand from the steering wheel and tapped nervously on his thigh. "He called and threatened me, said I'd better not go anywhere with you today. He told me about the appointment before you did. I said I wouldn't go." He shook his head. "I'm sure he's gonna kill me."

I huffed and stared out the window at a group of teens outside an Australian restaurant. Broken glass glittered on the sidewalk near them, a beautiful mess that no one noticed, that didn't belong there. Strangely reminding me of my life.

I turned back to Sean. "He's not going to kill you. He didn't like the way I dressed today, that's all."

Without skipping a beat, he turned and stared openly at my bare legs. "Yeah, I can understand that. I'd be pretty jealous if you were my wife and looking like that."

I tugged my skirt down as far as possible and used my hands to cover the rest of my exposed thighs. "And he didn't like me going to the abortion clinic, not even undercover." A sickening feeling crept over me as I mentioned the place.

Sean's gaze slid to my legs as we barreled toward slowing traffic.

"Watch the road, Sean."

He looked up in time to brake for a red light, slamming hard to avoid hitting the Hummer in front of us. It wouldn't have damaged the Hummer, but his little Ford Focus would've suffered a bit.

"I've been thinking, and..." He gave me an accusing glance. "...you must have told him."

"Told him what?"

"You know." He turned his baby blue eyes on me again and gave me a knowing look.

"About the kiss? Hmm." Maybe he did know. How long ago would I have told him? Right after it happened? Days later?

The light turned green. He drove to the next intersection and turned right, leaving the crowded streets of strip malls, gas stations, and grocery stores for a farm road, long and straight, that cut over to Indian Fort.

"Can we swing by my house? I'd like to change." The sooner I could change out of the trashy outfit the better. It would put an end to Sean's distraction and Jarret's irritation, and I'd be a hundred times more comfortable.

"Hell no, I'm not stopping at your house. What, are you trying to get me killed?" He turned to me with scrunched brows, looking offended. "Let him come to me. I am not taking it to him."

"Oh, Sean." I let out an exasperated sigh. "Stop being a baby. He's not going to do anything to you. Besides, he won't even be there. He's probably back at work. I want to change into some real clothes and scrape the make-up off my face. I feel silly."

"Not taking any chances."

I slumped in the seat. I would have to take a break from work and go alone. Candice wouldn't mind. She didn't even expect me to be working on cases until my memory returned. If I could only figure out what happened Friday night. Maybe facing what happened would trigger my memory.

Victor's revelation came back to me. *You did not leave work at five last Friday and neither did Sean... Sean has a crush on you.*

Sean stared straight ahead down the long, rolling farm road. The panic had faded from his expression. Maybe I shouldn't ask him now, but what other chance would I have? When else would we be alone?

"Sean, Victor said we stayed late Friday." I tried to sound casual.

He glanced. "What would he know? He was out on appointments all afternoon. He never came back to the office."

"Well, is it true or not?" His avoidance of a direct answer made it hard to keep an even tone.

He gazed at the road as we climbed a slight hill, his face as placid as it had been before the question. A long moment later, he answered, "Yeah, it's true."

"Oh. Were we working?"

He shook his head. "No, we were talking. You were mad at me. I wanted to know why so I could...fix it."

"Why was I mad at you?" The detective in me loved a good mystery, but not when it came to my life. Would I ever get the memories back, the missing pages from the book of my life? Or would I have to settle with piecing pages together, trusting others with their version of my life?

"I don't know. You never told me. You said you weren't, but I could tell you were upset. All morning you were distracted, like you had something on your mind. Then after lunch you were crabby." He flashed a grin after the word "crabby." "So after work, I tried talking to you about that..." A long pause. "And about, well, something else."

I waited and waited then finally said, "Okay. Are you going to tell me *what*?"

He inhaled and let the breath seep out his mouth. "I, uh, I ended up telling you...something...you know, that I have feelings for you." He rolled the last words out quickly, as if it were easier to get it out that way.

My stomach leaped. "Me? Sean, you can't have feelings for me. I'm married. And, well, it's awkward right now, me not remembering things—"

"Yeah, don't, Caitlyn. You told me all that already."

"I told you...?"

"You're married, you've never been in love with anyone the way you're in love with him, and I need to find myself a girlfriend and not think about you," he said with barely a pause and then gave me a sad sort of smile.

"I'm sorry, Sean. I didn't know. Well, not for certain." I sat stunned for a moment. Wow, to hear him say it like that... Could it be true? I'd loved Jarret enough to move across the country with him, away from family and friends. And start a family with him. Why couldn't I remember that kind of love?

"What are you thinking?" Sean said, looking pouty.

"Nothing. I just wish I knew why I was upset that day. I'll have to ask Jarret. Maybe something happened at lunch."

"Well, don't tell him what I just told you. He's jealous enough. He'd kill me for sure, unless..."

"Unless what?"

He gave me a narrow-eyed look. "You noticed it yourself, the way Jarret looks at me. What if he knows about me kissing you? What if you told him, like, at lunch Friday?" As he spoke he glanced back and forth between me and the road, a distant look in his eyes. "You were anxious about something all morning, and then you were mad at me, you know, for no obvious reason. But if you told him and he got mad or...started keeping a close eye on you... And that night we were there late, just me and you. Victor saw us. Maybe Jarret saw us too. You know? And what's more, on the way out your phone rang. You went back to answer it. I left. I swear, I didn't see his truck anywhere. But I wasn't really looking. Maybe it was him, checking up on you or calling from the parking lot across the street or something."

"You're not making any sense. I mean, supposing I told him and he was angry. Why would he call me?"

Sean shrugged and stared intently at the road for a few seconds. Then he faced me. "You said your car was found at a park. Maybe he called to have you meet him at the park, you know, to hash it out."

As he spelled out his theory, a chill ran through me. "What're you saying? That doesn't make sense. Why wouldn't we just hash it out at home?"

"Mmm, I don't know. Maybe the phone call was from someone else who wanted to meet you at the park. Or maybe he thought you and I were going to meet up there."

"So he followed me to the park and..."

"Yeah, and took it out on you in some way or another that gave you amnesia."

Annoyed by his suggestion, I let out a disgusted grunt. On impulse, my hand shot to the sore spot on my head. The bump had gone down considerably, but the skin was still tender. Sean wouldn't know about the bump. I hadn't told anyone at work about it, had I?

"I can't listen to you, Sean. Jarret would never hurt me." He did have a temper, and he was terribly jealous, but I couldn't imagine he would hurt me. Of course, when we were younger, Roland did come to school with unexplained bruises.

"Maybe he didn't do it on purpose," Sean continued. "Maybe he was angry and something happened, something bad. Then maybe he got scared and took off. Or maybe he didn't even know something had happened to you. Maybe you took off, angry at him, and he went home."

"Stop it! Just stop it!" Anger rising to the surface, I cut Sean a harsh glare, but he didn't turn from the road to see it. "I can't believe he would leave if something bad had happened to me. He'd feel instant remorse."

"Is that how he is? Does he apologize and fix his mistakes right away, or does he have to think about it? Does it take him awhile?" He pulled into the parking lot of Wright Investigators.

The instant the car stopped, I flung open the door. "I'm going home to change." I didn't look at him, didn't want to answer him. But I thought about it. The Jarret I remembered did make rash decisions. Was he still like that or had he changed?

I stomped three cars down and shoved the key into the lock of my dusty dark-blue Honda, forgetting again that the car remote could unlock my door. I'd never had a key fob before. Why did people call it a *fob* anyway?

Dropping into the driver's seat, I continued mulling things over. Jarret hadn't wanted me to talk to Roland, told me he needed to think about it. Fortunately, Roland sensed trouble and had flown clear across the country without being asked. But then, Jarret still didn't want me to call my mom or a friend to help get things straightened out in my mind. No, he didn't make quick decisions or fix his mistakes right away. But would he abandon me when I was hurt?

# Chapter 23

STANDING AT THE bathroom mirror, I smeared cold cream on my face. Maybe I should call Jarret to tell him; he'd be glad. I closed one eye and rubbed cold cream on it, making a disgusting gray paste. That glare on Jarret's face when he'd seen me all made up... My father wouldn't have given me a look half as bad. Of course, I had never put Dad to *that* test. I always hated make-up and skimpy clothes. Maybe because I had nothing to show off, as tubular as my body was. It wasn't a figure a girl would want to draw attention to. Still, I hadn't looked bad in the short jumper. Sean certainly couldn't take his eyes off me.

Turning from the mirror, I glanced at the denim jumper that lay crumpled in the corner. Jarret would want me to throw it away. I shrugged and slapped cold cream onto my other eyelid. I'd never wear it again anyway. It wasn't my style. Whether I looked good in it or not, I stood firmly against dressing to draw that kind of attention to myself. My mode of fashion was a skirt that came at least to my knees and a pretty, but modest, top.

After removing all traces of make-up, I worked on my hair, relocating the part to a more reasonable position on my scalp. Then I gazed at my reflection in the mirror to assess my overall appearance. With bone straight hair, I wasn't back to normal, but I looked fine. Maybe I would wear my hair straight every now and then. It made my green eyes stand out. Hadn't I woken with straight hair on Saturday? Did Jarret like straight hair?

The theory Sean had suggested came to mind. Could there be any truth to it? Jarret definitely showed signs of jealousy, but to suggest that he would follow me to a park and then—No. That would go beyond jealousy.

With a quick glance at the time, I swiped my keys from the back of the toilet and headed for the door. My stomach complained. If Sean had agreed to swing by the house, I would already be back to work and eating at my desk. Now I would have to pick up something for a late lunch. Sean had worried Jarret would be at the house, waiting for us. I giggled. He was so paranoid. Jarret was probably—

As I touched the doorknob of the front door, it turned. Heart leaping from my chest, I gasped and backed up.

The door swung open and there stood Jarret in tan khakis and work shirt. My heart returned to my chest. Of course, it was Jarret. Who else could it have been? I exhaled, unreasonable fear melting away, but the discomfort created by his presence replacing it.

"Hey." He gave me a head-to-toe glance and stepped inside. "You look good."

"Thanks." His compliment made my face warm.

I watched him strut to the kitchen, tempted to ask him a few questions, but I hadn't been alone with him since Roland arrived, and it felt weird now. Should I talk to him about Sean? If he knew about the kiss, did he blame me? If I'd told him, had I blamed myself? I decided to ask harmless questions instead, intending to leave after a few pleasant exchanges.

"So... what're you doing here?" Remaining near the door, I clasped my hands together and smiled.

"Lunch." His tone said I should've known, as if I shouldn't assume he was checking up on me.

"Do you usually come home for lunch?" The smile faded from my face, an accusing glare replacing it.

He pulled open the refrigerator and grabbed a few things. "No. Never. It's too far."

"Why today?" Did I really want him to answer that question? He'd seen me in Sean's car at the abortion clinic. He may have assumed Sean would've driven me home to change. The thought of me and Sean at the house may have been too much for him. Especially if he knew about Sean's kiss, and if he had seen our cars after hours at Wright last Friday.

But a strong relationship needed trust. Jealousy had no place in it.

"I thought you might be here." He set his lunch fixings on the island counter and dragged the bread closer. "Thought you'd want to change after your appointment."

"So, you're here to make sure?" I meant to sound playful, but it came out rude. This was my husband. Why should I find it so hard to talk to him?

He glanced, looking unsure of how to take me. "Noooo." He laid out two pieces of bread.

"Just like you showed up at the abortion clinic to make sure Sean hadn't come." Guilt and shame flooded my mind, making me regret saying this. I was not ready to discuss Sean with him. Not at all.

He opened his mouth and stared. Then he blinked and continued fixing his sandwich. "I came home because I wanted to tell you something." Another glance. "Hungry?"

"Yes, but I'll pick something up. I can't stay." I took a breath, relieved that he'd decided not to get into it. Then I went as far as the loveseat and stopped. "What did you want to tell me?" Wondering why he made me so nervous, I rubbed a seam on the back the loveseat.

He piled a mound of shaved ham onto the bread and opened a baggie of sliced Swiss cheese. "I'm gonna be late tonight."

"Oh, that's fine. No problem." I turned around. He'd missed a few days' work because of me, so I didn't doubt his boss would want—

He huffed loudly. "Ain't ya gonna ask me how late? Ain't ya gonna ask me why? Ain't ya gonna ask if you should wait for me for dinner?"

My heart prickled with compassion stirred up by the anguish in his voice, the accumulation of pain I'd caused him. Of course a wife would ask those things. If I could only remember being his wife. "Oh, I—I'm sorry. Why are you going to be late?"

Jaw clenched, he shook his head at his sandwich. Then he whipped the mustard squeeze-bottle, sending it flying down the counter. "You don't care about me at all, do you?" His words flew out rapid-fire. "Or about us. You go, against my wishes, into an abortion clinic—"

"Not to have an abortion." The words gushed out with shock and indignation. "I would never."

"I don't know, Caitlyn. I don't know you anymore and you don't know me. We don't talk. Are you even trying to remember?"

"Of course, I'm trying to remember!" I shrieked. "But you don't make it easy. You're practically stalking me. You won't even let me call my mom."

A moment of frozen silence passed. "I have a reason for that."

"Oh? Care to explain?"

He shook his head. No eye contact. Rigid as ever.

"Why are you so insecure?"

"Why do you think? The more people you turn to, the less you turn to me. Like now, you've got Roland. You go to your work. I go to mine. We have to see each other at dinner, but then you head to the bedroom, to *our* bedroom where *I* no longer sleep, and I'm outta your hair."

His words continued to sting that deep place in my heart. I didn't want to hurt anyone. I wasn't that kind of person. And this was my husband. "Jarret, don't."

Without thinking the action through, I ran to him.

He stepped back, an expression of shock turning to one of longing as I flung myself at him.

I wrapped my arms around his waist and tucked my head

in the crook of his neck. "I'm sorry that I don't remember how things were between us, and that this is so painful for you. I don't mean to hurt you." His cologne and the scent of him—of Jarret—the feel of his body against mine, his whiskers against my cheek, and my nose against the smooth skin of his neck overwhelmed me with a dizzying effect.

After a moment's delay, he encircled me in a firm, comforting embrace and buried his face in my hair. "I'm sorry too." Emotion laced his voice. "I know I've been acting like a jerk. I shouldn't have gone up to spy on you. I want to trust you again, but when you look at me like we're back in high school… I need you, Caitlyn, need you to remember what we have." He kissed my head twice. Dropping more kisses, he sunk his hands into my hair and guided my face up to his. He pressed a kiss to my cheek and, breathless, whispered my name.

My thoughts spiraled out of control and scattered, leaving only a sinking, helpless feeling. Then it dawned on me what signals I'd sent by running to him, by hugging him. I wasn't ready for what I suspected came next.

His lips grazed my cheek, tracing a warm, tingly path to my mouth.

Heart racing and overcome with a desire to flee, I retracted my arms from around his waist and withdrew from his embrace. "I—I have to get back to work," I whispered, touching my cheek, still warm from his kisses, and hoping the rejection wouldn't crush him. I wanted to remember my feelings for him, but I didn't.

Hurt flickered in his eyes, realization of the pain he'd risked by allowing himself to be vulnerable. Dropping his gaze, he rubbed a hand up his chest and over his face, then shoved his fingers in his hair. "Okay, then, I—I'll see you later. I missed a few hours today." He glanced, his arm swinging awkwardly to his side and his posture shifting as if he no longer felt comfortable in his own skin. "And I'm behind on a few things. Got deadlines. So I…I don't know how late I'll be but..."

He looked at the mustard bottle on the floor with a grumpy expression, resignation heavy in his tone. "Well, I'm sure you can find something to do. You and Roland."

# Chapter 24

"OH, PLEASE CALL him," I begged.

I walked backwards so I could read Roland's expression as we crossed the parking lot from Wright Investigators to my Honda. Heat radiated from asphalt that had baked in the sun all day, warming my ankles.

Roland's gaze flitted from me to Sean, who made a backward glance on the way to his car, to Mitch, who had just left the building, and back to me. Victor was out on an appointment and Candice was the only one who didn't seem anxious to leave at five.

Wanting to convince Roland, I grabbed his hand and clasped it between mine. "Ple-e-ease."

"I don't know." With the hint of a smile, he tugged his hand free. "I think *you* should call. He won't like hearing that question from me." Sweet Roland, gray eyes flickering with concern, always seemed so considerate of others' feelings.

Turning around, I fished the keys from my purse. "I don't want to ask him." A twinge of guilt struck me. I should be the one to ask, but I doubted Jarret would like my idea. "He gets so moody when I talk to him. I told you how he threw the mustard bottle." The entire incident threatened to invade my thoughts.

I quickened my steps to the car and lifted my key fob, remembering to use it this time to unlock the doors.

"Well, it's not like he threw it *at* you." Roland must've hated that I'd mentioned the incident, especially since I'd said it in the office, within earshot of Sean and Mitch. He'd caught the "I told you so" look Sean had given me, though he wouldn't have understood its meaning.

I hadn't meant to complain, shouldn't have brought it up at all, but I couldn't stand the emotions clashing inside my brain ever since seeing Jarret at the house. And I'd wanted Roland to know we had spoken and that Jarret had to work late.

"Let's stay home," Roland said. "We can rent a movie and make something for dinner."

Frustrated, I groaned. "Why should I have to ask permission anyway? He said he was going to be late and I should find something to do." I dropped into the driver's seat of my warm car and closed the door. In the few seconds it took Roland to walk around the car, the impression of Jarret's embrace came unbidden to my mind, the feel of his whiskers on my cheek, his skin, his scent, his kisses...

The passenger side door opened, swirling my thoughts like fall leaves in a little whirlwind. Roland got into the car, closed the door, and sighed. "Caitlyn, you know how Jarret is. If he comes home and we're not there, he'll think the worst. So it's not asking for permission, it's just... it's being married."

"Oh, ple-e-ease." Desperate to run from my thoughts, I twisted toward Roland and reached for the cell phone on his belt, but he grabbed it first. "Just call him!" I shouted.

Shaking his head, Roland sighed and made the call. A few seconds later he said, "What?" into the phone, sounding offended. "Nothing's wrong. Can't I call you?" He gave me a glance, then stared out the window. "Hey, Caitlyn said you're going to be late tonight, and she's tired of hanging around the house. You wouldn't care if we saw a movie, would you?"

"Please, please, please," I mouthed.

Roland shook his head and rolled his eyes. "Get serious, Jarret. It's not a date. She's my sister-in-law. I have a girlfriend and Caitlyn's got you... Ahhhh, you know it's not like that... Oh come on, Jarret."

"Exactly why I didn't want to call," I whispered. Jarret's jealousy outweighed every consideration. I needed to get out and forget everything. Kind of ironic considering that my forgetting everything *was* the problem.

Roland sighed hard. "She wanted me to ask you." He gave me a glance. I responded with a guilty smile. "She's probably afraid you'll get mad at her. She doesn't want you mad at her... I don't know... I don't know... All right. We'll try to catch an early one... Okay. Thanks."

He stuffed his cell phone into the holder on his belt. "Okay, it's a date."

Elated and tempted to clap my hands, I grinned over my shoulder and shoved the key into the ignition. "You told him it wasn't a date."

"What? I didn't mean— It's not a date. It's a *go*."

~ ~ ~

After a relaxing dinner at a barbecue joint, and a good hand- and face-washing to remove excess sauce, we found a nearby movie theater and a movie that had potential. Roland was less selective than I was. He didn't want to see a romance. I didn't want anything too violent or with constant swearing or with nudity or... We settled for a remake of Sherlock Holmes.

I gazed at the wide movie screen, paying little attention to the preview of yet another unrealistic, plot-less, violent movie with scene after scene of a bald man running, jumping, shooting, and shouting. My mind drifted elsewhere.

"Roland, I need to tell you something."

One hand in the tub of popcorn, he stared at the screen.

"And I don't want you to tell Jarret."

That got his attention. He dropped his handful of popcorn back into the bucket. "What?"

I took a deep breath and leaned closer. The volume in the theater boomed. The employee in charge of it must've thought we were all hard of hearing, or maybe he was hard of hearing, or maybe he wanted us all to become hard of hearing. Maybe he had a second job selling that medicine I'd seen advertised for incessant ringing in your ears.

"What?" Roland repeated.

"Sean told me something disturbing the other day."

"Sean? What?" Roland whispered as if we were in a library. I could feel him say "what" more than hear him.

"Promise you won't tell Jarret?"

"I didn't hear what you said."

"I didn't say it yet. You have to promise."

"Okay. You know me."

I nodded. In my present condition, he was the only person I did know. Sometimes I didn't even know myself.

"Sean said we kissed." Unfortunately, I spoke as a train blew by on the big screen and a man with a semi-automatic shot at it.

"Sean said we missed what?" He spoke louder this time.

"No. Not missed. Kissed."

"What?"

"Kissed! We kissed!" Typical of my luck, I shouted as the preview ended, my voice carrying to the far ends of the silent theater.

"Shhh." Roland glanced nervously around us. "Who kissed?"

"Sean kissed me," I whispered, shrinking down in my seat and burning with embarrassment. A group of girls in front of us turned to look at me. If there was going to be gossip, they wanted it. Who cared that they didn't know me from Nancy Drew.

"What? When?"

"Oh, a couple weeks ago, I guess." With my mouth to his ear, I quickly rehashed the story while the notice to silence your cell phone showed for an unreasonably long time on the screen. "I want you to find out if Jarret knows but without telling him."

He huffed and his head lolled back. "And how am I going to do that?"

"I don't know. Hint around. Ask him what he thinks about Sean. Maybe he'll say something negative and you can draw it out of him. If he knows. But don't tell him if he doesn't." No point in adding more tension between us.

"Wow." Roland looked me in the eye, mouth hanging open. "I can't believe you'd keep that from him."

His words cut through my soul, convicting me. At the same moment, the movie began, so I had an excuse to face forward and stop talking. I was keeping things from my husband. Was this something you kept from your spouse? What if a girl at his workplace had kissed him? Would I expect him to tell me? What type of person had I become? Of course, maybe I hadn't kept it from him before.

*I* should talk to him about it, not Roland. And not tonight. In the morning, when we'd both had a good night's rest.

## Chapter 25

THE FRONT DOOR slammed, jarring me from sleep. For a moment, I gazed at the sliver of night sky visible between the bedroom curtains, then I closed my heavy eyelids.

"Ahhh, there's my dear brother, come clear across the country to help out, workin' hard at it too, spendin' all day and night with my wife."

Hearing the sly tone of Jarret's voice through the closed bedroom door, a warning flashed inside and my eyes popped open.

"So, you're sleepin' on the loveseat? That's good. Dinner, a movie... I'z worried you might take your date to my bedroom." He spoke slowly, slurring every few words.

"What time is it?" Roland said through a yawn.

"Time for you to go, little brother."

Eyes wide and ears straining to catch every word, I bolted upright.

"What? It's after two in the morning." Roland sounded more awake now. "Where've you been? Have you been drinking?"

"You shouldn'ta come here. I don't know what you were thinking."

"What's your problem, Jarret?"

I grabbed my robe from the bottom of the bed and sprinted to the bedroom door. Hand on the doorknob, barely breathing, I resisted the impulse to yank open the door, deciding instead to eavesdrop. Maybe they'd sort it out quickly and go to sleep.

"My problem? My wife's in love with my little brother, don't want nothin' to do with me, can't even bring herself to kiss me."

I winced, recalling how I'd pulled out of his arms and fled. I should've kissed him. What kind of wife was I? One who didn't even know her own husband!

"On top of that, I'm gonna lose my job 'cuz I ain't going to work tomorrow or the next day, or the next day, or the next day..." His voice trailed off to a low mumble.

"Why don't you sleep this off?" Roland said. "Things aren't as bad as they seem right now. Let's talk in the morning."

The couch or loveseat squeaked, Roland getting up or Jarret sitting down. Then the sound of car keys plunking onto the coffee table.

"What're we gonna talk about? How you plan to get my wife to remember that she really loves *me*? Or why you left your Chinese girlfriend, dropped everything for your ex? How's she feel about this?"

"That's a load of bullshit!"

I blinked. *Roland said "bullshit"?*

"Bullshit? No, I'll tell you what's a load o' bullshit. My brother's *help* is pushing my wife farther away from me." Emotion flooded out with every word. "I know I never deserved her. And you did. But you had your chance. You didn't want her but I do. I want her and I want my baby. Don't..." His voice cracked and he continued in a desperate, pleading tone. "Don't you take her from me now."

Heart thumping and all my senses on high alert, I reached for the doorknob and turned it slowly. I should try to calm Jarret, keep him from doing something he'd regret. In a way, this was my fault. It wouldn't have killed me to kiss him. It might've brought a memory back. And maybe I shouldn't have gone to the movies with Roland. I should've respected Jarret's feelings, even as insecure and unfair as they were. Even though I couldn't remember, I was his wife.

"Jarret, I'm not—"

Something crashed.

My heart leaped to my throat. I cracked open the door. Roland lay sprawled out on the clean coffee table, the clutter that was on the coffee table having been cleared—by his body—to the floor. Jarret stood over him, shaking out his hand. Roland rolled over and dropped off the coffee table. As he righted himself, he stumbled away from Jarret, but Jarret grabbed him by the shirt and yanked him back.

A jolt of anger shot through me. This was the Jarret I remembered. Angry. Violent. How could I have married him?

Roland spun to face him and lunged. He flung his arms around Jarret in a great bear hug and forced him backwards.

Shocked speechless, I gasped. Roland fought back?

They landed together on the floor at the end of the loveseat. The coffee table moved. A pillow flew. Jarret wrestled his way to the top. Someone grunted. A second later Roland rolled to the top and Jarret went down. The coffee table slid into the couch.

In the next instant, Roland clambered to his feet and retreated behind the loveseat. "What are we fighting about?"

Jarret pulled himself up using the couch and the coffee table. His ponytail had come down and his hair fell in long dark curls that hid his face. As he lunged for Roland, I saw something in my mind's eye, everything else fading away.

*I had just stepped out of my car. As I slammed the door, I caught in the side mirror the glimpse of a man. He hurried toward me. Dark hair hung in his face. Black sunglasses hid his eyes. His face was all white where there should've been a nose and mouth. Did he wear a bandana over his mouth? Sensing danger, I bolted into the woods. Footsteps pounded behind me...*

Panic-stricken, I shrieked.

Jarret spun to face me, eyes wide with shock and worry.

~ ~ ~

"Maybe Jarret's right. It's better that I go." Roland stooped over his suitcase, which lay on the floor where Jarret had tossed it—at the end of the skewed coffee table. The zipper wouldn't budge. Roland had collected and shoved into the suitcase all his toiletries from the half-bath and a plastic grocery bag of dirty clothes that I wished I'd offered to wash. I'd been so self-involved lately.

I shook my head and scooted to the edge of the couch. "I don't want you to go." Emotion escaped with my words. Was he really going to leave me alone with Jarret? I shot Jarret an angry glare. "I don't want him to go!" Yes, having Roland here made things harder on Jarret, but I didn't know *this* Jarret—he was a stranger to me.

Jarret paced from the kitchen to the weight-room door, holding his forehead, his long curls draping over his hand.

"Don't worry, I'm not flying home, yet," Roland whispered. The suitcase zipper finally moved but got stuck halfway around. "I'm still going to help you. I'll just stay at a hotel. What's near here?"

"What's the name of your hotel?" I shouted to Jarret with a smarmy attitude. "Do you have a frequent-customer discount?"

We exchanged disgusted glances.

"Never mind. I'll find someplace." The zipper unhitched and sailed around the suitcase. Roland began to straighten, and I caught sight of the pink fist print on his jaw.

I slid off the couch and grabbed his arms, keeping him from standing. "Wait," I whispered, glancing to see if Jarret paid attention.

He didn't. He had extended the length of his pace, walking now to the patio door. His hand went up to his forehead, down to his chest and to each shoulder. Did he just cross himself?

I turned back to Roland. How should I word it to gain his support and not evoke his brotherly-protection impulse? "I was thinking and, um, I want to go back home. To my family."

Trouble flickered in his gray eyes. My words were like

pebbles disturbing calm waters.

"I'm not giving up on my marriage." I rushed my words, anxious to reassure him. "But I need to take things slow. What if my memory never returns? I can't just throw myself into this relationship without the feelings I should have as his wife."

"Marriage isn't only about feelings, is it?" He pinned me with a hard stare.

I sucked in a breath. He was right. But how could I live as his wife when I didn't remember falling in love? I remembered nothing but his bad qualities. I didn't even know how to talk with him or deal with his temper—which I always seemed to make worse.

Roland watched Jarret pacing and rubbing his face. Was he building up for an angry outburst or a display of remorse? I searched Roland's eyes for the answer. He would know. But his eyes showed only sympathy... for him, for me.

He leaned to whisper. "Give it a few more days. If I can't help you regain your memory, and you still want out of here, we'll go back together. But you'll have to give me time to help Jarret—"

"Are you still here?" Jarret stood in the empty dining room, his arms hanging at his sides like a gunslinger ready for a showdown.

Peeling my hands from his arms, Roland straightened. "I need to call a cab." He reached for the cell phone on his belt.

Jarret shook his head and approached, shoving a hand into his front pocket. "You can take my truck. I won't need it." He held his keys out to Roland.

Roland didn't take them. "Why won't you need your truck?"

Jarret tilted his chin toward me. "I'll just use her car." Grabbing Roland's hand, he slapped the keys into them and mumbled, "Take it. Go," both sounding and looking defeated.

Roland nodded. "I'll call you tomorrow. We'll talk."

Head down, Jarret nodded. "Okay, yeah, sounds good."

"And... you should probably get some sleep now." Roland

gave me a long look before leaving.

The front door clicked shut and my heart sank. Jarret leaned back against the door and dropped his head forward. With his hair draped over his face, I couldn't erase from my mind the image of the man who had chased me. He lifted his head and looked at me. "I'm sorry. I know you must hate me."

"Why would I hate you?" I said, my voice harsh. "Because you throw out the one person who makes me feel safe right now? Or because you keep me here like a prisoner?" Frustration made me want to go on, but a twinge of guilt put my anger in check and I whispered, "Of course, I don't hate you, Jarret. I don't hate anyone. But are you really so jealous and insecure?"

He shook his head but refused to look at me. A sulky child. What could he say? It was all true. Jealousy must've burned inside him and kept him from seeing straight. Maybe he'd been jealous Friday. Maybe he had seen my and Sean's cars parked outside our workplace after everyone else had gone. Maybe he had followed me to the park.

Gaining a burst of courage, I stepped toward him. "Where was my car found?"

His gaze lifted to meet mine.

I took another step. "It was a park I typically go to, wasn't it? Why didn't you want me to go there with Roland?" Something told me I shouldn't have asked, especially not now that we were alone.

He stomped to me and stared down through glassy eyes. "You can go to the park. You can go with me."

I shuddered and stepped back.

# Chapter 26

A JUMBLE OF thoughts kept me from sleeping. Rubbing my arms, I wandered around the dark bedroom. Jarret's jealousy knew no bounds. And what a temper! Why did he have to send Roland away? I needed Roland's help. I felt comfortable with him around, safe. And like Jarret had said earlier, Jarret and I didn't even know each other. He was a stranger. Or worse, he was the manipulative, selfish, womanizing bully I knew in high school.

The image of the dark-haired man in the sunglasses moved to the forefront of my mind. I remembered the moment, but only that moment, with clarity. Panic had raced through every nerve, but I knew I had to act. *Should I jump back into my car, fight him head on, or flee?* I remembered making a snap decision. I ran.

What led up to it? What happened next? Was it a memory from last Friday? From the night I'd bumped my head and gotten amnesia? It had to be. But was the man Jarret? Mike had told me memories might come back disjointed, not reflecting reality. But it seemed like Jarret was after me, and I'd desperately wanted to get away.

Maybe Sean was wrong about someone being after my camera. And maybe he was right about Jarret, my jealous husband, following me to the park. Maybe something so terrible happened that Jarret had even blocked it out. If so, my camera would've gotten lost incidentally and I should be able to find it at the park. I just needed to find out which park and sneak away or convince Jarret to let me go. He said I could go to the park with him. Should I take him up on it?

I shuffled toward the dresser. The glowing red numbers on the alarm clock showed 4:33 a.m. As drunk as Jarret seemed, he had to be sound asleep. I cracked the bedroom door.

Dressed in the same khaki pants and tan work shirt he wore yesterday, he lay on his back on the couch, one hand on his chest and one bare foot on the couch, the other limbs dangling to the floor. Moonlight streamed in through the front window and reflected on something, the only thing on the coffee table.

I squinted. Keys? Yes, my keys!

Before thinking it through, I yanked open the bedroom door and—careful to avoid the mess of papers, plastic bottles, and broken glass on the floor—tiptoed to the coffee table.

With closed eyes, a relaxed mouth, and dark curls surrounding a face free of the wrinkles of worry and agitation, Jarret looked as peaceful as a sleeping lion. One I would not want to wake.

Holding my breath, I reached for the keys. They scraped the table then clanked together as I lifted them. Keys held aloft, I froze. Now was not the time to do anything clumsy. I tiptoed backwards. My foot bumped a plastic bottle. *Careful!* With more caution, I picked my way back to the bedroom and eased the door shut.

I changed out of my nightgown and into one of my old favorites: a faded brown denim skirt and a chocolate t-shirt. Then I put on white crew socks and white tennis shoes, and I grabbed my purse and a denim jacket. I stuffed the car keys into the jacket pocket, lugged one of the antique chairs to the window, and stepped up.

The first time I'd attempted to escape through the window, Jarret had been sitting on the deck. He wouldn't even hear me this time. He'd sleep right through it. By the time he awoke in the morning, I'd be hours away. How far could I get on his eighty dollars? The credit cards would be useless. He'd said he canceled them because he thought my purse had been stolen. Was that the real reason? It would make it difficult for me to travel home without them. *Oh well.* I'd get as far as I could and figure the rest out from there.

I pushed the curtains back and inhaled a deep breath of the fresh night air that came in through the open window. It was a perfect night for running away. Once outside, I would race to the car and roll it out of the driveway. What if he heard the engine and woke up? That shouldn't matter. Having lent his truck to Roland, he would have no way of following me. Maybe he'd call a cab. He would probably assume I was going to find Roland or maybe to the park where my car had been found. He'd be wrong. I would be well on my way to South Dakota.

Heart pounding with anticipation, I lifted the screen and gave it a hard shove. The bottom corner popped right out. I laughed. *Easy.* The rest of the screen soon followed, but as it broke free—a high alarm sounded.

I gasped and my hands shot up to my ears.

The bedroom door flew open.

Jarret stood in the doorway, expressionless. "Oh, hey, I meant to tell you..." He staggered to me and offered a hand to help me off the chair. "I put an alarm on the windows, in case you, uh..." He looked me over instead of completing his sentence. I stood on a chair by the open window. What more needed said?

I took his hand and stepped down. "How do you shut the alarm off? It's going to wake the neighbors."

"Yeah, I got it. Gotta get it from outside." He sauntered from the room in no obvious hurry.

As soon as he disappeared, I dashed for the bedroom door and peeked around the corner.

No Jarret. Just the sound of the patio door sliding open.

Not giving up, I bolted for the front door, leaping over the mess on the floor and weaving around the skewed coffee table. I latched onto the doorknob. It didn't turn. I flipped the lock on the knob. It turned but the door wouldn't open. Two dead bolts held it shut. I unlocked one by hand but the other needed a key. I tugged on the doorknob, hoping the other one wasn't locked. It was.

Reaching into my jacket pocket, I glanced over my shoulder. The alarm still sounded. The sliding glass patio door and the screen were open wide, but I couldn't see Jarret.

Now, which key? Not counting my car key, four keys hung from the ring. Heart pumping hard, I grabbed one randomly and tried to shove it in. It didn't fit. My hands trembled. I dropped the keys.

The alarm shut off.

I glanced over my shoulder. No Jarret, yet. I snatched the keys. Which one had I tried already? I made a guess and shoved another one into the lock. It went in! I breathed and turned the key. As I wrapped my fingers around the doorknob again, I glanced over my shoulder and let out an involuntary, whispery scream.

Jarret stood a few feet behind me, hands on his hips and eyes droopy from lack of sleep. "You gonna run off to Roland? Leave me without a car?"

"I…" Guilt overwhelming me, confusing my thoughts, I pressed my back to the door and held the keys to my chest.

A look of defeat crossing his face, he raised his hands and stepped back. "That…that saying keeps running through my mind: if you love something… let it go…" He closed his eyes and shoved his hand into his hair, turning away. "God, don't ask this of me."

Was he saying I could go? All my ideas about him and all my plans of escape jumbled up in my mind. But this was my opportunity. I could get away from him. I could go home and figure this all out in peace.

My heart wrenched. No, I hadn't the heart to do it now.

Not sure what just happened, I tossed the keys onto the leather chair and shuffled back through the mess and to the bedroom.

~ ~ ~

Saturday morning. Weary after only a few hours of sleep but stomach growling, I sat slumped on the edge of the bed. Judging by the noise in the house, Jarret had somehow awoken before me. I'd have to face him to get breakfast. I stuffed my arms into a white robe, pulled it on over my nightgown and opened the bedroom door.

The washing machine chugged in some remote part of the house. Jarret held a plastic grocery bag and stooped over the mess he'd made in the living room. When he saw me, he straightened and opened his mouth to speak, apology written on his face.

Not ready to talk with him, I closed the door. Bits and pieces of last night flashed through my mind, with all the accompanying emotions: fear, anger, grief, anxiety… and shock. Was Jarret actually going to let me go last night? And I'd blown it.

I shuffled to the bed and pulled the sheet straight, wishing I knew what to do. My life had turned out much differently than I had hoped. With each passing year of high school, excitement and hope in my future had grown within me. I'd believed that God had a plan for me, and I'd wanted to make myself ready. I wanted to go to college, grow in faith, and meet others who shared my faith. Not knowing God's plan, the whole world had been open to me. I could go anywhere and become anything. True, it had always been in my heart to marry and raise children, but I had pictured myself marrying a godly husband... in the *distant* future. I'd had it all figured out— how had this become my reality?

After making the bed, I dusted the night table and dresser. As I dusted the jewelry box, the rag slipped and fell to the floor. Stooping to retrieve it, my hand brushed the pile of papers on the corner of the dresser. Catalogs, receipts, and bills rained down. With a loud moan, I dropped to my knees to gather them up. Could my life get any more frustrating?

The emotions and feelings I'd had in high school still felt so fresh, but here I was living the reality. Fast forward. *Abandon all hope, ye who enter here.* I had married a man as different from me as a lion from a house cat. In six months, I would deliver a baby into the world. Would I be fed up with Jarret by then and living at home with my parents? Could my marriage to this selfish, womanizing, jealous man possibly last? Or would I become another statistic, adding to the number of divorced, single-parent Catholics? Maybe I could get an annulment.

With a sigh, I slapped the papers onto the dresser and tossed the dust rag into the clothes hamper. *Get a grip. With or without your memory, you can make this work.* Right now, I just needed time to think things through.

After a long shower, I dressed in one of my familiar dresses. Then I stood before the bathroom mirror and played with my hair until it fell in pretty curls. As I admired my hair, my stomach rumbled. If it wasn't for the baby, I might have skipped breakfast. Who was I kidding? Jarret was right: I never skipped a meal no matter what.

I stuffed the comb, curling iron, and hair products back into drawers and cabinets. Then over the roar of the vacuum cleaner, a knock sounded on the front door. I froze and listened.

The vacuum cleaner went silent. The front door opened and Jarret mumbled something.

I raced to the bedroom door and cracked it open. Jarret walked away from the closed front door. He'd sent the unknown visitor away. Could it have been Roland? It was probably Bobby. I would've enjoyed speaking with Bobby for a while. He was such a sweet little boy. He had an awful lot to say. I could discover what else he knew about Jarret and about us.

One hand on the vacuum cleaner, Jarret gaped at me through the cracked-open bedroom door. "You look pretty," he said.

Not wanting him to think I'd fixed it for him, I returned to the bathroom and pulled my hair into a plain ponytail. A childish move, for sure, but I couldn't stop myself.

The smell of coffee tempted me as soon as I left the bedroom. I shouldn't have coffee, though, not with the baby.

As soon as Jarret laid eyes on me again, he shut off the vacuum cleaner. "Hey, I made waffles and sausage." He sounded extra friendly, no doubt wanting to make up.

"Okay." I needed to give him a chance, but I just couldn't smile. He'd thrown Roland out. And he so resembled the man in my memory. But then, too, he was going to let me go last night. Or was he?

"Food's in the microwave. The coffee's decaf." He turned the vacuum on and pushed it back and forth behind the couch.

After breakfast, not sure what to do with myself, I returned to my sanctuary and picked up the Louis L'Amour book. As I followed the cowboy in the story through his trials and tribulations, questions filled my mind. How could I regain peace in my life? What if my memories never returned? What important events did I no longer remember? Good things? Bad things?

Sometime later, I closed the book, slid off the bed, and opened the bedroom door. There Jarret was, heading my way with a basket of laundry. So, I sat on the edge of the bed and watched him put clothes away, my skin crawling to see him so comfortable in my underwear drawer. A part of me felt maybe we should talk, but I couldn't get myself to do it. Working silently, he didn't seem ready to talk either.

Laundry complete, Jarret carried the old boxes he'd brought from work to the table. He spent the next couple of hours spreading out and rearranging papers and charts until they covered the table like an ugly, patchwork quilt.

Deciding against interrupting his work and not sure what to say anyway, I picked up another book and made myself comfortable on the couch.

Lunchtime finally arrived. Jarret made turkey and cheese

sandwiches. I brought out a jar of dill pickles and a bag of cheese puffs. We said grace together and both bit into our sandwiches. Halfway through lunch, Jarret set the last bit of his sandwich down and took a swig of Coke.

"Hey, can we talk?"

"Uh..." My heart hammered. He wanted to talk? What direction would this conversation take? He'd already thrown Roland out. What would he want next? "Okay," I said over a mouthful of food.

Eyes on me, Jarret opened his mouth, took a breath, and a moment later said, "So...I messed up last night."

I stopped chewing. A glimmer of hope tingled inside me. Maybe he'd repent of booting Roland out the door and he'd invite him over today.

Sitting back, he ran a hand over his hair. "When I got home last night, late, and you weren't here—"

"But Roland called—"

He reached toward my hand but stopped shy of touching it. "I know. I knew you were still at the movies, but it triggered this..." He gestured, as if trying to physically grasp the right words from the air. "...this downward spiral of self-pity. And the guys from work were all meeting at the bar, so I turned around and went up there. And I didn't think I was drinking too much but..." He paused, a guilty grin flickering on his face. "Well, obviously I was. I—I said things to Roland that I shouldn't have. And I upset you, and—and I'm sorry."

"Oh, wow." His words having taken me by surprise, my voice came out whispery and my insides turned to jelly. The apology didn't fit into my idea of who Jarret was or what he was capable of.

"I just feel so powerless to make things right, powerless to help you. And I know, no matter what your feelings for him, for Roland, you wouldn't act on them." He paused. "You're better than that. And he is too. But with him around, the way you look at him..." He glanced, a vulnerable look in his eyes, and shook his head. "...the way you look at me, I can't shake this insecurity."

We both glanced down at our plates, my heart still hammering.

"I…I don't know what to say." His faith in me touched me. *Was* I better than that? Ever since Roland arrived, I'd been focused less on the mystery of my marriage and more on the mystery of my amnesia. How could I possibly develop feelings for Jarret when I still had feelings for Roland? Maybe he was right to throw Roland out.

"Tell me what I can do to make things better between us."

Stunned, I sat staring, my mind empty at first. Then everything I wanted flooded in all at once. I wanted Roland nearby. I wanted to keep going up to work. I wanted to visit the park where my car had been found… But I decided to ask for the two things I wanted most.

"Tomorrow's Sunday. I want to go to Mass. We won't get through this without prayer, without faith, without God."

He nodded. "Yeah, you're right." His voice was a hope-filled whisper. "We'll go to Mass."

"And I want to call my mother."

He froze, his gaze locked on mine and his face getting a shade lighter. "I…"

"Jarret." I used a firm tone to let him know this was non-negotiable.

He took breath and slouched back. "Well, what are you going to say to your mother? She wasn't exactly happy about you marrying me."

I didn't doubt that. Mom had probably judged him by his reputation. The West family, with their wealth and lack of involvement in the community, had had the reputation of being secretive and aloof. Due to a life of travel with their father, the boys had never set foot in a school building until their teen years. A cloud of strange rumors, most of them false, hung over them at school. I had never believed the rumors, preferring to give everyone the benefit of the doubt. Jarret had used the rumors to his advantage, convincing most everyone that he was to be feared and admired. He'd built *some* reputation.

I pushed those thoughts back, but still I wondered: how had I gone from helping him in his drunken stupor to falling in love with him? And what had Mom and Dad thought when I started seeing him? Mom had probably voiced a dozen objections.

*Why, oh, why didn't I listen to Mom?*

"And your mother doesn't like your job. You censor what you tell her, not wanting her to worry. If you tell her you've got amnesia and that you hate being with me..." He flung his arm around, gesturing wildly as he spoke. "...she'll blame me. She'll blame your job. Then when you get your memory back, it's gonna be a mess."

"You mean, *if* I get my memory back." I shook my head, tempted by despair but not wanting to compromise on this. "Well, I won't tell her I have amnesia. And I won't tell her I don't like being with you." Bitterly, I added, "I'll lie to my own mother." We stared at each other for a few long seconds, then a lump formed in my throat. "I just want to hear her voice."

Scowling, he gave a little nod, as if he understood.

"This is all still so strange to me," I whispered. "I don't remember any of this. I feel like I should still be living at home with my mom and dad."

He dropped his head into his hand and pushed the curls off his forehead. "Let me think about it. Just let me think..."

It wasn't the first time he'd said that. What was there to think about? Or was this just his way of stalling?

# Chapter 27

WITH FOLDED HANDS and bowed head, I knelt beside Jarret in a pew toward the back of St. Joseph Church. The choir sang, "O Lord, I Am Not Worthy," while people processed up to receive Holy Communion. I'd considered singing along but hadn't paid attention when the choir director announced the song number. I could always flip through the book, page after page, until I found it. Experience told me I'd find the song just as it ended.

Light crept under my eyelids. This church was so bright, compared to my cozy, traditional church back home. I'd only warmed up to this place—a modern structure with an odd mix of contemporary and traditional furnishings—in the middle of the Mass, during the prayers of consecration. My heart had stirred for a moment then, but I felt nothing now.

A cellophane candy wrapper lay in the pew in front of me, where my gaze naturally fell. By the shape of it and the pinkish tint around the creases, I decided it once contained one of those hot cinnamon candies that I'd never liked. Whose was it? No kids sat nearby. But an adult could've dropped it too. Some people didn't seem to care about the fast before Holy Communion.

Reeling in my wandering thoughts, I bowed my head lower. *Lord, sorry. Where were we? Thank you for letting me get to Mass this Sunday. Sorry about last Sunday, but you know it wasn't my fault. And please, please, please give me back my memory. There is sooo much I don't understand about my life. I promise I'll take advantage of this second chance I've been given, and I'll amend my life.*

A woman slipped into the pew in front of us and side-stepped to the very end. There she knelt, clasping her hands and making her thanksgiving.

A hint of jealousy struck me. Unsure of the state of my soul, I had remained in the pew during Holy Communion. Jarret did too. To keep an eye on me? Did he normally go up for Holy Communion? Next Saturday I'd talk him into taking me to Confession. Maybe he'd go too. A husband and wife should encourage each other in their faith, right?

I sneaked a peek at Jarret. My husband. *Why him?* my heart protested.

He knelt slumped over, with his butt resting on the seat and his forehead on his folded hands on the back of the pew in front of us. Was he even awake? He'd dressed nicely, anyway—with a gray tie, turquoise dress shirt, and dark gray slacks—the way his brothers and father always did. At least, anytime I ever saw them at church. I only remembered seeing Jarret in jeans. And that curly ponytail that refused to lay neatly on his back. Did he ever cut his hair?

*Argh.* I needed to direct my thoughts back to Jesus. I'd made a spiritual communion already and begged to get my memory back, but I couldn't focus on anything deeper.

*Lord, please, bring me through this. Make a way for me. Open a door.*

~ ~ ~

After Mass we drove straight home. Jarret changed into jeans and a striped t-shirt, while I made pancakes and decaf for breakfast.

Excitement, or maybe nervousness, fluttered through me as I ate breakfast. I couldn't wait to hear Mom's voice. And Dad. And maybe even my brothers and sisters. Jarret had kept his word, taking me to Mass. Would he let me make the phone call too? He'd said he needed to think. What was there to think about?

"Hey, so..." Sitting before a plate with a few streaks of syrup, Jarret twisted his coffee mug from side to side. "When do you want to make that phone call?"

A smile sneaked onto my face. My heart leaped. "How about now, I mean, after breakfast?"

He smiled back. "Yeah, okay. Sorry I didn't let you talk to your mother sooner."

"Really?" I whispered, again stunned by his apology.

He nodded. "We just gotta be cautious. Okay?"

"Okay. I won't tell her I have amnesia or that I don't like—" I pressed my lips together before "you" came out.

With a huff, he rolled his eyes and got up from the table. "Right, that you don't like me." Jarret gathered breakfast dishes and carried them to the sink. "So, there's one more thing you can't talk about." He turned and leaned against the countertop, resting his hands on each side.

"Okay. What is it?" I stepped into the kitchen, my gaze darting from the phone to him.

"Don't ask about your father."

I stared, dumbfounded and unable to formulate a reply for two whole seconds. Would I ever comprehend his ways? "Um. Why? That's kind of an unfair condition. Of course I want to talk to my father too."

"Please." He shook his head. "Just don't. I'll explain later."

A long moment passed, while I tried to read his expression and decipher his words. Vague explanations for his cryptic request flitted through my mind, but I could grasp none of them. Could my father have lost his job? Be suffering from an illness? And me so far from home, unavailable to offer comfort? Dad would never have left Mom. And he couldn't have—

Brick walls rose up in my mind, preventing me from considering other possibilities.

Jarret held my gaze, his warning and look of compassion reaching inside me.

A chill overcame me, dampening my excitement.

Shivering, I shifted my attention to the phone on the countertop and wrapped my fingers around it. I dialed the number I would always know by heart, amnesia or not, and three rings later...

"Hello?" Mom's sweet voice came through the receiver. She sounded a bit winded.

My heart stirred, and a great longing welled up inside. "Mom?"

"Oh, hi, Caitlyn. I was on my way out the door when the phone rang. I thought that was your number. What's up? Is everything okay?"

Wishing I could throw myself into Mom's arms, I leaned against the island countertop and wrapped my arm around my waist.

Jarret slinked over to the kitchen island and stopped two feet from me, his eyes on the countertop and a look of concentration on his face. He probably wished he could hear both sides of the conversation.

"I just wanted to hear your voice, Mom." Wanting to pour my heart out but knowing I couldn't, I struggled to keep an even tone. I didn't want Mom to worry. Maybe Jarret was right to try to dissuade me from calling. "How is everyone?"

Jarret lifted his gaze to mine, caution lights flashing in his eyes. He pulled a notepad and pen from a drawer.

I wanted to turn away from him and transport myself back home in my mind, but I also wanted to read his expression as I spoke and so remained facing him.

"Oh, we're all fine," Mom said. "Let's see, when did we talk last? What haven't I told you?"

"Um? When did we talk last?" I repeated Mom's question so that Jarret could give me the answer.

"Last month," he mouthed.

"I guess it's been about a month," I said. Worried I'd need more assistance with the phone call, I pressed the speaker button and replaced the phone in the cradle.

Jarret exhaled a deep breath, maybe seeing the move as a

sign of my trust.

"Well, not much new. Priscilla's still working at the Brandts' bed and breakfast and at the craft store, which you know she just loves."

Mind reeling, I tuned out Mom's next words. How could Priscilla be old enough to have a job? I calculated on my fingers. Priscilla was eighteen! And Stacey fifteen, David ten, and little Andy eight. Wow! My heart ached over the years I couldn't remember.

"I think she works too hard," Mom said, "but she seems to enjoy it, the Brandts love having her, and it really helps out around here."

"Oh." I could think of nothing better to say. And my mind had gotten stuck on trying to understand why Priscilla's job helped out around there. We'd never been rich, but Dad had always made enough to provide for the family.

"Stacey's talking about getting a job this summer too. She wants to help Mr. Brandt with his forest ranger duties." Mom laughed. "I think he'll humor her and let her help with a thing or two around their big yard."

"Stacey always did like outdoor activities," I said, "the dirtier, the better."

Mom laughed again. "So, did you call for a reason? Are you sure everything's okay? You and Jarret getting along?"

Jarret shook his head and sighed, then he glanced, maybe wondering how I would answer. He couldn't stop me now. I could say anything. But I wouldn't. I didn't want Mom to worry.

Not wanting to lie, I chose not to answer with a yes or no. "I just called to hear your voice, Mom. I miss you guys."

"We miss you, too, dear. Wish you didn't live so far away. I just know one day you're going to call and tell me I'm going to be a grandmother and that you're coming back home."

I shot Jarret a look and mouthed, "Mom doesn't know?"

He shook his head and wrote a note: *You wanted to wait.*

Still holding his gaze, I tried to understand why.

"Well," Mom said, "I'd talk longer, but I was off to your father's old workplace to see about getting our air conditioner replaced before summer. I don't know how he held the old thing together all those years."

Jarret stiffened and sucked in a breath.

Why would Mom worry about that at all? Dad was a registered heating and air conditioner technician.

"Guess we never realized how lucky we had it?" Mom's voice held a hint of sadness. "But his work buddies offered me his old discounts." She sighed. "I know they all loved your father."

Jarret sucked in another breath and blinked his eyes several times as he scribbled the note: *please don't ask.* He shoved the note to me and lifted his gaze…his eyes teary?

"A discount…" I repeated, mindlessly. "Loved?" Why past tense?

Heart thudding in my chest, I pressed my lips together to keep the questions from coming out. *What do you mean, Mom? Why doesn't Dad fix it? What's wrong with Dad?*

"We take so much for granted, you know? Your father always took care of all of that. No matter how harsh the winter or how hot the summer, we never had to think twice about heating or air conditioning."

Mom's melancholy voice brought waves of grief and panic to my mind. *Why could Dad no longer take care of it? What happened to him?*

Jarret pressed his lips together and turned away… as a tear slid down his face.

"Mom?" I whispered, unable to stop the question from coming out. "What happened—"

Jarret spun to face me and, grabbing me by the shoulders, pulled me to himself. "Don't, Caitlyn," he whispered in my ear. "Just tell her goodbye."

"Oh, well," Mom said, her voice strong now. "I have to get going. Love from all of us to both of you."

"I love you too, Mom," I whispered with my last ounce of

strength.

With one arm still wrapped around me, Jarret clicked the speaker phone off. “Come sit down and we’ll talk.” Squeezing my hand, he tried to lead me from the kitchen.

Desperate for answers now, I stood my ground and wriggled my hand from his grip. “What happened to Dad? Tell me.”

As if not sure how to answer, he bowed his head for a moment. Then he glanced up. “I didn’t want you to have to go through the pain again. I wish you could just remember. It was so hard.”

“Tell me.” I squeezed my hands into fists, bracing myself.

A pained expression overcoming him, Jarret sagged against the countertop. “A month or so before our wedding, we got the news.”

Anxiety mounting, I held my breath.

“Your father was diagnosed with a fast-acting cancer, given three months to live.”

*No*, I wailed inside but only a grief-stricken moan came out. Several puzzle pieces of my life shattered. Gone forever. Never to fall back into place. Nothing made sense. Why had I married Jarret after learning of my father’s cancer? Why had I moved away after that? Why hadn’t I remained behind to support my family?

Jarret moved in, reaching for me.

Not wanting his comfort, I pushed him back and shook my head. “Give me a moment,” I said, tears on the verge of erupting. Then I bolted for the sliding glass doors, slipped sandals on my feet, and stepped out onto the deck.

With my arms wrapped around my waist, holding myself together, I shuffled to a sunny spot by the far railing and peered through tears at the dense trees and bushes along the backyard. The sun-drenched wood of the back deck radiated warmth to my legs. A gentle breeze stirred the foliage and carried the scent of lilacs and other flowers. A distant radio played a sad country song. The peaceful surroundings did little to soothe my soul. *Dad is dead. I'll never see him again. What else have I lost that Jarret hasn't told me about?* It already felt like so much. Too much lost.

The screen door slid open. "Hey, I'll make you some iced tea, okay? I'll bring it outside to you."

After a quick wipe of my cheeks, I spared a glance and shrugged. I did not want his comfort. I wanted to blame him. If I hadn't married him, I'd probably still live in my home town. I'd be there for my family. And most likely, I wouldn't have had the accident that had caused my amnesia.

The screen door slid shut. A moment later, a cabinet squeaked open and pans clanked.

More than ever now, I wanted to go back home. I wanted, no, I *needed,* to mourn with my family. Sure, they might not feel the loss as intensely as I did now, having just discovered it—for the first time I could remember. But they loved him and must've still felt some pain.

I turned my head a bit, listening to a cabinet slam shut. Fragments of thoughts weeded their way into my mind. *Run. Leave.* He would be too busy making the iced tea to notice my disappearance. I could wander to the neighbor playing the country music... phone Roland from there and get a ride. Home.

I'd prayed for God to make a way. Could this be the door God had left open?

Heart thumping a warning, I crept down the porch steps and into the backyard. I didn't doubt Jarret had feelings for me, but our relationship had serious problems. In addition to not trusting him, I had too many questions, and I needed space and a good friend to help sort things out. And Dad was gone. Gone forever. Nothing made sense anymore.

Once past the lilac bush, I bolted, heading to the front instead of the back. I kept to the high wooden fence that enclosed the neighbors' backyard. Then I cut across their front yard and stopped in their empty driveway. My gaze snapped to the gate.

Jarret would notice my disappearance soon and come looking for me. I shouldn't be running away. He'd as much as told me I was free to leave him. But I'd lost my nerve when he'd said that. And if he said it again, I'd lose my nerve again. No, I needed to do this my way.

*Hide.*

He'd eventually tire of searching for me. Maybe he'd even drive around in my car. Then I could find the neighbor playing the country music. Phone Roland or call a cab. I would explain myself to Jarret later. If he was the man Roland claimed he was, he'd understand…

"Mrs. West?" Bobby's voice came from the street. "Whatcha doing?"

Scalp tingling, eyes ready to pop from my head, and anxiety mounting, I faced him. "Bobby..." I did not have time for this. "Why don't you go on home? I don't want anyone to know where I am. Mr. West and I are..." Biting my lip, I cut a glance to our house. No sign of Jarret yet. "We're playing hide and seek. Can you keep a secret?"

Bobby stood with his head tilted to one side and his thumbs in the front pockets of dirt-streaked jeans. He shrugged. "I s'pose."

"Good." I put a finger to my lips and said, "Shhhh." Then I dashed up the neighbors' driveway to the gate and lifted the latch.

"That ain't a good hidin' spot, Mrs. West," Bobby said.

As I cracked open the gate, Jarret called my name. He sounded near but not near enough to see me. I still had a chance. *Please, Bobby, don't rat me out.*

Heart pounding in my ears, I slipped inside the gate and pulled it shut.

A low growling came to my ears, making the hair on my neck rise.

I froze. Then with slow, deliberate movements, I turned.

A short, stocky dog with a shiny black coat bared its teeth and growled, its fiery orange glare locked on me. No more than a few feet away, it crept toward me.

"Nice doggy." My voice wavered and my blood ran cold. I wanted to reach for the gate and slip back out but feared the dog would attack at any movement. I lifted a trembling hand, inching it toward the gate.

The dog's growl deepened. He lowered his head.

My heart thumped hard in my throat.

Suddenly, the gate flew open and banged against the fence.

I stumbled back with a gasp.

The dog lunged.

Expecting sharp teeth to pierce my skin, I threw my arms over my face. But they never came.

A man grunted.

The dog went into a frenzy of wrath, barking, snapping, and jumping at his new victim: Jarret.

"Caitlyn, go!" Jarret flung himself onto the dog and pressed its snapping jaw to the ground.

Adrenaline surging, propelling me into action, I dashed through the gate.

The dog popped up and wriggled free to attack.

"Off! Down! Sit!" Jarret grunted, then cussed. A second later, he barged through the gate and slammed it shut. He set the latch and threw his back against the gate, breathing hard. The dog barked with fury, pounding its paws against the other side of the gate.

"They... got a fierce dog." Panting, Jarret looked me over. "You all right?" The dog had left long red gashes on his right forearm.

Startled by the sight and heart still racing, I reached but stopped myself from touching his arm. "He bit you!"

Jarret pushed himself off the gate, glancing at his arm. "Na, it's just a scratch." He tramped back down the driveway to where Bobby still stood.

"I told you that weren't a good hidin' spot." Mumbling to himself and shaking his head, Bobby turned and strolled away.

"We've been trying to make friends with Sparky," Jarret said, "whenever he's out for a walk, but..."

"Oh, so that's why we have dog treats in the cupboard?"

"It hasn't worked. Obviously." He gave me a little smile and a lingering gaze. A curl from his ponytail wrapped around to the side of his neck. His smile faded as he stuffed one hand in a pocket and stood with his weight on one leg and his head tilted to one side. Looking as cool as ever. Not looking like the man of my dreams. "I'm sorry about today. Do you wish I had talked you outta that phone call?"

Breathless and unable to answer, I gasped. Tears from a loss so unexpected and deep rushed out. A tidal wave of grief and emotion swallowed me up, destroying all reason, hope, and identity. I collapsed into his arms.

# Chapter 28

JARRET AND I strolled back to the house side by side. It had taken me an eternity to compose myself. Jarret had simply stroked my hair, kissed the top of my head, and held me the whole time I'd bawled in his arms. He never asked why I'd bolted from the house. Did he realize I'd wanted to leave him? Or did he simply chalk it up to my grief?

"Hey, so, I didn't get that iced tea made," Jarret said in a casual tone, as if we had just returned from a neighborly visit and not a heart-pounding attack by the neighbors' vicious dog. He stopped near the steps to the deck and made a sweeping gaze of our back lawn, which now rivaled the unkempt lawn of the abandoned house next door. "I was gonna cut the grass."

"Oh, you go ahead. I can finish making the iced tea." A bit numb from the experience, I climbed the steps. The screen door hung wide open, water ran from the kitchen faucet, and a pan lay on the floor by an open cabinet. Jarret must have heard the dog and noticed I was missing. Fearing the worst, he'd abandoned it all to rescue me.

I picked up the pan and took it to the sink. Within a few minutes, I made the iced tea and set a glass of it on the patio table for Jarret, along with peroxide, Band-aids, and cotton balls for his scrapes.

He stooped over the lawn mower, checking something. Then he yanked the starter and straightened as the lawn mower sputtered to life. One hand to the control bar, he glanced at me.

A bit of the numbness wore off at his glance, and my cheeks warmed with my embarrassment. I went back inside and watched him from the shadowy breakfast nook. In a moment of weakness and unwelcome vulnerability, I'd flung myself into his arms. Bawling against his muscular chest, encircled by his strong arms, his manly scent filling my senses, I'd felt safe and comforted and free to express my grief.

I sighed, more confused now than ever, and returned to the kitchen.

Wanting to think of something other than my father's death, I took a glass of iced tea and a bowl of prunes to the weight room to read more of the emails I'd sent to Roland that fateful summer. I desperately needed to know more about this man I'd married, now more than ever. So far, the emails had only given me the impression that Jarret was an arrogant drunk and I didn't like him much. But Roland had gleaned a different impression. Maybe I would see it too.

Computer humming and the email program open, I scooted my chair forward and picked up where I'd left off.

*Dear Roland,*

*Nanny's recovery is going well. She leaves her room more often now and sometimes tells me stories while she watches me work. She talks about you and your brothers, telling stories from when you were children. Sometimes we laugh so hard it hurts. It hurts my side, anyway. I'm sure it's worse for her healing body. I'll tell you the stories one day but not via email. I want to see your face. I want to watch your fine, pale skin turn a lovely shade of crimson.*

Stunned that I'd written "fine, pale skin" in an email to Roland, I sat back and laughed aloud. No doubt those words would've gone through my mind, but to write them in a message to him... Things must've changed between us.

My thoughts froze and I frowned. Changed from romantic to friendship? When? How? With a mournful sigh, I turned back to the email.

*Speaking of blushing, I saw Jarret blush for the first time in my life. Have you ever seen him blush? I didn't think he was capable of it, like he's too cool to blush or doesn't have any "blush" chromosomes. But he does.*

*Here's how it happened. Remember I told you how he came home drunk? Well, he's been asking me for several days and in several ways to tell him what happened that night/morning. When he realized I did not intend to tell, he began hanging out in whatever room I was cleaning. He pretended he had something to do, watch TV, read a book, drink a Coke, but all he really did was stare at me. I think he was trying to read my mind. But I guess that didn't work for him, because a few days later, he started asking specific questions. I gave vague answers or no answers. It was like a guessing game that I couldn't avoid playing unless your father or Mr. Digby saved me by coming into the room.*

*Then Jarret changed tactics. He stopped asking about that night and started talking about other things, trying to befriend me, I suppose. He told me his plans for the day, what he wanted to do with his life, or about some incident from his past. Then he asked me questions about things I've done or what I'd like to do, as if he cared. It broke up the monotony of my chores, so I didn't mind. Maybe he was lonely or bored.*

"Or maybe he liked you then," I whispered. Had I known of his interest in me?

*I finally gave in and told him what happened that night. We were having dinner at that new Thai restaurant. Don't worry, it wasn't a date. It's just that Jarret finally caved to your father's demand to either get a job or go on assignments with him, which he really didn't want to do. So when Jarret came home with the good news that he landed a job at the furniture store, he invited me to go celebrate with him. I asked why he didn't go out with his friends. He said they'd want to drink. I asked why he didn't celebrate with his girlfriend. He said he didn't have one. Can that be true? Have you ever known Jarret to be without a girlfriend? But he seemed so proud about landing a job the first day he set out to look for one, that I agreed to go.*

*At the restaurant, we talked and talked. It was strange. He was like a regular person. He was even fun. So, when he asked me again what happened that night, I told him. I knew it would embarrass him, but his reaction still surprised me. His gaze flitted around the restaurant. He squirmed in his chair, turning every shade of red. It was great! I know, you're dying to know what happened that night, but you'll have to ask him.*

*Gotta run,*

*Caitlyn*

"Wow," I whispered, stunned again, a strange tingly sensation washing through me. I did seem to like Jarret. I barely spoke two words to him now, and rarely a nice word. But that summer, we'd enjoyed talking to each other. Seemed like we talked about everything.

The last part of the email struck me most. I'd always loved seeing a guy blush. Especially if I liked the guy. What could've happened that night that had embarrassed him so much?

Sucking in a deep breath, I readied myself for more and clicked on the next email, this one from Roland.

*Caitlyn,*

*I can't believe you went out with Jarret. Maybe you shouldn't have done that. He's going to think you like him. He's going to ask you out again. You'd better be ready for that. He's very insistent with girls.*

*Roland*

I found myself smiling. Roland was so sweet. Cute. Worried.

The next email said nothing about Jarret. It was all about Nanny, the garden I had been working on with Mr. Digby, the horses—which I had learned to groom—and how I couldn't wait for summer to end so I could return to school.

I sipped my iced tea. The weight room had grown warm in the afternoon sun. And the lawn mower blared outside the window. I didn't mind the smell of cut grass, but the noise... I got up to close the window.

Reaching for the window frame, my gaze snapped to Jarret, who had taken his shirt off. My gaze lingered on his bare back, his curly ponytail, and his muscles shining with sweat as he pushed the mower diagonally away from the house. At the end of the lawn, he shoved the handle down and pivoted the mower around.

My stomach leaped.

He wore sunglasses, the kind with a mirror finish, not the black finish of the ones in my memory. But the sight of them made me queasy.

I shoved the window closed, yanked the blinds, and returned to the computer. Catching my breath and focusing on the monitor, I expected to find another email I'd written to Roland, since he'd written the last one, but I didn't.

*Caitlyn,*

*Hi. Ling-si's summer classes are getting tough for her. Mine too. I guess they have too much information to give in such a short time. We've been trying to pretend it's not summer and just study. But that's hard to do. It wouldn't be so hard for me, but she loves watching movies, taking walks, and shopping.*

*I'll keep this email short, but I have a question: Is Jarret still working at the furniture place? He won't answer or return my calls. Is he still living there? You didn't mention him in your last email and you haven't emailed in a while. Is something wrong? Email soon or I'm calling you.*

*Roland*

I sighed, enthralled with his kindness. Roland was so sweet, so concerned about me and his brother.

*Dearest Worried Roland,*

*Did I detect a threat at the end of your email? How unlike you. No, Jarret is not working at the furniture place. He was fired. And we aren't really talking, so I don't have much to say about him. I don't know what he's doing.*

*Worry not. All is well, your friend, Caitlyn*

*Caitlyn,*

*Unless you give me more to go on, I'm calling and you'd better answer the phone. Why was Jarret fired? Why aren't you talking to him? Why shouldn't I worry?*

*Roland*

*Roland,*

*Fine. Here it is: Jarret was fired for punching a customer. Oh, I don't blame him. The man asked for it. That's not what I'm mad about.*

*Need more specifics? Okay. Jarret was doing well at the furniture place, getting there on time, making good sales, etc. But a woman kept bothering him. He complained about her a few times, back when we were speaking. The woman came up every day to talk and watch him work. It sometimes interfered with his sales, but he didn't know how to make her leave without being rude. Well, her husband came up one day and accused Jarret of having an affair with his wife. The man started off shouting and ended up swinging. Jarret said he did all he could to avoid the punches and calm the man down, until the man's fist made contact with his chin. Then he lost control and slugged him back. He only threw one punch, and it wasn't his fault, but of course he was fired.*

*Your father didn't see things the way I did, but then Jarret doesn't explain himself well when he's under fire. They went around and around arguing, until Jarret finally blew out of here. He came back late, or rather early the next morning, drunk, I think. That's what made me mad. He told me he doesn't drink anymore, that he wasn't ever a drinker, that he only intentionally got drunk once and that was at a monastery. Like I'd believe that. Why can't he handle the setbacks of life without getting drunk?*

*It shouldn't really matter to me. It's not like I'm his girlfriend. But I thought we were friends, sort of. And I don't like my friends doing stupid, self-destructive things.*

*There. Now you have it.*

*Caitlyn*

"Hmph." I sipped my iced tea and shuffled to the window. I could not imagine falling in love with or marrying a man who drank. Had I really taken Jarret's side in that incident? I would not put it past him to flirt with another man's wife.

Lifting a slat in the blind, I peeked outside. Shirtless Jarret pushed the mower away from the house. Maybe I wasn't being fair. Maybe I was judging him again, based on his past mistakes.

*Roland,*

*Guess what? You'll never believe who's here! Okay, maybe you know. Your father said he told you already. Nanny and I have been getting ready for days. Yes, I'm talking about the Salazars and, in particular, Selena!*

Wait, wait, wait! Eyes wide, I straightened in the chair.

Hadn't Jarret said I'd kissed him before the Salazars' visit? I'd been preparing for the visit when I dropped the salsa and applesauce. He said we hadn't been speaking to each other.

I re-read the previous email. Okay. So I was mad at him because he went out and got drunk... again. Yes. If I liked him then, that would make me mad. But I must've forgiven him by the time he came to help clean up the mess. Hmm. So I'd kissed him before this email. I liked Jarret at this point, but I hadn't even hinted about it to Roland.

*I see why you liked her. She is so much fun! We do everything together. Oh, and Jarret hangs out with us too. Selena helps with my chores, so I can get done quicker and run around with her. The three of us work in the kitchen, dust, vacuum, do laundry... Jarret even cleaned a bathroom! We ride the horses every day. The first time we all went out, I was nervous, so I rode with Jarret. But that made me more nervous, if you know what I mean.*

Oh! What *did* I mean? The image of Jarret's sweaty bare back came unbidden to my mind and heat slid up my neck. I'd gone horseback riding with Jarret. Sharing a horse? Had I sat in front, his arms around me, or had I sat behind, holding onto him for dear life?

*I'm getting good at riding all by myself. I remember everything you tried to teach me about riding. We also go out to eat every other day, went to the movies once, rent movies to watch at home, play pool, take walks, etc. We even went to Peter's house the day he came home for a visit. I don't think he liked seeing Jarret with us. They bantered back and forth all night.*

*Gotta run, Selena and Jarret are waiting for me.*

*Caitlyn*

I leaned back in the chair and gulped the rest of my iced

tea. I giggled, picturing Peter and Jarret arguing all night. Then I read on.

*Roland,*

*Selena's gone. I miss her. I wish she could've stayed for the rest of the summer. And Jarret's mad at me now. I guess he liked how things have been lately, the three of us doing everything together. But I think he's interested in being more than friends, and I don't want to lead him on. Maybe I'm wrong and he only likes me as a friend.*

*Since I won't go out with him, I think he's trying to make me jealous. I don't know if he was out drinking. He said he wasn't. But he stayed out all night and came home in the morning. Then he accused me of thinking he was with a girl. Why should I care?*

*Your lonely friend, Caitlyn*

Ugh. I leaned my head back and stared at the ceiling, a strange sinking feeling inside my tummy. *With a girl?* Jarret and girls. Girls over to the house. Girls on the phone. Pictures of girls. I sighed. He probably *had been* with a girl. Why had I kissed him in the first place? It must've been a spontaneous action and I'd regretted it. But then... Oh, how had I ever wanted to marry him?

*Caitlyn,*

*I can't believe you like Jarret. He's not your type. He's too fast. And he can be an emotional train wreck.*

*Don't ever let him see this email. Delete at once. Anyway, is he going to get another job? I'm calling you. Answer the phone.*

*Roland*

"An emotional train wreck? Too fast?" I mumbled to myself, glancing over my shoulder in the direction of the window, now covered with blinds. I should've taken Roland's advice. I opened the next email in the vain hope that I'd read how I'd come to my senses. Of course, if I had, I wouldn't be in this situation.

*Roland,*

*I'm sorry I didn't answer the phone yesterday. I was in the garden with Mr. Digby. We have so many peppers, tomatoes, and squash that we're taking loads of them to the church.*

*I can't believe you think I like Jarret. I told you I don't. Get it out of your mind. Besides, he's leaving soon. He spoke to me this morning, just to let me know. He said he was going to hang out at an opal mine in Brazil. I said, that sounds fun. He said, no, it doesn't. Anyway, he's leaving in a couple of days. So you don't have to worry.*

*Caitlyn*

An opal mine? I studied my engagement ring, a fiery opal of red, orange, and pink set between two diamonds. Did he find the opal himself? We seemed to spend so much time angry at each other, how had we ever fallen in love?

# Chapter 29

THE FRONT DOOR opened, disturbing the silence. Then voices traveled to me in the warm weight room. Two voices? I then realized I hadn't heard the lawn mower in a while. I closed the file with the emails and shut the computer down. The screen went black as Jarret—wearing a shirt—stuck his sweaty head into the room.

"Hey, Mike's here. I'm gonna take a shower."

I leaned forward, about to get up, when Mike tromped into the room. "Hello there, young lady." He smiled down at me, his pale eyes glowing with creepiness.

"Are you my babysitter?" The thought scraped my peaceful mood, like sandpaper on porcelain. I stood, grabbed my empty glass, and brushed past him.

He followed me to the kitchen. "Why no, I thought I'd stop by and see how y'all were getting along."

As I brought the pitcher of iced tea to the island counter, something caught my eye. In the middle of the dinner table sat a round glass vase overflowing with perfectly arranged lilacs, their scent filling the kitchen.

My chest tingled. When had Jarret done that? *How sweet.*

"I am a bit thirsty," Mike said.

I snapped my attention to the iced tea, refilled my glass, and pulled another from the cupboard for him. "If you're here to check on me, where's your little black doctor bag?"

He smiled and nodded toward the living room. "Right there on the coffee table. Might you be so inclined as to allow a check-up?"

"Mm, I might." I dragged myself to the living room and settled myself in the leather chair. The sun had warmed it, and it felt good against my back.

Seeming a bit distracted, he set his glass on the coffee table and unzipped his black bag. "How've you been?"

I shrugged. What had Jarret told Mike anyway? How good of friends were they? Did they talk every day? Did Mike know about Roland's visit? Did he know Jarret and I didn't get along?

"Any headaches, blurred vision, hearing difficulties..." He pulled out a stethoscope and headed my way.

With a sigh, I sat up so he could check my heart. "I feel fine. No problems except for a little nausea. But I'm sure it's from the baby."

"Most likely." He slid the stethoscope down my back. "Breathe in for me."

I obeyed.

Mike let the stethoscope dangle against his chest and grabbed my wrist, holding it gently while he looked at his watch.

"Did Jarret tell you his brother came from South Dakota to visit us?" I said, to get a feel for how much Jarret had told him.

"His brother?" He glanced up from his watch.

"Yes, Roland."

Mike dropped my wrist and went to the bag. "Would that be his twin brother? He does have a twin, doesn't he? I seem to remember him saying—"

"Not that brother. His younger brother."

"Mm." Mike returned with a thermometer and a little black case. "So, his brother came out to..."

"Well, help me, of course, help me to get my memories back. Roland and I were always close, best friends even. I guess he thought he could help."

"And have you remembered anything?" He stuffed the

thermometer into my mouth, so I gave a shrug for my answer. He smiled. "You can answer that question shortly. And I don't have my fetal Doppler t'day, but I'll be sure to bring it next time."

He glanced at the bedroom door. It hung half open and the sound of the shower traveled through it. "I need to talk to you right quick before Jarret comes out." His pale eyes locked onto mine. "I do believe Jarret's job is on the line. Maybe you can talk some sense into him. He's told the boss he's not coming to work until you're all better. I don't think he understands: you might not get your memory back."

I might not get my memory back! What about the two brief memories I experienced? The thermometer slipped. I tried to keep it in place with my tongue. I had to get my memory back. I needed to understand our marriage and to understand Jarret. I had a baby coming in six months. If Jarret was a louse, I'd have to move back home. How would my mother feel about helping raise the baby?

Keeping my mouth closed, I tried to say, "Is it time yet?" while I pointed to the thermometer, but it came out like "hmm hm hmm hm."

"Almost time," he said. "You need to get Jarret to work Monday. I don't understand why he feels it imperative to remain home with you, do you?"

I rolled my eyes. *Yeah, he doesn't trust me.*

He finally took the thermometer.

"Mike, if I've had a few memories, is that a good sign? Do you think I might get more? Maybe all of it? I need to know if—"

"What memories?" He gave me a strangely intense look. "You've gained memories? Recent? Past?" The shower shut off and we both glanced at the half-open bedroom door.

"Well, one memory was more of a déjà vu experience, I suppose."

"Tell me." Mike sat on the end of the coffee table and leaned toward me.

"The other day, I was out on the deck and I dropped the pickle relish. As I looked at it, I remembered having dropped jars of salsa and applesauce. I remembered clearly the way I felt when it happened, but I didn't remember the specific incident or what happened before or after. But as Jarret came over to clean up the relish, I remembered him being there and helping me clean it up before. I also remember how I felt emotionally."

He gave the hint of a smile. Or was it a grimace? "The other memories?" He glanced over his shoulder at the bedroom door, then he leaned even closer. "You said you had a few."

Discomfort wormed its way into my mind. His eagerness to know made me reluctant to speak. Jarret hadn't told him about Roland or about how we didn't get along, so maybe they weren't that close after all. Maybe he'd only been called on as a doctor. I gave a casual smile. "So, is it a good sign? For me to remember?"

"A good sign?" His lips parted. Then a smile. "Why, yes, it is a very good sign. But I did tell you, you might get things messed up in your mind. You might mix up people and places without realizing it."

I nodded, an image of Jarret in his sunglasses flashing in my mind.

"So what other memories? Any that seem recent? Any that may've occurred that Friday—"

"Well..." Hesitant to answer, I fiddled with my rings. Would it do any good to tell him?

"How is she?"

I exhaled, relieved to hear Jarret's voice. First time for that.

He leaned a shoulder against the bedroom doorframe, his dark locks dripping on a white bathrobe tied at the waist but open at the chest.

Mike twisted around to face him. "Jarret. That was a right quick shower. She seems fine. She was just saying she got a few memories back." He threw me an encouraging smile and waved his brows.

"Oh, really?" Jarret stepped into the room, a seed of hope in his expression. "A few? You mean besides the mess on the kitchen floor?"

I nodded.

"What of?"

"Oh, I don't know. It's sort of confusing." I bit my lip, not sure how much to reveal. "Mike said I might get things messed up as I remember them."

"Well, what do you remember?" Jarret drew near and gripped the back of the couch, the seed of hope germinating. "Was I there? I'll tell you if it's messed up."

"I don't know. It was very vague." I slid to the edge of the chair, unease creeping through my veins. "Should I make dinner?" I didn't want to cook, but I had to get out of answering. I didn't want to tell either one of them about the man I'd run from. Which one made me more nervous, Mike or Jarret?

"I'll take care of dinner." Jarret moved closer and crouched by the chair, peering into my eyes. "What d'ya remember?"

Mike, sitting on the coffee table, leaned in again.

"I um..." A bead of sweat crawled between my shoulder blades. I shook my head, trying to think of how to avoid saying more. "I remember... Well, it wasn't much of a memory. It was just, well—"

A truck pulled up the driveway. All heads turned, and I exhaled and slumped back.

Jarret shot to the door and peered outside. "What's he doing here?" His irritated tone made me guess it was Roland. He yanked open the door and stomped outside in his bathrobe and bare feet.

Mike straightened and approached the screen door. "That must be Jarret's younger brother. He's awfully pale. Lives in South Dakota, you say?"

"Yes." I joined Mike at the door. Jarret didn't let Roland any closer to the house than the front bumper of the truck.

*Please, Jarret, let him visit.* I tried to send a telepathic message.

"Not today," Jarret said to Roland.

"When? I'm here to help her, here in North Carolina instead of being in school. You need to let me—"

Cold and unyielding, Jarret folded his arms over his chest. "Go back to school. That'd probably help her more."

Roland shook his head, then he peered past Jarret to the door. He looked directly at me, staring while Jarret mumbled something to him.

"Who's that?" Roland said, giving a nod.

Jarret glanced over his shoulder. "Mike. He's a friend of mine. See ya later."

My spirits sank. Jarret was sending Roland away. Again.

# Chapter 30

THE FIRST STREAKS of dawn appeared in the sky, and sunlight stole through the slit between the bedroom curtains. I woke with a stirring in my soul, a bud of joy that seemed out of place in my current situation. Perhaps God wanted to remind me that He was there and still in control of everything. I turned my heart to Him in a prayer of trust and asked Him to make a way for me and to open my eyes to His will. Hadn't I read something like that in the Bible? Or was it the lyrics of a song?

I slid out of bed and drew the curtains back. The scent of lilacs lingered on the cool, damp air. Inhaling deeply, I imagined myself back home, enjoying the fragrance of the Chinese Wisteria that grew outside my bedroom window. A few birds called back and forth. One sounded close, so I tried to spot it in the nearby trees.

Gazing at the cornflower blue sky, I took another deep breath. The early hour made me feel like the only soul awake in the neighborhood, the only soul awake in the house.

I turned my head to catch any noises in the house. Nothing.

Maybe Jarret was still sleeping. He looked exhausted yesterday, and Mike had stayed late last night. Jarret, not wanting to grill anything for dinner, had ordered Chinese and made Mike pick it up. The two of them talked work all through dinner, though Jarret seemed distracted. He kept casting long looks at me, probably wanting to know about the memories or wondering how mad it made me when he sent Roland away. It reminded me of what I'd read in the emails. He'd spent days trying to "read my mind" before finally asking what happened the night he came home drunk.

After dinner, my thoughts returned to Dad and to the ache in my heart, so I retired to my sanctuary. Treasured childhood memories filled my mind and after an hour or so I'd cried myself to sleep.

Stretching and deciding to make an early start of the day, I went to the closet. I flipped through "my" dresses, skirts, and shirts, but— No, I wanted to wear something different, something that would reflect my hope that everything would turn out all right. So, I rummaged through the clothes that I didn't remember but liked anyway. The yellow and pastel clothes didn't fit my mood but neither did the dark colors. A dress with tiny floral print in lavender, purple, and white caught my eye. It had a skirt of loose ruffles, a slim waist, and short frilly sleeves. As I pulled the dress off the hanger, a feeling of warmth and joy passed through me. It was such a pretty dress. I couldn't wait to try it on.

I washed up, dressed, and gazed at myself in the mirror. The lavender brought out the green in my eyes, and the ruffles complimented my wild red hair. I didn't look half bad when I stopped frowning. In fact, I felt pretty. I smiled at myself and then breezed from the room.

Jarret lay on the couch, both legs hanging off as if he'd fallen asleep sitting up and tipped over. My gaze drifted to the scratches on his arm, then to the key chain hanging from the pocket of his jeans. With a little tug, I could have them out and he'd never notice.

I shook my head at the silly thought. He'd probably wake the instant I touched the keys. I'd feel guilty. And maybe he wouldn't let me go this time.

Proceeding to the kitchen, my stomach growled, reminding me I was eating for two. I opened the pantry and scanned the cereal boxes.

A glance over my shoulder told me Jarret was still sleeping. Hadn't moved a muscle. He'd been keeping such a close eye on me, always up before me, staying up late, waking at the slightest sound all hours of the night. Maybe he *wouldn't* wake the instant I touched the keys.

Determination rushing into my veins, I grabbed a box of granola bars, closed the pantry, and turned around. Until I regained my memories or discovered by some other way the kind of man Jarret was, I would be better off living back home, surrounded by people I trusted and could remember. He'd said my mom didn't like him. I should find out why. He'd said my mom didn't like my career. Hmm. Oh well, I was having a baby. Forget the career for now. I needed to go.

Should I leave him a note? I took the notepad by the phone and wrote: *I'll call you soon. Please don't be mad. Caitlyn.* I could stop by Roland's hotel and have him call Jarret to help him understand.

I ripped the page from the notepad and turned, catching sight of the lilacs Jarret had arranged in a vase on the table. I lifted one out and brought it to my nose. It had lost none of its sweet fragrance. I tiptoed to the bedroom, found the money I'd taken from Jarret days ago, grabbed a purse big enough to hold the box of granola bars, slid my feet into tan sandals, and crept to the living room.

Jarret hadn't moved. His breaths came deep and long, drawing my eye to his half-unbuttoned shirt and the dark hairs down the middle of his chest. My fingers burned as I inched them toward the keys. Taking a breath, I slipped the keys from his pocket and set the flower and note on his chest. *Goodbye, husband.*

Careful to avoid stumbling on anything, I tiptoed to the front door. With a guess as to which key would fit, I separated one from the others. Based on experience, I expected the last key I tried to be the one. But the first one slipped in easily as if this was meant to be.

I twisted the knob, pulled the door open, and pushed the

screen, making barely a sound. My pulse thumped in my ears, but Jarret hadn't moved. Stepping outside, I closed both doors gently. Then I dashed for my dark-blue Honda Accord.

As I pulled the car door shut, something moved on the porch.

I slid the key into the ignition. The front door opened, and I froze.

The screen door flew open and Jarret stumbled out of the house barefooted. His hair hung loose around his shoulders and his half-buttoned shirt had come un-tucked from his jeans. Nearing the porch steps, he slid to a stop as if a forcefield kept him from going further.

I gripped the key, ready to crank the engine to life, but... Maybe he didn't run after me because he knew it wouldn't start. Maybe he'd done something to the car.

I cranked. The engine hummed and I breathed.

His mouth fell open but he didn't move; he only stared.

We locked gazes for a second, then I threw the gearshift in reverse and backed out of the driveway. Agony radiating from him, he looked heavenward, grabbed the hair on the top of his head, and dropped his head to his chest.

Cranking the steering wheel, turning the car, I backed onto the street. "Sorry, Jarret," I whispered, a pang stabbing my chest.

Jarret staggered to one side, lifted a hand as if to steady himself, and latched onto a post on the porch. Then he leaned, or more like fell, against it.

Clear of the driveway, I shifted into drive and rolled down our little street. He didn't follow. He just watched. At the end of the street, I peered in the rearview mirror at him standing still as a statue.

He didn't run after me. Had he given up? Then I remembered what he'd said. *If you love something, let it go.* I hadn't thought he meant it.

I glanced both ways, finding the cross street clear, but I couldn't get myself to step on the gas. Why should it bother me that he just stood there? I exhaled through my mouth, blowing the curls on my forehead. "Well, what do you think, baby?" I touched my belly. "He's your father. Should we?"

On impulse, I threw the car in reverse.

Jarret pushed off the post and straightened, arms dangling at his side.

I backed up past the driveway and swung the car into it.

His lips parted with a look of total shock.

I motioned him over, directing him to the passenger side.

A moment's hesitation, then he jumped off the porch and jogged to the car. With the press of a button, I unlocked his door and he climbed in without looking at me. Then he stared out the front window like a kid trying to hide his excitement when his dad let him come along for a ride.

Touched by the sweetness of it, I smiled to myself and backed out of the drive. At the end of our street, I turned right, the direction I had planned to take.

Now where would I go? What was I doing? I had my chance to head for home and surround myself with people I loved and trusted. Hadn't I prayed for this opportunity? And here God had given it to me. What *was* I doing?

A few miles down the road, highway signs became visible.

"Which way should I go?" I said.

He finally turned to me with a shy look that didn't fit the Jarret I knew. "Where do you want to go?"

I hadn't the heart to tell him I'd wanted to see Roland at his hotel, then head home to South Dakota. Those plans fizzled the instant I'd thrown the car in reverse. But I still wanted to go somewhere, somewhere I could think and relax, somewhere I could feel free. "I don't know. Where do you want to go?"

He shrugged. "Think I should've grabbed some shoes?" He lifted one of his bare feet.

I giggled, at first, but ended up laughing aloud. "I'll go back if you want," I said, gaining control. "Or we can go someplace where you don't need shoes?"

"Wanna go to the beach?"

I smiled in answer.

He smiled back, sending a spark to my heart. His expression showed no trace of the arrogant and domineering traits I'd come to associate with him. And his eyes, a dark cola brown, communicated something else that didn't fit my impression of him. I saw in them hope, vulnerability, and fear, the look of one given a second chance.

As I eased onto the highway, Jarret lowered his window, reclined his seat, and laid his head back. His long, dark curls whipped about his face like the mane of a running stallion.

I had never considered him handsome before. Maybe his attitude had blinded me. But I couldn't take my eyes off him now. I saw him as if for the first time. Even with his unshaven jaw, he looked handsome and dignified. His narrow nose, high cheekbones, and the arch of his brows reminded me of a Spanish nobleman from years past, like the ones in paintings I had seen in an art museum. His looks appealed to me more than I cared to admit.

Driving east, the sun blinded me as morning dawned. In the first hour, blue and yellow clouds and streaks of gold and pink colored the sky. I soaked up the beauty, resting in the unspoken prayer of my heart.

Every now and then, Jarret turned his head or repositioned his arms, but otherwise he rested heavy. For whatever reason, it made me glad to see him rest. And for a moment, I distanced myself from the situation and felt sorry for what his wife had been putting him through.

The two-hour drive passed peacefully, the wind increasing as we neared the ocean, the air growing thick and salty as teardrops. Anticipation grew, stirring inside me. *The ocean!* Having no memory of visiting the ocean before, I couldn't wait to see it. We were almost there.

A moment before I needed to decide which exit to take, Jarret lifted his head. He directed me, as if he had gone this way many times before, down to a particular beach. I parked in a small empty lot and leaped from the car.

A boardwalk separated the parking lot from a long stretch of sand and... the ocean! So beautiful, like an artist's watercolor painting with blended stripes of deep blue and aqua, splashes of white where foam bubbled up, and dots of gold from the sunlight. A group of seagulls glided overhead, uttering their mournful cry.

I inhaled a deep breath of salty air and smiled. I couldn't stop smiling.

Jarret walked around the car to me, his eyes on my chest. "What made you wear that dress?"

I looked at it. The skirt danced about my legs in the wind. "You don't like it?"

"No, I—I love it. I picked that one out. It's my favorite."

"Oh." My heart leaped, sending tingles through my body. Did that explain the sentimental feeling when I'd pulled the dress from the hanger?

He continued to stare, this time at my feet. "Take off your sandals." He sounded bossy, but it made me smile. "Go barefoot like me."

I obeyed. Then, abandoning my sandals, I gave him a playful grin and dashed for the boardwalk and the sand. My feet sunk into the warm granules, making it awkward to run, but I didn't stop.

The beach stretched out to the horizon in either direction. Umbrellas, sunbathers, and blankets claimed the sand to the right, so I jogged to the left. The sun glistened on the ocean. My hair flew like streamers in the wind, and my lavender dress of ruffles flounced about my legs. I felt like part of the artist's painting now, and it made me laugh.

"Hey!" Jarret called from behind me.

I turned, my long tresses blowing across my face. He ran after me but was still almost twenty feet away. I giggled and ran on.

"No more... running away," he said, gaining on me.

Happier than I'd been in a long time, I gasped in deep breaths of air and pushed my legs to run faster. The salty wind invigorated me. It felt familiar and comforting.

"You know..." He came alongside me. "You... can't outrun me," he said between breaths.

I smiled, breathing through my mouth, and I no longer tried to outrun him. We jogged side by side down the endless stretch of sand, coming upon and passing another group of sunbathers. We ran past a private-property sign and into the shade of a towering hotel. My legs and lungs could do no more. I groaned and slowed. A few paces more, I stopped to catch my breath.

He leaned over, breathing hard. "You can't be giving up."

I felt a pang of disappointment that he hadn't tried catching me, hadn't wrapped his strong arms around me. My feelings surprising me, I dropped to my knees.

"I surrender." I fell forward, rolled onto my back, and stretched out my arms in the sand.

# Chapter 31

MY HEART POUNDED against my ribs as I lay flat on my back in the sand, sucking in breaths of air and gazing at the blue sky. Puffy clouds shaped like unborn babies, chubby babies, dozens of babies, drifted miles above us. The ocean sang a lonely, soothing song as the tide rolled in and out. I was free. I knew in my heart that Jarret was not trying to control me. Whether I stayed with him or went back home, the choice was mine. Whether I wanted to talk with Roland or my Mom, the choice was mine. Had he changed or had I only just begun to see the real him?

Jarret sat a few feet away, staring at me through eyes the color of cola in the sunlight. "You surrender, huh? Does that mean...you're done running away... from me?" His chest rose and fell with his breaths and a breeze played with long flyaway hairs.

I smiled. Was I done running? Sitting up, I pushed my feet through the warm top layer and into cooler sand. A few yards away, waves rolled in and smoothed the sand, only to slip back to the ocean and leave a scattering of white shells and stones. "Why did you let me go this morning?"

He looked me over in a way that would've ordinarily made me self-conscious. "I don't know."

"When I saw you at the door, I thought sure you'd come after me."

With eyes narrowed in disbelief, he smiled. "Is that what you wanted?"

I shrugged. "Just expected it."

He bowed his head and traced a heart in the sand. "You ever feel like... like you're standing on a cliff and..." A pause. "And God's asking you to fall off it and into His arms?"

The depth of his question shocked me, preventing me from coming up with an answer. I couldn't look at him without fluttering my eyelids.

"Ever since you woke up with amnesia, that's how it's been for me." He stared at his feet. "I couldn't do it, though, not until today on the porch."

A salty breeze whispered across my skin, making a rash of goosebumps appear. His faith... How had I never noticed it before? "You fell into God's arms?"

"I let go." He gazed out at the ocean. "I saw you in the car ready to pull out of the drive, out of my life, and my only thought was tearing off after you." He flashed a smile. "Not sure how I was gonna stop you. Get in front of the car? Jump on it? Give chase? But before I took off, I felt God nudge me, so I—I gave it all to Him instead. Whatever happened, I was gonna trust Him." A crooked grin crept onto his face. "Then—miracle—you let me come with you."

With a sigh, his look turned sulky and his eyes shifted toward the ocean. He ran a hand through his hair, pushing curly locks from his forehead.

"Wish I could've trusted sooner, trusted God, trusted you. Instead of trying to control everything. Guess I still struggle with that."

He bowed his head, then lifted it and faced me, intense remorse coloring his features. "Caitlyn, can you…forgive me? I hate the way I've been acting lately. But, damn, girl..." A hard glance. "I don't wanna lose you."

His look, his words, and my heart... all three convicted me. I hadn't been fair to him either. While I believed any person, no matter how sinful, could change, I hadn't extended the possibility to him.

"If I had driven off, what would you have done?"

A flirtatious look danced across his face, melting into a sad one. "Bawl my eyes out, I guess. Then I'd find you. Find some way to make you fall in love with me again. Which, given your present memories, wouldn't be easy."

I smiled, his honesty and humor putting me at ease. I was ready to ask, ready to hear his answers. "So tell me, Jarret, tell me how we fell in love."

Solemn and thoughtful, he stood and brushed the sand off his jeans. Then he strolled to the wet sand where the waves had washed it smooth. He picked up something and stared at it as he came back, the wind playing with his hair and his half-buttoned shirt. Sitting beside me, he handed me a shell.

Our fingers touched, momentarily distracting me. Then I studied the shell, turning it over in my hand. Small, white, and decorated with thin ribs, it seemed insignificant compared to other shells along the shore. Did it mean something to him or to me? "What kind of shell is it?"

"It's a fallen angel wing."

"Fallen?"

"They're like angel wings but not as detailed, and they're smaller." He gave the hint of a smile but it faded like the ebbing of the waves. "They're not perfect."

I held the imperfect shell to my chest, treasuring it more now that I knew, but also wondering why. Roland had told me that I needed someone who needed me. A perfect man wouldn't need me. Could that have been why Roland and I drifted apart? He didn't really need me, but Jarret...

We both gazed at the ocean, time stretching out peacefully until he broke the silence. "Hey, uh..." Head bowed, he stared at the heart he'd traced in the sand between us. "...about your question. I don't know how you fell in love... with me. When you get your memory back, maybe you'll tell me."

"Roland said it happened the summer after my first year at college. He said I was living at your house, helping Nanny."

"Yeah, that's right, and I wasn't supposed to be there. I was supposed to be on a field study." He gave the crooked grin that I used to assume reflected some twisted thought but that I now found attractive. "I'm glad I didn't go."

"Roland showed me the emails I wrote to him that summer."

Jarret gave me a quick, worried look. "What'd you tell him?"

"Well, I guess I thought you were annoying. At first."

Amusement came to his eyes. "Yeah, I'm sure you did. I was bossy and rude."

Maybe it should've surprised me to hear him recognize his faults, but over these past few days—I allowed myself to admit it—I'd come to realize that he had changed. Still, I found myself pinning him with a glare and saying, "*And* you drank."

His hands flew up in protest. "Not really. I swear." He shoved a hand through his hair and his tone softened. "I don't know what you found in the emails, but... some of it might need explaining."

I watched as a seagull landed on the wet shore near us and poked at the sand. "So, when did *you* fall in love with *me*?" I felt as though I shouldn't have asked, as if it were none of my business, as if it were somebody else's life and not mine, so I watched the seagull rather than him. But I felt his gaze.

"We talked a lot, you and me. Every day. The more we talked, the deeper I fell. You're not like other girls."

I glanced to see the look in his eyes. Sincerity, vulnerability. Even with the breeze, my face warmed.

"You see the good in things, in people. You made me feel like I was good, worth your attention. Then I found out what you did for me that night I came home staggering drunk." He raised his hands again. "...which was not my fault."

Glad he'd brought it up, I proceeded with caution. "Do you mean how I helped you get your car?"

"Uh, no." He narrowed one eye, looking hesitant to disclose more. "That was nice, but *no,* that's not what I mean."

"What did I do for you?" A lock of hair blew into my face and I left it there, wishing I hadn't asked. I couldn't help thinking I'd compromised my virtue somewhere along the way. How else would I have ended up married to a guy like—my conscience struck me. I needed to stop thinking of him with preconceived notions and see him as the man he'd become.

"I don't know where to start. You took care of me, but I didn't remember any of it in the morning. I knew something happened, but I had to pry it out of you. And I really wanted to know 'cuz, uh, I found your flowered hair barrette and I couldn't imagine how it ended up... in my bed."

My eyes popped and my heart skipped a beat. "What?"

"I showed it to you the next day and asked you to guess where I found it, but you wouldn't. When I told you it was in my bed, you acted like it was no big deal. I hounded you for an explanation, but you wouldn't talk. Then Papa came around, so I took off. Me and him weren't getting along."

I remembered that from the emails.

"So, I'd wait until you were alone, working in the kitchen or cleaning a room, and I'd try talking to you. It became an obsession. I had to know." He glanced again. "You remember that you and I never liked each other."

I nodded. I'd had my reasons: he was mean to Roland, mean to my friends, and then the thing with Zoë.

"I couldn't understand how Caitlyn Summer would step foot in my bedroom, much less climb into my bed, and not be angry at me the next day." The look in his eyes intensified as if he were about to communicate something I ought to understand. "But you weren't angry. Not at all. And you always talked with me, just not about that. Then I got hooked on seeing you every day. I tried getting you to go places or take a walk, but you wouldn't." He smiled to himself, his eyes holding a faraway look. "Except one day, I was out riding my horse and I found you on the trail." He stopped talking.

"Then what?"

"I was riding alone, trying to quit thinking about you, trying to convince myself that there could never be anything between us. I'd made too many mistakes. You were pure. You deserved someone equally pure, like Roland." He glanced, looking sulky again. "But there you were on the path and I couldn't resist asking. I told you to get on the horse—"

"You *told* me?" I pretended to be offended, but I'd give him the benefit of the doubt.

He shrugged, giving a guilty grin. "Sort of. I didn't know how to ask, so I slid back in the saddle and offered my hand. You looked at my hand for two whole seconds, saying nothing, making me feel stupid. So I said, 'Get on the horse.' And you did."

I laughed. "I made you feel stupid, huh?"

"Anyway, we rode for a while, not talking at all. Then I took you back to the house. Maybe you liked me then, I don't know, but it cemented my feelings for you."

"So, at the Thai restaurant, is that when I told you what happened that night?

"Do you... remember?" Hope colored his expression.

I hated to let him down. "No, I read about it in one of the emails."

"To Roland? You told Roland?" His brows twitched and forehead wrinkled.

I bit my lip, trying not show amusement. "No, I told Roland about the Thai restaurant, how I had fun, how I liked talking with you." His worried expression faded as I continued. "I told him that we finally talked about 'that night,' but that he'd have to ask you if he wanted details. I guess you blushed when I told you about it, huh?" I wished I could remember.

His mouth opened then he smiled and glanced away. "I dunno."

Pushing my foot deeper in the sand, I gave him a flirtatious smile. "I guess you'd better tell me about it. I think I ought to know."

He sat with his knees up and pushed his feet into the sand the way I had done. Then he rested his arms on his knees and watched the ocean for a moment before answering. "Well, Papa was harassing me about getting a job, so I finally did.

And I used that as an excuse to ask you out, to celebrate." He gave me a sly grin. "I had to beg, but eventually you agreed to it. I'm glad you had fun. I wish you remembered it."

"Tell me the secret," I whispered, leaning into his space, giving him a playful nudge with my elbow.

He nudged back, shoulder to shoulder, leaning into me for a long second. "Okay. Here's what you told me: the night I was drunk, you heard my friend drop me off and saw me lying on the ground outside, wailing about my Chrysler. Your room was off the front of the house."

"In the email I told Roland I helped you get your car. What happened after?" I wanted him to get to the point before he changed his mind about telling me. Did he still find it embarrassing?

"Okaaay." He dragged the word out, seeming reluctant to share more. "We got back with my car and I couldn't walk straight, so you helped me upstairs and waited in the hall while I used the bathroom. But I never came out, so you came in and scraped me off the floor, took me to my room." Reluctance gone, he stared into my eyes as he spoke. "You took off my shoes and belt, turned down my bed, and got my PJs out of the dresser. I showed my appreciation by dragging you into my bed."

I gasped and looked away. "Oh!"

"I know and I'm sorry. You told me you tried to get away, but I pinned you down. Sorry."

My face burned. I found myself glaring sideways, not wanting to hear the rest.

He bumped my shoulder again, as if sensing my thoughts. "Relax. I didn't try anything bad. Apparently, uh, well, you told me I wanted you to, uh..." He cleared his throat. "I wanted you to sing to me."

"What? Sing?" I snapped my gaze to his.

He rolled his eyes. Was he blushing? "Yeah. This is where it gets embarrassing and the reason you wouldn't tell me sooner. You didn't want to humiliate me, but I had to know."

He ran his fingers through his hair, facing away from me.

I crawled to his other side to make eye contact and sat beside him. "Go on."

He huffed and smiled at the same time. "You sure you didn't tell Roland?"

I shrugged. "Not in the emails. I told him it was private to you."

"Good. So, I was trying to come up with a song my mother sang to me that you might know. I sang a few lines of this one and that." He paused, giving me a cautious look. "I was young when she died, you know."

"I know." My heart went out to him. He'd had to grow up without his mother.

"Well, after a few tries, we came up with one you knew: *Sing of Mary*."

"I love that song."

"So did my mother, and she used to pet my hair when she sang to me." His gaze slid to me, a sly grin on his face. "You did that, sang to me and petted my hair."

Totally entranced by his retelling, I could picture the whole thing and my heart delighted in every detail.

"A minute later, I guess I was out, and you got out of my bed. But you didn't leave. You stripped my shirt off." He rubbed his chest, a mischievous glint in his eye.

"I did not." I kicked sand at his leg. "You're making that up."

"You believe the rest of it? I'm not lying. I had crap on my shirt. Maybe I puked on myself. You could've left me like that, but you didn't. You put a clean t-shirt on me. Then you left."

I giggled, my heart melting at how sweet the secret was. He wanted me to sing to him.

"What's so funny?"

"Nothing." Not wanting to laugh, I covered my mouth.

"All right. That was a long time ago." He kicked sand at my leg.

I kicked back, laughing. "I know. I'm sorry." We

exchanged sand for a few more seconds then settled down. "So, you learned what I did for you and that's why you fell in love with me?"

He nodded. "Partly. I'd been nothin' but a jerk toward you, never treated you or your friends nice in high school, but you showed mercy and took care of me. Has anyone ever shown you mercy? It made me see you differently. You weren't one of Roland's annoying friends. You were a girl unlike any girl I'd ever met. Who would do that for somebody like me, after all the mistakes I've made?" He paused, his gaze flitting as if he were searching his memory. "You're like Roland in that way."

He had a compliment for Roland? Which reminded me... "You're kind of mean to him. You know he's only here to help."

"I know. And I was mean growing up but I've changed." He gazed into my eyes. "Really, I have. I know you can't see it when he's around, because I've reverted to my old ways with him. I guess it's my fear of losing you. And I'm trying to deal with that. But he was there at the lowest point of my life." His Adam's apple bobbed. "And I'll never forget that. I met Jesus through Roland's forgiveness, through his mercy."

I wanted to know more, but it seemed too personal for the moment. "Maybe you'll share that with me sometime."

"I already have." He smirked. "You'll have to get your memory back if you want to know about it."

"What if I don't? Will you tell me again?"

He shrugged. "Someday."

Seagulls cried in the distance. I tried to break from his gaze, but the depth of his emotion held me. I was like the seashell he'd handed me. And his love, like an ocean wave, washed over me.

A salty breeze rippling through his shirt, Jarret lowered his gaze and inched toward me.

The same breeze tickling my face and playing with my hair, I closed my eyes and held my breath. My lips burned, expectant.

"Wanna take a walk?"

My eyes popped open.

He stood over me, reaching a hand down.

Looking up at him, my mouth fell open with my disbelief. I thought sure he was about to... to kiss me. And I was about to let him. I took his hand and we strolled barefooted along the shore.

# Chapter 32

I SAT ON the edge of the bed, listening to the shower blast and smiling like mad. Everything felt different today. Jarret trusted that I would not run off while he showered. Or maybe…based on what he'd confessed to me on the beach, he trusted God, come what may. I never imagined this day would come. Maybe he would go to work and leave me home alone. Mike said I ought to talk him into it.

I reached for my bathrobe and got up to make breakfast. As I passed through the living room, I glanced at the bookshelf. My gaze lingered on the shells we'd collected from the beach. They looked nice sitting by the rocks, other shells, and pictures. Who were the girls in the pictures? It seemed strange that we had so many young friends with newborns.

We'd reached a new level in our relationship. I should ask him directly. And while I was at it, I would ask if he knew about Sean's kiss. A wife shouldn't keep secrets from her husband. So if he didn't know, he would find out today. My stomach clenched at the thought, but if I intended to do my part to make our marriage work, I would need to begin with trust and honesty.

With a sigh, I went to the kitchen to forage for food. We'd eaten all the bacon, and I didn't feel like sausage, but I remembered seeing a block of cheddar cheese in a refrigerator drawer. I could make cheesy scrambled eggs and toast.

After pouring the egg mixture into a hot skillet, I stuffed slices of bread into the toaster. As I pushed the toast down, the bedroom door opened.

Jarret strutted toward me dressed in white tennis shoes, gunmetal chino pants, and a short-sleeved white shirt that accentuated his chest and shoulder muscles.

Heart pitter-pattering, I lifted my gaze to his face. How had I ever *not* found him attractive? "You look nice. And you shaved."

"Yeah." He rested an arm on the island counter and rubbed his whisper-thin goatee. "Thought I'd clean up a little."

"So, you're going to work today?"

He opened his mouth to answer when the phone rang. We both looked at it, then at each other. "I'll get it. It's probably work," he said, walking around the counter.

A stab of disappointment made me sigh as he strolled into the living room with the phone. I was closer. When would he let me answer it?

Resting a hand on his hip, Jarret faced the front window. "I told you I wasn't comin' in... Well, I didn't think about it... No, I'm not. I scheduled this a long time ago... Can't... I don't care. Do what you have to do. I'm doing what I have to do... I'll come in this afternoon..." He glanced at his watch. "All right. I'll swing by and straighten that out, but I'm not staying." He strutted back to the kitchen, the phone swinging at his side.

"I really had fun yesterday." I bounced on my toes, feeling a bit shy.

"Me too." He returned the phone to its cradle, leaned against the counter, and watched me with a little smile on his face.

"I see you're wearing tennis shoes and not your new flip-flops." I carried plates of cheesy eggs and toast to the table.

"I hate flip flops." He sat at the head of the table. "I don't see the problem with bare feet in a restaurant, especially one near the beach. We should be able to come as we are."

I sat in the chair nearest him, smiling, thinking of last night. After our heart-to-heart talk on the beach, we'd tried finding a restaurant, but Jarret's bare feet had posed a problem. "It was fun, anyway. I haven't laughed that hard in a long time."

Once his smile faded, he led the Prayer Before Meals and took a few bites of his breakfast. Then he started patting his pockets. "I gotta find my cell phone, then I gotta run."

"Maybe you left it in the weight room." Oddly, it pleased me to feel I knew him well enough to guess where his phone might be.

"Yeah, probably." He glanced in the direction of the weight room, then back at me with a strange look in his eyes. "Hey, you probably heard me on the phone. I—I'm gonna swing by work, but I have somewhere else to go today. I'm kind of in a rush now, but I really want you—"

The phone rang again. I definitely sat closer. He needed to start trusting me. I pushed out my chair.

He popped up before I could stand and gave a bossy command: "Finish eating. I'll get that." Then he had to squeeze past me to get to the kitchen.

Disappointment fell like a timebomb in my stomach. If I didn't disarm it, it would go off.

"Hello?... Hey, what's up?" Jarret carried the phone to the living room. Stepping around the couch, he gave me a glance.

I looked away, but I listened.

"Nah. What'dya want?... No! What do you want?... What?... No, I'm sure of it. There's nothing on those pictures, just artifacts, tools, and dirt... A student? That young? I don't think so. You're getting your facts and theories messed up."

I shoved the last bite of eggs into my mouth and picked up my plate. Jarret watched as I carried it to the sink. He hadn't finished his breakfast, so I shouldn't start the dishes yet. I opened the pantry and stared blankly.

"Whatever... Yeah, you can look at them... No, not over here. I'll get them to you. I'll put them on a jump drive... I said *no*!"

When he shouted "no," I snapped out of the blank stare and my gaze landed on a box of chocolate chip cookie mix, so I grabbed it and mindlessly started looking for a mixing bowl.

"Okay, well, I'll tell her..." Jarret sighed and stepped into the bedroom, making it harder to hear his voice. It sounded like he said, "You can come over after dinner."

A moment later, Jarret returned to the kitchen with the phone. "Making cookies? Now?"

I gave a pleasant smile, pushing suspicion down, though I could almost hear the timebomb that had fallen in my gut ticking off the seconds. "Who was that?"

He opened his mouth then closed it again and slid the phone across the counter, toward the cradle. Then he stepped around to the head of the table.

"Jarret, who was on the phone?" I opened the refrigerator to get butter, trying not to look anxious for the answer. *Tick, tick, tick...*

A second passed. Another second. Another—

"Roland." He spit the name out and his lip curled up on one side as though the name gave him a bad taste.

"What did he want?" I smashed the butter into the cookie mix with a fork.

Jarret brought his half-eaten breakfast to the sink and scraped the eggs into the garbage disposal. "Look, I've gotta run up to work but—"

"Did Roland ask to speak with me?" Irritation wrestling with patience, I stopped mixing. *Tick, tick, tick...*

He glanced at me over his shoulder. "Uh... yeah."

"So, why didn't you give me the phone?"

He rinsed his hands and turned, reaching for the towel. "I took care of it."

I snatched the towel before he got it. "No. If someone calls to speak with me, I want the phone."

He shook his head, staring up at the ceiling. "He wanted to look at some pictures. They're *my* pictures from work."

The timebomb exploded in slow motion, anger radiating to every inch of my body. Folding my arms across my chest, I glared. "Maybe he knows something about what happened to me. Maybe he wanted to ask me questions or tell me something." My face tensed and my voice came out too loud. "Are you that jealous of him? Don't you want to find out what happened to me? Or do you think I'm going to run off with him? We all know he has a girlfriend."

He huffed. "And if he didn't?"

I shook my head in annoyance, spun around, and threw myself into mixing the dough.

He stepped behind me and spoke low over my shoulder, his breath warm on my neck. "And if he didn't?"

"I thought we moved past that." I dropped the spoon and faced him, putting my back to the counter. "Yes, I still have feelings for him. But things were changing. I—I really enjoyed being with you yesterday. And I'm amazed that you were going to let me... leave you. And our talk... I thought we were getting somewhere. But how can my feelings for you grow if one moment you're nice to me and the next..." I gave a little headshake in lieu of saying, "you're mean, jealous, and possessive."

Emotion rippled through his face, then he glanced at his watch. "I don't have time for this. I have to be somewhere."

"So, go. And I'll use this time to think. I don't have my memories and I can't help how I feel about things. You have to respect that. Respect who I am now. I'm obviously not the girl you married."

He blinked and averted his gaze.

"And you can't control me. If I want to talk to someone on the phone, to Roland or my mother, you have no right to stop me. And if I want to go home to my family... you need to let me go."

With dark brooding eyes, he shook his head as if he couldn't believe what I said.

But I had more to say. "I know you said it would ruin things for me to explain all this to my mother." I swung an arm out in the direction of the phone. "And I appreciate that you're looking out for me. But it's my life." I slapped my chest.

"And I need to make decisions for myself... even if I ruin things."

"It's your life. What about me? You're my wife." His gaze flicked to my belly. "And what about my baby? Are you going to leave me and take my whole life with you?"

"That's just it, Jarret. I'm not going to leave you. Not forever. I've begun to see qualities in you that I really like, but I need you to trust me and let me figure things out for myself. I still don't understand things about us, about *you*."

He stood speechless, his gaze flitting from me to the countertop to the floor. He shook his head. "All right." He threw his hands in the air and stalked past me. At the front door he stopped. "Did you ever call Kelly?"

"Who?"

"I gave you her phone number."

"Oh..." That's right, he had. What had I done with it? "No, I never called."

"I wish you would. You'd figure some things out about me. About us." He yanked the door open.

"Jarret, wait." I went to him, ready to push things even further. "I need to ask you something."

He stood by the half-open door, giving me a blank stare, waiting for the question I hated to ask.

I cleared my throat. "Did I ever tell you about..." I struggled to get the name out. "...about Sean... how he... kissed me?"

His stone face crumbled at his mouth. "Sean?" Gripping the edge of the door, he grimaced and gazed outside. "Great. That memory's come back to you, the one with him. None with me." His jaw twitched.

I closed the space between us, wishing I could ease his pain. "No, I don't have any memory of it. I found out. I just wondered if I'd told you."

His eyes narrowed. "Of course you told me. I like to think we don't keep crap from each other. Took you long enough, but you told me."

"How did you react?"

He snickered under his breath. "How do you think I reacted? Some guy kissing my wife?" His jaw tensed again.

"So, you were mad at me?"

"I was mad."

"Did we fight?"

He gave me a "What do you think?" look and stared outside.

But I needed more. I needed specifics. "I mean, Jarret, was there shouting, angry words... Was I crying?"

He met my gaze, stared for a moment, then nodded.

I only had one more question. "When did I tell you?"

As if not wanting to remember or wishing this conversation would end, he blinked a few times.

Stomach knotting, I forced myself to ask, "Was it that Friday? When you came up at lunchtime with my camera?"

His eyebrows twitched. Did he not understand the question?

"Was it that Friday I came home late?"

His lips parted. He closed his mouth and gave a slight nod.

"When I woke Saturday with amnesia, you asked if I was still mad at you. Is that what you were talking about? You thought I was mad because of how you reacted?"

"I..." His voice broke. "...go over it in my mind every day." He stared at the ceiling, his eyes welling with tears. "That was our park, where we always went together. Did you go there alone because of me? Because of my anger? Something happened to you because of me?" He closed his eyes and pressed his lips together. In a voice heavy with regret he said, "It's my fault you have amnesia, isn't it?"

I touched his hand but couldn't think of the words to say. Even if it were true, I wouldn't want him to feel such guilt. "It's not your fault."

Dragging an arm across his eyes, he turned away. "I gotta go. I'm gonna be late."

"Wait." I grabbed his arm before he made it through the

door. "I'm inviting Roland over."

His head moved. Was it a nod? I shouldn't need his permission. I was a grown woman. He was my husband, not my father, but I desperately wanted it to be okay with him. So I said it again.

"I'm going to call Roland and have him come over here."

He nodded for sure this time, then he asked in a soft, vulnerable tone, "Will you be here when I get home?"

"Yes." I meant it. If I was going to leave him, I wouldn't sneak to do it. We were past that now. He would have to respect my choices.

He dropped his gaze to my mouth then turned to go.

# Chapter 33

THE HONDA WHIRRED as Jarret backed out of the driveway. The car straightened, the tires squealed, and Jarret peeled down the street.

Jittery and sick to my stomach, I dropped the curtain and staggered back, bumping the brown leather armchair. "Wow, what just happened?" I said aloud. Everything we'd built yesterday on the beach had just crumbled in a few short minutes, like a sandcastle overcome by the rising tide.

Mind racing, I returned to the kitchen. Jarret said he was only stopping at work, that he had somewhere else to go. Where? And why? What could possibly be more important to him than his job? And what had Roland wanted when he called?

Growing in determination—I needed answers—I snatched up the phone. I tapped out Roland's cell phone number and pressed the phone to my ear. The first time I used this phone—that I remembered—I'd spoken with Roland. He'd heard the panic in my voice that day and had taken the first flight out to help me. What a friend.

Roland's phone rang in my ear. What did his girlfriend think about him taking off? How would I have felt in Ling-si's place, knowing he'd taken off to help another woman? An ex-girlfriend.

Then I remembered the airline ticket... Jarret had claimed he'd gone back to help Zoë. Did all the West boys feel the need to rescue every damsel in distress?

"Hello?" Roland's voice came through the receiver.

With a big exhale, I slid into a chair at the table. The view through the glass patio door attracted me. Morning sunlight illuminated the blooms on the lilac bush, bounced off shiny green leaves, and glistened on blades of mowed grass.

"Hi, Roland. Can you come over? We need to talk and I could really use a friend."

"Where's Jarret?"

I groaned. He *would* ask that. He wouldn't want to do anything to upset his brother. His unflagging loyalty almost annoyed me.

"Well, he's on his way to work and then I don't know where. He said he had somewhere else to go. I told him I was inviting you over. He said it was okay."

"Really? He was pretty adamant about me not coming over until tonight, when he's there, I guess."

"I know. We argued about it. But he's okay with it now." I winced, recalling Jarret's sad expression as he'd left this morning. "You can call and ask if you don't believe me."

"I believe you, Caitlyn. And I'll come over. I'm just surprised. But Jarret *can* be moody."

Placing the phone in the cradle, my thoughts returned to the beach, to our talk, to dinner, and to holding hands. I had to admit that Jarret had good reasons for some of his moodiness. This last week must've been torture to him. I had no doubt that he loved me. Maybe he wasn't moody so much as passionate. And maybe I liked that. If only I could trust him.

I made hot tea, got dressed, and baked chocolate chip cookies while I waited for the expected knock on the door. Heavenly aromas filled the house, but I wouldn't try one until Roland arrived. I arranged the cookies, two empty plates, and two mugs on the table. The lilacs still looked fresh and made a nice centerpiece. Sunlight streamed in through the patio door, shining on the vase and mugs, making everything picturesque. Of course, the kitchen had become a bit of a mess.

Maybe I'd have time to clean it. Jarret probably had dishes in the weight room too.

After setting the batter-crusted mixing bowl in the sink, I headed for the weight room. I stepped through the open doorway of the sun-drenched room and my gaze snapped to an empty glass and...the cell phone on the end of the computer desk. Oh, Jarret left without it.

I picked it up, my thumb accidentally brushing a button on the side, and it came to life. A message notification appeared along the top.

I froze, staring at the phone. My pulse thumped in my ears. Kelly had sent Jarret a text. *See you tomorrow.*

Kelly? The same Kelly Jarret had wanted me to call? Who was Kelly? How close of friends were she and Jarret? What were they doing tomorrow? *No, not tomorrow.* The text was dated yesterday, so that meant they had plans today. Now? Is that where Jarret was headed after he stopped by work? All dressed up to meet with Kelly?

Hand trembling, I swiped the face of the cell phone and tapped the text messenger. What other texts had Kelly sent? And what had Jarret sent her?

A knock sounded on the front door.

I jumped, jerking my head up and tightening my grip on the phone. *Roland!*

Anxious for a friend, someone to share this with, I raced through the living room and flung open the door.

Roland took one look at me and his dark brows climbed up his forehead. He ducked inside, giving me a quizzical look. "What's the matter?" Then his head swiveled toward the kitchen. "Something smells good. You make cookies?"

Unable to keep from frowning, I gestured toward the breakfast nook. "Help yourself."

Rather than head for the cookies, he drew closer to me. "What's the matter?" His gaze snapped to the cell phone in my hand. "You found your phone?"

"No, I found Jarret's phone. He was in a hurry and left

without it." I swiped the face of the cell phone again to turn the screen back on. Chest tightening with my anxiety, I tapped the text messenger again. Then I tapped the name at the top of the list: Kelly.

Roland peered over my shoulder and we read the most recent messages together.

Kelly texted: *Still on for tomorrow?*

Jarret texted: *Yeah, sure.*

Kelly: *Good. Everything ok?*

Jarret: *A little nervous.*

Kelly: *You have no reason to be.*

Then the message from Kelly that I had first seen: *See you tomorrow.*

Every word I read stabbed my heart. Jarret, my husband, and some girl named Kelly… Had yesterday meant nothing? Was our marriage built on sand? I staggered to the couch, flopped down, and let the cell phone slip from my hand.

Roland picked it up, sat across from me on the loveseat, and looked at it again. "You should just ask him about this. Maybe he has a job interview or something."

I looked at him in disbelief. "A job interview?"

"Well, I don't know. I mean, he's texting a girl, but we shouldn't jump to the conclusion that he's… you know."

I groaned, frustrated, but then an idea came to me and I got up. "You know what? Instead of jumping to conclusions, I'm going to find out exactly where he's going today. He's obviously meeting Kelly somewhere. Let's find out why." I stomped to my bedroom to change into something a little more presentable.

"How are we going to do that?" Roland's voice came through my closed bedroom door. "We have no idea where to look."

I yanked a casual black shift dress from a hanger and grabbed cute black heels. I rarely wore heels. But a strange sense of competition boiled inside me. After all we went through yesterday and all that we talked about, it sickened me to think he could have another love interest. A part of me hated to think he was the same playboy he was in high school, but another part of me wanted to fight for my man. "He said he had to go to work first, so let's drive up there and follow him."

"Do you know where his work is?"

"Sort of." I slipped my feet into the heels and gazed across the bed at my reflection in the dresser mirror. My hair was a mess of unruly curls. "He pointed it out to me once, when Sean and I met Melinda Meyers at a park." I tried smoothing a few curls, then bent over and flipped my hair, hoping it would all fall into place. Unwilling to waste more time on it, I stepped out of the bedroom.

After giving me the once-over, Roland tucked Jarret's cell phone into his chest pocket and dug out Jarret's keys from his jeans. "You look nice."

"Thanks." Mustering my strength, I led the way to the door. "Let's go."

# Chapter 34

"ARE WE GOING in?" Roland sat behind the steering wheel of Jarret's Dodge Ram, tapping a beat on his thigh.

I breathed, pushing back a mess of clashing emotions—fear, disgust, anger, and a desperate plea for hope—as I gazed at the two-story school building, Sacred Heart High.

We'd arrived at Jarret's work site just as he was pulling out in my Honda. Roland had cranked the steering wheel and turned down a side street just in time. Jarret had made no sign of seeing us. Then we'd stealthily followed him here and waited for him to go inside before we parked right next to the Honda.

"Why would he meet her at a high school?" I stared at the front doors of the building. "How old was Kelly?"

Roland shrugged and grabbed the door handle. "Guess we might as well find out." He looked at me, maybe because I hadn't made a move for my door.

My clashing emotions glued me to my seat. Discovering that my father had died had wounded my heart and soul. And while it had been hard to accept that I was married to Jarret, I didn't want to discover the death of my marriage too.

Roland took my hand. "There's got to be another explanation. Let's go find out what it is."

Not sharing his confidence, I gave him a weak smile and opened my door. "Yeah, let's get it over with." Nerves giving me chills, I followed Roland up the wide walkway to the front door of the school.

A thirty-something receptionist behind a high counter greeted us, sliding a clipboard toward us. "Here for the assembly? You'll have to sign in and wear a visitor's pass." She turned back to a computer monitor and picked up the phone.

Roland and I exchanged glances. Then Roland shrugged and scribbled our names on the sign-up sheet. I grabbed two passes. At least we didn't have to make up an excuse as to why we were here.

The receptionist put a hand over the mouthpiece of the phone. "It's in the gym. Just down that hall and to the left." She pointed.

Roland and I walked side by side down a long, empty hallway with tan and blue lockers on each side and few closed classroom doors. Light from big windows at the end of the hallway created a bright spot on the shiny floor.

"Now what?" My hope sank with every step. "Where could he be?" He and Kelly could've agreed to meet anywhere in the building, knowing that everyone else would be in the assembly today.

"I don't know. Let's just peek in the gym," Roland said. "Maybe he was invited to the assembly."

As we neared the end of the hallway, shouts, applause, and cheers traveled to us. We reached an intersecting hall, a sunny breezeway to the right and gym doors off to the left, the view through the doors dark.

"Apparently..." A woman's Southern drawl boomed over the sound system. "...you're a favorite of some of our students here." The applause grew louder.

Roland motioned for me to go in first.

Feeling out of place and worried someone would notice, I stepped through the doors. Students filled bleachers that stretched across the wall on the opposite side of the gym. More bleachers rose up on either side of me. Students also sat in rows of metal chairs in the middle of the gym, near the stage. Overwhelmed by the booming applause, I shuffled to an open spot next to the bleachers, where a few adults, probably teachers, stood. It provided a good view of the stage.

As Roland came up beside me, I focused on the figures on the stage, a middle-aged woman at a microphone and a young man strutting toward her.

"Is that…?" Roland didn't finish his question.

I saw what he saw, and my world turned upside down and spun out of control.

The young man strutting across the stage was Jarret. He walked with a little bounce in his step, the way he had in high school, then he pumped his fist and the kids went wild.

"What is he doing here?" I said aloud, not expecting an answer. We'd know soon enough.

"Oh, hey there, Caitlyn." A forty… maybe even fifty-something woman with a cute blond bob and a Southern drawl touched my arm. "I didn't realize you were standing right next to me."

"What?" Not recognizing the woman, I stepped back and accidentally bumped Roland. "I'm sorry, who are you?"

"Oh, my dear, Jarret told us about your memory loss." A look of intense compassion colored her face and she touched my arm again. "I met you two up at Shining Light Pregnancy Center, when you first came to volunteer. My name's Kelly." She stuck out her hand.

"Kelly?" My hand flew to my mouth while my mind tried wrapping around this. "Pregnancy center?"

"Why, yes, we provide counseling and support to girls and women who think they might be pregnant."

"We…we volunteer?" My heart tingled, filling with helium. "I guess that explains why we have so many pictures of girls with babies around the house," I said, thinking aloud. "And the phone calls."

I glanced at Roland, whose eyes held a confident "I told you so" look.

Kelly laughed. "Oh, my dear, yes. That could be troubling if you didn't realize—Now, you didn't think that man of yours was two-timin' you?"

"Well..." A wave of guilt washed over me.

"Oh, that man is so in love with you. Can't you see that?" Kelly gestured toward the stage, where Jarret and the woman at the microphone still exchanged a few words. "He does anything you tell him. I'm sure that's why he volunteers." She leaned close and lowered her voice. "Men don't typically volunteer for what he does, taking phone calls and such. But he's so good with all the girls. They can relate to him. He hasn't lost a single baby. He talks the girls right through their troubles."

Emotion formed a lump in my throat and I barely got out the word "Oh."

"You'll enjoy this." Kelly turned back to the stage just as Jarret took the microphone and the woman left the stage.

A strange rush of adrenaline made me alert to every detail, though I focused on Jarret.

Jarret squinted out at the dark bleachers. Lights shone only on him, probably blinding him, but he looked comfortable on stage, even in front of all these students. "Hey!" he shouted. "You ready for some straight talk?" Wild cheers and a few hoots came in response. He grinned. "Good."

My heart pounded and my hands had gone clammy. "What in the world is he giving a talk about?" I shouted into Roland's ear. He replied with a shrug.

The moment stretched out, but when the kids quieted down, Jarret began. "Some of you may've heard my talk at a teen event, so don't go to sleep." They laughed. "I've got the same message. But it's a good one, and you need to hear it."

He scanned the bleachers. "I gotta find my guys out there first. So, let me ask you a few questions." He grinned, looking like he was up to something. "You got a lot of hot girls here at Sacred Heart High?" Howls and hoots came from here and there but mostly from a top section on the far bleachers. Jarret nodded. "You showing them respect?" The howlers responded with a jumble of shouted comments and more howls.

"Okay, found my guys." Jarret pointed, his hand like a gun

on its side, to the top section of the bleachers. "I was like you. I'm talking to you now. Better listen good." A boy shouted something unclear and the group of guys laughed.

Jarret stared at the microphone for a second as if gathering his thoughts. "When I was in high school, would you believe I was popular with the girls?" He narrowed one eye as if he really wondered what they thought. Kids clapped. Some whistled. "Yeah, I had a few girlfriends. And I won't say I respected them, but I was a virgin in high school. Until I turned sixteen. Then I got the idea lodged in my head that I didn't want to be a virgin anymore. I wanted to try sex." One of "Jarret's guys" in the upper section of the bleachers hooted, a few others responded with unclear replies and shouts, but Jarret's expression remained grim.

"You see it all the time in movies and on TV. Everybody talks about it. Everybody does it, don't they?" He paused. "I didn't think it'd be that hard to find a willing girl, but I was particular. She had to be hot. So I found *the one*. She liked me. I liked her. We weren't in love or anything, but that didn't matter. And I'm not gonna lie and tell you it wasn't fun.

"But I wasn't seeing the big picture. I didn't know there *was* a big picture. Why do people have sex?" He paused and scanned the bleachers as if someone might offer an answer. "What's it all about? You know why you eat. To grow, to stay healthy. You know why you exercise or lift weights. To stay healthy, to look good." He got a few "yeows" from the girls in the folding chairs in the middle of the gym floor. He gave them an appreciative nod.

"So, what's the purpose of sex? Entertainment? Is it just something fun to do? Is it what you do when you're in love?" He shook his head. "If you eat too much, you gain weight. If you exercise a lot, you get fit, maybe bulk up. What's the natural consequence of a sexual relationship?" A few people shouted out answers, none of them clear. "Is there anybody here who doesn't know? We all know. We all *know* the natural consequence wears diapers, spits up, and sucks on a pacifier."

Giggles rolled around the gym.

"It's a baby. Surprise. My girlfriend got pregnant. Didn't see that one coming." The giggles turned into laughter. "Of course, I didn't want a baby. And she didn't want a baby. I told you we weren't in love. And even if we were, I was sixteen. She was younger. Neither of us had a job or a place to live, besides our family's homes. We were kids. What were we gonna do with a baby? A baby needs a mother and a father to take care of it. I was *not* going to be a father.

"Of course, I, uh, I didn't see that I already was a father. She was carrying my baby. But I didn't see it like that. She was *pregnant* and I didn't want her to be pregnant. So I gave her some money and told her to take care of it." He paused for a moment, probably to let the weight of it soak in. His jaw twitched as he let the moment stretch out.

"If you don't want to be pregnant, you don't have to be, right? You can take a pill or something and things return to the way they were. Right?"

No answer. Silence. He had them spellbound. He had me spellbound.

"Well, she didn't do it, because... I guess she was smarter than me. She knew that something living and growing was inside her, and it wasn't just a blob of tissue. It was a human being, a baby."

Lightheaded and tingling all over, I rubbed my belly. Was this really Jarret West? Was Jarret really saying these things?

"When I found out she hadn't done it, hadn't taken care of it... mm." He narrowed his eyes, probably giving a look like the one he'd given Zoë all those years ago. "I was mad. I knew, at the end of nine months, she'd have something that was mine, something that I would have to be responsible for. I didn't want that responsibility. So I told her again to take care of it. *Take care of it or we're through.*"

My hair stood on end. He had spoken the last line in a mean tone, the way he'd probably said it to Zoë. I couldn't imagine Zoë's grief.

"She got her appointment, and I stopped thinking about it. Until that day. The day she was scheduled to terminate her pregnancy." Jarret paused. The gym fell entirely silent. He frowned and turned his gaze upward to the darkness above him and then to the overhead stage lights.

"Now, I don't know if God worked it like this to wake me up, but that day, I was surrounded by babies. Little ones with round eyes and tiny hands and chubby faces. I had to drop my brother off at a church function, and they were everywhere. They were crawling out of the woodwork."

A few giggles came from the girls up front.

"And as I stood listening to a youth band, one of them babies stared me down. I didn't even hear the music. It was like that little guy knew what I did, what was happening to *my* baby that day." Jarret's voice cracked. He glanced at his feet. "So I had to get away from that punky little accuser, but I couldn't shake the feelings... of guilt. Guilt overwhelmed me, guilt, anger, sadness. Utter grief. And before long, I jumped into my car and raced down to the abortion mill.

"And I call it a 'mill' because of what they do there. They want you girls in there." His eyes turned to the girls in the front. "Their profits depend upon you. It's a multi-million-dollar industry. They bring in over eight-hundred and thirty million dollars a year, killing over a million babies. That's thirty-seven hundred babies a day in our country. Don't be fooled. They aren't providing you a service. They don't care about you at all. They're using you. They want you to be sexually active, want you to use birth control, and they know that birth control is going to fail.

"So anyway, I raced down there to stop her. But when I got there, I found her sitting on the clinic steps leaning on a woman, crying her eyes out. I was too late. It was done. My baby was dead." He paused. "Her heart started beating eighteen days after conception, and I just had it stopped. I killed my baby."

Visibly trembling, he swallowed hard and stared at

various points in the gym before steadying himself and continuing. "At seven weeks a baby can suck its thumb. At nine weeks, she can wrap her fingers around an object. As early as sixteen weeks she can hear her mother's heartbeat and noises like my music."

He lowered the microphone and took another moment to compose himself. Then he lifted it and spoke again. "What happened next, I see it as a miracle. Any of you ever pray outside an abortion clinic?"

A few people clapped, then more and more until applause came from every side of the gym.

He nodded, looking pleased. "Sometimes people drive by and shout obscenities at you, right? Some people think you're crazy. But you keep on praying and holding those signs," he shouted. "You're making a difference."

More applause erupted, making him wait. He nodded again, signaling his approval, then waited patiently for everyone to quiet.

"That day, a bunch of people were out there praying for my girlfriend, maybe for me. And, thank God, my girlfriend changed her mind. She didn't go through with the abortion. When I saw her sitting on the steps, she was crying in the arms of one of those crazy people, a crazy woman trying to save a life." He paused. "They saved three lives that day. My baby's. My girlfriend's. And mine.

"Everything changed for me that day. I stood by my pregnant girlfriend until she had the baby. We were too young to raise her, so we placed our little girl for adoption. I think about her all the time. Her adoptive parents send pictures sometimes. She's cute."

Girls throughout the gym said, "Awww."

"Ever since that experience, I've stopped looking at sex the same way. I wasn't about to go through that again. I began to realize sex isn't some form of entertainment. And if you think it is, you're being selfish. You're thinking of what you want and not what you're doing to your partner, and not how you could be creating a whole other person.

"It's kind of awesome, really. God creates. But he lets us create too. A man and a woman get together and, bam, there's a third person. Kinda cool." A few kids clapped.

"Doesn't it make sense that sex belongs in marriage? Only in marriage does it become a true expression of love between a guy and a girl, two people ready to bring a new life into the world and take care of it, love it. So I changed my view and I became a virgin again."

He got some laughter and comments from his guys in the top section of the bleachers.

"Really?" I whispered to Roland. "He stopped having sex?" I never imagined he had used self-control from that day on. Roland shrugged, his eyes as wide as mine.

"Yeah, go ahead and laugh," Jarret said, gazing toward the upper bleachers. "I know you can't go back, can't erase the past, but you can start over. I started over. Everybody makes mistakes. I was man enough to admit it and then do what I had to do from then on." He got some cheers and applause.

He brought the microphone closer to his mouth. "People can change. So, to those of you who have given up your virginity, if you see what I'm saying, if you understand the value of life, the value of sexuality, the value of love... you can change. You don't have to keep doing what you're doing. Don't let anyone tell you, you can't change. To those of you who are still virgins, good for you. There's no greater gift a guy can give his future wife, or a girl can give her future husband on their wedding night than your virginity. Wait for your husband. Wait for your wife."

He paused, lowered the microphone, and stepped back. The applause started on one side of the gym and soon spread. A group in the bleachers stood, the applause growing in intensity. Soon over half the students in the gym were standing and clapping.

My heart swelled with affection for this man. I shook my head in joyful disbelief. Was this the same Jarret West I'd known in high school? Was this really my husband?

When the applause quieted, Jarret brought the microphone back up. “Even after I changed my ways, I had a hard time living with the guilt over what I’d told my girlfriend to do, even though it didn’t happen. Having an abortion, deciding to take the life of your baby, it’s not something you do and forget about. I don’t know how I ever would’ve forgiven myself if—” He pressed his lips together, dropped his gaze, and shook his head. The hand with the microphone swung to his side.

My breath caught in my throat. My face warmed, embarrassed for him. Would he be able to finish the message?

He turned away, wiped his eyes, then his pant leg, and turned back to the audience. Microphone to his mouth, he said in a voice that filled the gym, “But we have a God of mercy.”

People started to clap but he kept talking. “And if any of you, or someone you know, made that terrible mistake, we have a God who forgives. And maybe he’ll send someone into your life who can help you heal, help you see yourself without looking at all your past mistakes. That’s what God did for me.” His voice cracked. “And I know I don’t deserve her... my wife...”

My heart leaped and my eyes welled with tears. I moved away from the bleachers and stepped toward the stage, but he didn’t see me.

“She’s my treasure. She was a virgin until our wedding night. She couldn’t be here today or I’d introduce her to you. She’s—”

“I’m here,” I shouted and more than a few heads turned. I waved as I strode to the stage.

He squinted in my direction. “Caitlyn?”

“I’m here.” I neared the stage and tried to smile, but emotion forced something more like a frown.

He set the microphone down and jumped off the stage, meeting me in the aisle, stopping a few feet away. “You’re here,” he whispered, disbelief and joy on his face.

Fighting back tears, I nodded. With my next step, my

three-inch heel wobbled and threw me off balance. I flung my arms out and fell against him. His hands shot up to my waist, helping me regain balance while making it look like a lover's embrace.

"I'm here for you, Jarret." Moved by an uncontrollable desire to be held by him, I threw my arms around his neck. He pulled me to his sweaty, trembling body and kissed my cheek. The assembly cheered and applauded.

I turned my head to find his lips. A tingly thrill of excitement coursing through me, I kissed him as if for the first time.

When our brief kiss ended, he pulled back, his expression a cross between shock and joy. And for an instant, we stood alone in the gym, in the world, clinging to one another, husband and wife.

"You're trembling," I said, still in his arms.

"Yeah, talking about this—how many years later?—always shakes me up."

"Why do you do it?"

"You." He gazed into my eyes, conveying love, admiration, and things deeper yet. "You told me I should. You said my story might help others, maybe save a life. You thought I could help kids like me, like I used to be."

His arms slid from around me. He jumped onto the stage, snatched the microphone, and hopped back down. Then he took my hand and said, "I'd like you to meet my wife. Caitlyn. She's three months pregnant with our baby." The applause made it impossible for Jarret to say more. He dropped the microphone to his side, pulled me close, and kissed me again.

# Chapter 35

TOO ELATED TO think straight, I sat on the couch in the living room, smiling at the loveseat. Jarret had looked so confident, so handsome, strutting back and forth on the stage. Although the things he said brought obvious discomfort, it didn't stop him. How many times had he given the talk? How many schools had he gone to?

"These cookies are good. I'm getting addicted." Roland carried a plate of them into the living room. He set it on the coffee table and flopped down onto the loveseat, sitting across from me. "What's with the smile?"

Snapping out of it, I focused on him and sighed wistfully. "I'm thinking about Jarret. I can't believe his talk. He's so brave. I could never get in front of people and do that. All that personal stuff he shared... He didn't seem the least bit nervous, did he?"

Roland shook his head. "A little emotional now and then. But the kids loved him."

"Oh, they did. I wonder how many were truly affected by his talk. It was wonderful. I'm so amazed. Jarret. My husband." I smiled at the loveseat again.

"You aren't falling in love, are you?" Roland gave his sweet little smile, the one that had always made my heart flutter.

I giggled and shrugged, happy with the thought of falling in love with Jarret and aware that the idea pleased Roland too. "Maybe. I like the things I'm learning about him, about who he is now. I never realized how he changed, especially after Zoë."

"Yeah, I guess I didn't either. Keefe's probably the only one who knew, being his twin and all. I knew he'd changed in some ways. But he kept up his bad boy image all through high school, didn't he?" He pushed the plate across the coffee table, toward me. "Have a cookie."

I took one. At the beach, Jarret had said that Roland's forgiveness and mercy brought him to Jesus. Did Roland know? What an amazing brother and friend. Roland had dropped everything and flown out here to help his brother, to help me, and to support our marriage. Somehow, my affection for him had deepened, but also changed. I loved him as a friend, no longer wishing for more from him. And my feelings for Jarret... Some strange excitement made my heart race.

"Aren't you going to eat that?" he said, making me realize I'd been staring at him.

"Yeah, I was just thinking." I placed the cookie on my lap. "What's Jarret's favorite food?"

"Huh?" Roland took another cookie and shoved half of it in his mouth.

"You remember how upset he got when I made your favorite meal."

"Lasagna. Yeah, that really bugged him. He likes Mexican, not like fast-food so much as real Mexican. I'm sure there's a restaurant around here."

"No restaurant. I want to make it myself. I'll find recipes on-line." I ate my cookie and thought. "You know, now I'm sorry I considered Sean's theory about Jarret. Jarret would never—"

"Sean's theory... about Jarret? He never shared it with me." Roland's steel gray eyes flickered with curiosity and suspicion.

"Well, maybe he didn't think I told you about the kiss. Maybe he didn't want you to know. I think he's embarrassed about it." I grabbed another cookie and scooted to the edge of the couch. "And, well, he was right about Jarret knowing. I had told Jarret. And he's also right that I told Jarret on Friday." I stood, cookie in hand, and walked around the couch to the bookshelf.

"Wow. You told him on Friday? What Friday? The Friday before last?" His voice held a touch of urgency.

"Yes, that Friday, *Amnesia Friday*." I gazed at our silver-framed wedding picture on the bookshelf and bit into the cookie. We looked happy on our wedding day. Oh, what I'd give to remember it.

"Wow. How'd he take that?" With a half-eaten cookie in one hand, Roland leaned forward and rubbed his other hand down his thigh. "I mean, you told him Sean kissed you? How'd he respond to that?"

"Oh, not good. He said he got mad. I'm sure he was jealous."

"I bet he asked if you kissed him back. Did you?"

"What?" I glanced. Roland's dark eyebrows slanted upwards like two caterpillars lifting their heads. His eyes betrayed the depth of his worry. "How would I know? I don't remember."

"Sean has a theory? What's his theory?" Roland still held the half-eaten cookie.

Returning to the couch, I took another cookie. "Well..." How had he worded it? "Sean suggested that I told Jarret about the kiss that Friday at lunchtime, which turns out to be true, and that Jarret saw our cars outside work, after hours. Did I tell you about that?"

"No." He shook his head, eyes blinking. "You mean you and Sean were working late and Jarret drove by?"

"I don't know if Jarret drove by, and we weren't working. But we were at work, talking for an hour or so after everyone else had gone."

"Just you two?"

I nodded, his anxiety deflating my high.

He set his half-eaten cookie on the coffee table and ran both hands down his thighs. "So, what's the rest of his theory?"

"Well, I'm sure you can guess. Jarret followed me to the park or told me to meet him there or whatever, then he got angry. Something happened, and I ended up with amnesia."

Roland gave a stone-faced stare and shook his head. "How well do you know Sean?"

"What?"

"I'm sure he's a nice guy and all. Don't get me wrong. But what if he's not playing with a full deck? What if he's not being honest with you?"

"Roland, I didn't say I believed him. It's just a theory. He's trying to help me consider possibilities." I flung an arm out, making a gesture of frustration. "I told you I was sorry I'd even considered it. As I get to know Jarret better, I don't think it's possible he could get so angry that—"

"Jarret can get angry." He said it under his breath but then glanced at me as if to see if I caught it. Then, as if to keep me from dwelling on it too long, he said, "What do you know about Sean?"

"What do you mean?" Sean was a nice young man who loved being an investigator. Of course, Victor thought Sean was a bit on the obsessive side, especially when it came to me. Didn't Victor even say he'd confronted Sean about that? Sean obviously couldn't accept what Victor had said since he'd continued to pursue me, admitting his affections only that Friday.

"Okay. I mean..." Roland stood and walked the length of the coffee table. "What'd you and Sean talk about when you stayed late Friday? Do you know? Did he tell you?"

I nodded but hesitated to answer. "I guess Sean confessed that he had feelings for me, and I told him I was in love with my husband. I told him he needed to find himself a girlfriend and get me out of his mind."

"What if he couldn't handle that? Since you can't remember a thing, it's his word what happened next."

"Roland, please. I don't think Jarret or Sean had anything to do with my amnesia."

"You should consider everything."

"Should I?" *Even the theory about Jarret?* I couldn't bring myself to say it. Roland was only trying to defend his brother. He was no doubt annoyed that Sean had made him a suspect.

"There is something I haven't told you, since you haven't been around," I said, and he gave me his full attention. "The night Jarret came home drunk and fought with you, the reason I freaked out, I had a flashback, regained a memory." A chill ran down my spine, making me wish I hadn't brought it up. With reluctance, I continued. "When I saw Jarret's hair down and falling about his face, I knew I'd seen an image like that before. Then I remembered something clearly." So, I relayed the entire memory to him, including the way it had made me feel.

Roland made no immediate response. His face appeared strangely calm. "It could've been a disguise."

"A disguise?"

He eased onto the loveseat again and leaned back, looking exhausted. I'd never noticed dark circles under his eyes before. "You said he wore sunglasses and something over his mouth and nose. Not wanting to be identified. Because maybe you know him. If it were Sean, maybe he wanted you to think it was Jarret. Then—"

"Stop!" I folded my arms in protest. This was really too much. "Sean just happened to have a dark wig?"

"They've got more than surveillance equipment and cameras in the supply cabinet at Wright. They have disguises too."

"Roland! I can't believe that." Frustration eked out in my voice. "Sean's a nice guy. His feelings are misplaced. He wouldn't do anything to hurt me."

"Maybe he didn't mean to hurt you." Totally out of character, Roland raised his voice to match mine. "Maybe it just happened."

"I've heard that already, only difference is Jarret was the suspect in the other theory."

Roland shook his head, disgust written on his face. "Yeah, Sean's theory."

"What about you? Do you have a theory?" I forced myself to lower my voice. Wanting to break his increasingly agitated mood, I got up from the couch and sat beside him on the loveseat. As calm as he had always been, it disturbed me to see him so troubled. Why had Sean's theory bothered him so much, anyway? It was just a theory.

Roland picked up his half-eaten cookie and set it back down. "I don't have a theory. We've been exploring all possibilities, going over the cases again, the pictures, the people you've had contact with lately. Oh—" He turned to me. "I think I know who you meant to meet at the park."

"You do? Who?"

"Her name's Adeline. Over a year ago, she had an abortion. She's eighteen now, and your notes in the computer said she'd make a good witness, but you've been unable to contact her."

"What makes you think I was going to meet her on Amnesia Friday?"

"Remember your notepad? Her name was on it. Her name and nothing else, as if it were a last-minute note."

"Oh." I vaguely remembered a notepad with a name on it. It sat on the edge of my desk and I'd moved it because I thought it might fall.

"Maybe it's a long shot, but I'm going to check it out. If she was supposed to meet you at the park, maybe she saw something."

"Good idea. We need to find out what park it was."

Roland gave a confident nod. "I'll ask Jarret tonight."

"Yes, let's. I really think a visit to that park will help me regain my memories."

Roland returned to Wright Investigators and I puttered around the house, cleaning, organizing, and counting my blessings. I was about to grab another cookie when a car pulled in the driveway.

I glanced at the clock. I was after five and I hadn't put dinner on!

As I rounded the loveseat, the front door opened and Jarret came in.

"Hi." He gave me a cautious smile, stirring my heart.

I wanted to throw my arms around him and give him a wifely kiss, but I couldn't make myself do it. How did a girl ever break through that apprehension?

"Hi, Jarret." I twisted my arms behind my back. "I'm sorry I lost track of time."

He shook his head as if he didn't understand.

"I don't have dinner on," I said.

"Oh, don't worry. I'll make it. I'll throw something on the grill."

I followed him to the kitchen and leaned on the island counter.

Working methodically, Jarret pulled a pound of ground meat, ketchup, mustard, and eggs from the refrigerator and proceeded to wash his hands. "I'll make hamburger patties." He brought down a bag of breadcrumbs and the salt and pepper shakers from an overhead cupboard.

"You were great today," I said, practically whispering and tingling with awe. "Your talk."

"Yeah?" He gave me a crooked grin.

"Yeah. I'm so amazed." I watched him for a moment, appreciating his smooth moves as he worked. "I—I wish you had told me that we volunteered."

"You wish I—" He froze and narrowed one eye.

Regretting my comment, I put up my hand. "I'm sorry. I know you tried. I wish I had listened to you. I didn't really give you a chance to explain."

A look heavy with emotion colored his face, but it passed as he immersed himself in his work. By the time his hands were entrenched in the mixing bowl, doing the messy job of forming the patties, the phone rang. He didn't look up. It rang again. He gave me a glance.

"My hands are a mess." He held them up. Then he locked gazes with me and the hint of a smile passed his lips, as if in acknowledgment of our newfound trust.

The phone rang again. I slid around the counter island and picked it up.

"Hello?"

"Caitlyn? What a surprise. I full well expected that husband of yours to answer."

"Hi, Mike." I leaned against the counter, near Jarret. He glanced at Mike's name but kept forming patties as if the phone call did not concern him.

"Mind if I speak with him?"

"Jarret can't come to the phone right now. He's... indisposed."

Jarret gave an amused grin, then leaned toward me. At first, I thought I stood in his way, but then I realized what he wanted. He gave me a quick kiss on the cheek, which had the surprising effect of making me feel just like a happily married woman.

"May I give him a message?" I said, smiling from the kiss.

"Sure, Caitlyn. I simply need to know: is Jarret coming to work tomorrow?"

I lowered the phone. "Mike wants to know if you're going to work tomorrow."

"I don't know. What do you think?"

"You'd better go to work." I was half-playing, using an insistent attitude, but I was half serious too. "I haven't been going. How are we going to pay the bills? And with a baby on the way—"

Gaze dropping to my mouth, he leaned to kiss me again.

I turned away playfully, flipping my hair in his face, and put the phone to my ear. "He'll be there, Mike."

"Well, that's good. The boss is none too pleased with his recent attendance. And besides, I understand Jarret found his camera. He needs to bring it to work. There are some pictures on there that I need, uh, *we* need to complete our assignments here."

"Okay. I'll tell him."

"Make sure he brings it."

"Okay." Eyes on Jarret, my husband, I hung up the phone and leaned in for a kiss.

# Chapter 36

LYING IN BED on my left side, I stared at the bedroom door. Roland had come back over and stayed late, sharing his theories and making suggestions for our next course of action. Words from our conversations rolled around my head like clothes in a laundromat dryer. I closed my eyes and tried to shut off my thoughts.

My knees pressed against each other, bone to bone. I flipped onto my other side and stuffed part of the blanket between my knees. *No good.* Now my hipbone dug into my skin. I shifted my weight. *No use.* I rolled partially onto my tummy, but the thought of how my back would ache in the morning gnawed at me. So, I rolled onto my back and gazed at the ceiling, at the strip of blue light that crept into the room through the inch-wide gap between the curtains.

My gaze traveled to the bedroom door. I could barely find comfort in bed. How could Jarret find comfort on the couch? It wasn't fair, really, that he should have to sleep on the couch every night. It wasn't his fault I had amnesia. We could take turns on the couch. I could sleep just as uncomfortably on the couch as I could in bed.

Or... he could sleep in bed with me, the two of us, the way it must have been for almost a year. We were married, after all. I'd seen the marriage license and the wedding albums with my own eyes. No doubts remained. I no longer suspected him of kidnapping and drugging me.

I giggled at the paranoid thoughts I'd once had. Then I

rolled onto my right side, facing the window.

We were married, united in a permanent covenant. He was my husband. I was his wife. I had no right to keep him out of the bedroom.

I threw the blanket back and tiptoed to the window. Pushing the curtain aside, I inhaled a breath of cool night air. The tree by the deck looked like a tall shadow of trembling leaves, black against the royal-blue night sky. Above it shone a few points of light from distant stars.

Did I love Jarret? He wasn't at all the man I had at first assumed he was. Yes, I loved him. It felt like a new love, though. If only I could remember our marriage, or at least a moment or two of the wedding, an exchange of vows, the bouquet toss, the chicken dance... How would I ever fully resume my role as wife?

A wife shouldn't keep herself from her husband. I no longer belonged to myself but to him. Isn't that what it said in the Bible? And he belonged to me.

I wanted to make him happy and to make our marriage a good one, a fruitful one. I liked the idea of children. In fact, I wanted a houseful of them. My hand and my gaze dropped to my slightly rounded belly. Why should the thought of nuptial love make me nervous? I had obviously done this before.

Jarret wasn't unattractive. My false opinion of him had blinded me to his appearance. I'd only seen the person he used to be, the person I assumed he was still. In reality, Jarret was handsome, once you got past the sneer. And his body, the way he worked out... Other girls saw it. They probably considered me lucky to have him. Now that I knew him better... I *was* lucky, or rather *blessed,* to have him. But to give myself completely to him...

I sighed and let the curtain fall. If I could only remember our wedding.

My memories might never return, but we were married. I would have to start acting like his wife sooner or later. I turned toward the door, inhaled deeply, and forced the air out, cementing my decision.

It took an entire minute to cross the room, but then I flung the bedroom door open and it banged against the doorstop.

Jarret popped up from where he lay on the couch. He grabbed the remote and muted the TV. “Hey, you okay?” His ponytail hung loose and low as if the band had nearly come out.

“Okay? Oh. Yes, I’m fine.” I leaned against the doorframe, attempting to appear relaxed.

He got up from the couch, concern in his eyes. He wore the same white shirt, un-tucked now, and the chino pants he’d worn all day. “You got a headache or something?”

“A headache? No.”

“TV too loud?”

I glanced at the muted TV, then at him as he slowly approached. He came to stand, as had been his habit lately, about five feet from me.

“Did you...” Hope flickered in his eyes. “... remember something?”

Glancing at my feet, I spoke softly, almost whispered. “No, I wish I had.”

“So...” He let his mouth and his sentence hang.

“Well, I thought...” How should I say it? Maybe I should’ve just sat next to him on the couch for a while, but he was up now, standing there, staring, waiting for an explanation. Once I went to the bedroom for the night, I never came back out. Of course, he was worried. “I thought you might, um, want to sleep in our bed?”

He gave me the hint of a smile, kindness in his eyes. “I don’t mind sleeping on the couch.” He paused. “I’m not letting you sleep on the couch.”

“Well, I didn’t mean to.”

It took a few seconds for my words to appear to register in his mind. He opened his mouth to speak, shut it, gave the dark bedroom a glance, and then, with his eyes locked on mine, closed the distance between us.

I didn't regret inviting him, but my heartbeat quickened with every step he took.

He moved into my personal space, pushed a tangle of hair from my face, and rubbed his fingertips down my cheek. "Are you sure?"

My heart fluttered at his touch. I breathed and nodded. "We *are* married," I wanted to say but found myself unable to speak.

With his gaze connected to mine, he took my left hand, brought it up to his mouth, and kissed my wedding band. Then he turned my hand over and kissed my palm once, twice, three times. After each kiss, he met my gaze as if getting my permission to go on. What look my eyes held, I had no clue, but each kiss made me dizzier than the first.

When he finally brought his mouth near mine, he stopped before our lips touched. What was he waiting for? Did he doubt that I wanted this? That I wanted him? Or did he want me to make the first move? My lips burned for his, but he seemed unable to draw nearer.

So, I did it. I made the move, pressed my mouth to his, and kissed him with a passion I didn't realize I had.

He took my hands and played with them, caressing them as we kissed. Then he withdrew and gave me another searching gaze.

I wanted to smile to let him know it was okay to go on, but I only panted for air and tried keep the world from spinning out of control.

His next kiss came soft and short, then another like it. As he kissed me this way, he brought my hands to a button on his shirt and left them there.

Did he want me to take off his shirt? Could I manage it? I fumbled with a button before it finally slipped through the buttonhole. As he continued to kiss me playfully, and my lightheadedness increased, I went to the next button and the next.

At the fourth button, he pushed his hands into my hair.

Then he stroked my collarbone and my neck up to my chin. He probably meant to please me with gentle caressing… but the feel of his hand against my neck sent a dread chill through me.

I froze.

He pulled back, his gaze shooting to mine then dropping to my hands motionless on the fourth button of his shirt. He inhaled deeply, exhaled a trembling breath through his mouth, took my hands into his again, and kissed me on the top of the head. Then he backed away.

"I love you, Caitlyn." He released my hands. "I can wait. I just want you to..." He didn't finish his sentence but I knew what the rest would be. *Love me.* He turned away.

I wanted to say something—to apologize or tell him that I did love him—but I only watched him return to the couch.

His hairband must've fallen out when we embraced. His hair hung free. So dark and so long for a guy. How it had swung about his face when he and Roland had fought. It so resembled the hair of my attacker, if my memory served me right.

I slunk back into the darkness of the bedroom before he had a chance to settle on the couch and turn my way.

Leaving the door ajar, I took a few steps toward the bed, but I couldn't get myself to lie down. Still dazed, I touched my neck. The feeling had come with such strength at his touch. My attacker, he had touched my neck roughly. Something of the fear of that moment returned to me, turning my blood to ice.

Trembling, I crawled under the covers and tucked the blankets under my chin. Jarret had kissed me so sweetly, but I had felt such passion.

*Passion.*

*Jarret stood inches away, confusion and hurt in his eyes. The desire to kiss him overpowered me, the desire to be safe in his arms. I flung my arms around his neck and pulled him close. His kiss sent a thrill through me that merged with the pain in my head, resulting in a dizzying effect.*

I gasped at the memory. When had that happened? I remembered it clearly! Closing my eyes, I tried to recall more. Perhaps all the memories would return if I concentrated.

*I stumbled into the bathroom. The glowing nightlight reflected in the mirror. I pushed my weight against the bathroom door to close it. Jarret tried to block it but made no real effort. With a good shove, it clicked shut. He shouted something, his voice loud and angry, though muffled through the door.* What did he say? *Water blasted from the faucet. I splashed it on my face. Cool, soothing. Leaning over, my head reeled and the pain increased.*

The rest of the memory came in pieces. It was mostly Jarret's anger that I remembered. He had grabbed my wrist and glared down his nose at me.

*"You got something you wanna tell me?"*

*I twisted my wrist from him.* What was his problem? *"If I did, I would've told you."*

*"You cheatin' on me?"*

Did he just say— *I glared. "You don't really think that?"*

*"I don't want to. But why won't you tell me?"*

Breathing hard, trembling, I sat up. When had this happened? At that time, I couldn't think clearly, but the memory itself... it was clear. It had to be real. It had to have happened to me.

I slipped from bed and retraced my steps to the dresser, to where Jarret had stood. Was this the night I'd lost my memory? What had happened before? What happened after? Why was he so angry?

Before I reached the dresser, a memory of darkness filled my mind.

*A strange humming sound rang in my head, so loud it hurt. Not in my head. Outside me. Surrounding me. I knew the sound. The sound of crickets and night bugs. I opened my eyes and blinked a few times to make sure they were really open.*

*Darkness surrounded me. The odor of dirt and decaying leaves permeated the air. I shivered from the coolness of the night. My head throbbed with pain. Cold and grit pressed against my cheek. Rocks poked into my legs and hip.*

*Unable to see, I reached out with both hands and swung at the air. I hit something hard and cold. A rock on my left, a big rock. I gripped the boulder and pulled myself up. It stood nearly as tall as I did.*

*Where was I? What happened to me? How did I get outside? My heartbeat quickened and my breaths came hard. Panicking would get me nowhere.* Calm down!

*Clinging to the boulder, I forced myself to take slow, deep breaths. My heart rate slowed and my breathing calmed. I heard other sounds, distant ones. Every few minutes came the faint rumble of a semi-truck driving over an open road. It came from my left. I would go that way.* Get out of the woods.

*Reaching into darkness, I stumbled along at a slow pace, tripping on roots and getting my legs tangled in vines and weeds. Moonlight shone through the canopy of leaves here and there, revealing outlines of trees and bushes and occasionally reaching to the ground. Too often, I walked with no hint of light. Darkness. Indistinct shapes. The sounds of the road grew louder; I was headed in the right direction.* Keep going. *I would soon get back to civilization and find my way home.*

*My mind tingled, grew numb.* Get out of the woods. Get out of the woods. *Finally, the trees parted and a road lay before me. How long had I been walking? My head hurt. I needed to lie down.*

# Chapter 37

THE BIRDS' SWEET songs traveled through the open window, inviting me to wake. I stretched and rolled toward the window, a beam of sunlight finding me. I opened my eyes, squinting. The left side of the curtain hung open a bit. I hadn't bothered pulling it closed after standing at the window last night.

I pushed myself up, sitting out of the sun's reach. I yawned and stretched again. A tempting aroma wafted on the air, making my stomach growl, but my body ached and sleepiness clung to me. I hadn't slept well. I couldn't find a comfortable position and strange dreams had haunted me all night.

My eyes popped open wide. No, not dreams. Flashbacks. I hadn't been able to shut my mind off to the disturbing flashbacks. Even now, I remembered the night sounds and the distress of wandering in the dark. I shook my head, not wanting to think about it again.

Folding my hands and bowing my head, I turned my thoughts to God. I offered my day to Him, come what may. And I asked for His strength and wisdom. The memories made no sense and I wanted to interpret them correctly, rather than jump to conclusions. I'd misjudged Jarret terribly so far. I wouldn't do it again.

My stomach growled, turning my thoughts to my baby.

"Okay, I hear you." I stumbled out of bed. After washing up, I pulled my bathrobe on over my nightgown and opened the bedroom door. I was dying to know what Jarret had made for breakfast.

On my way through the living room, something caught my eye. The old box of files and slides from Jarret's work sat on the coffee table, closed with the flaps tucked one under the other, Jarret's camera and keys sitting on top. He must've finished organizing the contents and planned to take it back to work. I turned my attention to the kitchen.

Jarret didn't see me coming or he probably wouldn't have cussed over his mishap at the stove. He jumped back as a flame leaped from the skillet. Then he snatched an oven mitt and swung the flaming skillet from the stove. The flames died quickly. He slid the skillet back onto the stove, still unaware of me, and leaned over a cookbook, mumbling to himself. He was dressed for work, already, wearing blue work pants and a burgundy button-front shirt, his hair in a neat ponytail.

"Smells delicious." I rested my arms on the countertop to watch him work.

"Oh, hey, you're up." He glanced then did a double-take at my robe. "It'll be done in a minute. It's, uh, apple crepe."

"Wow. That's impressive. And you said you couldn't cook."

He gave a sly grin. "You better try it before you think too highly of me." He stirred the simmering apple mixture in the skillet. "You going to work today?"

"I don't think so. I'm just going to hang around the house, work from home. I want to call Melinda, that girl I met at the park."

"Yeah, you and Sean." He dumped the apple mixture into six crepes in a crude but successful manner.

I nodded, refusing to acknowledge his jealous tone. "Melinda would make a great witness if she wouldn't mind telling her parents. Because of her age, we would need their permission."

He filled the last crepe and dropped the skillet into the sink.

"Mainly, I want to focus on getting my memories back.

Roland's going up to Wright. Maybe being alone here, relaxed, thinking about it, and going over the few memories and impressions that I have..." I shrugged, pushing back discomfort from last night's memory. "I don't know. It's worth a try. And I have other phone calls to make."

That made him look, but he just as quickly turned away, as if he had made a personal commitment not to interfere with the way I chose to handle things. He folded the crepes, sprinkled them with a crumbly streusel topping, and put two on each plate. Plates in hand, he skirted around the end of the counter. "I thought we could eat out on the deck." He nodded for me to go first.

"Oh, that sounds nice." As I squeezed past the big table, my gaze fell on a romantic scene of purple, lilac, and white on the deck.

A white tablecloth covered the patio table, swelling with a breeze. In the middle of the table stood a tall vase of lilacs and a short crystal vase of violets. Glasses of milk, coffee cups, utensils, and napkins were all in place. A dark green umbrella hovered above all, casting a shadow on the chair that missed the shade from the tree.

"Oh, wow, Jarret." Heart tingling, I pulled out a chair and inhaled the fragrance of the lilacs.

He set the plates down then jerked his face toward the house. "Oh, wait!" He dashed inside, mumbling, "I forgot... I need to get..."

The crepes, the flowers, the umbrella... everything so picturesque. I felt a bit out of place in my nightgown and bathrobe. Maybe I could throw on a dress before he—

Jarret hurried out onto the deck, slowed his pace, and sat in the chair across from me.

"You didn't try it." He reached toward the vase of lilacs, but his eyes were on my plate, disappointment on his brow.

"I was waiting for you. Everything is so lovely. What did you forget?"

"You'll see." He raised an eyebrow, then bowed his head

and made the Sign of the Cross.

Together we prayed the traditional grace before meals, the same prayer I'd prayed every day of my life, before every meal with family, friends, and even alone. I prayed with my husband. *He prayed.* The godly husband I'd hoped to marry.

Overwhelmed with thankfulness, I lifted my fork and smiled at the sky. The sun peeked through the leaves and sent hazy beams to the dew-laden grass. "You must've gotten up awfully early."

"Yeah, gotta get to work on time. Before they decide to fire me. But I wanted to, uh..." Fork in hand, he stared at his plate but made no move to eat. He glanced. "I—I wanted to tell you how we got engaged."

My heart did a somersault. "I'd like to hear that."

"Okay, but try the crepes." He cut his own crepe and took a bite, watching me.

Trying hard to eat like a lady, I slid a forkful into my watering mouth. My taste buds went wild over a sweet, savory taste with a hint of tang. "Oh my, these are delicious."

His crooked smile said he liked my response.

We both took a second bite before he began our story. "Didja know about my trip to South America and the opal mine?"

I nodded, chewing, unwilling to speak with food in my mouth.

"Well, while I was there I called you—"

"I thought..." I swallowed. "...we weren't talking."

"Yeah, we weren't. But I needed to hear your voice." His glance made him look vulnerable. "So I called the house. You answered but I, uh, I didn't say anything."

I put on a pretend angry face. "How rude."

He smiled and shrugged a shoulder. "You kept talking into the phone, thinking whoever-it-was could hear you and trying to get whoever-it-was to call back, as if we had a bad connection. After we hung up, my cell phone rang. It was you. You asked if I called, then told me you couldn't hear me. I told you I didn't say anything. So that made you mad, and I thought you were gonna hang up on me. But then..." His nonchalant manner faded with the flicker of his eyes. "I confessed needing to hear your voice, so you stayed on the line. We talked awhile. I told you about the work I was doing in Brazil, how muggy and buggy and uncomfortable it was there. Felt like I wore wet clothes all day long."

While he retold our conversation and toyed with his food, I finished my first crepe and cut into the next.

As his story wound down, he leaned forward. "Anyway, we talked till my battery ran dead. And we agreed to see each other when I returned home."

"I thought I didn't want to go out with you." Finishing my second crepe, I set my fork on the empty plate.

He took my plate. "That's what you *said*. But that's not what you *wanted*." He gave me a crooked grin and went inside, returning with the last two crepes on my plate. "You said..." He still grinned. "...you really liked me, but you were afraid of your feelings. They were too strong. And you didn't want to do anything wrong."

"I did not." My face warmed.

"Yes, you did. So, we agreed to some rules, like, we wouldn't kiss unless someone was around. So, while you lived at my house, we spent an awful lot of time around my father."

I felt the blood rushing to my face, knowing that I'd turned beet red. "You mean, so we could kiss?"

"Yeah." Eyes narrowing with a defensive look, he folded and unfolded his arms. "Hey, it wasn't all physical, and our kisses were sweet, innocent. What we had was good, really good. You were good. You made me want to be good." He shook his head. "Within a couple of weeks, I couldn't think of anything else but making you my wife. So I had an engagement ring made with an opal I'd brought back from the mine."

I gazed at the ring as he spoke. Two glittery diamonds flanked an oval opal that sparkled with blue, orange, and pink.

"I figured that's where the opal came from when I learned about the mine."

"I carried the ring around with me for days, afraid to ask you."

"You... afraid?" His confident air all through high school and even while giving his talk to hundreds of high school kids made it hard to imagine.

"Well, your parents had, uh, reservations about me." He shifted in his seat, pushed his crepe around with his fork, and gave me fleeting glances. "Some of your friends... Well, you can imagine their reaction to us being a couple. And we'd only been seeing each other for a short time, and you hadn't ever told me you loved me."

"Did you tell me?"

"No. Well, yes, when I called from Brazil, I told you I thought I was falling in love with you. And, of course, I told you when I proposed."

"Tell me about that." A longing struck my heart. Of all the memories I'd lost, I would love to have at least this one returned to me.

"Okay." He set his fork down and leaned forward, resting his arms on the table. "I meant to propose over dinner in a fancy restaurant. But I didn't. I didn't want you to be uncomfortable with all the people around, especially if you wanted to say *no*. So we just ate and talked. You kept asking if something was wrong." He smiled at his plate. "Next day, we took a walk in the woods behind my house, and I almost asked you then, but... I don't know why I didn't.

"A couple days later, we were at your family's house, and your father had a little talk with me. Maybe he knew we were getting serious, I was getting serious. He asked me all these questions about my plans for the future. I realized I couldn't answer him, because I needed to know if you were gonna be in it with me. So I tore you away from a board game with your sisters and took you for a walk."

Jarret reached toward the vase of lilacs as he spoke and

picked up a little box I hadn't noticed sitting there. "We walked to that playground down the street from your house. Sat on the swings for a few minutes, you swinging and talking, me thinking about how to word my proposal and trying not to freak over the possibility of rejection. Then I got off my swing and stopped yours."

He got up and dropped onto one knee before me.

My fork fell from my hand, a strange sensation washed over me, and my heart threatened to burst from my chest. I saw nothing but love in the deep brown eyes looking up at me.

"Caitlyn, I love you, and I want to spend the rest of my life with you, have a family with you. You make me want to be better than I am. And I know I can make you happy. I want you to be my wife."

I opened my mouth to speak but my breath caught in my throat.

He smiled with his eyes as if my reaction pleased him. "So, that's what I said."

I breathed. He was only retelling how it went. He wasn't actually proposing. *Calm down.*

"Oh," I whispered, wishing I could think of a better response but unable to think of anything except how sweaty my palms had become and how violently my heart was beating in my chest.

He took my hand and pushed a little black box into it. Then he lifted the lid. Diamond earrings with opal drops rested on black velvet inside the box.

"I love you more today than when I married you," he said. "And I want you to remember our wedding. Maybe we can start over. Marry me. Again."

My gaze flitted back and forth from his eyes to the earrings. *Did he just propose?*

"I was gonna give you those for our anniversary. You already have an engagement ring. What would you do with two? So, I thought those could be engagement earrings, or whatever. You used to wear the necklace I gave you. It matches too."

I touched my neck. "I'd like to see it. These are beautiful."

"So..." His gaze intensified. "What's it gonna be?"

Emotion formed a lump in my throat, making it difficult to speak. "We're already married. How can we marry again?"

"Father Zac, the priest at our church, said we could, well, renew our vows, anyway." He knelt on both knees and his gaze dropped to the earrings. Was he trying to avoid eye contact? "What I really want you to think about is—and you don't have to answer me now but—do you *want* to marry me? You know you *are* my wife, but do you *want* to be? If you do, I thought it'd be nice for you to have a wedding you could remember. What if you never—"

"I will, Jarret. I'll get my memory back." I set the box on the table and took his hands, his eyes rising to mine. "I get bits and pieces every day. Sometimes it's just a bit of knowledge or a feeling but..." I slid off the chair and knelt with him.

He gave me a funny look and his mouth fell open.

My heart overflowed with emotion. Words came together in my mind and left my lips without my thinking about it. "I love you, Jarret. I'm starting to see who you really are. I realize I've misjudged you and I'm sorry. I guess I've been seeing you for your past mistakes and not for the man you've become."

Squeezing my hands, he smiled and pressed a kiss to my forehead. "Do you realize you did this the first time I proposed?"

"What?"

"When I asked you the first time, you slid off your swing and dropped to your knees with me. Then you told me 'yes' and said you thought God brought us together."

I'd done this before! A joyful laugh escaped me. I wrapped my arms around his neck and pressed my cheek to his. His arms slid around my waist, pulling me close. "I do think God brought us together," I whispered.

"So, is that a *yes* or do you want to think about it?" His

voice, a warm rumble in my ear, stirred me deep inside.

# Chapter 38

RUNNING OUT OF places to search, I rifled through my underwear drawer. Beneath everything, I found several prayer cards, a birthday card from my parents, and a little plastic bottle of holy water from Lourdes.

*Not there.*

I had already checked the jewelry box, which held mostly Jarret's jewelry, and the bathroom drawers and the bookshelf in the living room. Where could I have put my opal necklace? How could I have been so careless with it? Didn't he say I wore it all the time? Maybe my purse!

I dashed to the closet and grabbed the first purse. Empty. I tossed it to the floor. The next one? Empty. Next? Empty. Next— I tossed each empty purse to the floor. Why did I have so many purses anyway? The last one I checked had my wallet, lip balm, comb, an empty granola bar box, and— Oh! The spy pen. *Oops.* I had forgotten to return it. Hands on my hips and totally frustrated, I sighed and made a quick prayer to St. Anthony. Maybe I should've asked him first.

Trusting it would turn up, I took the spy pen and stomped to the table to get back to work. I liked the way Jarret had taken full advantage of the table the other day, spreading out all his papers and slides to organize them. So I decided to do the same thing. I drew pictures for visual reminders, laid out photos of witnesses and contacts, and arranged pages of notes. I then made new lists to help organize the facts concerning Amnesia Friday or anything remotely related.

My memories had begun to return, and I was certain more would follow if only I could find the right triggers.

I decided upon the most reasonable way to start my search: determine potential motives. I ripped a sheet of yellow notepaper from a pad and wrote the word "REVENGE" at the top. Then I scribbled down everything that came to mind for that motive and set the sheet in the center of the table. I wrote the next motive on another sheet, continuing the process until I'd written every possible motive I could imagine for an act of violence against me. With one hand on a hip and the other on my chin, I studied the motive sheets.

*<u>Motives</u>*

*JEALOUSY - Sean likes me and seems unable to take "no" for an answer. Jarret hates Sean, learned about the kiss, and maybe saw us at the office after hours. Has a pattern of drinking when faced with "setbacks." (I had written that note thinking of the emails and of last Friday when he had thrown Roland out.)*

*REVENGE - who has suffered from my work on a case? Arthur Jordan: man involved in fraudulent worker compensation claim, or family member of Arthur Jordan who suffers from his jail sentence. (My photos and evidence had formed the key proof against him.)*

*RAPE - no, thank God, no. (I was fairly certain I had not been violated.)*

*MUGGING - not likely since car and purse untouched. Note: Camera, cell phone, and keys still missing.*

*INCRIMINATING PICTURE ON CAMERA - Tamara Eber, underage girl in the bar. Tamara's boyfriend. One of the men involved with illegal drugs at 1419 Danbury. Gary Nicolan, the embezzler. Adeline's boyfriend? Was he there that night at the park? Was he worried I had taken or was about to take a picture?*

As I reviewed the possible motives, Sean's theory came to mind. With reluctance, I considered it. Jarret had admitted feeling responsible because of his anger toward me, but he hadn't mentioned going to the park. What if he'd been drunk and couldn't remember?

I shook my head. It didn't seem possible. Of course, if my cell phone and camera were found at the park, wouldn't it rule out the MUGGING and INCRIMINATING PICTURE motives? But it would leave as possibilities the REVENGE and JEALOUSY motives.

We had to go to the park.

Something else came to mind, so I jotted it down on a clean sheet of paper and set it with the motives. *Question: Why is Victor so against our work on the abortion case?*

I placed lists around the motives, along with transcripts of interviews and pictures that might've been related. I made a section on the table for recent witnesses and contacts, with pictures if I had them, and another section for the pictures that were on my camera Friday.

I grabbed a fresh sheet of notepaper and a pen, deciding to write out the events as they may have happened that day, based on what people told me and on my bits of memories. I titled it "Amnesia Friday."

> *Morning - before work, Jarret took my camera by accident. At work, I contemplated telling Jarret about the kiss and was edgy all morning. Sean noticed.*
>
> *Noon - Assuming we had switched cameras, Jarret came up to Wright Investigators to trade cameras. He had mine. I didn't have his. His was in the old box. I told Jarret about the kiss. Jarret got angry. Sean saw me in Jarret's car. Anyone else see?*
>
> *Afternoon - annoyed at Sean. Went to print pictures with Sean.*
>
> *Five o'clock - everyone left work except Sean and me. Sean*

*wanted to talk, wanted to know why I was upset, ended up confessing his love. I rejected him. Victor saw our cars. Anyone else see?*

*Six o'clock - Adeline called? I went to meet her at the park? Which park? Why? Probably to get her story and make her a witness. Did anyone follow? Who else was there? Roland will soon know more.*

*At the park - MEMORY: getting out of my car, I saw a man in a disguise, got scared, and ran into woods. Can't be Sean. No time to get a wig? Can't be Jarret. He wouldn't disguise himself, would he? Maybe the image is mixed up, the way Mike said it might happen.*

I set the pen down but picked it up again. What about the new memories? Those would've had to happen later, after the incident. I scratched the memories down on a separate paper, which I placed near Amnesia Friday.

Tapping my lip with the pen, I gazed at the spread of pictures and notes. What was I missing?

A knock sounded on the front door. *Roland!*

I tossed my notebook over the 'Jealousy' motive and went to the door. Roland wouldn't like to see Jarret's name there. Besides, I had ruled out jealousy as a motive. Neither Jarret nor Sean seemed capable of violence against me. I might as well crumple up that page and throw it in the garbage.

The knock came again, the instant before I opened the door. Roland lowered his fist and smiled. "Hi. Am I too early?"

I laughed. "Isn't it after ten? How lazy do you think I am?" I held the door while he came in, then I closed it behind him. "I'm glad to see you." I hugged him. "Are you hungry? Want something to drink?"

"No." His gaze snapped to the table and his body, as if drawn by a magnet, moved toward it. "What're you up to?"

I followed, trying to think if I'd written other notes I wouldn't want him to see. "I've been sorting through my notes, trying to piece things together. What'd you find out about Adeline? Were you right? Did we have an appointment?"

He nodded and stopped by the table, his eyes roaming, taking it all in. "Adeline said you tried to contact her the week before, but she hadn't wanted to think about the abortion. She finally decided to call back Friday about ten to six. You agreed to meet her at the park. She waited for you for an hour, she said. Then she tried to call the office again, but no one answered. After that, she just put it out of her mind, until I called."

"Wow. Did she see anything suspicious?"

"No." Roland touched a paper on the table. *Which one?* He turned it so he could read it.

I came up beside him and glimpsed the paper. *Oh.* I gulped. He was reading the description of my new memories. My hand nearly shot out. I wanted to snatch the paper and flip it over. Instead, I folded my arms across my chest. I wanted his help.

"Adeline saw nothing out of the ordinary," Roland said, squinting at the note. "And she'd come alone, too. But the pavilion you agreed to meet at doesn't have a view of the parking areas, so—"

"What's this?" He lifted the paper and turned his gray eyes to me.

"Oh, that." My face burned, knowing the personal details he'd just read. I forced a smile, trying not to look freaked out, and then I snatched the paper from him. "I gained more memories."

"About Jarret?"

I nodded.

"About Friday?"

I nodded again. "I don't think they came to me in order, but my head hurt in all of them, so I believe they occurred after the incident. They're kind of confusing." I stared at my notes as if I needed them to remember, but the memories were as fresh as when they had first flooded my mind. I returned the note to its place on the table and said without emotion, "I was kissing Jarret in one of them, arguing with him in another, and wandering alone through the dark woods in the last one."

"Hmm. Yeah, that sounds mixed up. I'd think you'd be kissing after the argument, uh, making up."

I giggled.

Blushing, he turned his gaze to the table.

"If I try to fit them together with the first memory, I'd say, I ran into the woods, something happened where I hit my head and maybe passed out, then I woke up in the dark and stumbled through the woods to get home."

"Right. And when you got home, you argued with Jarret over something. What do you remember about the argument?"

I didn't want to say. It didn't look good for either of us. "Oh, um, well, he asked if I was cheating on him."

Roland shot a glare, opened and closed his mouth, looked away. "That had to be a bad argument."

"I think it was. But I do remember kissing him, so obviously..."

"Unless the kiss was from some other time."

"I don't think so. My head hurt in all the memories, and I remember standing in the bedroom by the bathroom when we argued and when we kissed."

He reached for the notepad in the middle of the table.

Not wanting him to see the note under it, I grabbed his hand and turned him to face me. "Jarret proposed to me!" I knew my eyes were wide and crazy, but I couldn't control it.

"What?" Roland said. "You're already his wife."

"I know. But isn't he sweet? He wants me to have a wedding I remember. I think he did it because last night I—" No, that wasn't something I should share. "Well, he said he wants me to think about my feelings for him, for us. I guess he wants to know if I would do it all over again."

"So, what'd you tell him?" Roland's expression and the slant of his brows betrayed a combination of amusement and worry.

"I didn't answer." I played with my engagement ring, recalling the somewhat dejected look in Jarret's eyes, but I'd had a few things I still needed to sort out.

# Chapter 39

I SAT IN the front passenger seat of my car, watching Jarret drive. His face was as emotionless and still as a stone statue. He wore his hair in a ponytail, the black sunglasses I had picked up at the store last week, and a white Armani pullover shirt with a thick gray stripe across the chest and down one side—but that shouldn't matter. It should still work.

The setting sun sent beams of light through the trees, making a strobe-light effect as we passed by. Patches of sunlight fell on the new blacktop road. The winding road, which resembled a great mottled serpent, took us deeper and deeper into the woods.

"Where would you have parked?" Roland slid forward in the backseat and rested his arm on the back of my seat. Wind from Jarret's open window made Roland's dark hair dance on his forehead and drew attention to the investigative squint of his eyes. The inner workings of his newly-trained detective's mind showed through pupils surrounded by steel gray irises.

"There're three or four parking areas," Jarret said before I got a chance to shrug my shoulders.

While I loved parks and walking in the woods, I didn't remember this park at all. North Carolina's woods seemed different, lighter and thinner than the forests of South Dakota. Nothing looked familiar.

Jarret glanced over his shoulder at his brother. "She would've parked in the back one."

"What makes you think that?"

Jarret's eyes narrowed as he made a second over-the-shoulder glance. "She's my wife."

"Well—"

"Whenever *we* met here, that's where we parked. We never parked anywhere else. And if she was meeting that girl here, she probably told her to meet at the back pavilion. It's the nicest one."

Roland nodded but didn't look convinced.

We parked in the back lot at the end of a row of a dozen parking spots that butted up to the woods. One other car sat on the opposite end, its driver and a yellow lab staring out the windows. Across the road, sat an empty playground. The quiet swings, slides, and sprawling tan climbing structure were probably crawling with children an hour ago, parents watching from the surrounding benches. The sign at the park entrance informed that the "park closes at dusk," which explained the lack of people and why no one had reported suspicious behavior that night.

"You left work around six, right?" Roland cracked open his door.

"I think so," I said. "You're thinking this is the time I would've been here that Friday."

He nodded before getting out of the car.

Jarret stood next to the driver's side, scanning the area, hands on hips and sunglasses folded and stuck in the collar of his shirt.

As I walked to him around the front of the car, a familiar but uncomfortable feeling washed through me, and goose bumps broke out on my skin.

"Where's the pavilion?" Roland came up behind us.

"You can't see it from here." Jarret pointed. "It's back that-a way. There's a short path."

"Jarret..." Standing before him, I hesitated to ask my question. I'd heard that the best way to regain a memory was to try to recreate the incident. "Would you let down your hair?"

A faint grin flickered on his face as if he thought I was

flirting. He glanced at Roland, who turned away.

I pulled the shades from his shirt. "And put these on."

His eyebrows drew together. "Why? The sun's going down." He obediently pulled the band from his hair as he spoke. Then he let me put the glasses over his curious and confused brown eyes.

"Caitlyn." Roland's tone sounded firm, like a parent's warning. He came closer as I ran my fingers through Jarret's hair, arranging the curls around his face. "You don't think—"

I gave him a glance. "No, Roland. I don't think that. I just want to recreate what I remember. He has long dark hair. So—"

"Think what? What're you talking about?" Jarret whisked the hair from his shoulders with one quick sweeping motion, messing up the image I was trying to create. I reached for his hair again, but he grabbed my wrist. "You want to tell me? What're you talking about? Why's my hair down? Why am I wearing sunglasses?"

I wriggled my hand free and touched the front neckline of his shirt. "For the same reason you're going to pull this up over your nose."

He opened his mouth as if to ask but said nothing. Instead, he faced Roland, perhaps thinking he stood a better chance of getting a straight answer from him.

Roland shrugged and shook his head. "Caitlyn, are you going to tell him?"

"Oh, I guess so." I backed up and folded my arms. "I had a memory of, well, I was getting out of my car. And I think you're right. This feels like the spot, maybe the exact spot I parked in." I turned in a circle, scanning the area. "As I got out of the car and closed the door..." I faced him again. "... I saw a man in the side mirror."

Jarret whipped the glasses off, worry or anger flashing in his eyes. "What? Why didn't you tell me? What man?"

I stepped back. "I don't know. He was tall. He wore sunglasses and a handkerchief covered his mouth. And, well, he had long dark hair."

Jarret's expression turned hard. He stepped toward me.

I didn't step back. "His hair covered most of his face."

He glanced at Roland then scowled at me.

"I don't think it was you," I said, defensive. "It's just the memory I have. Mike did say I might get pieces of my memories mixed up, so maybe the image of the man has nothing to do with anything. But it's what I remember."

"Maybe you came here because, because of me, but I didn't hurt you." His fiery eyes burned with hurt and betrayal.

I took his warm, calloused hands into mine, and his expression immediately softened. "I know you didn't. I don't suspect you. I just want to recreate my memory. Maybe I can remember who did hurt me?"

His gaze bounced around, as if he found it hard to look at me, as if I had flat out accused him of attacking me.

"Please?" I touched his cheek and ran my fingers along his stubbly jaw. His gaze became mine. "I think it'll help."

He nodded, gave me a quick kiss, and put the shades back on. I arranged his hair again and had him stand a short distance behind the car.

"I had just climbed out of the car." I opened the driver's side door. "As I closed the door, I saw him in the mirror." I moved the door enough to catch Jarret's reflection. Startled, I gasped.

My attacker's hair hung like a curtain. The bandana hid other features that would've identified him. But it was the black sunglasses, aimed at me, that chilled me to the bone.

"Why didn't you get back in the car?" Jarret said. "If I, uh, if *he* was standing right here—"

"He wasn't standing. He was moving toward me and I had closed the door. I only glimpsed him in the mirror as the door swung shut. The door was closed and locked by the time I sensed danger. I purposely didn't look directly at him. I didn't want him to realize I had seen him. I thought he might rush me."

Roland turned, scanning the area. "So you dashed into the woods?"

Jarret stepped toward me, increasing the uneasiness that prickled my soul. "Yes, I think I did." Since that was how I remembered it happening, I slammed the car door and dashed into the woods.

I tried not to think of Roland's presence, or of Jarret being Jarret. I tried to think of the man in the shades chasing me. The undergrowth of weeds, vines, and prickly plants scraped my bare legs, tried to trip me up, and made running difficult. I had to cut over to the path. The path... Where was the path? Instinctively, I headed to the right. A few yards later, I stumbled out onto a trail.

Branches cracked behind me.

Jarret swore and muttered something. Roland's response was too loud to ignore. "Chill out. She's trying to recreate that night. Just go along with it."

I squelched the desire to laugh and tried to assume a panicky frame of mind.

Their footfalls came fast. They—*he* was gaining on me. I couldn't stay on the path. He'd see me. He'd overtake me in no time.

I peered through the woods, hoping to catch sight of someone, a lingering walker, anyone who hadn't left the park yet, anyone who could help. But it was dusk and the park was closed. There wouldn't be anyone. We were alone.

An impression formed in my mind. A major road ran along the woods a few miles east. I knew the woods. Maybe I could lose him. I couldn't let him see me leave the path.

I risked a glance over my shoulder, then stopped... to laugh.

Jarret and Roland jogged side by side, thirty yards back. Jarret still wore his hair down, but the sunglasses were folded and hanging from the neckline of his shirt again. He shoved Roland. Roland shoved back. They were bickering about something.

"Are you guys going to help?" I folded my arms across my chest. "Or are you just going to bicker like a couple of kids?"

They caught up to me, panting.

"Is there a major road this way?" I pointed east.

Roland looked to Jarret.

"Yeah, I think so," Jarret said. "These woods are pretty big, but I think a road— Yeah, if you were gonna run through the woods to get help... You wouldn't want to head back to the park. It'd be empty so, yeah, you'd probably go that way."

I gave a satisfied grin.

"You remember that?" Jarret said.

"I remember thinking he was gaining on me, going to catch me, if I didn't outsmart him. So I wanted to leave the path and, I guess, sneak to the road."

"It's still pretty far."

"Well, let's go. Let's find a good, sneaky path."

When the path rounded a bend, the three of us left it and pushed into the woods. A group of elm trees with thick trunks grew close together a few yards in. I would've probably headed for them. They would hide me from my pursuer's view. Then I would've angled back, trying to weave from one hiding place to another.

Roland pointed out an overgrown hawthorn bush. The surrounding short bushes and clusters of plants and weeds made it the only choice. We jogged to the hawthorn bush. The sunlight peeked in here and there through the canopy of leaves, but shadows and darkness grew with each passing minute.

From the hawthorn bush, we spotted a cluster of pines. But as we crunched over the needles and cones, we decided it would've been a bad choice. Maybe there was a better hiding place. We stood under the pines, peering into the woods around us, searching for hiding spots.

"Over there." Jarret pointed to an outcropping of rocks.

My heart skipped a beat. I would definitely have run to that if we were still headed in the right direction. I glanced up to find the angle of the sun. Yes, the rocks lay east of the path.

We forged ahead to the rocks, heaviness growing within me.

Jarret walked beside me, his fingers brushing mine a few times, as if he wanted to hold hands. But I made no move to take his hand. I needed to recreate the feelings of that night. I must've felt alone and frightened, running for my life. Had he hidden his face to avoid being identified later? Was it someone I knew?

We reached the outcropping of rocks. I stopped and let Roland and Jarret investigate. At the far end of the outcropping stood the tallest rock, one about four feet high, rectangular in shape, and just the right size to hide someone. The other rocks were lower and flat and stretched out as long as a car.

The outcropping would make good climbing rocks for kids, a good place to make believe. How easily it could become a pirate ship on the ocean, a frontier home in the wilderness, or a temple to some strange god. Or. A good place to stop and see if you're still being followed.

A tingling sensation crawled down my spine. I glanced over my shoulder. He had followed me here. This is where we fought. I had stooped to hide, and he stepped out from behind—

I spun around.

Three trees, joined at the trunk, stood eight feet away. He had been waiting behind them, I'd realized too late. I had crouched to catch my breath behind the rock. A shadow moved. Before I could straighten up, he stepped out from behind the tree.

"Caitlyn, look!" Jarret said, his voice distant.

I gazed at the three trees that had grown into one and in my mind...

*I saw him. A shadow. Not a shadow. My pulse pounded in my ears and throat, hard like a warning drum inside me. Dressed all in black, his face concealed by a handkerchief, sunglasses, and dark hair... He meant to harm me. Screaming would do no good. No one would hear me. We were well inside the woods, though not yet halfway through, by my estimation. I would have to fight him.*

*"What... do you want?" I said, trying to catch my breath. "My purse... is in the car. I have no money."*

*He shook his head.*

*I shouldn't take my eyes off him. He was tall, so much bigger than I was. I would need something for a weapon. I glanced away, my gaze darting to the ground. If I could find a rock or a branch... A fist-sized rock lay at my feet. I stooped. My finger brushed the rock—*

*Hands landed hard on my shoulders, pushing my back against a rock. My feet flew out from under me. Pain shot through me and the air left my lungs.*

*Sitting with my back to the rock, I gasped to breathe. No air would come.* Need to breathe.

*He crouched, hovered over me, leaned one arm against my chest and groped through my jacket. "Where is it?" he whispered in a harsh tone.*

*Overwhelmed with fear, I dragged in a breath of air. I wanted to ask him, "What? What do you want?" but no sound came out.*

*His arm weighed heavy on my chest. His face, now hidden in the darkness of night, hovered inches from mine. Had he removed the glasses?*

*Gaining an ounce of courage, I spat.*

*He drew his hand back as if to slap me, while I forced my body into action and thrust my knee to his groin. He cursed but barely swayed. Then he jerked his hand back again.*

*I turned away, bracing myself. His hand struck the side of my head with a sharp pain. A groan escaped me.*

*He reached for my neck.*

*I shrieked, clawing at his hand. I twisted, turned, tried to wrestle free, but his weight...*

*He pushed me against the hard rock, holding me captive*

*with one arm, searching me with his free hand. "Ahh..." He unzipped my jacket, yanked the camera that hung around my neck, and lessened his grip on me.*

*In an instant, I twisted away and flung myself face first to the ground. Free of him, I groped the ground for the rock—*

*Hands clamped to my arms. He yanked me to my feet.*

*Gripping the rock I had snatched from the ground so tightly my fingers ached, I raised my hand.*

*He saw it. He grabbed my hand and forced the rock toward me.*

*I opened my fingers to let the rock go, but he held it now. It came down fast and with great force.*

*Pain. Pain shot through my head. White light blinded me. Darkness.*

I gasped.

"Caitlyn!"

The memory faded and Jarret stood before me, his features barely visible in the dwindling light. He clutched my shoulders. "What's wrong?"

I shook my head, unwilling to speak of it.

"Hey, look what else I found." Roland crouched by the outcropping. He straightened with a necklace dangling from his hand. "Isn't this Caitlyn's?"

Jarret snatched it from him and stood with his back to me, staring at it. He slowly turned to me, his face twitching all over. "Do you know what happened? Do you... remember?"

I inhaled and nodded. "He caught me here." I pointed to the trees. "He came out from behind there and..."

"And what?" Jarret approached me again. Two sunglasses hung from the neckline of his shirt, one dirty and cracked.

"Those are his." I backed away.

"What happened? What did he do to you?" Jarret locked me in his gaze.

"We found your keys and your phone." Roland broke into the uncomfortable moment. "It's smashed. Deliberately. What else would you have had on you?"

"Let's get out of here. It's getting dark." I took off without waiting for their assent.

Jarret came up behind and snatched my hand.

I gasped and tried to pull away, but he wouldn't let go.

"Wrong way," he said, clinging to me.

I looked around. He was right. The path headed west. But I remembered going the other way. I remembered waking up by the rocks, seeing only darkness, trembling from the cold, my head throbbing with pain. I remembered the sound of distant traffic and staggering in that direction, staggering over roots and through brush, groping my way through the shadows of the night until at long last, I reached the road.

# Chapter 40

I MOVED MECHANICALLY, spreading out my notes and the papers and pictures that had possible connections to Amnesia Friday. My recovered memories left me uneasy and wanting to pore over my notes alone. With Jarret at work, I had the house to myself and the perfect opportunity.

As I laid out the pictures that had come from my camera, my gaze drifted to the patio doors and through them to the white billowing tablecloth and vases of lavender and violet flowers. Jarret's romantic proposal and the wonderfully unexpected talk he gave at the high school now seemed like distant memories that barely related to me. The experience at the park overshadowed everything and weighed on my mind, making it difficult for me to focus on much else.

The flashback had been so vivid, as if I had re-lived the moment. And my attacker... I had not recognized him, yet he seemed familiar. I couldn't help thinking I knew him.

My attacker wanted my camera. And since we couldn't find it anywhere in the area, he must've been successful. All other motives became irrelevant. I whisked from the display every motive sheet but that one and dropped them into a pile on the floor.

The "JEALOUSY" motive sheet lay on the top of the pile. Did I still feel any lingering suspicion about Jarret? Every troubling assumption I'd made about him had turned out to be wrong. I knew the real Jarret now, and I liked what I knew.

Something about Friday and him still made me uneasy.

He'd admitted worrying that he was responsible for my amnesia. The memory of our argument came to mind. Could he have been drunk and not able to remember the night any more than I could?

No. My attacker wanted the camera. What would Jarret want with it? He'd had it earlier that day and gave it back. My attacker had something to fear in one of the pictures on my camera.

I rearranged the pictures on the table, knowing I would have to dig deeper into the cases related to them. It was lucky that Sean and I had prints made that afternoon. The attacker wouldn't have known that, but wait... Had I taken another picture after that? Without my memory, I had no way of knowing.

After a quick review of Amnesia Friday, the outline of how I assumed Friday went, I jotted down the note: *Someone wanted my camera and followed me from work to the park.*

I looked at the pen in my hand and smiled at my absent-mindedness. I would have to return the spy pen to Wright Investigators before someone missed it.

Maybe I would ask Victor again if he noticed any other cars in the parking lot or across the street. I glanced at the note with his name on it. *Why is Victor so against the abortion case?* Should I keep the note? Yes, I'd keep the reminder until I understood his agitation. It might have nothing to do with Friday, but still...

I flipped open the file labeled "A-Z Women's Choice Clinic" and arranged pictures of witnesses and contacts, pairing them with transcripts of interviews. Maybe after making some tea, I would sit down and skim the transcripts.

Melinda had given us good information. We would need to convince her to talk to her parents and get permission to use her testimony in the case. Would I find anything useful in the testimonies, anything that could help me piece Friday together?

I sighed and got up to make tea. The memories I'd gained

gave me a good picture of Friday, unfortunately without getting any closer to knowing who attacked me or why. The memories of kissing Jarret and arguing with him must have occurred after the attack. Had he really thought I was cheating on him?

I set a pan of water on the range and turned on the flame, as a knock sounded on the front door.

My heart skipped a beat. I had told Roland to come by after lunch because I wanted to work alone. He and Sean planned to go over the pictures on Jarret's camera this morning anyway. Maybe he had found something.

I sprinted to the door and yanked it open.

Mike stood on the porch, dressed in a tweed sport coat and jeans, arms behind his back and head down, possibly staring at the smudge of dirt on his brown designer shoes. His shiny black Mercedes sat in the driveway.

He lifted his head and gave me a broad smile as he peeled black sunglasses from his face. "Well, hello there, young lady."

I shuddered, perhaps at the sight of the sunglasses. The image of my attacker still lingered in my mind. "Mike. Hi. What're you doing here?"

He swung his little black doctor bag around from behind his back. "I was in the neighborhood." He dragged his arm across his forehead and exhaled through his mouth, as if the mild seventy-six-degree day was unbearably hot. "Mind if I come in?"

I should've used the peephole. I did not like the idea of being interrupted, much less of having *him* in the house... alone. Clutching the half-open door, I glanced at my outfit—a comfy knitted skirt and over-sized t-shirt—then squinted at the tinted windows of his Mercedes. "Is Jarret with you?"

"With me? Why, no. Didn't he call you?"

"Call me? No." The phone hadn't rung all morning.

"Oh, well, we've been so busy, what with the move and the deadlines and the time he's missed. We're all behind. Especially Jarret. I guess he forgot to call but, well, why don't

I come in and we can talk about why I'm here?"

I hesitated. "Um, well, the house is a mess and I'm in the middle of something. Give me a second and I'll give Jarret a quick call?" I swung the door closed.

Like a battering ram, his hand shot out and stopped the door mid-swing.

I jumped at the impact, a little flutter of anxiety rippling through me.

"A quick call?" His pale eyes flashed with a look showing he'd taken it as an insult. "We've been friends for how long? Now you're acting suspicious of me? Do you have a reason for that?"

"I'm not. I'm sorry. It's just that Jarret..." Not sure how to best complete the sentence, I let it hang.

"Yes, that husband of yours is a jealous one." He gave a knowing look. "But he sent me over here, so he must trust me. And it was me he called upon to help you Saturday, was it not?" He waggled his eyebrows and smiled. "But if it'll make you feel better, I'll get him on the phone." He pulled out his cell phone, tapped it a few times, and put the phone to his ear, turning as he waited. "Oh, well now, doesn't that figure." He faced me. "Jarret is on another call. Honestly, he sent me over, so why don't you let me in? We don't want Jarret angry at us, now do we, Catie?"

*Catie?* No one had ever called me that, not even my brothers and sisters when they were too young to pronounce my name. Kay-wyn, they called me. I stepped back as he pushed his way inside.

"I had to drive out your way, anyhow." He strolled to the kitchen, his gaze sweeping through the house. "So I told Jarret I didn't mind stopping." He glanced in the direction of the patio door or at the cluttered table, and then at me. "You alone?"

"Um, yes." I closed the front door and joined him in the kitchen area. "He wanted you to check on me?" Jarret and I had reached a level of trust, so I didn't want to believe this.

He leaned against the counter island, his gaze grazing

over my body before returning to my face. "Not exactly, but how are you doing?"

"I'm fine."

"Your head?" He brought a hand up, touched my hair, and pulled a curl down over my face.

I blew the curl away and stepped back. "Really, I'm fine."

"I don't imagine your memories returned."

"So, why is it you stopped?"

"Right down to business, huh?" He gave a lopsided grin. "Pictures, my dear. I believe you have some pictures on your computer that I need."

"Pictures?"

"It's work related. Jarret took pictures at work and they are no longer on his camera. You don't mind if I sit down at your computer?" Doctor bag in hand, without waiting for the answer, he proceeded to the weight room. "I won't be long."

I followed him into the little room. If he hadn't come to check on me, why the doctor bag?

Mike plopped down and the desk chair sighed. He turned the computer on and swiveled the chair toward the weights.

"I am jealous of Jarret's weight set. But I'll wager he doesn't have time to work out like he used to. My guess is you keep him pretty busy." He grinned and gave me an obvious once-over in a way he wouldn't dare do in Jarret's presence.

I narrowed my eyes and spoke in a cold tone. "I don't really know."

"That's right. Your memory." He continued to stare, nodding slowly, like a doctor thinking over a patient's symptoms. "How are you and Jarret getting along? It must be strange not remembering your husband."

"We're fine." The computer booted up and was ready for him to use, if only he would turn around. I stared at it, hoping he would take the hint, get his stupid pictures, and leave.

"I suppose it could be kind of exciting, sort of like being with a man you're not married to. Since the amnesia, have you and Jarret..." He gave a look as if he assumed I knew what he was talking about, which I probably did, but it disgusted me that he would ask such a personal question.

I folded my arms and exhaled loudly. "Are you really a doctor?"

"What? Why, yes. That's an odd question." He spun to face the computer, grabbed the mouse, and clicked through files.

"A doctor makes good money. Why are you working at an archaeological site?"

He chuckled. "You sound a little suspicious there. Haven't you ever found yourself in a situation you'd rather not be in? Maybe you will find it hard to believe, and I hope you won't share my secret, but I don't really enjoy being a *doc-tor*, listening to a person's gripes, touching rashes and old, wrinkled bodies and looking into various orifices. It was my father who wanted me to become a doctor. Maybe 'want' is not the word, more like 'insisted.' He paid for my education and would tolerate no other vocation. He monitored my grades, arranged my internships... He was a doctor, as was his father before him, and I guess he felt it vitally important for his only son to follow in his footsteps. Why, he even spoke to me of having a son to carry on the tradition."

"What does your father think of you studying archaeology, or doesn't he know?"

He ran his hand over his hair, as if to smooth it back, though it seemed more like a gesture of habit. "Well, my father died a few years ago."

"I'm sorry." A pang of grief over my own father's death struck me, and my heart softened to Mike.

"Yes, well, now I am no longer imprisoned by my father's whims. I am free to pursue my own interests. And my own interest, Caitlyn..." He leaned and I backed up. "I like a little more adventure. So, I returned to college to study archaeology. I guess I pictured myself traveling the world on expeditions." He returned his attention to the computer. "But I've stayed pretty close to home." Mouse in hand, he searched our computer, clicking on various file folders.

"You wouldn't mind getting me a little something to drink, now would you?" He cleared his throat. "I'm a little dry."

"Oh, sure." As much as I wanted to keep an eye on him, I appreciated the opportunity to step away.

"Some lemonade or a soda. Anything would be mighty fine."

I stepped into the kitchen and my gaze snapped to the phone. If I hadn't been so set on working alone, I would've invited Roland over earlier. He would be with me, with us, now. How long would Mike stay? He'd be gone by the time Roland came over, even if I called him now. I picked up the phone and tapped his cell phone number anyway.

With the phone to my ear, I opened a cupboard for a glass. I had no reason to feel uneasy. Mike would be gone in a matter of minutes. Jarret had wanted him to stop by for the—

"Hello?"

I sighed at the sound of Roland's voice, the muscles that had grown tense in Mike's presence relaxing. "Roland, it's me. Do you think you could come over, like, right away?" I opened the refrigerator and glimpsed movement out of the corner of my eye.

"Sure. Is something wrong?"

"So, what do you have to drink?" Mike appeared beside me, too close.

I lowered the phone and forced a smile. "Oh. I'm getting it." I peered into the refrigerator. "We have juice, milk, water... Oh, here's a Coke." I grabbed the red can and handed it and a glass to Mike.

He set the empty glass on the counter and grinned at me as he cracked open the can. "Is that Jarret?"

"No." I held the phone at my waist.

He took a long sip from the can. "I'll be another minute in there. Then I'll be out of your hair."

When he said "hair," it triggered something in my mind. So when Mike turned away and strolled back to the weight room, my gaze snapped to his hair. He wore it pulled back in a ponytail that seemed a bit longer than Jarret's. And he didn't have bangs, so if he wore it down, it would probably hang in his face. And if he wore black shades...

My pulse kicked up a notch and fear slithered up my spine.

"Something wrong?" Mike stood in the doorway of the den, staring at me.

"No." I turned away and put the phone to my ear. "Roland?"

Silence.

"Are you sure you're all right?" Mike came up behind me.

I shivered and turned to face him, trying to keep my expression calm. "Phone's not working."

"And I meant to ask when I arrived, where's your car? I didn't see it in the drive. After all you've been through, you didn't get in an accident, now did you?" His questions sounded familiar, so familiar.

I looked at him but my vision blurred and his features faded into his pale face... dark circles for eyes... My head grew light.

*I had been staggering down the road when, by chance or the grace of God, a cab stopped and picked me up. The address I gave the driver rolled off my tongue without my even thinking about it. I repeated the address to myself, wondering whose it was. The cab driver said I'd been walking in the wrong direction. And he said other things, talking, talking, but my head ached so, and I desperately wanted a warm blanket and to lie down. I woke as the cab pulled into a driveway and the driver announced the charge.*

*The driver twisted around to face me and repeated the charge, so I reached for my purse. I had no purse. I asked the driver to wait.*

*As I headed for the house, the door opened. Jarret stepped outside and met me on the front porch, worry in his eyes. "Are you okay? Where's your car? You get in an accident?"*

*"Do you have any money?" I looked over my shoulder at the*

*cab.*

*"Yeah." Jarret put a hand to his back pocket and dashed down the driveway.*

*I stumbled inside. My head was pounding like mad and my body ached with exhaustion. I considered collapsing onto the couch, but I wanted my own bed.*

*The front door slammed. Jarret spoke over my shoulder. "Man, you're late. I tried calling your cell phone. What happened to you? Something go wrong?" He followed me into the bedroom and turned on the light.*

*"What? No." I squinted from the light and turned to him. Something about him seemed strange.*

*"Nothing's wrong?" He spoke loudly and looked me over with half-crazed eyes. "Your hair, your clothes..." He gestured. "What happened to you? And where's your car? Did it break down? Did you get in an accident?"*

*"What? No."*

*"So, where's your car?" He stared with intensity.*

*"My car? I don't know." I turned away and stepped into the bathroom.*

*He slammed a hand to the door, keeping me from closing it. "That's it? I'm here worrying about you for three hours, you don't call, you come home in a cab, and you've got nothing to say?"*

*"What do you want me to say?" I rubbed my forehead. I wanted to lie down.*

*"I want you to tell me why you're late."*

*I threw my weight against the bathroom door, forcing it shut.*

The memory connected with the one I had gained the other night. Jarret was angry, but he wasn't drunk. I could hear him shouting through the bathroom door. He was upset because I was late with no explanation. He had no idea where I'd been, because he had nothing to do with it.

# *Chapter 41*

I SAT SLOUCHED on the couch, holding a wet washcloth to my forehead. When the memory had hit me, I'd zoned out. Mike led me to the couch, brought me a washcloth, and told me to rest. I vaguely remembered telling him I felt lightheaded and that he had said I'd be fine. Then he must've returned to the weight room, but I hadn't seen him do it.

What triggered the memory? Mike's hair? I'd never paid much attention to it—anxious as I'd been to avoid him—but it was long enough to pull into a ponytail, maybe longer than Jarret's.

Could he have been my attacker? No. What motive would he have had? Could he have been involved in one of my cases? No. How would any of them pertain to a doctor and part-time archaeologist? He worked with my husband. He had nothing to do with Amnesia Friday. I wasn't thinking clearly.

Taking a deep breath, I closed my eyes, but my mind continued to turn. It wasn't Mike's hair that triggered the memory so much as what he said. *Are you all right? Where's your car?* Jarret had said that. He was so worried about me.

Guilt pricked my conscience. Until a few days ago, I had misjudged him.

The lightheadedness passed, so I set the washcloth aside and pushed myself up. I should get back to work. Roland would be over soon, and we could review each other's notes and ideas.

I stepped to the table at a leisurely pace, not wanting the lightheadedness to return. My gaze fell on the pictures I had laid out.

*Pictures.* What pictures did Mike need from our computer? Was he looking for a particular picture? Something he at first thought was on my camera...

I shook my head. *Drop the paranoia.* He came for pictures from Jarret's camera: pottery, fields, dirt... They had nothing to do with my cases, and there was nothing suspicious about them in the least.

I scanned the faces of the girls in the pictures spread out on the table, then picked up one of the files. I wanted to review the transcript of Melinda's conversation. Then I would review Roland's notes from his conversation with Adeline.

*Melinda.* Why had she looked familiar? I flipped through the pictures of the girls related to the A-Z Women's Choice Clinic lawsuit. Melinda's picture was not among them, but I felt certain I'd seen her before. The pictures on the bookshelf!

I dashed from the table to the bookshelf in the living room. Maybe I'd met Melinda through the pregnancy hotline. Maybe Melinda had had a baby before she lost one to abortion.

I glanced at one and then another picture. *No, wait...* I thought back to our meeting at the park. Melinda hadn't known me at all. And she hadn't recognized Jarret, either. We had never met before.

"How are you feeling, my dear?" Mike stood near the doorway of the weight room, his sport coat draped over one arm and his black doctor bag in hand.

"All done?" I rested my hands on the back of the couch, relieved at the prospect of him leaving.

"I believe I am." He moseyed into the living room and let his coat slide onto the leather armchair. "What do you say I check that baby's heartbeat before I go?"

"Oh." I glanced at the door, wanting him to leave but... The baby's heartbeat? I couldn't turn down the offer. "Okay. Can I hear it?" Hands clasped, I walked around the couch.

"Why, sure." He set his bag on the coffee table, eased it open, and withdrew something from it. "This here is a fetal

Doppler monitor, an ultrasound device that transmits the sound of the baby's heartbeat." He showed me a white hand-held monitor with a probe attached by a coiled cord. "Now this'll work better if you lie down, and I generally use a dab of gel." He pulled a small tube from his bag—and blew it off?—while I stretched out on the loveseat.

I lifted the bottom of my over-sized t-shirt and shoved the waist of my knitted skirt down enough to expose my belly.

Sitting on the coffee table, he hunched over to work. "This'll be a bit cold." He squeezed the gel onto my abdomen, then placed the probe under my navel and slid and tilted it back and forth.

A moment later, a heartbeat sounded through static.

I sucked in a breath and laughed, sheer joy bursting from my heart to hear the heartbeat of my baby. Tears filled my eyes. If only Jarret were here. He'd want to hear it.

"See here..." Mike angled the monitor so I could see the screen. "That fluctuating number is your baby's heart rate. That's a good strong heart rate. Your baby's doing fine." He shut the Doppler off, wiped the probe, and stuffed it back into his bag. "You still question that I'm a doctor?" He handed me a wipe.

I smiled, wiping my abdomen as I sat up. "No, I'm sorry. I guess I'm a bit paranoid lately. It's been difficult, not remembering so much about my life. I'm confused about everything."

"I imagine it would be confusing." He stood and, leaving his bag, returned to the weight room.

"Well, I promise I won't ask for your credentials again."

Looking amused, he disappeared through the doorway.

As I stared in the direction of the weight room, a thought pushed its way to the forefront of my mind. I remembered where I'd seen Melinda's picture. *No, it couldn't be. That would mean—* "Mike?"

"Mm-hmm? Did you want me to shut the computer down?" he hollered, then peeked out of the room.

Heart racing over the theory that bounced around my mind, I forced myself to remain calm. Maybe I was mistaken. "You can leave it on."

He tapped the doorframe and emerged from the room. "Well, I guess my job is done here."

We met in the empty dining room, me stepping closer than I would've preferred. But I would need to see...

"Hey, my phone's not working. Can I use yours to make a quick call? I wanted to invite Roland over." I gave him a friendly smile.

"Oh, sure." He pulled his cell phone out and tapped the screen.

I leaned in. The image of the girl appeared for a split-second before the phone pad popped up. But I'd had enough time. Straight dark hair, heavy make-up…it was Melinda.

My heart shimmied in my chest. I should've been reaching for the phone he held out to me, but I found myself unable to move. Something didn't make sense. Melinda had referred to her boyfriend by a different name.

"Caaaitlyn?" Mike stretched out my name, his tone heavy with suspicion.

Snapping from my trance, I met his gaze and forced myself to reach for his phone. I needed to act normal.

His pale eyes, gleaming with intensity, were locked on me. A grin crept onto his face. The instant my fingers brushed his phone, he yanked it back and shoved it into a pocket. "You didn't really want to make a phone call, now did you?"

"What?" Heart hammering, I backed into the middle of the empty dining room. Too late to try to act normal.

"You wanted another peek at the photo of my girlfriend. I gather you've met her."

"I—I guess I have. Melinda, right? Why does she call you Tony?" Wanting more distance between us but unwilling to turn my back to him, I continued backing up.

"My father's name was Michael so my family used my middle name, Anthony. Tony for short."

"Melinda's awfully young, don't you think? What is she, like ten years younger than you?"

"Well, now, that's your concern, is it?" Mike stared, seeming to study every inch of my face. "I'm not sure how to explain to you... When a man uncovers a treasure, he does not ignore it. An archaeologist searches and searches but, most of the time, discovers nothing."

Mouth going dry, I wrapped my arms protectively around my belly.

He gave the hint of a grin, his pale eyes shifting as his gaze roamed all over me. "But on that glorious day that a man comes across a rare and valuable find, would you expect him to simply leave it in the ground? As an archaeologist's wife, I should think you would understand. I can no more pretend that my heart has not found a treasure, than I could leave an artifact buried in the dirt."

Not sure how to respond, I shook my head. Trepidation grew within, and I found myself unable to tear my gaze from his pallid eyes.

He inched toward me.

I backed to the dining room wall.

"I say, who can really control the heart? The heart is free. It does what it pleases. It finds in one a friend, in another an enemy, and in yet another..." Moving into my personal space, he licked his lips. "... a lover. You can no more stop the yearnings of your heart than you can the sun from shining or lightning from striking. Love is not ours to decide. It's a gift." He smiled. "And I think God puts love in our hearts, don't you?"

Heart pounding in my throat, I slipped from between him and the wall and dashed into the kitchen. I grabbed the island countertop and turned to face him. "Love?" I said. "That's not love."

He resumed his slow pace toward me.

Wanting to get to the other side of the counter island, desperate to have something between us, I backed up. "You took advantage of a young girl's vulnerability. Melinda doesn't know what she's doing. You got her pregnant and forced her to do away with her child. For you. Do you know how that scarred her? Are you even still seeing her?"

"We'll get back together, when all this settles down. Perhaps I should've done the procedure myself, then your agency wouldn't have known about her, but it's so easy for a girl to get rid of her problem at a clinic, I didn't feel it necessary."

I shuddered at his choice of words: "the procedure," "her problem." He made it seem so ordinary and little, as if it did not involve a sacred human life.

He ran his hand along the counter as he continued his slow pursuit. "Now, the mind is something altogether different from the heart. The mind can be educated, convinced, manipulated, or controlled with logic, sweet words, or drugs."

*Drugs?* I backed into a chair, banging my calf. Trying to maneuver around it, I stumbled and lost my balance, a tingling sensation rippling through my entire body.

He laughed, watching me flail.

I flung my arms out to steady myself and accidentally swept a pile of papers and a pen from the table to the floor. Regaining my balance, I was about to dash to the other side of the counter island.

The pen—*the spy pen*! It rolled under the table. If I were to stoop for it, I would have to take my eyes off him. He could get me.

I scooted around a chair and grabbed hold of it, clutching it like a shield between us.

"Is that what you did? Did you drug me?" I asked. Then with all the strength I could muster, I thrust the chair at him and dove under the table. Papers slipped under my hands and knees. Fumbling in my long, knitted skirt, I flopped onto my side and groped for the pen. My fingertip brushed it, pushing it farther away. I got up on all fours.

Mike laughed and made a guttural grunt. The chair

crashed onto the table—above me.

Startled, I shrieked and jerked my arms up over my head.

The chair slid off the table and smashed into the patio doors, bouncing to the floor. Papers and photos rained down.

I stretched, reached and... got it! I clicked the pen, hoping to turn it on, and crawled backwards to get out from under the table.

Mike lunged and latched onto my arms. The pen slipped from my grasp as he yanked me to my feet. He spun me to face him and forced my back against the counter island. Clutching my arm with a merciless vice-grip, he rested his other hand on the counter and stood in a posture of intimacy, a feigned look of hurt in his eyes.

"Drug you? Why now, Caitlyn, I'm a doctor." He clicked his tongue in disapproval. "Perhaps you assume that because I am a doctor, I could easily get my hands on dangerous pharmaceuticals. Why, that would be malpractice. I certainly did not drug you. And it was not my intent to hurt you. You were the one who grabbed that rock."

"Then it *was* you? You chased me in the woods?"

"Ah..." He smiled, a pleasant expression that belied his cruel behavior. "So you do remember. And here you've been denying all recollection."

"You didn't want to hurt me? What did you want? My camera? I had no pictures of you." I tried to wiggle my arm free from his painful grip.

He released me but blocked my escape with his arms, his hands resting on the counter on either side of me.

"Well, now, there you're wrong. I didn't want *your* camera at all. But I guess that's what I got. I never checked. Jarret told me the two of you switched cameras. So, I thought I took care of my little problem when I took yours. I only recently realized my mistake."

I grabbed his arms and pushed, but he only smiled. "What was on Jarret's camera?" I wished I'd looked at all the pictures. I must've missed whatever he was after.

"Nothing now. And every trace of the pictures on your computer is gone."

I could find out. Sean could recover it. I gave Mike a smug look. "Then I guess you're done here."

Mike returned the smug look but added a creepy laugh. "Don't think your friends down at Wright Investigators can retrieve the pictures either. Not even with their fancy recovery software. I cleaned them off good."

My hope melted. We'd have no proof of his involvement with a minor. I would have to get him to admit it. I turned to glimpse the spy pen, hoping that it was turned on, working properly, and now recording our conversation.

"And what's more, now that our dirty laundry hangs in the open, I have to say, I don't want my name brought up at all in the work you're doing for that attorney. Do you understand me?"

"Worried about statutory rape?" My face tightened in another smug grin, which I really ought to control since we were alone, and he towered over me.

He smiled. "That's really an unfair and outdated law, don't you think? In the not too distant past, it was common for a man to marry a girl, younger even than Melinda was at the beginning of our relationship."

"Fair or not, Mike, it is the law."

The eye above the scar twitched. Anger flashed in his eyes.

It was time to make my move. I twisted and rammed him with my hip. He staggered back a step. Then he grinned and lifted his arms as if to wrap them around me.

I wouldn't give him the chance. I thrust my elbow to his chin.

He staggered back several steps this time.

I sprinted for the door.

In an instant, he was behind me, grabbing me by the hair, jerking my head back.

Searing pain shot through the bump on my head. Groaning, seeing stars, I stumbled and smacked into him. He wrapped his arm around me from behind and enveloped my body. Grasping, twisting, I struggled to free my arms.

"These outdated, unfair laws ought to change, but be that as it may." He yanked my hair again, a pain-inducing tug that forced me to face him.

I stifled a whimper and stopped struggling. I needed to think.

Holding me close, he pressed his cheek to my forehead and spoke. "You want to go after the abortion clinic, go after them. But you are not going to mention my name, dragging me into it, painting my picture as some pervert child-rapist to that attorney or to your client. I will be in none of your reports. And I'm going to tell you why. Your husband, as it turns out, has been stealing artifacts."

What was he talking about?

He yanked my head back further.

I groaned, the pain bringing spots to my vision.

"And since I know about it..." His mouth, twisting out lies, hovered inches from mine. "... I have the responsibility to report him. So, when you falsely accuse me, I'm going to make it clear that you are motivated by revenge. You will no longer be reputable and perhaps your company with you."

"You're going to ruin Jarret's career over this?" My jaw trembled as I spoke. "He has nothing to do with it."

"He has everything to do with it. He's your husband. But if we keep all this between ourselves, you can save his career and yours. You talk to Jarret about this or mention my name to Wright Investigators, and I will ruin you both. I will not go to court or to jail for statutory rape. Our society may see things differently, but I have done nothing wrong."

"Let me go." I wriggled to get some space between us, but he only laughed in my ear. If I had a little space, I could—

The screen door squeaked and the front door flew open. Jarret stood in the doorway, his face contorting with a series of spasmodic tics. "Get your hands off my wife." He spit the words out and formed a fist on his way over.

Heart beating wildly, I heaved a great sigh, thankfulness and confusion flooding my thoughts. How did he know to come?

"Easy now, Jarret. Caitlyn and I are simply having a little talk." Mike laughed. "Unfortunately for you, your arrival changes things. Leaves me little choice." He released my hair and relaxed his hold... enough for me to get the space I needed.

I turned a little, jabbed my hipbone into him, and spun to face him. Before he understood my intent, I thrust my knee into his groin. He doubled over, groaning. I brought my elbow up to strike his chin but, in mid-motion, found myself shoved away.

Jarret's fist ripped across Mike's chin. Mike swayed but then retaliated, throwing his body weight into Jarret, slamming him against the wall. A good fifty pounds heavier and half a foot taller, Mike had the advantage.

Desperate to help, I glanced around the house, trying to come up with an idea.

Mike punched Jarret in the gut with his right fist, his left, his right. Jarret groaned, his body convulsing.

"Stop!" I shrieked.

Jarret pushed off the wall, lodged his shoulder in Mike's abdomen and rammed him into the countertop.

I jumped out of the way.

Jarret drew his fist to throw a punch. Mike blocked it and grabbed his arm. Jarret made a move with his other fist, but Mike blocked that too. They wrestled, arms locked, heads together, moving through the house in an awkward dance. They bumped into the loveseat, the coffee table, and then the couch. Jarret cracked his head against Mike's and broke free. He threw another punch. Mike swayed and smashed into the bookshelf. Pictures, rocks, and books slid along the shelves and crashed to the floor.

Rocks! I dashed for the bookshelf. I swiped up the grapefruit-sized amethyst geode and lifted it over my head.

Mike had Jarret down on his knees, his arm around his

neck in a sleeper hold.

I brought the geode down.

As I did, Jarret broke the hold and traded places with Mike, his hands grasping for Mike's neck. So when the geode struck a skull... it was Jarret's.

I gasped.

Jarret fell to the floor. Rubbing his neck and breathing hard, Mike climbed to his feet and stooped over. He laughed as he straightened.

I dropped to Jarret's side, rolled him onto his back, and pressed my ear to his chest. *Please, be alive.* His heart beat strong and fast.

Mike gripped the couch for support and continued to laugh, wiping a tear every few seconds. "I was running out of energy, thought Jarret was about to own me. So, I thank you, Caitlyn. I'm much obliged."

I grunted in disgust.

"I guess... my job is done here... so I'll be going now. I've got some business... to attend to at work," he said between breaths as he headed for the door. "Remember what I told you. You can keep your job or lose it. Either way, my reputation will not suffer."

He pushed open the screen door and disappeared.

"Oh, Jarret." I sobbed over him. "I'm so sorry. I can't believe I did this to you."

He lay still and peaceful, sleeping like a gentle lion.

I wiped the sweat from his hairline and kissed his forehead. *Please, God, let him be okay.*

# Chapter 42

THE SOUND OF Mike's car rolling out of the driveway sent a wave of relief through me. A few seconds later, a car pulled in. My heart, which had only begun to calm, pounded again. A car door slammed, making me jump. Footsteps sounded. I held my breath. The screen door squeaked open and a dark figure stood in the doorway, the bright sun behind him.

"Caitlyn? Jarret!"

I exhaled, relieved that Roland had come.

Roland shot to my side and dropped to his knees. His gaze flitted from me to Jarret to the mess in the house. "What happened?"

"He's unconscious. But I think he's okay. Mike came over..."

Roland nodded and popped up. "He was after Jarret's camera, not yours."

He disappeared into the bedroom. A moment later, he returned with a wet washcloth, which he handed to me. His gaze snapped to the dining room, where papers lay strewn on the floor and a chair on its side, then he swiped a decorative pillow from the couch and joined me on the floor.

"We enlarged Jarret's pictures at work. Mike's in three of them, in the background with an underage girl. His girlfriend."

"Melinda." I cradled Jarret's head in my arms as Roland stuffed the pillow under it. "You have the pictures? Mike came here to erase them from our computer. I figured he already took care of Jarret's camera." I cleared the floor around Jarret's head, pushing books, pictures, and rocks away.

"Yeah, Jarret gave me the pictures on a jump drive. Remember?" He scooted aside and leaned against the backside of the couch.

"That's good to know. We need proof because Mike said— Hey, how did Jarret know to come home?"

"When you called me, I heard Mike in the background. Sean and I were putting it all together, and I figured you shouldn't be alone with him. Jarret was closer, so I called him before I headed out."

"I'm glad you did." I explained everything Mike had threatened me with.

Jarret stirred and we both looked down.

"Maybe I should've called the police, huh?" Roland said. "But I didn't know for sure. Do you think he needs an ambulance?"

Jarret groaned.

"Jarret?" I hovered over him.

He touched his head and squinted at me. "Man, what happened?"

"Oh, it's my fault." My heart ached with remorse.

"What's your fault?" He pushed himself up, rested on his elbows, and glanced around. "Where am I?"

"Where are you?" Worry shot through me. Maybe he didn't recognize the house from his point of view on the floor, between the couch and the bookshelf. Of course, I had brought the geode down hard. "You don't know where you are?"

Sitting up all the way, he touched his head again and raised an eyebrow at me. "What're you doing here?"

"You came home to save me. Don't you remember?"

He stared without blinking, his face unreadable.

"Don't you know who I am?" My voice came out high.

He huffed and glanced at Roland with a crooked grin. "Uh, yeah. You think I don't know you? You're Caitlyn Summer."

I gasped. "Caitlyn Summer? No, Jarret, I'm your wife."

He smirked and looked me over. "Right."

"I am." This could not be happening. We couldn't *both* have amnesia. "Tell him, Roland."

Sitting comfortably with his back to the couch, Roland shrugged. "What can I say? I couldn't convince *you*. You two as man and wife? It *is* a bit hard to believe."

Disbelief tangling my thoughts into an impossible knot, a strange grunt escaped me. I turned to Jarret.

"Jarret, please believe me." I squeezed his hand. "I'm your wife, and this is our home."

He gave me a sly grin. "Prove it."

"Prove it?"

"If you're my wife, kiss me."

"Oh, I can do that." I leaned forward, my eyes on his mouth. My lips tingled and my heart raced.

The corners of his lips trembled as if he was trying to suppress a grin. But when my mouth touched his, he made a little gasp as if he hadn't expected me to do it. Then he leaned back.

I continued to prove my status, sinking into him and kissing him, thankful he was mine and he was okay.

Leaning back more, he bumped the bookshelf. A row of dark brown books—the entire Louis L'Amour series—slid off a shelf, landing directly behind his head, one after another.

I pulled away, giggling.

He smirked and sat up again, draping an arm over one raised knee. "Why don't you finish proving it to me in there?" He tilted his chin, indicating the bedroom.

I gasped and then narrowed my eyes. "You're faking it. You don't have amnesia. You know exactly who I am." I whacked his arm with a book.

"Yeah, you're my wife."

Roland shook his head and stood. "Why don't you lie on the couch? And keep the washcloth on your head. I'll get some ice. Do you think you should go to the hospital?"

No sooner had I assisted my aching husband to the couch,

settled him into a mound of pillows, placed an icepack on the unfortunate part of his head that had received the brunt of my ill-aimed blow, and brought him a Coke, than a police siren erupted. The siren grew louder. I rushed to the door as the sirens ceased and two police cars with flashing lights pulled up in front of the house. Before the officers flung open their car doors, I stood waiting for them on the porch.

"Wow! That was quick. I'm so glad you came," I said to two officers, who approached with synchronized steps. "I didn't know if we should call or just go up to the station, but I guess Roland decided..."

"Ma'am, we're looking for Jarret West." The taller of the two officers had a thick blond mustache and spoke with a strong Southern drawl. Tan biceps bulged from under his tidy, black uniform as he removed his sunglasses and revealed his scrutinizing glare.

"Oh. He's inside." I yanked open the screen door and stumbled out of the way. "He's okay. I guess we should file a police report, huh? Don't we have to go down to the station for that?"

The officers brushed past me and met Jarret inside the door. He had gotten up from the couch but still held the icepack to his head. Roland came to his side.

"I'm Jarret West." He switched the icepack to his other hand so he could shake their hands, but they weren't interested. "Did you call the police?" Jarret said to Roland. Roland shook his head.

"Jarret West—" the shorter officer said.

"Mike's the one who did this to Jarret." I pushed between Jarret and the shorter officer. He barely gave me a glance. "Michael Caragine. He's a doctor, but, well, he attacked me two weeks ago, only we didn't know until today. He was seeing an underage—"

"Sir, we need to take you down to the station for questioning."

Jarret's eyes and mouth twitched. "Questioning?"

"Englehardt Cultural Resource Management believes you are in possession of stolen artifacts—"

"What!" Jarret tossed the icepack and clenched his fists. "Me? Stolen artifacts?"

I grabbed one of his fists to keep him from looking irate in front of the officers.

"Relax, Jarret," Roland said and then whispered in his ear. I caught bits and pieces. Roland was summarizing events, explaining what Mike had done.

"If it's all right with you, we'd like to search your home?" the taller officer said. "We don't have a search warrant yet, so you have a right to refuse but—"

"His doctor bag!" I gave Jarret a wide-eyed look.

He responded with a clueless shrug and turned to Roland. Roland nodded as if what I said made perfect sense. Then he whispered more details to Jarret, whose expression grew increasingly perturbed.

I dashed to the weight room. One of the officers followed me. The other officer said something to Jarret. Jarret gave an annoyed, whiny reply.

"Mike came over to get pictures off our computer," I said to the officer, "and he had me get him something to drink." I yanked open the closet doors, catching a whiff of dry cardboard. "I left him alone in this room." Empty boxes for the DVD player, CD player, computer, and television filled the closet. "And also, I sat on the couch for some time." I searched between and behind the boxes. "He would've had plenty of uninterrupted time to hide— What are we looking for?" Finding nothing unusual, I turned my attention to the overhead shelf, but I would need a chair to—

I glanced. The taller of the two officers stood behind me. He could search the top of the closet easily enough while I searched other places. "Officer, you're quite tall. Would you mind?"

"Oh, sure, ma'am." He stepped up to the task.

I scanned the room. Jarret's weight set took up most of the

room and had no hiding spots. The desk! I whipped open drawers one at a time and slammed each one shut when I found nothing suspicious.

Hands on my hips, I blew out a breath. "I can't imagine where he would've hidden it. I know he sat at the computer. Of course!" I shoved the swivel chair out of the way, dropped to my knees, and crawled under the desk.

There among a tangle of cables and cords, lay an old clay pot, brown and grainy as dried dirt. It had a narrow opening at the top that probably had a cork stuffed in it back in its day and two rough spots where a handle might've been.

"I think I found it." I crept out from under the desk and sat back on my heels.

The tall officer squatted beside me and peered, making a face that said he couldn't believe anyone would've stolen it. "So, that's it?"

"I guess so."

"I'll get an evidence bag." He darted from the room.

A moment later, the officers stood outside by one of the two police cars. The officer by the open driver door spoke on a radio. Roland watched from the front porch, arms folded, eyes squinted.

Jarret paced in the dining room, from the den to the kitchen. "I can't believe Mike did this. All this time I trusted him. Like a fool, I brought him over here the day after he hurt you." Jarret cussed and kicked the backside of the kitchen island. "I brought the man who hurt my wife into my house to make sure she was okay."

When Jarret switched from talking to me to swearing and talking to himself, I tore myself from the front window and went up to him. "Jarret, stop."

He stopped pacing and looked at me.

"I'm okay. You're okay," I said. "Mike will soon be in jail."

"Will he? What if they believe him and not us? Roland told me what he was gonna say, that we made up the crap about the girl because I'm a thief." He emphasized the word "thief" then turned to resume pacing.

I grabbed his arm. "There'll be evidence. They'll get a search warrant. I'm sure they'll find particles of the artifact in his doctor bag. I'm sure that's how he brought the artifact in here. And maybe they'll question Melinda. Maybe she'll admit to their relationship."

He shook his head. "I'm going to jail. Jail! I never imagined I'd find myself in jail. I've made some mistakes, but I'm not a bad guy."

Suppressing a giggle, I tried to look compassionate. "You're not going to jail. Maybe they'll bring us to the station for questioning. They won't put you in jail. You didn't do anything."

"Jail," he whispered, obviously still picturing it.

"You know, Jarret, I thought my memory would return once I discovered my attacker. Why didn't I recognize him that night?"

"You'd only seen him once or twice before all this. I don't think you ever spoke to each other."

"Really? He acted as if we knew each other well. He called me *Catie*." I released his arm and returned to the front window. The officers still stood by the police car. "I was so sure I'd get my memory back." My voice broke. I was thirsty, that was all. Everything would work out. Would I have time to make tea before our trip to the station? I ambled toward the kitchen.

Jarret stared at me. As I neared, he grabbed my arm and swung me to face him.

"Marry me."

The desperation in his eyes, the tone of his voice... He seemed to think it was the key to unlock the door that would make everything right. I'd get my memory back. He wouldn't go to jail. Life would return to normal.

Holding his gaze, I realized that the intense look in his deep brown eyes had a way of pulling me in, drawing me deeper into his world. I wanted to believe as he seemed to, that renewing our vows would be the answer. I wanted to throw my arms around him and rest in the safety and warmth of his embrace. I did want to marry him. "Jarret, I—"

"Mr. and Mrs. West." The taller officer stood by the front door. "We need to bring you in for questioning."

# Chapter 43

"RELAX, CAITLYN," ROLAND said. "Stop pacing. It'll be fine." He sat in a row of chairs that lined one wall of the detective and administrative area of the police station.

I unclenched my fists and wiped my sweaty palms on my gray knit skirt. "Oh, all right." I flopped into the chair between Roland and an old, whiskery man. "I'll try."

Officers worked at desks in the middle of the open area, a phone to one man's ear, others gazing at computer monitors. Every few seconds, someone marched past us, going to or from halls on either side or stopping at one of the desks. A group of officers stood talking around the desk nearest me, making it impossible for me to hear anything else.

I didn't want to listen to them. My attention was glued to the far corner of the room, where an officer sat behind a desk, interviewing Jarret. Jarret jumped up for the third time, making an angry gesture and jerking his head from side to side with an attitude. The officer motioned for him to sit back down.

My heart thumped against my ribs like a gorilla trying to bust free of a cage. "Oh, my, look at him."

Roland grabbed my hand. "Relax. It'll work out."

"What do you think he's saying?"

"I don't know. He doesn't really know anything except the little bit I explained to him." He sat there cool as a breeze, serenely undisturbed as if he were watching a movie and not his own frantic brother digging himself into a hole.

I took a deep breath to calm myself. Ten minutes ago, I'd had no problem explaining things to Officer McDuffie, the officer questioning Jarret. I told Officer McDuffie about Wright Investigators' work on the abortion case, Mike's involvement with the underage girl, the pictures on Jarret's camera, how Mike had attacked me, and about the threats he made against Jarret. I thought it explained perfectly why the stolen artifact was found in our house. I turned over the audio pen recorder as evidence and asked them to contact Candice for pictures and other case information.

Jarret's angry voice carried across the room, though I couldn't make out what he said. Officer McDuffie raised his hands, palms out, in a take-no-offense gesture.

I winced and turned away.

Ever-steady Roland squeezed my hand. "Sean and I think we put it all together. Want to hear it?"

"Hmm?" I faced him, locking my gaze onto cool gray eyes as placid as an undisturbed pond. The look in his eyes, his touch... they no longer set off sparks or butterflies in my stomach. Jarret alone stirred those feelings in me now. But Roland did comfort me in a way no one else ever could. "Sure."

Releasing my hand, he leaned forward. "The Thursday before Amnesia Friday, Mike's underage girlfriend showed up at the dig site to talk. We suspect that's when she told him a private investigator wanted to speak with her." He glanced. "One of you guys."

"How do you know it was that Thursday?"

"The properties of the picture files."

I nodded. "Oh. Do you think he knew I was the PI or that I was working on a case against the abortion provider?"

"Maybe. But he definitely realized Jarret had accidentally caught him and Melinda in his pictures that day. Then Jarret took the camera home and unintentionally brought yours back on Friday. So Mike couldn't delete the pictures yet. And instead of waiting to get the camera from Jarret the following Monday, he decided to get it from you that night."

I shivered, an unpleasant feeling weaseling its way into my tummy. "He didn't realize we'd switched cameras back at lunchtime."

"Right. So he waited for you to leave work and... well, he got your camera, thinking it was Jarret's, not realizing his mistake until days later. Jarret had stopped going to work by then."

"Keeping an eye on me." I dragged in a deep breath and exhaled, my gaze traveling to Jarret. We'd come so far.

A second later, Jarret jumped up and slid a hand into his back pocket. The officer shoved him back into his chair and shook a finger at him, as if scolding a child.

"Jarret always makes himself look guilty," I said by way of placid observation, determined not to let it get to me. As Jarret's wife, I should probably learn to assess a situation with a bit of distance and prepare myself to help him, the way Roland did.

"Yeaaah, I know." Roland combed his fingers through his hair and sighed. "He always has, especially when someone wants him to explain himself."

We watched the spectacle for another moment, then Roland continued. "When Jarret finally brought the camera to work, Mike cleaned the pictures off but he figured they might also be copied to your home computer. So he came over today to erase them and for Plan B."

"Plan B?"

"Right. In case either of you suspected him, he wanted to plant evidence to frame Jarret."

"Which he's done with that old pot."

"Artifact."

"Right, that old pot. And that's where we are now. Jarret's accused of stealing and I'm only trying to smear Mike's name in retaliation."

"Rascally young man," said the whiskery old man beside me. He had a hound dog expression with long vertical folds in his cheeks that deepened as he spoke. "He yours?"

"What?" I glanced from the man to Jarret, who sat gripping his hair and shouting. "Yup. He's mine." My heart sang at the thought.

"Mine's in there." The old man pointed a big-knuckled finger toward one of the two doors marked "Interview Room." He shook his head with the tired look of someone who had *been there* too many times. "Granddaughter. Takes after her mother."

"What did your granddaughter do?" Maybe I was being nosy, but he seemed to want to talk. And he had called my husband *rascally*.

Before the man could answer, two figures entered from the foyer. They moved at a pace that stood apart from other passersby, not hurried like the officers and not haltingly like first-time visitors. It was more of a grand entrance.

"I am certain we can clear this up in a matter of minutes." Mike's cordial Southern drawl carried over the chatter in the station. He wore his hair slicked back into a smooth ponytail and the same sport coat he had on earlier but with dress pants rather than jeans. "I will cooperate in whatever way I can. I full well expected Jarret West to find some way to retaliate." He laughed. "I cannot wait to hear what he has accused me of."

Mike strode into the area alongside the arresting officer, taking no notice of me and Roland as he passed. The officer led him to an interview room.

"I think Jarret's done." Roland popped up.

Jarret stood—without being shoved back down—next to the officer, the two of them conversing casually. They shook hands. Then Jarret crossed the room, looking drained but regaining his cool with every step.

A black female officer escorted Melinda and a woman with bleached-blond hair from the other interview room. Melinda wore a tight yellow-and-white shorts outfit and sauntered like a runway model, sparing no one a glance. Her mother wore an equally skimpy black outfit and heavier make-up.

The old man and I stood up together.

"Good luck with yours. Here's mine," he said to me, then to the blond woman, "How'd that go?"

"These people here are all confused." The woman gave an annoyed headshake. "They thought my Melinda here was seeing some doctor. I mean really. Can y'all imagine? That would be some catch, but I don't know where they get their information. Come on, girl. You should be in school."

"Hey." Jarret stepped into Melinda's path. "That looks like the—" His gaze snapped from her neck to her eyes. "Where'd you get that?"

Melinda's hand shot to her neck, covering the necklace, the dull blue crystal she'd worn when Sean and I interviewed her. "My boyfriend gave it to me."

"Your boyfriend? Can I see it? It looks like—"

Melinda lowered her hand, but the black police officer took a warning step toward Jarret. "Back off, lover boy. This girl's done had enough trouble for one day." She grabbed Melinda by the arm and led her to the foyer.

Jarret followed them with his eyes. "But she's got..." He glanced at me. "Who is she?"

"That's Melinda, Mike's underage girlfriend, who probably lied and denied their relationship." I sighed with disgust.

He huffed, disbelief on his face. "She's wearing a stolen artifact. We found that sapphire at the site. It's probably part of a late 18th century necklace or an earring, judging by the... That's Mike's girlfriend?" He craned his neck to see through the windows in the doors that led to the foyer. "What is she, like twelve?"

"No, but she's too young for Mike. Unfortunately, I think she denied knowing him. I wonder if I got anything with the pen recorder." I looked at Roland. He shrugged. "I hope the pen worked."

"You're a free man, huh?" Roland said to Jarret.

Looking awkward and unsure, Jarret shook his head and

shrugged.

"Good," Roland said. "Let's go. We can call Sean or Candice and see what they found out."

# Chapter 44

THE SAVORY AROMA of authentic Mexican food pervaded the house. Adeline carried two baskets of tamales to the patio table, which now sat in the formal dining room with both patio chairs and the swivel chair from the computer desk. I had Mitch and Sean carry it inside so there would be enough seating for the dinner party.

"Place looks great, Caitlyn." Mitch sat on one of the barstools that I had the luck to find at a garage sale on the return trip from the ethnic foods store.

I pulled plates from a cupboard and set them near the tamales that still lay out on the counter. "Thanks, Mitch. Why don't you help Victor with the lights?"

Victor had grumbled about the assignment of hanging the chili-pepper party lights, but Candice convinced him to do it. Having hung a string of them over the patio doors, they were now working on the dining room.

"You're just trying to keep me from the tamales." Mitch chuckled in his odd, expressionless way.

"Maybe she don't like y'all watching her work," Sean said. He sat hunched at the dinner table, his back to the patio doors, eating tortilla chips out of the bag instead of dumping them into the bowls like I had asked him to do.

Bobby sat at the table, facing Sean, babbling as he mindlessly grabbed chips from the bag. "... an' we done seen them doing it, too, so when them neighbors come back to..."

"No, Sean, that would be you," Mitch said. "You're the one

who always—"

Tired of Mitch referring to Sean's obsession with me, I intentionally interrupted him. "Sean, are you going to dump those chips in the bowl before Bobby eats them all?" Sean had shown interest in Adeline, and maybe something would come of that.

"Sorry, Mrs. West," Bobby said. "I won't eat no more." He skipped to the dining room and said something to Victor and Candice as they worked on hanging lights.

"So, when is the guest of honor scheduled to arrive?" Mitch stroked his scrubby beard, obviously dead set against helping. Even Bobby had helped by setting out pitchers of water.

I handed him a stack of red paper napkins. "Please put these around, one at each place."

Mitch took them. As he slid off the barstool, Adeline came over and stole his seat. She leaned forward, her thick-lashed eyes sparkling with mischief. "Your life is going to be different from now on."

I counted out forks and spoons, a thrill of anticipation stirring inside. After all he'd gone through, Jarret deserved this party. Yes, things would be different from now on.

"Different? What do you mean?"

"Now, you are one of the few. Making authentic tamales is a rare art. You're like a member of a special club." She gestured with her thin tan arm, her French-tipped fingernails glittering under the kitchen lights. "All these people here know you can make tamales and they'll tell their friends. People will beg you to come to their parties. *You* are now an authentic-tamale cook." She leaned forward again and shared a giggle with me.

"I could never have done it without you. I'm so glad we met. And I'm so-o-o glad you offered to help." After leaving the police station yesterday, Roland, Jarret and I swung by Wright Investigators. Candice had been interviewing Adeline. She introduced us and we became instant friends. When Adeline's Mexican heritage came out, I couldn't believe it. The timing! Right when I'd decided to cook Jarret's favorite food, Adeline came into my life.

"I love making tamales." Adeline grabbed an empty basket and picked up one of the tamales that lay out on the counter.

"Who could love making tamales?"

It was exhausting. Yesterday, we had driven an hour to an ethnic store, where we bought strange ingredients like cornhusks, masa flour, and cumin seeds. Today, Adeline came over early. We had a pot of pork roast and another of chicken simmering on the stove all morning. Before long, savory smells filled the house and my stomach wouldn't stop growling no matter how many snacks I ate. Then we soaked cornhusks and shredded meat, by hand, and made a strange dough out of lard and corn masa flour. Adeline made assembling the tamales in the cornhusks and rolling them up look effortless, but I never got the hang of it. It took forever.

Wanting to surprise Jarret, I was glad he decided to go to work. He said he needed to salvage his job and thought he could wrap up their project in one day. Roland went with him. He had specific instructions to keep Jarret from coming home for lunch and to give a warning call before they returned at the end of the day.

He'd called a few minutes ago.

My heart skipped a beat. They'd come home any minute now.

Everything was ready: sweet corn cake, Mexican rice, chicken taquitos—which Adeline called flautas—and tamales. I only had to dump the salsa and bean dip into bowls.

I scurried to the pantry to find what I needed.

"Get olives, too," Adeline shouted. She took the bag of chips from Sean and dumped it into a big bowl. Sean said something, and the two of them laughed.

I stepped away from the pantry with an armful of jars: three different salsas, bean dip, and green olives. I stopped in the middle of the kitchen.

"Oh, you mean the black olives." I spun around.

And there was Mitch! Lurking directly behind me. As we collided, the jars slipped from my grip and crashed to the floor.

*"Oh, no!" I fell to my knees to clean up the mess. This couldn't be happening. If only I wasn't such a klutz. My heart wrenched. I was already behind in preparing the menu Nanny had given me.*

*My hand brushed a piece of glass and smarted. Ignoring it, I turned to grab one of the empty plastic grocery bags. "What a mess, what a mess," I whispered, my voice strained. I scooped the bigger pieces of glass into the bag. "Oh, what a mess."*

*Tears blurred my vision and streamed down my cheeks. My hands, my entire body trembled, and hopelessness raced through my mind. Nothing was working out. I'd already forgotten to pick up the drinks on Nanny's list. The menu was too complicated. And now...*

*I moaned aloud.*

*"Hey, are you all right?"*

*Startled, I looked up.*

*Jarret stood over me with his head titled and one hand stuffed in the front pocket of his faded designer jeans. He crouched, the big ugly mess between us. "Let me get that." He picked up a piece of glass and dropped it into the bag. "Hey, you're bleeding." I thought he meant my hand, but he stared at my knees.*

*I had knelt in the middle of the salsa and applesauce. And broken glass. Most of the red on my dress came from the salsa but—Oh! A patch of dark red.*

*"Blood," I whispered, my mind numb with frustration.*

*He grabbed my arms and pulled me up. "Go take care of that. Get washed up. I'll clean this. It's no big deal."*

*How could he be so nice? We hadn't spoken in days.*

*Still sniffling, I shuffled to my room and peeled off my wet, disgusting dress. After taking the fastest shower I could and sticking Band-Aids to my knee, I slipped into a clean dress and stood before the mirror.*

*The white, sleeveless sundress flattered my thin, shapeless figure. I hated that I'd picked the dress to look good for Jarret. Why should I have feelings for him? He wasn't my type.*

*I returned to the kitchen as Jarret closed the door of the broom closet. The floor was spotless and completely dry. Only the dishtowel lay on the floor. Had he used it to finish up? A dishtowel? Why not a cleaning rag from under the sink? Still, he'd done this for me.*

*I stepped to the counter and stood in the exact spot where I had dropped the jars. "Thank you," I whispered, so grateful I could burst.*

*He came up beside me and grabbed a notepad and pen from a drawer. "You need salsa and applesauce. What else?"*

*Melting at his kindness, my heart spiraled out of control. I loved him. I could no longer pretend I didn't. Unable to control myself, I threw my arms around his neck and pressed my lips to his. Warmth. Longing. Love. He wrapped his arms around my waist and pulled me closer. My heart pounded. A faint moan escaped me. I kissed him with a passion I never knew I had, the passion of a love too long suppressed.*

*A low voice came from the hall. We pulled away from each other. Jarret snatched the pen and leaned over the notepad. Mr. West came around the corner, holding a cell phone to his ear. He gave us a casual nod.*

*"So, what else do you need at the store?" Jarret appeared calm except for the base of his neck, which throbbed with the beating of his heart. He loved me too.*

*"Um, um..." I wiped my mouth, intensely aware of the impression of his kiss, and ran a hand through my hair. It wasn't as easy for me to compose myself as it seemed to be for him.*

*He scribbled something on a scrap of paper and placed it in my hand.*

*"That's my number. Call me when you think of what you need." He gave me a slight smile and held my gaze until his father turned around from the refrigerator.*

*I nodded and watched Jarret leave through the side door, excitement, longing, and fear racing through my veins. And the conviction that my life would never be the same.*

"Get a wet washcloth." It was Candice's voice.

I sat on the couch. Sean squatted nearby but jumped up at Candice's order.

"Are you okay?" Candice sat beside me, deep concern in her Nancy Drew eyes. "I think you blacked out for a minute there."

"Don't worry about the mess." Adeline sauntered from the dining room and spoke over the loveseat. She pointed a thumb over her shoulder. "I have Mitch cleaning it up."

"Thanks a lot." Mitch's sarcastic voice came from the kitchen. "Just what I wanted to do. I get invited to a..."

"Mr. West uses plastic grocery bags..." Bobby's voice also came from the kitchen. "... whenever he cleans up after Mrs. West's accidents." A cabinet door squeaked. Bobby must've been helping.

"And don't worry about the salsa." Adeline propped her hands on the back of the loveseat and grinned. "I sent Victor to the store."

"Victor?" I smiled. *Victor.* I understood why Victor hated the abortion case. Several years ago, he'd tried to fight an abortion provider in Arizona. His own underage daughter had made a mistake and suffered greatly for it. The abortion provider won and, in the process, tore his family apart. Victor lost his wife and daughter through the destructive tactics of the abortion provider's lawyers. He shared this with me one night while on a covert surveillance operation, during the long hours of waiting and watching in a dark van.

Sean returned with a washcloth and handed it to Candice. *Sean.* I never realized he'd a crush on me until last Friday, even after he kissed me on that undercover assignment. I had only thought he was a nice, sensitive, "slightly obsessed with investigative equipment" sort of guy.

Sean's surfer-boy gaze flitted from me to Candice and then to Adeline. Adeline stepped around the loveseat and took him by the hand. "Come on, Sean, let's give her some space." She led him to the dining room.

"What happened there?" Candice pressed the washcloth to my forehead.

"I, well, when I dropped the salsa... I think I got my memory back."

I remembered vividly our first kiss. I remembered what happened after, how Jarret had called me from the store and I tried to apologize for kissing him. He wouldn't let me.

"You're not gonna erase it. It happened. It was good. You like me and I like you."

We didn't kiss again the entire two weeks Selena and her family visited, but we did everything together.

"Your memory?" Candice said. "A particular memory?"

I realized I was smiling. "No, all of it."

I remembered going to college with Roland, meeting Lingsi, and working that summer for Nanny at the West house. I remembered first laying eyes on Jarret when he dragged his luggage into the foyer, and his arrogant attitude. I remembered him coming home drunk and noticing me in the shadows of the foyer, then lying beside him in his bed, stroking his hair and singing to him.

How peaceful he had looked when he'd drifted off to sleep, peaceful like a sleeping lion. I'd felt sorry for him then, sorry that he seemed so sad, that he still mourned the loss of his mother, that he probably missed his twin brother, and maybe felt alone in the world. I made a personal commitment to treat him with kindness no matter how rude he might get. I hadn't expected to fall in love with him, but over the days, that's what happened. He brought me into the intimacy of his inner world and there I felt uniquely loved, needed, and special. There I wanted to remain.

My mind lingered on the memory of his proposal. He'd stopped my swing and dropped down on one knee. I first thought he needed to tie his shoe, but the nervousness in his eyes told me otherwise. As he proposed, my heart, mind, and body turned into a feather, so light I could have floated away.

Our engagement lasted one year, its length intensified by the few visits we shared: Thanksgiving, Christmas, and Easter holidays. I had returned to South Dakota University to complete my associate's degree, and he'd gone back to Arizona to get his bachelor's. We talked to each other and sent emails every day.

My parents weren't comfortable with either my decision to marry Jarret or my career choice, but after many discussions, they supported me. We married last summer at St. Michael Church and held the wedding reception on the Wests' property. It was beautiful. How could I have ever forgotten it?

"How do you feel? Do you want a drink of water?" Candice refolded the washcloth and pressed it to my forehead again.

I smiled and pushed the washcloth away. "I'm fine." I was more than fine. I remembered it all! Every memory of every event of the past few years had returned to me.

"You like Victor, don't you?"

"Caitlyn!" Candice shook her head, the look in her eyes saying she wanted to keep it secret. "I'm glad you're feeling fine. I'll get you something to drink." She jumped up.

I laughed. Then the front door flew open. Jarret was home! Roland followed him into the house, gave me a nod, and headed to the dining room.

Jarret stepped into the living room and looked at me with a question in his eyes. "What's with all the cars in the—"

His eyes shifted to Sean, who stood in the dining room sipping a drink. Roland came up to Sean and the two started talking.

"What's he doing here?"

I got up. "My, but don't I have a jealous husband." Not sure how to tell him that my memory returned, I gave him a sly grin and sauntered to him. "Don't you know I love you?"

I pulled him close and gave him a little kiss, contemplating how I had fallen in love with him twice. I gazed into his gorgeous brown eyes. He gazed back with love but also with the protective, jealous undertone that had always amused me.

"How was work today?" I asked.

"Ahhh..." He shook his head and broke away from my embrace. Then he gave Sean a narrow-eyed glance and scanned the red-pepper lights before returning his attention to me. "I got the project wrapped up. But, uh, they don't want me coming back."

"What?" My happy mood shattered. "Why? Are you fired?"

"On leave until they clear up the situation with the stolen artifacts." He gazed at the red-pepper lights again and rubbed his unshaven chin.

Candice carried two wine glasses toward us and, judging by her knitted brows, she'd heard what he said. "What about the evidence against Mike? They found particles of that clay pot in his doctor bag."

She handed a deep red, fragrant drink to Jarret and one to me. Adeline had called it "Jamaica" (pronounced ha-mike-ah) and said it was made from hibiscus flowers.

"Now that I think about it." I glanced from Candice to Jarret. "I should've been suspicious from the start. It wasn't a doctor's visit, so it didn't make sense for him to have the bag or to take it into the den. He only offered to examine me as an afterthought."

Jarret's eyes twitched. "He examined you?"

"Only the baby. I heard the baby's heartbeat." I rubbed his arm, feeling something of the excitement I'd felt then. "You should hear it. Come with me on my next baby appointment."

His expression melted. "You want me to?"

"And Mike's motive..." Candice said. "It's a good thing you had that recording device. He completely spelled out his motive and his plan." Her forehead wrinkled. "Why did you have that anyway? Did you suspect him?"

"No. I didn't know he was coming over. I accidentally brought the pen home."

"Well, it's a good thing you did. And when Melinda finally told the truth—"

"Can you believe it?" Sean approached.

Jarret snatched my hand possessively. "I thought Melinda denied knowing Mike."

"She did," Sean said, "until she was told about the necklace, you know, that it was a stolen artifact. Boy, was she mad. Hell hath no fury..." He grinned and gave Jarret a look of camaraderie.

Jarret smirked, then he must've remembered his own fury and he glared.

Sean blushed and stepped back before he continued. "I think she spilled it all, told everything. She'll be a great witness for the abortion case, if she's still talking by then."

"Well," Candice said to Jarret, "it should leave no doubt as to Mike's guilt. Your name should be cleared."

"I don't know." Jarret took a swig of the drink Candice had given him. "I'm tired of working for them anyway. Their next assignment is an hour south of here. I'll look for another job, but I want my name cleared. Stealing artifacts won't look good on my resume." He grinned and took another sip. "What is this?" He lifted his drink. "And what's that wonderful smell?" He glanced at the kitchen as Adeline came to join us.

"Caitlyn made tamales," Adeline said. "Just for you."

"No way." He gave me a teasing glance. "They smell like the real thing."

"They are," Adeline said. "Your wife is an authentic tamale cook."

"How long did that take?"

"All day," Adeline and I answered together and giggled.

A moment later, Victor returned with the salsa and bean dip. I led Jarret to the dinner table, which—I now remembered—we had specifically put in the eat-in kitchen so we could enjoy the view outside. And because we didn't have the money to waste on a second table, one more suitable for the smaller area. It bothered Jarret that we struggled to make ends meet, but he didn't want to rely on his father's wealth. I admired him for that.

"I want you to enjoy our dinner party," I said to Jarret. "I made your favorite food. And don't worry about finding work. When I have to quit for the baby, you can work for your father. I'm sure his offer still stands."

He shrugged and sat at the head of the table, eyeing Sean at the opposite end.

Sean fidgeted in his seat as if he were trying to avoid looking down the table. Then he scraped his chair out and carried his plate to the kitchen. He and Mitch did a little dance in the middle of the kitchen to get around each other, then Sean sat at the patio table.

"Eh," Jarret said. "I don't wanna work for Papa." Then he gave me a one-eyed glare. "Hey, how do you know about my father's offer? Did you get another memory back?"

I smiled and took our plates into the kitchen. Adeline had already made plates for Bobby, Victor, Mitch, and Candice. I returned with plates loaded with taquitos, Spanish rice, and sweet corn. As I set one in front of Jarret, I said, "Poor Sean."

Jarret gave Sean a disgusted glance. "Poor Sean?"

"Well, look at him." I flung a hand in Sean's direction. "He sits as far away from you as he can. I'm surprised he even accepted my invitation today. He's so afraid of you."

"Not as afraid as he should be."

"Jarret." I used a scolding tone. "You don't mean that."

"Oh yeah?"

"You're not going to hurt him. Besides, I talked to him for a long time... that Friday." His sudden glance at the words "that Friday" reminded me that I had never mentioned that conversation to him. I'd meant to, just as I had meant to call him from the park to tell him when I might be home. Mike, in his disguise, had changed all that. "Sean seemed really sorry. He said it would never happen again, and I believe him."

Jarret shrugged and folded his hands, ready to say grace. "Whatever. I don't have to like him." Bowing his head, he mumbled the *Prayer Before Meals* with me. Then he stabbed his taquito. "And I don't mind him being scared of me. Maybe he'll consider what I might do to him next time he's tempted to touch my wife."

I hid my smile behind a napkin, not wanting to show approval of his machismo, but touched all the same.

"We all make mistakes." I took his hand. "Isn't that what you told those high school students? God sends people to help us see ourselves anew without always dwelling on our past mistakes?"

"Oh no you don't." He pulled his hand back and shook his head. "God ain't sending *me* to him. He can send someone else." He gave a nod toward the kitchen.

I peered over my shoulder. Adeline carried two drinks to the patio table and gave one to Sean.

"Hey..." Jarret pushed the hair from my shoulder. "You're wearing the engagement earrings. That your way of saying *yes*?"

I smiled and took his hand again. "I love you, Jarret, and I would marry you again, but let's wait until our anniversary to renew our vows."

"Our anniversary? That—that's weeks away. Not that I—I can't wait." He squirmed, glancing outside, at the ceiling, and back to me. "I can wait. If that's what you want to do. You want to wait? I'll wait."

I giggled. "Jarret, you don't have to wait to sleep in our bed again."

"What? I thought..." He glanced at the others at the table. Mitch and Bobby talked over each other. Candice and Victor seemed to be struggling to follow both conversations. No one was paying attention to me and Jarret. "I thought you'd want to wait." He scooped up a forkful of rice and polished off his taquito.

I shrugged and tried not to smile. "If you want to."

His eyes narrowed with suspicion. "Okay, you're keeping something from me."

"What?" I tried to look naïve.

"You got your memory back."

I shoved a forkful of corn cake into my mouth and feigned interest in whatever Bobby was saying. My ears perked. Wait! Was Bobby talking about me?

"... and Momma and Mrs. Patterson thought Mr. and Mrs. West weren't tryin' hard enough, what with their careers and all, but they was wrong." He laughed. "Y'all know Mrs. West is in a family way?"

Victor shook his head and gave Candice a look. Candice laughed.

"Did you tell Bobby?" I spun to face Jarret, pretending it bothered me.

He glanced down the table. "What, that you're pregnant? Course not. That kid picks up everything." Jarret leaned close, suspicion in his eyes. "Don't try to change the subject. You got your memory back, didn't you? I can tell. You're different. Well, not different, but the way you were before. You're messing with me, aren't you?"

"Do you want seconds?" I glanced at his empty plate.

"Okay, that's the way you want to play, huh?" He grinned, pushed his chair back and stood. Then he frowned and sat back down. "Hey. Do you remember that summer two years ago?" His eyes held a look of longing so intense that I could not continue my charade.

"I do remember, Jarret."

"... falling in love with me?"

I nodded.

The tension drained from his expression. "So, uh, since the other day on the beach, I can't help but wonder: how *did* you fall in love with me?"

I took his hand and played with his fingers while thinking of how to word my answer. "I fell in love with you when I saw how you really tried."

"Tried what?"

"I know you've made mistakes in your life, but by the time we met, you wanted to do the right thing and you really tried. That's important to me. It seems easy for some people to be good, maybe because of upbringing and circumstances. But what happens to them when faced with tough challenges? Like me? When I woke up in our home and couldn't remember us or how I got there, I immediately judged you."

My voice broke and my eyes watered, but I held back the tears. "Trying to accept that you were my husband... I couldn't see past the mistakes you'd made. I couldn't see you for who you are. I guess it was easier for me to avoid judging when you were more of a stranger to me. Maybe I'm harder on the people closest me."

Repentance weighing heavy in my heart, I squeezed his hand and whispered, "I'm sorry."

He dropped his gaze and shook his head as if he didn't deserve the apology.

I leaned closer. "But you, I know you've struggled to do the right thing. And even when it's a challenge, you don't give up, you keep struggling. It matters to you. And that's partly why I fell in love with you. I'm also drawn by the strength of your love for me. It never seems to waver, no matter how I treat you."

He laced his fingers through mine. "I hope you know how much I love you. Tell me you remember marrying me?"

"I'll tell you later." I gave him a sly smile.

A crooked smile crept onto his face. "Are you saying what I think you're saying?"

I shrugged.

"You're still messing with me." He got up. "I'm gonna grab me another taquito or two." He pushed his chair out and gave me a quick kiss. "Want anything?"

I shook my head.

Minutes passed and he hadn't returned, so I turned to see what kept him. I didn't see him at first, but when I did, my heart did a somersault.

Jarret was leaning against the far end of the kitchen island, holding a drink and talking to Sean. Sean smiled and laughed about whatever Jarret said. If I hadn't known them, I would've assumed they were friends. I never would have guessed that one of them had kissed the other one's wife.

My heart stirred over his act of mercy and I rejoiced that I had married him. Then something fluttered inside me. The baby? Dropping my hand to my belly, I rejoiced again. He was the father of my unborn baby. Jarret West, my husband.

Now that I thought about it, I couldn't imagine being this happy married to anyone but him.

Did you enjoy this book? If so, help others enjoy it, too! Please recommend it to friends and leave a review when possible. Thank you!

Every month I send out a newsletter so that you can keep up with my newest releases and enjoy updates, contests, and more. Visit my website www.theresalinden.com to sign up. And while you're there, check out my book trailers and extras!

Facebook: https://www.facebook.com/theresalindenauthor/
Twitter: https://twitter.com/LindenTheresa

## About the Author

Theresa Linden is the author of award-winning *Roland West, Loner* and *Battle for His Soul*, from her West Brothers series of Catholic teen fiction. An avid reader and writer since grade school, she grew up in a military family. Moving every few years left her with the impression that life is an adventure. Her Catholic faith inspires the belief that there is no greater adventure than the reality we can't see, the spiritual side of life. She hopes that the richness, depth, and mystery of the Catholic faith will spark her readers' imagination of the invisible realities and the power of faith and grace. A member of the Catholic Writers Guild and the International Writers Association, Theresa lives in northeast Ohio with her husband, three boys, and one dog.

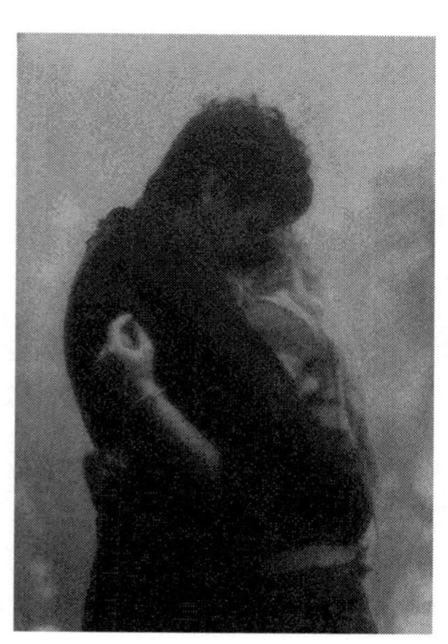

Made in the USA
Middletown, DE
19 June 2019